THE ULTIMATE DECEPTION

THE ULTIMATE DECEPTION

A LIFE of LIES

Delbert Moad

iUniverse, Inc.
Bloomington

The Ultimate Deception
A LIFE of LIES

iUniverse books may be ordered through booksellers or by contacting:

iUniverse
1663 Liberty Drive
Bloomington, IN 47403
www.iuniverse.com
1-800-Authors (1-800-288-4677)

ISBN: 978-1-4759-5288-9 (sc)
ISBN: 978-1-4759-5287-2 (hc)
ISBN: 978-1-4759-5286-5 (e)

Library of Congress Control Number: 2012918331

Printed in the United States of America

iUniverse rev. date: 10/17/2012

Chapter One

THE HEAVY, MAHOGANY DOOR quietly clicked, shutting out his opulent suite of rooms as Paul turned slowly to face the uncertainty of his future. The angular planes of his face were etched with the inner turmoil that he usually managed to hide. The deep brown eyes, which more often reflected a thoughtful nature, today, were shadowed by the doubts that plagued him. With his bronze complexion and wavy, black hair, he had grown to match his father not only in stature but looks as well, but even at six feet tall, he had yet to reach his full maturity. That would come in the next few years. His physical appearance did not concern him. He had learned years earlier that intelligence and the ability to use it wisely were the true mark of a man, not looks or even wealth, although admittedly both could be vital assets.

Like his father, he knew that at first most of his friends were drawn either to his out-going personality or his handsome, rugged features, but they remained friends because his money insured a life of privilege and prestige that they expected. He realized their friendship was conditional. He had few true friends; his position in the family didn't allow for close ties. Paul understood his place and fulfilled his responsibilities accordingly. Even if he desired more personal freedom, especially at his father's compound, he had learned the need for restrictions, for precautions. More important issues crowded his thoughts this morning, however.

Slowly he surveyed the elegant expanse of hallway, his eyes automatically drawn to the portrait of the man whose harsh features dominated the landing at the head of the twisting staircase. Like everything else in this lush twenty-acre compound, sprawling across the rugged slopes of the Andes, secrets lay hidden in the depths of those piercing black eyes. Stately, seductive, sinister, Raul Contreras radiated the autocratic authority of the early Spanish conquistadors, who had stripped the verdant land of its riches and enslaved its people. There, too, beneath the harshly-etched planes of his face, lay the thinly-veiled, absolute power of a dictator, a modern drug lord, a man set on conquering new worlds of his own.

On meeting his father for the first time, Paul had failed to fully comprehend Raul's true power. At fourteen, Paul had been awed by the beauty of his surroundings, seduced by his youthful desire for wealth, subdued by the harsh reality of subtle threats, and had easily succumbed to Contreras' charm, his ambitions—his dream.

That innocent summer vacation to the island paradise of Aruba with his parents, Lawrence and Janette Stevens, had unleashed a chain of events that even now, years later, were far from complete. His sudden and unprecedented departure for Bolivia, alone with Alberto Nunez, a man he had only recently met, had left Paul confused and scared. The shock of meeting his real father, Raul Contreras, hours later and learning that his parents were not who he had believed them to be had been overwhelming for a boy his age. The following days had left him reeling, as he found himself stunned by the barrage of facts Raul had revealed.

Before many years, Paul learned that Raul's expectations for him had far greater ramifications than he had been able to grasp at that first meeting. Now, however, he saw the true magnificence, the brilliance of a mind setting into play a series of events so calculating that they could shape the destiny not only of men, but of entire nations.

Raul Contreras was a man of vision, a man of infinite patience, but most importantly, a man of action. His expectations were simple, unemotional, even diabolical, but unreservedly mandatory, the penalty for failure to comply—inevitable. Paul didn't want to consider what Raul would do to his adoptive parents if he failed to comply with his wishes. Regardless of how confused and hurt he had felt at their betrayal, they were his family. Now that he realized the true extent of Raul's power, he could finally forgive them for their earlier deception.

As he walked slowly toward the stairs, Paul tried to view Raul's scheme dispassionately, but Paul recognized his own fatal flaw. Standing before his father's portrait, staring into the cold, soulless black eyes, Paul knew he could never be as heartless, as emotionlessly detached, as his father. Even so, he realized that, with his youth ripped from him, he had become a man conformed to his father's image, a man whose destiny lay charted for him, a man who was, after all, Raul Contreras' son.

In the years since that first meeting, Paul had learned much about his father. With his summers spent in Bolivia at Raul's compound, he had pieced together most of the plan that Raul viewed as his vision. Begun twenty years earlier, that vision was finally coming to fruition.

Not born to wealth and prestige but rather a simple, working-class family, Raul, at an early age, had had the foresight to learn how to gain an advantage. His father's position as personal driver to Don Gonzales, head of the Bolivian drug syndicate, had paved the way for him. Accompanying his father any time he was permitted allowed Raul the opportunity to study the man behind the money and the power of one of Bolivia's largest drug cartels.

It wasn't long before Raul began running errands for Don Gonzales. He wasn't too proud to do even the most menial tasks. Don Gonzales laughed at Raul's eagerness to learn; he recognized the hunger that burned in Raul and joked that someday Raul would have his job. Raul laughed with the aging Don, but secretly he hoped his words would be prophetic.

With encouragement from Don Gonzales, who opened his private library to him, Raul became an avid reader, a student of learning. He devoted much of his study to famous world leaders. He soon realized that excessive pride and a lack of foresight had been the downfall of many great men. He focused on his studies. He watched; he listened; he learned.

Don Gonzales enjoyed the attention of the young Raul; he prided himself on being a good role model and decided Raul would make an admirable addition to the *family*. Raul's father was hardworking and loyal. Don Gonzales recognized those same traits in Raul. His decision to enroll Raul in the prestigious Comillas Pontifical Universidad in Madrid, Spain altered Raul's life dramatically and opened an unknown world to him. Raul quickly seized the opportunity and vowed to make Don Gonzales proud of the trust he had placed in him.

Raul couldn't have been happier. He traveled to Spain with his aunt, who was to maintain his residence, and with his expenses provided for by Don Gonzales, Raul was assured the time needed to focus on his studies. But Raul was wise enough to know that Don Gonzales expected more than just a good return on his investment. His returning to work for the cartel was a given, but bringing added influence through a network of European connections would be a windfall. Using his rugged image, intellectual acumen, and Don Gonzales' money, Raul soon formed life-long associations with the sons of influential men all across Europe.

Raul's thirst for knowledge was only exceeded by his need for excitement. He made friends easily. Women were drawn to his self-assured attitude, and men to his no-nonsense demeanor. Like most young men, he never backed down from a challenge, but, unlike many of his friends, he was smart enough to know how to circumvent problems. For privileged youth with too much money and not enough responsibilities, Raul became the friend to have. If some of their problems were manufactured by Raul himself, who was to know? Deception added an element of excitement. To manipulate a situation and achieve the desired outcome sent a rush of adrenaline coursing through his body. To them, Raul was a magician who could make all their troubles disappear. To him, they were potential allies for the future. He partied with them all, he played their games, but he never lost sight of his goal. If there was a problem, Raul would find an answer. He asked nothing in return for his help, but he never forgot what was due him.

After completing his studies, Raul received his degree in international business and finance and corporate law. He returned to Bolivia and accepted a position in the prestigious Melendez Law Firm, which existed primarily to protect the investments and interests of the Bolivian drug cartel and especially those of Don Gonzales.

Raul worked hard and seized every opportunity to ingratiate himself with his superiors. He was determined to learn every aspect of the drug trade, to know every person connected with the cartel. He studied the weaknesses, the strengths, the habits, and especially the vices of everyone he dealt with. He secretly compiled files on business transactions and those involved. He recorded anything and everything that might one day benefit him and ultimately guarantee his success. He never doubted himself once, but neither did he leave anything to chance.

Raul became an indispensible advisor to Don Gonzales. He uncovered weaknesses in security, streamlined business transactions, and introduced modern technology to track supplies, shipments, even people. But he also made enemies, men who were working for their own advancement, men who envisioned themselves as a replacement for the aging Don, men who would, if given the opportunity, easily remove any competition. But Raul was no shortsighted idealist; he recognized the potential threat he was, and he planned accordingly.

Paul stood before the portrait; his eyes traveled down the image of his father to where Raul's hand lay carelessly placed on a world globe. Only Paul recognized the true significance of that stance. Raul planned to someday rule all that lay beneath his touch.

Paul's phone hummed softly in his pocket, a quiet reminder that he was never truly alone, that nothing escaped Raul's attention. He was expected downstairs. His eyes moved toward the secluded camera, discreetly placed within the ceiling molding. He smiled slightly. Ramon would be on duty now. Paul had learned much from him, yet he knew that was only because his father wanted him to know; otherwise no one would have revealed anything about Raul's life, not even to him. The price for disloyalty was too high for any man to pay.

Paul glanced back at his father's portrait. There had been others who had been as ambitious as the young Raul. But Raul was a man of foresight. He had befriended Rafael Salta, a man as ruthless and focused as Raul, a man who could help shape the empire Raul planned to command, two men that only fate could bring together, kindred spirits, *compadres.*

Even in his limited experience, Paul had often witnessed the unspoken communication between the two men, minds so attuned to one another that words were unnecessary, yet polar opposites—Raul, the educated man of privilege, wealth, and power—Rafael, the worldly man of desperation, poverty, and determination. Both had risen in the ranks of the cut-throat, die-young drug world by different means. Raul the elite, authoritative lawyer, Rafael the sinister, powerful enforcer; together they wielded the ability to rock the drug world, to manipulate nations, to create their own empire. Together they were unstoppable. Raul's skill at recognizing threats and analyzing future needs was equally matched by Rafael's talent at eliminating those threats and meeting those needs. Where one used prestige and privilege, the other used finesse and force. Raul's vision was no grandiose delusion of a madman—it was the diabolical scheme of a master mind. With Rafael's help, Raul was almost guaranteed success.

The unexpected deaths of Raul's father and Don Gonzales, however, had left the cartel in turmoil. When a head-on collision with a truck, on one of the treacherous mountain roads, caused Don Gonzales' car to careen down the rugged mountain slopes and burst into flames, Raul was forced into swift action. Even though he was distraught over his father's death and the loss of his mentor, he quickly seized this long-awaited opportunity.

Raul joined forces with Rafael and together, the two men effectively silenced any opposition to Raul's assumption of rule, in a power play of coercion, negotiation, and intimidation. Rafael, equally as forceful in his own right as Raul, commanded the underbelly, the dark, sinister elements of the drug world. Together they held the power of life or death, riches or poverty for all those around them. With Raul's political and legal expertise and Rafael's subversive army of underlings, they presented a united front no one could or would dare oppose. In a matter of days, Raul and Rafael dominated the Bolivian drug trade.

Under the strict leadership of Raul, the illicit trade in cocaine soon flourished into a multi-billion dollar industry. Seeing the advantage of aligning forces with Raul's cartel, many competitors were lured into his organization by the promise of greater profits, stronger alliances, and fewer problems. Those less far-sighted were forced into submission. Nothing was beyond the scope of Raul's reach.

Under Rafael's leadership, loyalty to the cartel was insured through an elite army headed by Alberto Nunez. A throwback to the early Catalan Spaniards, Alberto's light coloring and stylish good looks hid a soul devoid of human feeling and compassion, a heart hardened by all-consuming lose and overwhelming devastation, a mind scarred beyond redemption.

Paul glanced at his watch. Why was he being so introspective? Usually he would be racing down the stairs to embrace the day. He started to frown then caught himself. He didn't want to betray his feelings, his confusion. Everything was reported. Even Ramon would do what was expected. There were no options. Paul's mind returned to his father and all Paul had learned over the years. Maybe it was the significance of the day that had him replaying the past. Maybe, but the hair on the back of his neck rose as he took one final look at the portrait. Even Paul had to admit, his father was a genius at envisioning the future.

Always with his ultimate goal in mind, Raul had decided, early on, to create his own army, one that would rival any elite force on Earth. Thus, he began his campaign to build a force of well-educated subordinates, trained in vocations suited to their temperaments and abilities. Raul wanted a force unencumbered by any outside ties. Habitually, he scoured the echoing halls of the nearby Catholic orphanage, searching for those young boys who had been rescued by the local priests and were desperate enough to sell themselves into his service for any chance at a future away from the deprivation and loneliness of their present existence.

Raul had been drawn especially to one quiet, reserved little boy, standing alone among the scraggly group of orphans, all refugees from the violence of the neighboring villages held hostage by the disbanded forces of previous drug lords. Those who survived the senseless death and destruction had been left to aimlessly wander the isolated, rugged mountains of the Bolivian countryside until, if they were among the lucky few, they were rescued by local priests.

Counted as one of the fortunate ones, Alberto had gone unnoticed among the noisy, older boys, unnoticed by everyone except Raul. In Alberto, Raul recognized a deep, desperate despair. From the priests, he learned this angelic-looking, little boy had not only been severely injured and left for dead by the pillaging troops but had also witnessed the savage destruction of his entire family.

Left helpless, blood seeping from his frail body through the jagged bullet wound in his chest, Alberto had watched, frozen in agony and horror, as his father's tongue had been ripped from his throat for defying the soldiers. In silent terror he had witnessed the rape and the brutal disfigurement of his mother and sisters, their screams mingling with the sense of hopelessness that raged through his body. The smell of blood, death, and despair had consumed him as he saw his father's eyes gouged from his head and his throat cut, at last silencing the final, desperate, agonizing moans. Left by the marauding band of militants to slowly bleed to death, Alberto ultimately succumbed to the hollow, empty void of unconsciousness. The few remaining villagers, who had escaped the brutal attack, rescued Alberto and took him to the only place of refuge, the last vestige of civilization that remained in this war-torn area, a nearby Catholic orphanage.

With the help of a neighboring doctor, the priests were able to successfully treat Alberto's physical injuries, but they were unable to reach the little boy emotionally. He now appeared devoid of all feeling, all emotion. He did as he was told, but rarely spoke. Nothing penetrated the cold exterior. Nothing moved behind the vacant stare. For Alberto, living held no meaning; dying held no fear.

It had been an easy task for Raul to gain guardianship of any of the orphaned boys. The orphanage was packed and finances limited. Raul's patronage meant survival for those left behind. The priests remained stoically silent about Raul's affairs. Even in the church, money bought results, and Raul always paid well. As the most powerful man in Bolivia, he could offer advantages to these boys that they would never realize otherwise, and Raul recognized the value of an educated work force. Ignorance bred failure. Failure was unacceptable. Raul wanted only the best in his organization, and he was willing to pay for it.

The boys were introduced to a life of privilege, where luxury was the norm. But their lives were not easy. They were expected to follow orders, meet strict requirements, and assume demanding responsibilities. This allowed Raul and Rafael to scrutinize their abilities and assess their talents. Though no one was forced to adhere to Raul's wishes, their former lives of destitution and deprivation always lay in the forefront of their minds, insuring their adherence with Raul's decisions for their futures and their undivided loyalty to him.

He became the father-figure in their lives and made sweeping plans for their education and introduction into his organization. The boys were tutored in the compound by special instructors who prepared them for lives outside the limited scope of their previous existence. They were groomed and trained, exercised and drilled. A good education was a must. Raul's expectations were high, and he was seldom disappointed. He challenged them then rewarded them well for their success. They worked hard; they played hard; they grew up into an elite force of trained intellectuals. They were soon ready to be sent out to further their education in selected universities around the world. Raul did not underestimated the value of expert linguists trained in every conceivable field of business and finance—his own personal army of executives and advisors. After their successful training, Raul's money allowed them to easily move into the elite societies of the privileged and powerful. Within a twenty-year span of time, Raul began reaping the benefits of his endeavors.

Whenever possible these young men accepted positions within traditional businesses and organizations. When this was not an option, Raul opened a legitimate enterprise and established a power base from which to operate. As businessmen, they were expected to ingratiate themselves into the lives of the rich and influential through honest and honorable means, if possible—dishonest and dishonorable, if absolutely necessary. They were to seek out alliances and uncover weaknesses, providing a wealth of vital information for Raul.

During his early years as advisor to Don Gonzales, Raul had developed a network of computer and technology experts whose sole job was to track the movements of individuals, government officials, heads-of-state, syndicate bosses, business magnets, anyone and everyone who might even remotely benefit Raul. Satellite imaging, global position tracking, resonance sound recording, and telecommunication devices so acutely tuned that they were able to provide detailed visual and auditory surveillance records many times placed the very futures and lives of these men in Raul's hands.

The subtlety with which Raul manipulated the lives of those around him was the work of a true genius. Through coercion and intimidation, Raul brought men to heel. Then he rewarded them suitably for compliance with his wishes. Women, drugs, jobs, nothing was beyond the scope of Raul's influence. For most, it was considered an honor to serve him, a wise business decision. However, there were always a few who opposed his terms.

For those few, Rafael stepped in. Any meeting of importance included both Raul and Rafael. Decisions appeared to be by joint consensus, although Rafael rarely voiced an opinion. Raul led the discussions, but Alberto learned early that when Raul became silent Rafael had assumed power, an unspoken shift more deadly than any man's anger.

Alberto watched and learned. It was only after Raul felt that Alberto truly understood how to influence men through their weaknesses that he turned his training over to Rafael. No one knew more about retaliation than Rafael. He had spent a lifetime perfecting his art. Just as Raul was a master of negotiation and manipulation, Rafael was a master of punishment and death. The same network of intelligence that allowed Raul the means to influence also allowed Rafael the means to punish. Family members, friends, business acquaintances were all accessible to Rafael. There was no place safe enough, no distance far enough to provide sanctuary. Examples were made of those foolish enough to deny the scope of Raul's power and the reach of Rafael's hand. Few dared stand against them, but no one ever forgot the end result. Not even Paul, himself.

Dark memories flooded his mind as he turned from his father's portrait to descend the broad staircase. His hand slid effortlessly over the intricately carved mahogany railing. A cold chill swept over him. Terror threatened him for a moment. He shook his head to clear the images and glanced at the grandeur surrounding him. The moment passed.

Like everything else in Raul's life, nothing had been left to chance. His home reflected the power and prestige of the man. The luxury of the rooms rivaled any grand European palace. Marble floors reflected a thousand tiny lights from the crystal chandeliers, suspended from the upper reaches of the second floor; the rich fabrics of the furnishings echoed the vibrant colors of the heavy brocades, draping the massive, floor-length windows, which fronted the house. A matching staircase twisted gracefully along the opposite side of the foyer, easily dividing the upper regions into two completely separate residences.

The second floor housed Raul and Rafael's private suites of rooms with adjacent guest apartments further down each corridor. Privacy was insured by digital entrance pads and monitoring at entry levels. Only the most trusted household staff was allowed on these floors.

The compound itself housed an infirmary with a staff and the latest in medical technology. Emergencies were transported to a nearby city in one of the private helicopters housed in a hangar at the rear of the compound where Raul's private fleet of jets was also stored. Isolated by the rugged terrain of the Andes, a remote valley between mountains formed the perfect landing strip. The compound boasted repair and maintenance shops for the vehicles and aircraft. Raul recruited only the best workers and paid them well. By housing them on the grounds, he restricted their movements. No one left without his knowing.

All cartel vehicles were equipped with tracking and monitoring devices, but only a select few knew of the true reach of Raul's power. Training of personnel stressed the necessity of knowing as little as possible about the details of everyday operations. Abductions were few, but not unheard of and government-sanctioned undercover operatives occasionally caused minor difficulties. The less any one person knew about the operation, the better for everyone involved.

Raul didn't flaunt his power. He preferred to remain disassociated from government interference. He knew a well-placed word would insure the results he wanted. Few men viewed Raul's organization as a threat unless they were foolish enough to oppose him in some way; then retaliation was fast and final. Otherwise, he was viewed as a great man. It was common knowledge that he used his abundant resources to help those connected with his operation, much like a feudal lord. His people worked and lived on his land, providing services and meeting his needs. In return, he took care of them.

The compound even housed a small chapel as well as a resident priest. Raul often attended services; he believed in a heavenly God, but he felt that same God had given him the ability to shape his own earthly realm, his personal manifest destiny. Most days he felt truly blessed; the more money he put into his organization and his people, the more benefits he reaped. He never cluttered his mind with concerns about those who might suffer at his hands. Retribution was all part of Rafael's realm. Raul felt justified in any action he took. He had an empire to build, an organization to run, people to protect. He slept well at night.

It amazed Paul how easily his father disassociated himself from the darker elements of his world. Would he ever learn to distance himself from the true nature of Raul's empire? Would he eventually become hardened to the reality of his father's expectations? Even his limited knowledge of Raul's power left him in no doubt as to the ultimate outcome of defying Raul's wishes. Paul frowned as he wondered if he could ever truly become his father's son.

A fluttering movement caught his eye as he stepped into the foyer. Cascading, silver-blonde curls shimmered in the reflected glow from the chandeliers. Soft, silky fabric billowed gently around slender, tanned legs. Paul's dark eyes traveled up the exquisite form descending the opposite staircase—another of Raul's surprises. But this one was completely unlike any of the previous ones. Paul walked to the bottom stair, his eyes riveted on the beauty of her face.

Their eyes met, and Paul felt somehow removed from the moment. His hand automatically reached to grasp hers as she descended the last stair. Nothing was the same; he felt his destiny shift, his life reshape. Somehow on some innate level, he recognized his future. The slow, seductive smile that played around the corners of her lips sent Paul's blood racing.

"Well, well, we meet at last," she calmly responded as she deftly slipped her hand from Paul's. "I'm Caroline, and you must be Paul. I've heard quite a lot about you," she smiled softly.

For a moment Paul felt perplexed. Why hadn't he been told about her? Was this another in a long series of tests? Recovering quickly, Paul responded deftly, "I'm sorry that I can't say the same. But maybe we can rectify that situation over breakfast."

"Certainly," her deep blue eyes danced with mischief as she walked beside him. Caroline felt his discomfort and reveled in her ability to momentarily stun the heir-apparent. She had her own agenda, and things were falling into place nicely. Her lips curved into a knowing smile. She let her eyes drift slowly over Paul. He wasn't nearly as handsome as his father, but there was definitely hope for him. Besides, what choice did she have? But she planned to have her own way just the same. What could Raul really do to her? After all, Rafael was *her* father. A bubble of laughter escaped her well-shaped lips.

Paul felt a moment of unease at the discordant sound. He glanced at the beauty walking regally beside him and wondered how she fit into Raul's scheme. If he had learned anything in the last few years, it was that nothing happened by chance—not in Raul's realm.

As Paul seated himself across from Caroline, he questioned his good fortune. Instantly his senses went on alert. She had descended from the opposite staircase, Rafael's dominion. How did she fit into Raul's plans? Why did he feel he would have even less say in his future now?

"Haven't you figured it out?" Her lips curved gently as she slid her hand over his across the table. "It's all arranged, you know."

No, he didn't know. Anger surged through him, but he refused to let her see it. Carefully, he turned his hand over and captured hers. "Why don't you tell me, and we can compare notes," he suggested giving her, his own slow, seductive smile. Why give the game away so soon. He had watched Raul long enough to know how to play. To allow her the victory in this opening skirmish would be tantamount to losing the battle, and he had no desire to let that happen. He recognized that predatory gleam she had tried to hide in those deep blue eyes. He had witnessed the same in women who thought to influence Raul. Everything in life was about control, and it lay in his hands now.

Firmly, his fingers tightened over hers before dropping her hand back on the table to pick up his fork, a small power play, but effective. His unconcerned attitude momentarily distracted Caroline. She expected him to be overwhelmed by her beauty; others always were.

Quickly she pulled her hand from the table and placed it in her lap. He didn't need to know how angry she was becoming.

"Don't you know who I am?" she questioned, the slight vibration in her voice revealing more than she realized. Even though her soft lips were curved in the semblance of a seductive smile, Paul wasn't fooled. His attitude had fired her blood. She wasn't used to being ignored. He knew how to use that anger against her. He had watched a master.

Paul ignored her question as he finished his meal and placed his fork carefully on the table, "I'm sure that you will tell me in due time." He signaled the attending servant for more coffee, his apparent unconcern only fueling her anger more. "I have a busy schedule today. If you would care to meet later, perhaps we can continue our discussion." He rose swiftly from the table, "Enjoy your meal." With a slight bow to her, Paul walked quickly toward the open French doors, leading to the lush gardens and outer compound beyond. Not for anything would he allow her to dictate this conversation, not until he knew what was really going on. There was no place better to find that out than the surveillance files Raul kept on everyone significant. Hadn't he learned about his own life from them? Why not hers?

Deliberately, Paul slowed his steps. He had learned not to rush into anything. To show too much interest would send a red flag to Raul immediately, and he didn't want Raul to know that his interest was captured by this latest addition. What had she meant by everything being arranged? He knew that his life for the next few years was mapped out for him, that he was expected to continue his education, but that plan hadn't varied much from his own personal goal. The difference lay in what was expected of him during that time. Raul had revealed enough about his own educational experiences and how he had developed his circle of friends and contacts that Paul knew what was expected of him. He hadn't needed the added reminders about the welfare of his adoptive parents to encourage his cooperation. Paul knew that, as Raul's son, he would always be answerable to his father.

Of course, that was something that he had learned to live with, but even now, he struggled against the restraints his position placed on him. As he turned to walk down the pathway connecting the main house to the outer buildings, he knew that in all honesty, he appreciated the respect afforded him. Regardless of how restricting his life seemed, he wouldn't change it. He was too much like his father in that regard. He liked power; that was what made his present situation so irritating. Caroline, for all of her soft-spoken ways, wanted the same thing. He recognized the determination she tried to hide behind a beguiling smile and caressing hand. Now though, he needed answers, and he planned to get them.

Pushing open the heavy oak doors that held the outer world at bay, Paul entered the quiet confines of the logistics and technology compound, a mini-fortress that shielded the innermost secrets of the most powerful people in the world from the prying eyes of everyone, but Raul's elite forces. Even then, very few, other than Raul and Rafael, had true access. The information that Raul housed here could topple nations and destroy global economies. It was not something to treat with a lack of respect. Raul knew the value of a well-guarded secret. His elaborate encoding system helped to assure access to only a few. The lives of these men were so entangled with the cartel that thwarting Raul's wishes would never be considered. Everyone knew Rafael's role in the cartel. No one doubted his abilities; no one wanted first-hand experience in his methods of retaliation. Raul was the man fathers spoke proudly of knowing; Rafael was the man fathers whispered of in warning.

Paul glanced at the ornate clock dominating the inner wall. He had time for a leisurely stroll through the offices, something that he did on many occasions. No one would think anything about it. He often stopped by to chat with the personnel, a habit he had developed from watching Raul interact with his workers. No man was slighted. No matter how menial the task or how inconsequential the job, if a man performed his duties well, he was a man worthy of praise. Raul made sure all his workers knew their value to his organization; without their help, his empire would crumble—a chain was only as strong as its weakest link. Trite but true.

Paul quietly pushed the inner office door open. He knew that the men had been following his progress on the screens. Had he been a stranger, he would never have been able to open the door.

"Hola, Ramon. Anything new on the horizon?" he smiled at the tall man seated behind a massive desk. An elaborate bank of monitors filled the interior wall, constantly shifting positions as movements around the compound were detected and analyzed. Hundreds of images filled the screens at any given time. Recording devices burned encoded discs of each day's activities. Microchips filed away every transaction.

"No, Senor Paul, not today," he smiled in return.

Propping one hip on the desk, Paul leaned forward conspiratorially. "I met Caroline this morning, but, of course, you knew that." Paul allowed his soft laugh to resonate slowly around the room. "What do you think about her?" Paul held the man's eye. He knew he could trust Ramon. Paul had known him since that first summer years before when Ramon had shared Paul's past with him. Paul had been shocked to discover how every aspect of his life had been documented and recorded. Ramon had shown him the need to have such records for his own protection. They had been friends ever since. Ramon would help him, if he could.

Ramon chuckled, "That's a young lady to be aware of. No, wary of," he corrected, smiling at his own joke. Ramon sobered suddenly, "You do know who she is, don't you?"

"I can guess," Paul answered. "What does she have to do with me? Or do I know already?"

Ramon glanced quickly around the room. No one was paying them any undue attention. They were used to Paul and Ramon talking together. This was one of the few rooms that were not monitored for sound, although it was visually recorded. "It has been told that you and she will someday form an alliance between the two partners."

Paul refused to allow himself to show any emotion. His reaction would be discussed quietly among the family. He had to hold his own now, more than ever. "Well, well, what an interesting idea!"

His smile broadened as he contemplated the reasons for this decision. "She certainly is beautiful," he added. "Where has she been all this time? I've never seen her here before."

"True. She rarely comes to the compound. Rafael prefers it that way. But this was a special occasion. After all, it's your birthday." Ramon clasped Paul's shoulder tightly, "Be careful that you don't lose more that your heart," he advised quietly.

Dropping his hand from Paul's shoulder, Ramon asked in a slightly louder voice, "Have you seen how this new camera works?" he asked. The personal conversation was over.

Paul returned to the main compound some time later by a more circuitous route. Although his steps were unhurried, his mind raced with the possible implications of the information he had gathered. He forced himself to appear at ease and carefree, staying with his usual pattern of behavior. His mind raced with questions. He couldn't formulate any cohesive plan of action. What did he do now? Should he do anything, or just wait and see what would take place? He had learned from Raul not to wait for someone else to manipulate the situation.

He was still searching for answers when he rounded the corner of the main building and was confronted with the slender, bathing suit-clad form, which had suddenly become the focus of all his thoughts. The secluded patio was the perfect place to recline in the early morning sun.

Caroline tipped the amber-rimmed sunglasses up, as she watched Paul stroll toward her. She smiled provocatively, angling her shapely body toward him. Inwardly, she still burned from his earlier attitude toward her. Was she doomed to be surrounded by men she couldn't influence? Caroline's teeth clinched. The ache in her jaw forced her to take a deep breath and assume a more pleasant visage.

Inwardly at least, she allowed herself to feel a small victory. He hadn't known about her or her role in his life. She would bet anything on that. He had covered his reaction well, but she had seen the second of stunned surprise flicker in his dark eyes. Did he know how much he truly resembled his father? It was more than looks. It was that vague something that set them both apart, an inherent characteristic that eluded capture, the electric feeling pulsing in the air before an approaching storm, the excited thrill of expectation before a momentous event, the icy chill of dread in a moment of terror. Anticipation—one always felt there was something more to come—something monumental. Even the trivial took on an aspect of importance when Raul or Paul was part of it.

Caroline allowed her hand to fall languidly to her side, drawing attention to her slender waist and the soft flare of her hips. She knew her charms and how to make the most of them. She had become an expert in the last year. Rafael had seen to that—a priceless education, formal training, a personal coach, whatever it took to create an impeccable, faultless work of art. Caroline felt the constraints of her life many times, but she had learned early that the silk bonds that held her could change to steel cables at a moment's notice if Rafael so decided. She had witnessed that cold, hard darkness once in her life, and that had been enough. Never would she go against his wishes again.

The incident had seemed so innocent to her. She had defied her chaperone's orders and had left on her own to investigate the city's night life. She and a few friends had arranged to meet at a local restaurant.

After a leisurely meal, they had gone to the movies. Caroline had arrived home later that evening escorted by a fellow classmate from the private school she attended. He was handsome, sophisticated, wealthy, and much too old for her. Her chaperone sat waiting. Nothing was said as she entered the room, but Caroline quickly sent her escort on his way. The silence that followed was more devastating than any tirade.

The next day Rafael had arrived. Caroline's chaperone was dismissed, and a stolid figure resembling a prison warden assumed her role. No more motherly chats, or late night movie sessions, Caroline was now isolated from everyone who had formed a family connection in her life away from home. Rafael, whose dark eyes had glistened like fire-hardened obsidian, had spoken little and then only to say that his disappointment in Caroline's behavior was great and would not be tolerated again. It was that very dearth of words that had conveyed the true import of Rafael's meaning. She had crossed the bounds of acceptable, her punishment was isolation.

No longer was she allowed the freedom she had once enjoyed. Now her every move was monitored, her every word recorded. She felt the brunt of Rafael's anger through his total lack of communication with her. He no longer talked with her except through the "Rock," as Caroline secretly dubbed her new chaperone. For a girl with her personality, who lived for contact with others, she learned that limiting that interaction could be very devastating and that psychological punishment was more effective than anything physical could ever have been.

Her rebellion taught her something else too. She soon realized that any reaction to her isolation only revealed weakness, and she refused to allow that to happen. She worked harder at her studies, filled her time with music and books, and forged a bond with her new chaperone, not by subservience, but by standing up for herself while always following the rules.

It took finesse and fortitude, but Caroline managed it quite nicely and earned the grudging respect of her new "jailer." Of course, Caroline was intelligent enough to know that her actions were all reported. Caroline wanted to earn Rafael's forgiveness, but she knew that it would be a long time before she would be able to do so. Still, she was determined to succeed.

She had known early in their relationship that Rafael had something planned for her life, and she was vain enough to want to know just what that was. She realized that Rafael wielded much power, and that in his part of the world, he was formidable. His attitude told her that he answered to no man. His actions told her that no man wanted to displease him. Now she knew that meant no woman also, at least not a smart one.

Where once she had enjoyed the warm feeling of belonging, of being pampered, now she endured the cold harshness of isolation but endure it she did. After all, she was Rafael's daughter; she would show him just how strong, how determined she could be.

Caroline was unaware of how much of her inner turmoil she revealed as Paul slowly neared the lounge chair where she lay. He had become adept at analyzing people, a prerequisite for his position. He could tell from the set of her lips that she was forcing her friendly attitude, and she was still inwardly angry about their earlier confrontation. It had not gone as she expected, and she was trying to regain her lost advantage. He knew she realized that she had caught him off guard with her bold statement, but he had recovered quickly.

This was going to be a very rocky relationship, if they both tried to assume leadership. Paul really wasn't worried. He knew his role, and Caroline was just another step on the ladder. A broken rung could be easily replaced. She would have to fall into line or be thrown aside. He almost felt sorry for her—almost.

Caroline recognized the assessment Paul was making; she smiled more leisurely, thinking she had his attention now. But she had misread his thoughts. He wasn't like any of the other young men she had met. Laughing to himself, Paul smiled, letting her think that she was his sole interest, that he was beguiled by that sexy little smile. This might be fun after all.

"Hot enough for you?" he asked. He eased into a nearby chair. Stretching his long legs in front of him, he reached for the pitcher of lemonade. "Want some," he asked provocatively.

"No, thanks," she smiled sweetly. "How has your day been?"

"Oh, I can't complain. How was yours? Learn anything new?"

"Only that you don't seem to be very excited about your birthday. Why is that? Doesn't reaching such a milestone, the big 21, turn you on?"

"Why should it? It's just another day like any other." He smiled to take the bite out of his words. He didn't like talking about his birthday. At times like these, he felt the sting of being a pawn in someone else's game. He was too much like Raul to want to feel powerless. No matter how much he learned, how much he studied, he still felt that Raul influenced every aspect of his life—even his very thoughts were dominated by what Raul expected. It was not a feeling that he liked.

He could only hope that someday that feeling would subside, that he would be in total command, that his thoughts would be his own, and that he would be able to take Raul's place. But did he really want to do that? Had he ever really been given a choice? Subtle threats had kept him from any defiance even from his very first meeting with Raul years before. Now, it was just assumed, expected. He had been a willing participant until now, so why was he questioning everything today?

Maybe his birthday was affecting him after all. Wasn't twenty-one the mark of a man, a time when a man took charge of his destiny? Was that the sting that he felt at any reminder of the significance of this day? Or was it the less-than-subtle, scantily–clad form stretched out before him that had him feeling restless, unsure? Was this another ploy in Raul's plan?

Somehow, he didn't see Rafael thinking along those same lines. Rafael with his cold, dark eyes wasn't an enemy that Paul ever wanted to have. He would have to tread carefully until he fully understood what the future held for him. Caroline might seem worldly, but Paul would bet his last dollar that it was all show. Rafael wasn't the type to countenance any disreputable behavior, especially from a daughter.

Paul had heard how the upper rooms had once held a harem of beauties that even a Maharaja would have been proud of. Both Raul and Rafael had entertained lovely women from all over the world. The closely guarded apartments were filled with every conceivable delight where the women were reputed to vie for the two men's attention.

Over the years as Paul had begun staying at the compound for longer periods of time, the family had begun to accept him as one of their own. He was no longer considered an outsider, and he had learned more and more about the early days of the Contreras Empire. Stories that he had once deemed improbable, he now realized were more than likely only shadows of the real truth. Only Raul and Rafael knew the whole plan. Had they secretly maintained their own private harem? Were the girls really selected to produce the desired children? Had other children who fit Raul and Rafael's preordained criteria been sent away and raised by carefully chosen parents, just as he had been? What had happened to the women? Was there someone else waiting to take his place if he failed to meet Raul's expectations?

None of this had ever been revealed to him, but suddenly the grueling years of training, of dedication to Raul's wishes began to make sense. If there were others, where were they and what was their role in his future, in the future of Raul's empire?

Paul's lips curved in a cynical smile. Pandora, that's what he would call her from now on. She had opened the lid on the carefully hidden box of secrets. He wouldn't be able to rest until he had the answers he needed, and he knew for certain that some of the answers weren't going to be easy to discover. Maybe this was just another test to try his determination, his strength of will. If so, he was definitely going to pass because he realized these questions had been lurking in the recesses of his mind for months, ever since Raul had sent Alberto for him this last time.

Even then he had noticed a subtle change in Alberto's behavior; some inexplicable barrier had sprung up between them. Alberto, remote at the best of times, had been even more withdrawn, as though waiting for something to happen. Yes, she was definitely Pandora. He almost laughed aloud. Would she be shocked if he told her what he was really thinking? Did she know how dangerous their fathers were, or had she deluded herself as he once had?

Raul never left him in any doubt as to his role, nor had he ever been less than brutally honest about his expectations for Paul, but Paul no longer felt the sting of rejection that had plagued him as a young boy. He had finally realized that Raul's emotionless behavior toward him was an inbred characteristic of his personality. Emotions were messy and could lead to poor judgment. Raul never let emotions affect his decisions. It was this same cruel, brutal, heartless demeanor that clutched at the very souls of those who incurred Raul's wrath.

Paul glanced at the suntanned body stretched before him. "Let's go for a drive."

"What? You mean to say that we can leave this oh, so lovely prison?"

"Not getting a little claustrophobic, are you?" he laughed, the sound trailing across the compound, making more than one head shake knowingly. Most thought he might have met his match. It was, after all, the common belief that the children of the two patrons would someday marry and create a combined empire, the likes of which no one could imagine.

"I might have a little influence," he laughed as he reached for her hand and pulled her to her feet. As she rose, she let her body fall toward him, but he quickly dropped her hand and stepped to the side. He wasn't having any of that. She might as well learn now that he would make the moves, if and when he chose. He wasn't going to be manipulated by some spoiled little girl, even if she was Rafael's daughter—no, especially since she **was** his daughter.

"Get changed and let have some fun." He was already moving toward the mansion as he spoke, leaving her to follow in his wake, assuming that she would abide by his wishes.

Caroline wanted to stomp her foot in frustration at his attitude, but she forced her hands to unclench and hurried after him, acknowledging that she was tired of the grand isolation of this place. That was the only reason she was doing as he wished, the only reason!

"I'll meet you downstairs in fifteen minutes. Don't be late!" he warned.

Caroline bit her tongue to keep from asking, or what, but she already knew the answer, and she didn't want to be left behind.

As they entered the open foyer, each went a separate way up the twisting stairway leading to the private apartments above. Paul couldn't help but note the symbolic nature of this divide, two separate worlds converging to form one unstoppable force.

Raul kept to his usual schedule even when Paul was at the compound. He didn't want Paul to think he deserved any special consideration. He wanted him to know that he must always rely on himself, that no matter how much money or influence he had, ultimately, it didn't matter if he couldn't rely on his own abilities. He had taught Paul from the beginning that he must always think about every decision he made, no matter how small or seemingly insignificant. Success was many times determined by addressing the slightest details.

He flipped the computer screen to another view of the compound. Things were shaping up nicely. Preparations for the party were well underway. The staff, of course, had everything in hand. Paul was well-liked, and they would all see to it that he had a spectacular birthday. Raul was proud of his son. He had made the right choice, just as he knew that Paul would also.

Caroline was a different matter, but Rafael had taken charge of that situation. Her small rebellion had been managed quietly and successfully. She had learned that her behavior would not be tolerated. Raul could rely on Paul to manage her. He almost laughed at the way his son had handled this morning. Raul had deliberately kept certain elements of his plan from Paul. It would never do to let him become complacent, to think he knew everything. Then he wouldn't be prepared for the unexpected problems that would present themselves.

Raul had made it his special task to learn everything about his son. He had known that Paul would go straight to the communication compound to seek answers to the questions that Caroline had unknowingly revealed. Paul, like himself, didn't want anyone else to have the upper hand. He wouldn't ask Raul directly, but he would find them in his own way. It wouldn't matter; the outcome was assured.

He had listened to their conversation on the patio. He didn't often invade his son privacy, but today was different. He had smiled when he watched Paul handle Caroline's obvious little antics. They would make a good team. He was actually impressed by Caroline. She hadn't shown any outward feelings of boredom, but her statement revealed she had been feeling isolated.

So they planned to leave the compound, he mused. That would be good. Raul pressed the button that connected him directly to Rafael's office. Of course, just as he did, Rafael would already know Paul's plans. Tonight, Raul and Rafael would reveal the next phase to them. From this point on, Paul and Caroline would be a team, inseparable, tied together forever, and more securely bound than by any marriage vows.

He had thought of everything, hadn't he? Was there any situation that he hadn't contemplated, imagined? The only true test would be time, and the only true victor would be Raul. He felt assured of his ultimate success. How could he not succeed with Rafael at this side?

"Rafael, do you have everything prepared?"

"Of course," the deep timbre of Rafael's voice echoed across the room. "He is too much like you to have waited for explanations. Independent, isn't he? You chose well."

"We will see." Raul knew better than to be overly confident. "Take care," he advised.

"Always." The conversation was at an end. There was never any need for wasted words or further discussion. Each man knew his part. Trust was implicit.

Rafael tapped his pen on the hard desk surface as he scanned the monitor in front of him. In front of the massive doors stood the ancient, four-wheel drive, dust-covered Jeep that Paul had ordered for the day. Rafael smiled. Paul had changed dramatically over the past several years. He no longer asked permission or sought advice. Now, he simply ordered what he wanted and went where he pleased. Of course, he had learned the limitations that were inherent with his position, and he had never overstepped the boundaries after that one incident. Invisible as they were; there were definite limitations to Paul's freedom. But there were even greater rewards. Soon, he and Caroline would learn what the future held for them.

Rafael laughed softly as he watched Caroline descend the staircase, her sundress swirling around her legs. Somehow he didn't really think she was prepared for an outing with Paul. But Rafael knew Paul well enough to guess what he had in mind. He wasn't the least bit worried about Caroline's safety. Paul would never do anything to warrant Rafael's interference or incur his wrath. Raul had made sure Paul understood Rafael's role in the organization from a very early age. But more importantly, Rafael and Paul had a bond that even Raul didn't share.

Rafael leaned back against the soft leather of his chair. His dark eyes traveled around the bank of monitors lining the opposite walls. Satisfied with the destination Paul had in mind for his outing, Rafael pressed a button on his computer and the wood paneling slid silently across the wall, closing off visual access to the monitors.

Rafael was still concerned with Caroline's attitude, but she had done nothing further to warrant his displeasure since her earlier transgression. He was almost certain that she had learned that her willful disobedience would not be tolerated. But he had to admire her stubborn tenacity. She had accepted the changes in her circumstances and had proven herself willing to change and able to adapt quite well.

Although Caroline had done nothing terribly wrong, it was her choice of friends and her willful disobedience that Rafael had seen necessary to correct without delay. Their plans left no margin for adolescent misconduct. However, he could see from her attitude toward Paul that she hadn't lost any of her earlier confidence. He was glad; he didn't want to curtail her exuberance for life. He just wanted to insure her compliance with his dictates.

He swung around in his chair and clicked off the computer screen. The festivities would begin soon. Raul would be expecting him. Rafael, himself a ruggedly handsome man, never allowed any hint of softness to betray his emotions, but after viewing the interaction between Paul and Caroline, the slight appearance of a smile lingered around the corners of his mouth. He could be proud of his daughter. She would fulfill her role admirably, of that he had no doubt.

Paul swung the beat-up, old Jeep around the twisting curves of the mountainous road with practiced ease. He had been driving through the valley since his first summer at the compound. Even at fourteen he had been expected to begin assuming his role. This had been his first vehicle, and even though it had seen much better days, it was kept in excellent repair just for Paul's personal use. He much preferred it to the massive vehicles Raul and Rafael both used. It had seen him through more than a few tough scrapes, unconsciously his hand slid over the bullet holes still evident along the window's edge.

His short, dark hair blew wildly in the hot, sultry breeze streaming through the open windows, and he laughed silently as he watched Caroline fighting to keep her hair in place. In exasperation, she whipped her scarf from around her neck and secured the windblown curls. Her smug look of satisfaction caused his laughter to burst forth. Her eyes darted in his direction. She tried to remain aloof, but his apparent light-hearted gaiety was catching, and she laughed aloud with him. It felt good to be free of the confines of the compound and the all-knowing eyes that seemed to follow her everywhere.

Paul glanced at Caroline. He understood what she was feeling. Even though he knew they were never truly alone, it still felt good to be free, even if that freedom was monitored. The workers at the compound were family, but even family could become stifling at times. Out in the open, flying down the mountain slopes, he felt more at ease, less on display, less as though he had to be perfect. Just for a few minutes, he could be himself.

He wondered if Caroline truly understood the restrictions placed on her. Maybe she didn't know the extent of their fathers' surveillance of their lives. Somehow, he didn't think that she would like it, not even a little bit. He could almost hear her ranting again the injustice of it all. She seemed to be the sort who would make a stand and stick to it until the death, if necessary, just to make a point. He hoped that he was wrong in his assessment. Death was all too real in the cartel's line of work—and all too permanent. People were an expendable commodity, easily replaced. Paul had seen and heard too much in the last seven years not to appreciate that fact.

He swung off the main road on to a less-frequented track. The Jeep bumped and swerved as he raced down the trail. Caroline gripped the edge of the seat with one hand and the door frame with the other. Her well-manicured finger nails dug into the material as she struggled to keep her seat. Her seatbelt cut into the upper portion of her body as she bounced around. Paul seemed to be unaware of the discomfort he was causing her, but she would die before she made one sound of complaint. If this was some sort of test, he needed to learn that she had been trained by a master, her father. She would be the last to give in; she was determined. Paul slammed on the brakes and skidded expertly to a halt just feet from the sheer drop-off that overlooked the valley below.

The scene spread out before them was breathtaking. Sultry wisps of vapor rose from the valley floor and floated majestically in the air, suspended between earth and heaven. Lush green foliage covered every conceivable inch of land. Vibrantly colored birds flitted back and forth, squawking noisily in their flight. The soft lulling sound of water flowing nearby added background to the picturesque scene.

Paul stepped from the Jeep and started down the steep path that wound toward the valley floor. Caroline struggled to release her seatbelt and hurried after him. She knew he wouldn't wait for her, and she was determined to prove herself to him. The short heels she had chosen to wear were unsuitable for the terrain, but she refused to be intimidated. Shoes could be replaced. First impressions lasted a lifetime. If she fell and broke her neck, then he could answer to her father. Now that could prove interesting. For a moment she felt light-hearted. Then she sobered; the thought of Rafael's reaction did give her a momentary boost of energy, but she wouldn't want that to ever happen. She had witnessed Rafael in action. The memory of his cold demeanor still sent chills racing through her blood.

Paul smiled. He had to give her credit; she hadn't complained—not that he had given her much of an opportunity to do so. For that matter, he probably couldn't have heard her if she had with them racing along in his worn-out old, bucket of bolts, but soon they would reach the valley floor. Then he would see. He picked up his pace. This day was definitely taking a different turn from the way that it had first begun.

Chapter 2

ON THE SOUTH SIDE of Memphis, the oppressive weight of the sultry, summer air felt laden with hidden danger. Drug Enforcement Agent, Tim Richards, slumped against the dingy, crumbling brick wall. His quarry had gone under; now he would have to squander the little time left in what would probably be a fruitless effort. A smoking cigarette dangled lazily from his lowered right hand. His left remained out-of-sight behind his back. His fingers lightly gripped the handle of his concealed 38, crammed in the waist of his torn, faded jeans. Being left-handed sometimes gave him an advantage.

To anyone paying close attention, he gave the impression of slovenly disdain for his surroundings. His scruffy beard and stringy hair added to the picture of disrepute. He blended well with the lackluster, slow-paced morning derelicts just beginning to wake from their late-night rambles. He wanted to keep it that way. He rarely spoke; his sometimes street-friends thought that he was shell-shocked, a too-often-seen casualty of an earlier war, not a participant in the daily war that raged in the streets around him. He let them think that; it added to his aloof aura of disinterest. He knew that his life depended on his ability to blend in, to remain uninvolved.

Richards had seen so much during this undercover operation that, most nights, sleep was difficult. Remaining detached from the criminal elements that surrounded him had forced him to witness unimaginable abuses. He didn't really care what the slime that the Mighty Mississippi dredged up did to each other, but the innocent lives caught in the crossfire, that was what caused him to hate his job, to hate that he couldn't afford to break his cover, but more than a few innocent lives would be lost if he didn't accomplish what he had been assigned to do. He had invested three years of his life, of his own freedom, to see the end to this operation. He couldn't let anything interfere now, not after all this time.

He also knew that he couldn't last much longer uncover; he was losing touch with his former life, with his own identity. Some days he actually felt that he was who he claimed to be. Now it was becoming too easy to play the part and harder to recognize the reality, to separate fact from fiction. That was why this meeting today was so important.

Richards' fingers unconsciously tightened on the handle of his weapon as he envisioned the upcoming meeting. Jared Strong, a man to be reckoned with in his own right, a man not to underestimate, but not the only man he soon hoped to bring down. Richards pushed away from the wall and glanced slowly around. The mostly empty street held no apparent threat, but he was savvy enough to take nothing for granted. He glanced at the cheap knock-off watch he wore—time to move. He would be expected.

He deliberately kept his movements slow, even awkward, as he ambled toward the corner. His lack of coordination, at first, had made him a target for the local street punks, but when they forced him into action, a few well-placed kicks had taught them to steer clear of him. Over time they had left him to brood silently in his accustomed spot. The vacant stare that he had perfected only added credence to their belief that he was harmless to them and their enterprises. He simply became a fixture on the street, as unimportant as the street light with its broken bulb and just as useless.

It was his ability to move undetected within the city that had first brought him to the attention of Strong. Richards had let just enough information slip to whet the interest of those in power. He knew they needed men to carry out sensitive jobs, silent, withdrawn, well-trained men, men who were disillusioned with and disenfranchised by society. His training as a special-forces operative and the falsified record showing his discharge, brought about by his psychotic actions as a result of a supposed injury, gave him the needed cover for his withdrawn behavior and his willingness to succumb to Strong's enticements to join forces with his organization.

Even then Richards played a cat and mouse game with Strong. He didn't want to appear too eager; nothing signaled trouble faster than someone overly eager to join forces with the likes of Strong. Only after lengthy discussions did he allow himself to be persuaded to join Strong's organization.

He had something that the streets couldn't give them; he was a well-trained assassin, one trained to take out his quarry while he lay sleeping next to someone else without creasing the covers. Anybody could kill, but very few could do so without detection. Strong wanted someone who could instill fear in the hearts of the fearless—a phantom.

Richards knew there were serious problems developing between Strong's organization and the new syndicate, which had begun operation in Atlanta, New Orleans, and Houston. There were always rival groups springing up around the country, but they were usually easily dealt with. This group, however, seemed too deeply entrenched to give up without open warfare. Strong didn't want that. It brought unwanted attention on the whole operation. Richards also knew that today's meeting would be with Strong's boss, Alexander Graham. Richards had waited a long time for this; he had sacrificed over three years of his life. Now he was finally going to achieve what he had vowed to do.

He wasn't proud of some of his actions during this operation, but he had succeeded in bringing several men to justice, men who would have otherwise escaped. Some might see that as vigilante style retribution, but he didn't lose sleep over any of those. It was the innocent ones that he couldn't help that gnawed at his insides.

Richards slipped quietly down a back alley, always checking behind him. He changed directions several times, winding back on his own route. He hadn't made it this far just to slip up now.

He didn't trust Strong; he knew that Strong tried to keep tabs on him and was secretly afraid of him. The very skills he possessed were the same skills that made Strong wary of him. If Richards hadn't been useful to them, he knew Strong would have tried to eliminate him.

But Richards had become indispensible, at least as much as anyone in the criminal world could be. He faded from sight until he was needed. He never asked questions. He followed orders and accepted whatever was given. He was rewarded generously, but he never pursued any of the usual pleasures of those around him. He kept to himself and continued his life of seclusion.

His sent the majority of his earnings to an orphanage out of state. Richards knew that Strong had had the money transfers traced, and he had made it easy for him. The dummy account appeared legitimate, and there was an actual orphanage located in the area, which received regular anonymous gifts, but most of the money was re-deposited by a special agent into a federal account, awaiting the conclusion of the operation.

Richards made his way unobtrusively to Graham's office building. Silently, he slipped passed the lounging guard stationed at the building's entrance. He had tied his hair at the back of his neck as he walked, slipped his weapon into his leg holster, and eased his awkward gait to a more normal pace. He blended well with the early morning crowd rushing to fill the elevators. Richards stepped off one floor above his destination. He always varied his means of entry although he recognized early on that Strong's men were inept at subterfuge.

Using the back stairs, he walked to the floor below, which housed Graham's private offices. He waited in the silent stairwell until Graham's secretary left her station. Strong knew that Richards would be in the building and that he wouldn't enter Graham's office if anyone was in the outer office. Strong always sent the girl on some errand. Neither Graham nor Strong wanted anyone to recognize Richards, and that suited him. The fewer people involved in his plans the better for his own safety, as well as theirs.

Richards knew that the trucking and transportation enterprises, which Graham ran out of his office, were legitimate. He sincerely doubted that any of Graham's office staff or business acquaintances really knew what his actual business involved. People rarely scratched below the surface to see what lay beneath, especially if the person was charming, seemingly compassionate, and philanthropic. Graham was all of these.

Within the organization, he kept a very low profile and limited his association to issuing orders through Strong. Very few people knew his true involvement. Something very important must be in the works for Graham to send for Richards and especially since he was to meet with them in Graham's private office. He had rarely met personally with Graham.

Richards could sense the tension in the room as soon as he eased the door open. Graham paced angrily back and forth between his massive desk and the window-lined outer wall. Richards remained just inside the closed door, not advancing into the room. The early morning light streamed through the tinted glass casting a haze over the surroundings. He had never seen Graham this agitated before. Richards assumed his normal pose; his cold, empty eyes stared vacantly at Strong; he appeared unaffected by the tension filling the room.

Strong immediately stood and motioned Richards to take a seat. Richards ignored him. He knew that his silent refusal angered Strong, but it was a necessary tactic. Richards had long ago learned never to become too complacent, never to let his guard down. Even such a meaningless power play could signal weakness. He had to maintain his air of disdain for authority. It was this very element of fearless, intractable obstinacy that made him ideal for the jobs he carried out for Graham's organization.

Graham failed to share Strong's dislike, and even fear, of Richards. To Graham, Richards was a burned-out reject from society, with little personal initiative. He believed that Richards had been so well conditioned during his military training that he had lost touch with reality and assumed the "duties," as assigned by Strong, to be covert military operations. Richards played up this idea whenever possible. When he did break his usual silence, he purposefully used military jargon to refer to the target and any possible deterrents or obstacles to accomplishing his goal.

Angrily, Graham swung around to face Richards. This time he would issue the orders; this time he wanted to personally bring an end to his rivals. He had lost countless contracts, suffered major financial losses because of their interference, because of their threats to his people. He wouldn't be patient any longer. It was time that he made them all aware of the risk of trying to take over his territory. He didn't want open warfare, which seemed to be his rival's ultimate goal. He liked the appearance of respectability that his social position offered. But the time had come to stand his ground. If they wanted warfare, then let them deal with a war unlike any they had ever seen, one that they couldn't possibly win.

"Richards, I have an operation unlike any that you have been assigned before," Graham's voice vibrated with pent-up anger. "I want an all-out assault of multiple targets," he was in his element now. He liked the feeling of power he felt when issuing orders to Richards, a general leading his troops. "I want it staged simultaneously. I have mapped out the details. You can work out the logistics. You will have everything that you need at your disposal—everything." Graham's rage vibrated around the silent room as he slammed his fist onto the dark mahogany desk top; the silver in-laid pen holder rattled noisily.

Richards remained silent as he ran various scenarios through his mind. This must be bigger than even he had thought. He remained impassive throughout Graham's tirade against his enemies. When Graham finally burned off his excessive rage and flung himself into his leather desk chair, Strong began filling in the details. Strong couldn't stand Richards' silence; it made him edgy. Richards knew Strong would fill in the missing pieces, often betraying more information than was necessary for Richards to carry out a job. Richards had accumulated a rather detailed portfolio on the organization just from inadvertent slips that Strong had made.

Richards had also seen how often Strong displeased Graham and prompted him to believe, that if Graham ever felt truly threatened, Strong would be in serious trouble. Richards was smart enough to know that he was expendable as soon as his usefulness ended. He had only himself to rely on and a few within the department who actually knew about his operation.

Richards' having been undercover for such an extended time, left him vulnerable to shifts in departmental strategies. To maintain his cover, he had virtually broken all ties with his former life. Few people even knew who he really was or what he was doing. It had to remain that way for his protection. But money talked, and so did men who needed it. It didn't matter what color their uniform, if the need was great enough. Richards had seen too many good men make bad decisions. Even the upper echelons of the force were accountable to Graham and his political allies for their benevolence. Deals were brokered; favors were given; funds were supplied. Graham's ties to local, state, and even federal government made serious problems for ever proving his involvement with the drug syndicate.

Up until this meeting, Graham had disassociated himself from actually issuing orders. Simple conspiracy wasn't enough; Richards wanted undeniable proof that Graham was the syndicate head and that he was not the generous, caring man he portrayed himself to be.

What was that old saying, "You can't have your cake and eat it too." Well, he was certainly going to try.

Apparently, Graham was willing to sacrifice anything and anyone to accomplish his goal—eradication of his enemy. Graham had approved an elaborate scheme to purchase large quantities of cocaine from rival sources throughout the south and the west. His idea was to use his personal contacts within various local and state governments to coordinate raids on the strongholds of as many local dealers as possible. He wanted not only their merchandise, but he also wanted their people off the streets. He wanted to cripple their organizations, to disrupt the flow of cocaine in their areas, to discourage the reestablishment of rival groups. He wanted Richards to form a unit of men able to assassinate the leaders, annihilate their operations, and eliminate the competition. Only then would he be satisfied.

In his rage, Graham divulged plans to include police officials and government sources to bring about the downfall of these groups. He was willing to allow some of his own people to be used to bait the trap. Already plans were underway for the protection of his people after they were convicted as part of the group. Plans were made for the dispersal of funds to families whose members gave up their freedom to bring about the results Graham wanted. Such a sweeping drug bust operation would make the War on Drugs a rallying cry for every would-be politician and deceive the public into believing that illegal drugs could be effectively managed. This was such an elaborate operation that Graham had called in favors from every influential person that he knew.

He had devised a cover for his involvement, one that implied his discovery of his trucks and shipping enterprises being used for the illicit trafficking of drugs throughout the United States. The fact that this was one way his own drugs were distributed, didn't faze him or lessen his determination to reveal many of his own methods for distribution. He felt the loss of some of his men and revelation of some of his techniques were well worth the cost involved. Setting up the downfall of so many people at basically the same time was a demanding task, but one that stimulated Richards' ingenuity. After learning the names and locations of those most sought-after members of the opposition, Richards demanded time to devise his own plan.

He didn't want to presume too much. This operation would take an incredible amount of thought. To take out the leaders and disable the operations in so many different locations, using police and government agencies as the instruments of destruction, was almost laughable. To think that one of their own was willing to sacrifice so much just to prove his power was a sobering thought. Was Graham suffering from a Napoleon complex? Had he remained behind the scenes so long that he no longer feared discovery? Did Graham think that he had acquired so much prestige and power that he was untouchable, unstoppable? It was beyond Richards' understanding what the human mind could convince a person to believe or to do.

After arranging the next meeting time, Richards slipped as effortlessly from the office as he had entered. He didn't quite understand why Graham had been so upset. Competition was always a threat. Why was he reacting this way and why now? Richards needed to check his sources and find out what information Graham had withheld. He hated to surface now, but he didn't really have a choice. He needed to know more, and he needed help. Coordination was the key; surprise was the trick. Could it be done, and could it be done swiftly enough to capture as many key players as Graham wanted? Richards was willing to do his part even if it only meant a momentary interruption in drug trade. Graham's scheme was good, but how good remained to be seen. There was a wide margin for error between devising and doing.

Richards removed his hair tie and shook out his hair, letting its straggly links hide most of his features. Assuming his usual awkward gait, he paused briefly to scan the crowded street before mingling with the passing mass of people. Caution was more important than ever. He slipped quickly down a deserted ally and slid his revolver back into its usual place. The feel of the cold metal against his spine eased some of the tension that had been building inside him ever since he had entered Graham's office. He was used to dangerous situations, but something about today felt off. He couldn't figure it out. He needed more information and fast.

Entering an unimpressive, shabby looking building, Richards moved quietly up the deserted stairwell. He quickly entered an empty office and locked the door. Pushing a well-concealed mechanism on the adjacent wall gave Richards access to a hidden recess and a wide assortment of devices. Grabbing a preprogrammed phone, he punched in a series of numbers and waited. Rerouting the call would take a few minutes.

Chapter 3

PAUL LOOKED OUT OVER the panoramic view and silently laughed as he heard the underbrush snapping and cracking behind him. She was gutsy he had to admit, but he hadn't failed to hear her muttering under her breath as she slipped and slid precariously down the twisting trail. He would bet just about anything that if she could, she would push him right off this mountainside. He kept his expression somber as Caroline skidded to a staggering halt at his side. It really wouldn't do to antagonize her too much. He had a definite feeling that their lives were going to be intricately tied together from now on. It would be much smarter on his part to make her an ally rather than an enemy.

"What do you think?" he asked as his hand swung out to include the vista before them.

Gritting her teeth, Caroline thought that he didn't really want to know what she thought at this exact moment. She took a calming breath and scanned the majestic beauty of the mountains and valley below. Even she couldn't remain hostile in the presence of such magnificence. Okay, so maybe she wouldn't be able to walk for a few days, the splendor before her was worth the sacrifice. She would just make sure that he bought her a new pair of shoes at least. Caroline felt the tension of the last few days slip away. A sense of being alone in the world with no one except Paul flowed through her, a feeling of peaceful serenity. Would that feeling remain after the party tonight? Would she want to be alone with Paul after Raul and Rafael revealed their great plan for their futures? What would she do if she didn't agree with their plans?

She almost laughed aloud. She knew better than to thwart Rafael once he issued an order. She wouldn't dare voice a complaint.

Caroline forced herself to relax again and enjoy the view. "It's breathtaking," she replied in an awed voice. Paul heard the sincerity and was relieved. He would have been disappointed if she hadn't understood the significance of this place. It was his solace, his refuge. He never took anyone here, but somehow it had just seemed appropriate to share it with her, even if he thought she still had a lot to learn. Of course, he would never tell her any of that. Too much information personal or otherwise was a dangerous tool in the hands of others. Didn't his father use just such information about others to manipulate them? The more he kept to himself the better for all concerned.

He was impressed; she didn't feel that she needed to fill the silence with meaningless conversation. Maybe there was hope for them. If he only knew exactly what Raul intended, but that would be soon enough. He knew the importance of this birthday. He felt the subtle shift in those around him. Did they know more than he did, or were they just guessing? He seemed impervious to the deep sigh that escaped him.

Caroline glanced in his direction. She had been lost in her own world of conjecture. His sigh summed up exactly how she felt. Maybe they would work well together after all. She smiled briefly. Only time would tell—and their fathers.

A multitude of lights encompassed the main compound. Sultry rhythms vibrated through the warm night air. Music and voices blended harmoniously as a myriad of sounds pulsed across the open spaces. Every inch of the compound seemed to come alive with lights and music. People gathered everywhere. The subtle smells emanating from the food-laden tables mixed with the soft fragrance of the flowers lining the walkways and spilling from the hidden gardens. A kaleidoscope of colors, sights, and smells filled the early evening hours. Paul walked among friends. He felt at home with these people. They knew him and who he really was. He didn't have to pretend with them. He could be himself. But he knew instinctively that was about to change. Still, he planned to enjoy this night. Too many people that he admired and respected had worked to make this a special night, and he wouldn't ruin it for them, regardless of what surprises the evening might hold.

Raul watched silently from his suite of rooms as Paul moved among his family and friends. He was proud of his son, but tonight would be the true test of his mettle. Paul had proven himself already. He was an exceptional student, well respected at Harvard, and friends with some of the most influential heirs to America's fortunes, its oldest, most prestigious families. He had distinguished himself among his peers, but like his father before him, he had learned quite early how to manage situations, especially those that his friends seemed to constantly find themselves caught up in.

Raul was pleased how quickly Paul had comprehended the intricacies involved with manipulating situations and people to his own ends. Paul had built a tight circle of elite young men; all of whom owed Paul, sometimes for something trivial and other times for something more critical. Like his father before him, Paul never accepted anything in return for his assistance. If needed, his private collection of files would someday be worth a king's, or a New England blue blood's, ransom. Of course, Raul's elaborate computer system safely housed all of the crucial documentation, evidence of youthful indiscretions, pampered willfulness, and complete disregard for the law.

Paul had had little trouble fitting into the prestigious circle of the Eastern elite. His adoptive parents had been well placed in Texas society with their oil money and ancestral ties to the founding fathers of the Lone Star State. Raul considered it a stroke of genius that he had devised the plan to institute his own private adoption agency in the States. He had been able to place the children with the best parents from the most influential backgrounds. Their all-consuming desire for children left these childless couples easy prey for Raul and even easier to manipulate once they had developed a strong bond with their baby. Having agreed to the special conditions the agency, under Raul's close direction, set for the adoptions, the couples agreed to allow their children to be introduced to their real families at a future date.

Of course, for the prospective parents, the agency related Raul's heart-wrenching story of how the mother of the child had been deceived by some man and left to suffer the results of her indiscretion alone. It was only to save the young girl's reputation, her family's good name, and to protect the innocent child that these influential families allowed them to give their children up for adoption.

Raul smiled; he had realized at a very early age that desperation drove people to make irresponsible decisions. Had these couples not been desperate for a child of their own, they most likely would have questioned more closely the restrictions and stipulations placed on the adoptions. However, Raul had seen to it that everything was legal and above reproach. If one couple refused, there were always a dozen more to replace them. The very private and elite nature of his agency appealed to the more affluent and prestigious families.

Having accomplished his first goal, his dream finally lay within reach. Years of planning were taking shape, and the distant future now seemed very near.

In his own apartments, Rafael watched his daughter laughingly accept a drink from a smiling young man, who seemed awed by her sparkling beauty. He was proud of his daughter. She had excelled in every aspect of her life. She was an accomplished linguist, an excellent student, and a talented, independent young woman. She definitely had her mother's beauty; for that he was glad. Caroline radiated the same vitality that had drawn him to her mother over twenty years earlier. Raul's plan had exceeded both of their expectations. They had the living proof before them tonight, and now it only remained to continue their dream.

Rafael closed the monitor and walked toward Raul's apartment. Tonight the meeting with their children would be private. There was much to discuss, plans to be made. With their help, their children were destined for a future of unimagined greatness. For Raul and Rafael, the future held the promise of immeasurable power.

As the lavish celebrations came to a close, Raul sent word for Paul and Caroline to come to his private office. There was much speculation as to the changes that all felt were about to take place. Paul, leaning against a low rock wall leading to the upper patio, waited patiently for Caroline to make her way across the vast area of the outer courtyard. The grounds of the compound were extensive, and tonight they looked almost like a small city ablaze with lights. Well-wishers continually slowed Caroline's progress as she moved toward Paul. Paul wasn't the only one celebrating a birthday, even though her birthday was still a week away. She and Paul would no longer be at the compound after tonight. Tomorrow they left to begin their last year at Harvard.

Strange that they had both attended the same university and had never met before this. Caroline somehow felt they might have been kept apart deliberately. Even though Caroline had finally won Rafael's approval again, she had still been kept on a very short leash. Her degree in business law and her minor in political science would definitely benefit her if she married someone with political ambitions or if she pursued a political career herself. She had not wasted her collegiate career with the trivial pursuits of Sorority Houses and elitist organizations but rather had become completely immersed in campus politics and had made more than one influential acquaintance.

Although, she had to admit her adopted father knew just about everyone who was anyone in the political arena. She had not used his influence to ingratiate herself with her politically-minded friends but much preferred to be valued for her own abilities. Her confident demeanor and in-depth understanding of key issues soon earned her the respect of her colleagues.

At first they had assumed she would just fill the slot of the "token blonde" with more money than sense, whose primary role in the political process would be to elicit funds from rich contributors. It hadn't taken her long to dissuade them of that false notion. Anyone who took the time to really get to know her was pleasantly surprised by her political acumen. But that was not to say that she felt herself too important to seek financial contributions. After all, God had given her the gift of beauty, and she felt there was nothing wrong in using that gift, especially for a good cause. Most people soon realized that she was a force to be reckoned with, as intelligent as she was beautiful, and she liked that.

Her father, on the other hand, favored moving behind the scenes; he didn't directly involve himself in campaigns but preferred to support those whom he felt were worthy representatives of his own personal interests. Caroline had rarely met those men since she was usually away from home attending school. In fact, she had rarely been home after that summer when she had first met her real father, Rafael Saltas. From that moment, her life had virtually ceased to be her own. She often felt that her life, after that eventful summer, had become a never-ending series of subtle learning experiences laced with unspoken expectations. Nothing she did was simply for fun or entertainment. Even activities, which most people pursued for pleasure, were tasks which she must accomplish to charm and captivate those around her.

While there were few decisions made for her that she didn't actually concur with, just knowing that someone else held the reins caused her to want to throw off the traces and run free. But she wasn't stupid. She understood, now, that Rafael had great plans for her and going against his wishes could be very dangerous. She had felt the underlining tension which filled a room any time he entered, and she recognized that Rafael had unlimited power at his disposal. She loved her parents; they had been good to her and had given her every possible advantage in life. She didn't want to repay their love with a childish rebellion, one which might harm them, as well as her. She was a smart girl—at least, most of the time.

Caroline glanced at Paul, lounging negligently against the patio wall. Had he ever done anything really stupid? Would she ever know if he had? He was so quiet, so secretive. No, that wasn't quite right. He was cautious; he seemed to weigh each word before he spoke, a trait she probably should emulate. She knew that she would have to be very careful around him. That carefree pose he had assumed didn't fool her. Caroline sensed the same vigilance in Paul that appeared to be the hallmark of his father. But now, the hour of truth lay before them. Taking a calming breath, she walked toward him.

When Caroline reached Paul's side, he motioned for her to precede him up the outer stairs. As they made their way across the open expanse of the entry, for a fleeting moment Paul felt the overwhelming compulsion to hum a funeral dirge in time to their steps. Was he more concerned about this meeting than even he had realized? Or was he just feeling the weight of his obligations?

Caroline certainly appeared to be unconcerned. Paul absolutely refused to let her appear more composed than he. Did his father ever have misgivings about his decisions? Paul almost laughed. No, Raul would have covered every contingence and uncovered every weakness before undertaking any plan. He was methodical, shrewd, and dispassionate, all important qualities for a man in his line of work, and especially for a man with his power.

As Paul opened the heavy, mahogany door to his father's private office, he knew that this was a momentous occasion, one that would shape his destiny and determine his future, as well as Caroline's.

Chapter 4

THE NEXT DAY AFTER several hours in flight on one of Raul's private jets, Paul and Caroline landed without incident at the bustling airport. Quietly thanking the captain and flight attendants for their services, Paul stepped confidently through the doorway and walked directly toward the waiting car. His driver would collect their baggage. Having safely delivered its cargo, the plane would refuel and return to the isolated beauty of Raul's compound.

Paul was not concerned with petty details; his mind raced with unlimited possibilities. Now he finally understood, and it made perfect sense. It was a masterful plan, one that had taken years of planning and execution, an incredible investment in the future.

His mind was already focused on his part. His pulse raced when he considered the multitude of details which had to be worked out before they could move forward. His heart pounded with excitement when he thought about what the future held. Only time would tell just how successful they would be. Failure, even for a son, was not an option in Raul's world.

Caroline followed behind Paul and smiled at the rush of happiness she experienced at being back in the States. Her trips to Rafael's always left her feeling smothered. The lush tropical beauty of the compound was breath-taking, but she could never really relax when she was there. She always felt as though she were poised on the brink of some great discovery yet plagued with uncertainty, at the mercy of unseen forces.

Now she understood the true nature of those forces, at least as much as the Raul and Rafael allowed her to know. After a somewhat curt explanation of her role in their plans, she was advised to return to her apartments and pack for the next day's return flight to the States. Paul would be in charge from now on and would fill in any details necessary for her to know at a later time. She tried with some difficulty to cover her irritation at being summarily dismissed.

She was an intelligent girl and had deduced much more about their lives than she had ever revealed to anyone. She really didn't want to believe certain aspects, but neither could she deny the obvious. No one had ever directly stated what the family business was, and she had never asked. Some things were best left unsaid. But after the elaborate and far-reaching plans, which had been revealed last night, she could no longer hide from the truth. How did she really feel about this entire operation? What choice did she have? She couldn't refuse to do her part; that had never been an option. She might not like certain aspects of their plan, but she would follow orders, because that was exactly what they were—orders, direct and inflexible.

Even the bright sunlight of the midday sun seemed dim now as she crossed the tarmac. No, she would not let any of this affect her. She would focus on doing her part and try to remain as detached from as she could. This was just another assignment, and the benefits would be unbelievable. She had always excelled in any challenge she faced, and she would this one. Besides, she wasn't attracted to anyone special. The only downside was her inability to choose for herself and the fact that she had been wrong about her future with Paul; that irked her; she hated being wrong.

Instead, she was to be the inducement, the necessary enticement, to lure the right man into their scheme. Had this been an earlier century, she would have experienced less frustration at the way the men had dictated her role, decided her future without regard for her wishes, but then she had always known that her wishes were of little consequence to Rafael. Just as she knew that there was never any question that she would disobey. The consequences of any rebellion were too frightening to consider.

As she watched Paul striding confidently in front of her, she could not help drawing an obvious parallel between their lives now and the future. She would always be the woman behind the man, never out front. Her role was decided, and there was no point in trying to change it. She had been groomed for this position, and modern ideas of equality played no part.

Paul, as well as she, had at first been surprised by their fathers' plans, but Paul seemed to change right in front of her. His boyish charm and nonchalant attitude had disappeared. When the men began discussing the details the night before, Paul had been adamant that he already had the perfect candidate in mind. He only needed a little time to work out a few finer points. Surprisingly, Raul had left that decision in his hands.

Caroline, they said, was a natural for her part. She had the training, the expertise, and the background to be the perfect wife—to be Paul's perfect accomplice. Not the role she had envisioned, but she realized her heart had never been involved. It was merely an idle fancy brought about by the subtle hints of the *family*. Like her, they probably had had no idea how her life and Paul's were to be connected, and marriage uniting the two families would have seemed obvious to them. But Raul and Rafael's plan far exceeded that limited view.

Robert Billing stood out among his fellow classmates. It wasn't only his boyish good looks and sincere, charming manner, but more his confident attitude. Although his family had always been honest, hard-working, rural farmers, they were by no means wealthy. His bronzed skin and naturally gold-streaked, light brown hair and owed nothing to a fashionable salon, but more to a youth spent helping his father. But he didn't let that fact, or the fact that he was attending Harvard on a scholarship, make him feel inadequate even when surrounded by the country's elite and privileged future leaders. His superior intelligence and phenomenal memory distinguished him from most others. His charismatic personality and the ease with which he could recall information made him a favorite among the students and facility. He was more than willing to share his knowledge when someone needed help. His involvement in campus politics and the ability with which he could debate most issues with comprehensive understanding and astute observations soon led to invitations to the homes of some very influential people.

He became the man to know, and he liked that feeling. He realized that his classmates paraded him in front of their parents as a means of showing how studious and civic-minded they were. Robert didn't care what their ulterior motives were. These were golden opportunities for him to make contacts and to impress the men in power, men who worked behind the scenes and often determined the country's future.

Robert meant to be a part of that future. He had chosen his path, and nothing was going to alter his course.

He knew that his classmates were using him to impress their parents; he didn't care. He was using them as well. Life was filled with users. Their personal agendas might be different, but they all did it. He wasn't a gullible country hick or some down-home, good ole boy, and he wasn't really impressed by their affluence. He had something that none of them did. He had power that few possessed, and he planned to make the most of his ability.

With his phenomenal memory, he far exceeded most men's ability to debate issues. This brought him to the attention of those looking for someone outstanding to lead their party to victory. He was a handsome, young man with a charming personality, a prestigious education, and the skill to verbally annihilate almost any opponent.

Robert laughed at the ease in which he was able to maneuver his way into their inner circle. Others, who held secret beliefs in their own power to impress, soon fell before Robert's shrewd political and economic prowess. His understanding of issues, his ability to see far-reaching consequences, and his skill at forging bonds between disparate groups solidified his acceptance by the elite and his future role in the Democratic Party. He was on his way.

However, Robert had few true friends. He understood that to some he was a threat. Intellectually, they couldn't compete with him. Most of them came from families of power, privilege, and prestige. With that, he couldn't compete, but he was a man on the move, a force to contend with. Before long he would have those things also. He had met one person whom he considered a true friend. He never asked anything of Robert. He was a friend Robert could trust, someone who was almost as brilliant as he.

Robert smiled at that thought. They were both talented, but their fields of expertise were definitely different. Worldly wise in a manner which Robert almost envied, his friend had brought sophistication into Robert's life. With his help, Robert felt at ease among the rich and powerful; he knew he only had to ask if he really needed anything, and it would be his. What more could a friend want?

Robert wasn't dumb. He didn't ask for anything, but any time Robert needed to fit in, to become part of an inner circle, to mix with the right people, his friend was there to pave the way. He was Robert's security blanket against the cold winds of rejection and the empty wasteland of failure. Failure was not acceptable. He might face a slight set-back from time to time, but never a failure.

His peers all thought that everything was about money—who had it and who didn't. Life was more than that, much more. Money was important; he didn't deny that fact, but power was much better. Power, and those who held it, drew money like a magnet. Power and influence—however they were achieved—those were the real forces. All that Robert had to do now was keep his focus. He couldn't afford to let anything derail his plans. His future was at stake but, before long, would be within his reach.

Robert closed the book he had just finished speed reading, one of his many talents. He laughed softly to himself, causing several heads to turn. Nodding apologetically to his fellow students, he smiled, displaying his boyish grin. While others pursued sports and girls, he used his time to improve his knowledge and to be seen in the right places. He wasn't opposed to having a good time, and he knew how to party, but he also knew that to create the wrong image, at this point, would be political suicide. Somebody would always remember, and he didn't plan to give anyone the upper-hand in his life, not if he could prevent it.

Robert glanced around at the students gathered for the fall term. He recognized several faces. The calm quiet of the enormous university law library was the ideal spot to meet those who favored a scholarly approach to political and economic problems. It also formed another potential power base for him to gain support in future years.

If possible, when the time came, he wanted to draw everyone that he could to his side and offer a platform that would address the concerns and issues of all demographic sections. Many in the party viewed that as an unrealistic dream, but Robert knew that great men of the past had been able to see beyond the limitations of their time and had created for themselves a new reality and had reshaped the world around them. If anyone could draw people together, Robert felt that he could. He truly believed that he had the skill and the resolve to be a great leader, a man who could change the destiny of his party and his country.

Robert realized he had one shortcoming; he needed experience. People wanted someone tested, tried and true, to lead them, someone who had faced adversity and overcome, someone who had known despair and not succumbed, someone who had suffered injustice and persevered—someone that the average person could identify with.

Those in power wanted someone they could shape to their wishes, who would fall in line with their personal agendas and not upset any of their long range goals. Robert knew the art of compromise and excelled in diplomacy. He knew that with time and patience he would succeed in bringing them all together in support of him.

First, though, he had to make a name for himself with the people, and he had a plan. This was his final year at Harvard. He would graduate with honors in the spring, and with his law degree, he planned to establish himself in one of the prestigious, old law firm in his home state of Arkansas. He had already received several lucrative offers from prominent firms around the country. His credentials were impeccable, and with his double major in international and business law, he would be a valuable asset to any firm.

But he hoped to launch his career and pursue his political ambitions from the state ranked forty-ninth in almost every conceivable area. Robert wanted to use his own state's desperate need for whole-scale reform to shape his future, to become his personal battle ground for change, and to make a name for himself.

Robert stretched his long legs out in front of him and rubbed his neck as he leaned back in the upholstered chair. He was tired and needed a break. It was time to meet with his friends at the student center across campus. Everyone would be back now. Time to see what changes the summer had brought. He had used his time to clerk for a prominent federal judge. It had been well worth the investment. He had meet several influential men and worked closely with some of the country's top lawyers. It was an unforgettable experience, and, hopefully, one that had brought him to the attention of some important people.

Chapter 5

Paul entered the noisy student center with a purposeful stride. He needed to find his man as soon as possible. His heart raced with excitement. This was a challenge of such magnitude that he felt almost breathless in anticipation. He had to remind himself that this plan would take years to bring to fruition, but what were a few more years especially when he contemplated the time that had already been invested. The mere magnitude of the entire enterprise was almost inconceivable. When he considered that the man behind this vision was his father, he almost felt unworthy. How could anyone compete with a visionary of Raul's caliber?

Only Rafael understood the true character of his father; only Rafael comprehended the singular magnificence of Raul's dream. Paul was still perplexed by the sheer enormity of integrating so many details into a unified plan of action. The number of people involved over the years must have been staggering, yet nothing had ever been revealed to anyone outside of the family's most loyal, inner circle. Paul had never had even a remote suspicion of the scope of their family's involvement in other enterprises. Yet as he thought about it, he realized that he should have known Raul's powerbase was of world magnitude, simply from the training and personal instruction he had received from Raul.

Had he not shown Paul how to build a network of individuals who were indebted to him? Had he not indoctrinated Paul in the compilation of detailed biographies on the lives of anyone of worth, of possible future value? Biographies laced with the intimate details of the peccadilloes of youth, the obsessions of maturity, and the idiosyncrasies of old age—the good, the bad, and the illegal. Now Paul understood the value of those files and the extent to which most people would go to make sure that their contents were never revealed.

Briefly he scanned the laughing, jostling groups of America's most privileged sons and daughters, searching the crowd for his face. Most people were so predictable that it was easy to monitor their movements, easy to locate them. Maybe that was why he tried never to do the predictable, to alter plans, to change his routine often. He laughed out loud. Those around him glanced his way, and many waved in recognition. Maybe his very unpredictability was the element that made him predictable. He laughed again, a deep soft sound, rumbling up from his inner core. Maybe he was predictable because he was unpredictable. That was a new twist.

Another more sobering thought filled Paul's mind. He knew that his own life had been monitored since the day he had been adopted by the Stevens. Ramon had shown him his file; Paul realized now that Raul would have sanctioned this action as a means of initiating Paul into the intricacies of his scheme. Over the years, he had learned more and more about the family's operation and the far-reaching consequences of involvement in Raul and Rafael's organization.

Raul had relentlessly trained Paul to observe before speaking, to think before acting. After watching his friends and acquaintances make regrettable mistakes and demonstrate poor judgment, Paul could understand the logic behind his upbringing. There were few notable people in the room that Paul didn't have information on that someday might prove very useful.

As he walked across the crowded entrance, Paul wondered if he had ever truly made a decision of his own, or if he had been manipulated by a master-mind into doing what his father thought best for him? At this point, it didn't really matter. He liked his life; he enjoyed the thrill of working behind the scenes in people's lives, and he expected his future to be—what? Unpredictable—at this thought, Paul really laughed, causing those close by to turn, nothing like creating a scene the first day back to get everyone's attention. He had to admit it was out of character for him to display emotions so openly. He was definitely acting out of character.

He swung back to scan the room once more. Then he saw his man. He was leaning against a low, flower-filled planter which ran the expanse of the far wall, the bright splash of colors surrounding him like a lush, royal entourage, his demeanor in keeping with the fun-loving group gathered around him. As soon as he saw Paul, he straightened and walked toward him, his hand extended in cordial greeting.

"Paul, how good to see you. How was your summer? Meet anyone interesting?" his light-hearted banter drew his friends' attention. They waved to Paul in greeting.

"No one I would share with you," Paul laughed. "How was your internship? Meet any interesting criminals?"

"You know me—only the best."

"Really?" Paul played along. He knew where the conversation was headed.

"Yeah, the ones who got away." It was a running joke between them that justice in the criminal courts was only meted out to those who couldn't afford the best defense attorneys.

"That's why I'm in business law. The lawyers are always the winners regardless of who the criminals are." Paul slapped him lightly on the back as he maneuvered him away from the group to talk more privately.

"I need to speak to you privately. I have a proposition for you."

"Paul, I'm shocked. I would never have dreamed you felt that way," his voice shook with laughter as he raised one eyebrow suggestively.

Paul's eyes narrowed. "This is important. Come by the apartment the first chance you get. We'll talk then." He started to walk away then turned back. "Seriously," he added.

"Sure thing, I'll be there in about an hour." He watched Paul leave then turned back to his friends. What was that all about? He was used to Paul being serious, but he had seemed even more reserved, more secretive than usual. He had better make arrangements with his friends for the next day's meeting and head out. His curiosity was definitely roused.

His eyes traveled around the student center. More than his curiosity was roused as he glimpsed this year's bountiful crop of new arrivals. They were always ready for an evening of fun. Beauty, encased in the harsh, cold reality of Daddy's money, seldom warmed permanently to the likes of him. He was used to the double standard, a man good enough to be a friend for the son, but never for the daughter. Old money married old money. It was almost Victorian, daughters still bartered to the highest bidder. Whether it was name, wealth, or social position, there was always a price. He couldn't be too critical, though. He would do the same if it meant achieving his own goals.

In less than an hour, Robert Billings knocked on Paul's apartment door. He didn't know that from that moment, his life would never be the same.

Quickly pushing her long, blonde curls back from her face, Caroline juggled the cascading pile of books in her arms, trying desperately to maintain her precarious hold of them. She mumbled irritably under her breath as she tried to manage the sliding texts. Why had she decided to carry everything at once? She didn't really need all of these today. She could just have easily waited for some of them until later.

The silken, blonde strands slid back across her eyes just as she bumped head long into a solid wall of flesh. Her muddled brain registered warmth through the strong hands that gripped her arms to steady her after the stunning impact. Books began to slip free in every direction at once. Caroline screeched in a panic-filled voice and grabbed at whatever she could. Just as the man she had literally run into did the same thing. Between them they managed to grasp several books while the others scattered at their feet.

Caroline's eyes snapped angrily to the ruggedly handsome face before her. Irritation flooded through her, but she restrained the impulse to complain. Instead, she took a calming breath and assumed her characteristic pose of poised refinement. A Southern belle should always thank a gentleman for his assistance, even if he had been responsible for the problem. But in all honesty the fault had been hers.

"Thank you for your help, and I'm sorry that I ran headlong into you. I'm afraid that I really couldn't see." She shifted the books left in her arms to a more comfortable position and extended her hand.

"I'm Caroline," she smiled her most winning smile, knowing from past experience the effect that it would have.

Feeling his blood warm at the sight of her singular beauty, he accepted the slender hand and smiled in return. "It's a pleasure to meet you. I'm Robert." He released her hand then frowned quizzically. "Haven't I seen you at some of the political rallies on campus?" She smiled.

"I've been to several, so you might have. I'm usually in the background handing out pamphlets," she shrugged. "I've heard you speak. You're very persuasive."

He grinned, "Enough to convince you into going out for a drink with me?"

She laughed at his direct approach, "Maybe some other time. As you can see, I've got a lot to do."

"I'm really sorry that I caused such a mess." He bent down to collect the remaining books and papers rustling in the breeze around their feet.

As he stood with his arms laden with the last few books, she flicked her long hair back across her shoulder. "It's this hair. I can't keep it out of my face today, and this fall breeze doesn't help. I should have remembered how windy this campus can be."

"To be honest I wasn't paying as much attention as I should have been. I'm afraid that my mind was on something other than where I was going. So really the fault was mine."

Caroline laughed. "We certainly sound as though neither of us should have been out walking today. But there's no harm done, and thanks for helping. I'm afraid I got a little overly ambitious with the books."

"No problem," he smiled, one corner of his mouth lifting in a self-deprecating slant. "I've been guilty of the same thing a few times myself."

Caroline quickly looked him over and raised one finely arched brow. "I can just imagine," she laughed softly, the sound flowing across the early evening air. Somehow he didn't strike her as the bookish type. When he laughed too, she knew she had been right in her assessment.

"Okay, I'll admit that hasn't happened too often," he grinned sheepishly, making good use of his own charming manner. He rarely had to bother with books. His ability to remember just about everything didn't leave the need to study. But most people didn't want to know how easy things were for someone else. They wanted others to suffer along with them. He'd learned not to reveal too much. He much preferred to use his charm until he needed to prove himself.

"Why don't I help you with these?" he suggested.

"Well, under the circumstances, I don't think I can refuse," she smiled up at him and began walking toward her apartment complex. "But I have to warn you. It's a rather long walk."

"I'll let you know if I need to stop for a breather," he laughed, matching his longer strides to hers. At least she hadn't turned down this offer.

Caroline smiled. It was nice to walk beside a man for a change, not one step behind. Maybe she could figure out a way to spend—she stopped. No, the thought was untenable. She had been chosen for a special role, and she couldn't do anything that wasn't approved, no matter how innocent her actions might be. Still, she couldn't help being drawn to his good looks, boyish charm, and gentlemanly manners. He was a hard package to resist.

Maybe she had just spent too much time around the men at the compound. They were always extremely polite, but she knew that she was considered an unimportant, but necessary, component in the men's grand scheme. That attitude grated on her nerves. She must be tired. It was too late, metaphorically and literally, to consider such thoughts. Her future was charted. She glanced at Robert and sighed. Life was so unfair at times.

Paul almost laughed as he watched the two of them. He couldn't have set this up better if he had tried. Now all he had to do was make sure that Caroline knew her part. He had been on his way across campus to find her when he saw Robert and her collide. Paul knew Robert's reputation with women. He wasn't overly promiscuous, but he got around. Actually now that Paul thought about it, Robert was rather selective, but that charm of his worked wonders on the women. What would Caroline's reaction be, he wondered? He heard her distant laughter.

Paul decided to follow at a safe distance and see how things progressed. If this all came about naturally, that would just make everything easier. After several minutes, they made their way to Caroline's apartment. Paul watched as she deftly removed her books from Robert's hands and entered her apartment without missing a step. Robert turned with a smile and started back across the street. Obviously, she had captured his interest. All Paul had to do was make a few suggestions and arrange some more seemingly innocent meetings.

When Paul met with Caroline later that evening, he didn't mention what he had seen. He wanted to know how she felt about Robert but decided to wait until she brought the subject up. Paul had agreed to come to her apartment. It was strange to think they hadn't met before, but not unusual when he considered her more sheltered lifestyle and his more sophisticated pursuits. But then he had to remind himself that Rafael would restrict not only her activities but also the people that she came into contact with. Raul, on the other hand, had encouraged Paul's sophisticated pursuit of Harvard's most influential and powerful.

Caroline had lived almost in a vacuum, a void filled only with people and activities approved by her father. Everything in both their lives had been made to fit into Raul and Rafael's preconceived plan.

As Caroline moved around the apartment bringing refreshments for them, Paul wondered how she had felt about this whole idea. She was an essential element to their success. What if she refused to comply with Raul's wishes? Would they really do anything to her personally? Ah, but then they didn't have to, like him, she had another family. She would comply whether she wanted to or not. Maybe it was better to be the son instead of the daughter. He had a lot more leeway than she was given, and he knew that Raul listened to his ideas. He doubted either of their fathers would be concerned with anything Caroline had to say.

But he was interested in what she thought and how she felt. He knew for personal experience that a plan was only as good as the people who carried it out, and he didn't want a disgruntled team member. Life went much smoother if everyone had the same priorities.

"I know when we got back that we didn't really have much time to talk, but I want to know your feelings about all of this," Paul's serious tone revealed his sincerity. Caroline placed his drink on the low table in front of him before answering. She measured each word carefully before speaking. Even if his concern sounded genuine, she didn't want to reveal too much this early. She took her glass and sat down across from him on a matching leather sofa.

Unconsciously, her eyes traveled across the room to the closed door. She knew her conversations were relayed to her father. Did they think that she was so ignorant that she would not know? She suspected the rooms were monitored just like everything at the compound. Maybe this was another test of her resolve.

"I hadn't given it much undue consideration," she smiled sweetly. "Is there a problem?"

He laughed. "No. I just thought that before we get too involved with the details, we should come to some basic understanding ourselves." He leaned forward to place his drink on the table again. He had seen her glance toward the closed door. He knew how to eliminate part of the problem. "Listen, I've been stuck inside all day, and I could really use some fresh air. What do you say to a walk around the park?"

The bright gleam in her eyes gave her feelings away. She would give anything to get out of this place. She hated being restricted and her every move timed so that she never had a chance to veer from her schedule. It would be a definite improvement if she could just get a little freedom. There were times when she wanted to scream just knowing that every detail of her life was scrutinized.

Today she didn't care what anyone thought. She jumped up. "I'll get my jacket. The wind was really blowing earlier." With that she raced to her room. Her companion met her in the hallway with her jacket. Caroline didn't miss a beat. "I'll be out. I'm not certain when we will return." She didn't bother to explain or ask permission. She was stepping free, at least for this short time; no one was going to get in her way. She raised one brow in question as she faced her companion who only smiled. Impulsively Caroline gave her a quick hug. Today she wanted to taste freedom without any restrictions.

Paul smiled at the speed in which Caroline returned. She definitely felt the pinch of her limited existence, the gilded cage. This bird obviously was ready to fly. All he had to do was position the players in this game, and the results were almost guaranteed. Paul smiled as he held the door for Caroline. She noted the amused look in his eyes but refused to be concerned. He was in charge of their futures now. She would soon be introduced to an entirely different circle of people their fathers felt it necessary for her to cultivate.

Paul laughed at her exuberance as they walked crossed another busy street. "Not quite like the mountains, but the park has its own peaceful beauty." When they finally reached their destination, the rippling sound of water cascading nearby lent an air of nostalgia as Paul remembered the serenity of his mountain retreat, his solace in the midst of chaos.

Suddenly Caroline stopped and turned toward him. "I know that we might not have much time, but could I enjoy just a few days of freedom before I have to give my life over to this scheme? I don't plan to do anything foolish." She turned away, trying to compose her next words carefully. "I just want to know how it feels to rule my own life—just once."

Paul reached for her hand. "I wondered if you knew how regulated our lives have been. I've spent a lot of time piecing together our pasts and specifically how involved our fathers have been in them." He started walking farther down the trail, drawing her with him.

"I'm sure that you know our adoptive parents agreed to allow our real families to meet us when we were old enough." He glanced at her. She simply nodded. "I don't know about you, but I was sure confused. It took me several days to finally understand what had really happened with our adoptions. You've got to admit, Raul thought of everything." They walked along quietly for a few minutes, each remembering that first eventful meeting.

"That summer changed everything. At first, I was too scared to ask questions. If it hadn't been for Alberto, I'm not sure what I would have done. He helped me see that Raul had been concerned with my welfare when he had sent me away. But it was hard to think of myself as half-Bolivian, the son of a drug lord, a prime target for his enemies. I always thought of myself as the all-American boy." He laughed. "I can tell you, it was quite a shock. But before long, I learned to accept my dual life. My parents weren't thrilled when I spent my summers in Bolivia, but the information they were given was above reproach, government certified, and gave them no reason to be concerned. Raul saw to it that they received detailed reports on my well-being and schedules of summer activities. We talked regularly through computer link-ups and by telephone. They never suspected who my father really was." He frowned. "I wasn't about to tell them any different either, and after a few summers, it wasn't so bad. As I got older, I learned to appreciate what I had—two families who cared about me, just worlds apart literally." He laughed when he thought just how far apart his two lives were. Which would he choose if he actually had the chance? He didn't know. Things had gotten more complicated with each passing year.

She glanced at him. "My story's not much different. I just had a chaperone with me all the time. I finally figured out that she was a member of Rafael's family. My parents never knew. They thought they had hired an American to travel as my companion. Of course, I rarely went to the compound. Rafael and I met on one of their island retreats, and he spent days with me discussing his expectations and his plans for my education. I didn't have much free time. My life revolved around becoming the perfect, sophisticated, enlightened young woman, who always followed orders." She laughed. "Well, most of the time, but I learned quickly."

He waited for her to explain. When she didn't, they continued further down the path. A light breeze was blowing; the fall leaves were tumbling around their feet as they walked, both lost in thought.

Caroline couldn't help musing as they strolled down the flower-laden trail, that this just might be the proverbial 'garden path.' She chided herself. This was not the time to let her mind wonder. She had a part to play, an established role; she had to keep her focus. Every decision she made from this point on impacted the future, their future.

Suddenly Caroline took a deep breath then let it out loudly, "Okay, so what's the plan?" She tried to exude the right amount of acquiescence and charm. She had a job to do and would have to live with the choices Paul made. "Lead on Mac Duff," she quipped. She would trust his judgment; she just hoped it was sound.

"There's no need to be so dramatic. Let's have a party to celebrate our final year?" He laughed as she spun around on the path, her laughter rippling on the wind.

"What do you have in mind?" she asked in an offhanded manner, but her eyes were alight with excitement. She usually attended political functions or obligatory family celebrations. She hadn't been given the leeway to party with casual acquaintances, and her free time had been limited. Her education had come first. She had once believed she would have a lifetime to celebrate after she received her degree, but those dreams disappeared the night Raul revealed his plan. Her life had now assumed a complicated craziness that left her reeling. When she let herself dwell on the future, she fluctuated between excitement and panic.

Chapter 6

RICHARDS WASN'T SURPRISED BY the information he received. But he was surprised by the extent to which Graham's competition had gone to take over his territory. They must have taken a deep cut in profits. Financing coke parties would be costly, but then the potential growth in demand would offset the initial outlay. What Richards couldn't figure was why. They had flooded the streets with powder and cut the price. Those actions alone would have achieved the desired results. Why were they going to all this hassle? They couldn't be more harmful to Graham's organization if they gave the stuff away. In fact, he wouldn't doubt that, in many instances, they had.

Private parties hosted by the elite of the business world and financial wizards of the market opened an entirely new avenue for growth, a power base with an endless supply of funds. No one had been excluded. From high school and college Rave clubs to smoky, dimly-lit dives, everyone had been lured into the web. Richards just wasn't sure exactly what this spider had in mind. Making the product enticing and readily available usually obtained the desired results. Distributing free "highs" was typically all it took to attract the unwary, the maladjusted, the alienated, the forgotten of society. Then there were always the bored, spoiled thrill-seekers in search of the next ultimate experience. Why use these extreme measures? No one he contacted had an answer. Someone was going to a lot of trouble to bring Graham down. Who had that kind of power? Who had that amount of merchandise?

Richards replaced the equipment and locked everything away. This had been a wasted afternoon. He had more questions now than when he started. According to his sources, the major cities being "flooded" were former strongholds of Graham's organization. His street sources said that no one would talk. The word was out; talk and pay. Less than subtle hints about the consequences of divulging information were linked to a surge of deaths, previously considered gang-related, but now ascribed to the new drug operation. The gruesome details of these deaths led many to believe that they were connected to the sudden surge in drug activity.

Cautiously he slipped from the building and made his way painstakingly back to his apartment. He spent several minutes backtracking, retracing his steps to confuse anyone taking an interest in his activities. Strong's men weren't very adept at following him, but even the least intelligent got lucky once in a while. He couldn't afford a mistake now. He had to come up with a plan that would help Graham carry out his scheme but put Graham out of commission at the same time. He had a lot to think about and little time to do it.

Ambling awkwardly down the back alley, Richards waited. He took precious minutes to light a cigarette and lean back against the dingy outer wall of the building. He couldn't break from his usual routine. It was more important now than ever not to draw suspicion to himself.

With his last drag, he tossed the cigarette aside and pushed open the outer door leading to the stairs. Even now his heart raced in anticipation. One mistake would be all it took. He scanned the stairwell and carefully began his ascent. He stumbled against the far wall as though he had lost his balance. From his crouched stance, he could check out the upper landing. All appeared safe, but nonetheless he felt uneasy.

Straightening, he continued stumbling awkwardly as he made his way to his landing and pushed open the door. Everything was just as he had left it. The trash was still piled outside his apartment. The overhead light was still broken farther down the corridor. The smell of decay and neglect still permeated the dank, evening air. Even though everything appeared normal, Richards felt his skin prickle, the hair rise on the back of his neck. Those were reactions that he had long ago learned to respect.

Carefully he checked to see if his apartment had been entered, but the almost invisible filament had not been moved or broken; the tiny sliver of paper remained poised above the door. He almost breathed a sigh of relief, but not before he entered and made certain that no one had come through the outer window. Suspicion raced through him when he realized the dust on the window sill had been disturbed. So they weren't giving up yet.

Strong had never really trusted him, and his underlying fear of Richards made Strong a dangerous man. It was a shame that he hadn't hired men with more aptitude for their jobs. They were careless, leaving several telltale signs that they had rummaged through his belongings. They wouldn't find anything; he wasn't stupid, not when his life hung in the balance, not when he had spent this long uncover, and especially not when he had given up over three years of his life for this operation. That's what made him good at his job; he didn't get in a hurry. Acting before thinking could be deadly. And he planned to live to reap the rewards of this assignment.

Quickly he put things back in order then sat down at the scarred wooden table to map out a plan of action. He knew from his earlier phone calls that he could expect limited support from the police, and even then he couldn't reveal what he knew without giving away his connection to Graham's organization. Graham had most of the police and federal agencies involved in his pay. All Richards had to do was stay out of the way and take care of his part.

Removing those in power would be no easy task, not when what he really wanted was to take them into custody and bring them up on charges. He would have to find a way to remove them from the scene and keep them hidden until he could safely reveal his own identity. Because once he broke cover, there was no going back.

After learning about everyone Graham planned to involve in his own scheme, Richards wasn't sure that there was anyone left in the department that he could trust. He wouldn't be able to rely on the police or the feds. If they weren't on the take, they might inadvertently reveal something to the wrong people. He couldn't risk that. But he knew who he could trust, who would help him. There wasn't much time though. He would have to move quickly if he expected to achieve the results he needed.

Caroline could hardly believe her eyes. The spacious rooms glittered with an array of lights and colors; music played softly in the background; tables displayed artfully arranged flowers; waiters moved discreetly among the elegantly-dressed crowd. Caroline held her head high as she mingled with the university's assorted elite. She knew many of those gathered tonight, but there were several that she hadn't met.

Tonight was to be her initiation into Paul's inner circle, but if this crowd was anything to go by, then his inner circle was extremely large. He had been serious when he told her that she would meet everyone of importance tonight. She should have realized Paul moved on an entirely different plane than she did. But that was all about to change. After tonight, she would be the woman everyone wanted to know.

The only damper on the evening was the fact the she had to meet the man Paul had selected for her. She was resolved to make the most of the night first and not let that fact hinder her from having a great time. She watched Paul standing across the wide expanse of the ballroom talking with a crowd of friends. He always amazed her with his negligent air of sophistication. Nothing seemed to disturb him. She wished that she could adapt such a nonchalant attitude.

Accepting a fluted glass from a passing waiter, Caroline moved in her own graceful manner around the room, talking with friends and meeting others, laughing about summer exploits and the upcoming term. Everyone was feeling light-hearted and carefree. It was the first social event of an event-laden year, one which would bring many changes in the lives of all those gathered.

When Caroline accidently bumped into someone standing behind her, she turned, automatically ready to apologize, but the words froze on her lips. He had reached out to stead her, just as he had the first time then laughed at her stunned expression.

"We seem to do this a lot." The sound of his voice rippled across her skin. "How have you been? It seems like only yesterday that we met." He couldn't keep the laughter from his eyes or his voice, and she laughed with him.

"You might be right," she responded. But it's been weeks actually, she thought to herself. She moved slightly, stepping out of his grasp; he let his hand fall to his side. "I haven't seen you around. Have you been busy?"

She hoped that her voice didn't betray too much interest. She lifted her drink to her lips, drawing his attention to their lush fullness; she wanted to appear unconcerned. She let her eyes roam over the crowded room. She had thought of him often, but now that he was standing before her, she wasn't sure that he would live up to her imagination. Why was it that the reality was never as good as the dream? He was handsome though, and he did have a charming personality. Maybe there was hope for him yet, but what was she thinking? After tonight there wouldn't be another opportunity. This was her moment; she should seize it.

Hooking her arm through his, she began to lead him across the room. He only smiled at her when she looked up at him. He wouldn't object to anything she had in mind. He was putty in her hands, at least for tonight. He slid his hand down her arm and grasped her hand, twining his fingers lightly around hers. She was a knock-out. He couldn't do better than this. If only he knew something about her background? What would Paul say if he knew that he was about to leave with someone? After all, he had arranged this evening for him to meet some very important people, people who could help chart his future.

Why was fate so cruel? He had finally met someone who truly captivated his interest, and he couldn't pursue the relationship. Paul had made it clear that his help hinged on Robert's total commitment to his plan. His life-long dream was within his reach; all he had to do was follow the path laid out before him, and he was almost guaranteed success. How could he give in to temptation now? As he glanced down at the sultry beauty walking beside him, he wondered how he could not.

Caroline could tell the instant he began to withdraw. His body tensed; she felt his fingers tighten briefly on hers. She knew instinctively that something had changed. She glanced around the room. No one was paying any special attention that she could see, so what had happened? She was a pro at anticipating people's actions; she wasn't about to let him dictate this situation.

"Let's sit over here and talk." She deftly maneuvered him toward a group of plush seats strategically placed to allow more intimate conversation while still remaining part of the gathering. "We haven't really had a chance to get to know one another." She quickly took a seat in an oversized chair, leaving him to sit across from her. Well, that was that, she concluded.

"Tell me, where are you from, and what are your plans after graduation?" She didn't even give him time to formulate an objection before she launched into her interrogation mode. She could do this for hours if need be, but she suspected he wouldn't last that long.

He sat quietly watching her for a few minutes before he answered. So she had picked up on his reticence. He had to give her credit; she was a very astute person. Most women he knew were too self-involved to recognize the subtle nuances that signaled a change in someone. He almost laughed. Some of them couldn't recognize a change in another person if they were told about it directly.

He smiled his most charming smile. He was going to call her bluff. This might be fun.

Paul watched from across the room. As he scanned the gathering, he knew that things weren't going as Caroline had expected. She exuded the same beautiful radiance as always, but the inner spark, which usually radiated around her, had dimmed. She was definitely putting up a good fight, but he didn't think that she would win against Robert. He almost laughed; she really didn't know Robert, and she certainly didn't know his role in their future. Maybe he should intervene. His mind ran through a series of potential problems and the consequences if he remained silent.

He quietly removed himself from the group he was with and made his way across the room, stopping along the way to speak to several friends. There was no use in setting her against him from the start. That would definitely disrupt his plans; he might as well get this over with and let them reconcile their differences before they grew in magnitude.

From Robert's relaxed pose and Caroline's ramrod stiff posture, Paul easily deduced that she was not winning in whatever game they were playing. He had to admit though he was impressed. She wasn't retreating from the battle, and she was holding her own. But he could tell that she wasn't used to these circumstances. Robert wasn't easily led, and he was rarely defeated in any debate in which he chose to participate. Paul had seen him in action too many times not to know the devastation of crossing him, even if it were a verbal battle. He had a killer instinct and could verbally demoralize an opponent with astonishing ease, often defeating them before they even realized the battle had begun.

Caroline was good; he had to give her credit, or she would never had lasted this long. Of course, Robert could be toying with her just to keep her attention. From the smug smile hovering around the corners of his mouth, Paul would bet that was the case. Robert might need to hide his pleasure a little better, though; it wouldn't do to make her too angry; after all she was Rafael's daughter. Paul had a feeling that she was more like her father than even she knew. Paul could see her physically regroup as she leaned back in the chair and crossed her legs. He couldn't help but grin at the patently obvious, womanly wiles she was employing to distract Robert. This could prove to be a match made in heaven, or much more likely, one that would toss them all in hell.

Caroline glanced up as Paul walked over. Was he checking up on her? Had she spent too much time with one man? She couldn't help but panic a little; she was not used to having any freedom or making her own decisions. She didn't really know how lenient Paul would be with her. "Relax," she silently chided herself. She took a calming breath and smiled at him, letting her countenance reflect her pleasure at seeing him.

Robert turned to see what had distracted her. Quickly he stood and shook Paul's hand. "This is a terrific gathering. Thanks for inviting me. I've met some very interesting people." He let his eyes travel over Caroline's exquisite features. She was so beautiful that it almost hurt to look at her. It had been so much fun keeping her involved in their discussion by playing on her obvious prejudices. He hated for it to end, and he had to admit, she was a worthy opponent. However, he had come tonight for a specific purpose. Now he had to turn to the work at hand.

Caroline looked at the two men standing before her and wondered how they had become friends. They were both rather devastating to the female mind, incredibly handsome, each one in his unique way. But Paul was so reserved that he made Robert seem outspoken. In truth, he wasn't, and she had really enjoyed some of their verbal sparring. Still, she had the demoralizing feeling that through most of their conversation he had just been toying with her, stringing her along. Whatever, it had been fun—well sort of—she had to admit honestly. Smiling her most radiant smile, she stood with the men.

"I see you two have met," Paul said watching the interplay between the two. Caroline glanced at Robert before she spoke.

"Yes, we just keep bumping into one another," her voice held the hint of laughter.

"Well, it just so happens that I wanted to introduce you to one another tonight. Now you've saved me the trouble." Robert glanced quickly at Paul. Was he implying that Caroline was the woman chosen for him? Robert couldn't believe his good luck. His glance swung back to Caroline. She looked as stunned as he felt. Did she know what this evening meant; did she know about Paul's plan?

Caroline abruptly recovered from Paul's little surprise. Her mind was working at warp speed. How did she feel about this change in events? She had never dreamed that she would have anything to do with the choice Paul made. Now it seemed that she wasn't to be sacrificed quite as boldly as she had assumed. She really liked Robert; enough to spend her life with, she wasn't sure, but she didn't have much choice in that matter. Still, she wasn't about to complain. Things were already so much better than she had ever thought possible. Hoping her face didn't reveal too much of what she was thinking, Caroline turned to Robert and extended her hand. "It's a pleasure to formally make your acquaintance," she smiled sweetly.

Robert laughed, "The pleasure is all mine. A truce then?" He took her hand and held it as she studied his face. She could get to like this man with a little practice and patience. But he couldn't win every discussion. That just wouldn't do.

Caroline laughed too, the soft sound floating across the crowded room. "A truce, but I expect to win the next round." Robert laughed again at her adamant voice. He would let her win anything she wanted if she was the prize he received for losing. Gallantly, he lifted her hand and kissed the back lightly. A courtly gesture sure to please; his lips formed a smile as he straightened. Caroline arched one shapely brow at him. Did he think she was so easily won?

Her own smile revealed that she understood exactly what he was thinking. She was set to stand her ground. He couldn't assume the upper hand in this relationship unless she conceded defeat, and that wasn't going to happen. It would be joint control or nothing—her skin prickled—unless Rafael deemed otherwise.

Robert interrupted her thoughts, "Would you like to dance?" His question made her realize that she had forgotten that this was to be an enjoyable evening. She glanced around to see couples moving gracefully to the melodious strains of a popular love song. She smiled bewitchingly, "Only if you let me lead."

"No way," he laughed. Then he grabbed her hand and led her across the room to join the others. As he whirled her around and pulled her gently into his embrace, he whispered softly in her ear, "We'll take turns." With that thought, he easily led her into the dance. Caroline didn't care. She felt lighthearted and carefree. She was enjoying the moment. Let the men worry about tomorrow. It would come soon enough. With that sobering thought, she let Robert take complete charge of the evening.

Paul stood back and smiled. Things were progressing nicely, but he knew from experience that nothing went well all the time. Those were the moments when clear judgment and a finely tuned plan were essential; he had both. He had already made definitive plans with several key people tonight. His list of contacts was growing; the future looked very promising.

As Paul watched, Caroline and Robert solidified their partnership with a cordial evening together. Glancing around the crowded room, Paul took note of those present. Every step they took from this point on assumed greater importance. Every action must be weighed carefully. Every possible contingence must be considered. Time was critical.

Earlier Paul and Robert had discussed the first steps in carrying out their plans. Robert shared with Paul his thoughts about returning to his home state to begin his career. After several days investigating, Paul agreed it would be a good place to start. The state was wide open for change. Between Paul's abilities and business connections and Robert's intellectual expertise, they were almost assured of success for the first part of their plan. Money and, if necessary, coercion appropriately applied would further insure the results they wanted.

Caroline, with her grace, poise, and intelligence, would provide the stabilizing force necessary to insure the family appeal to voters at the appropriate time. Her inclusion would also provide the solid foundation that aspiring young lawyers were supposed to demonstrate. Old established firms portrayed an image of stable, often conservative, values. To develop a base of operation within the state, it would be essential to cater to those time-honored institutions. The time to assert more liberal ideas that would sweep the state with change and institute radical transformation would be after developing their own base of power.

After talking with several key figures from the region, Paul viewed Robert's idea as a masterful stroke of genius, almost worthy of Raul. Between the two of them, their future looked very bright. All that remain was finishing the year and applying for positions at the proper law offices. Paul had the names of two prestigious firms, both located in the sprawling capital city, either of which would provide the ideal platform from which to launch a suitable law career and, more importantly, an eventual political career. Everything now had to be scrutinized for its future impact. As he watched Caroline and Robert moving gracefully around the dance floor, he hoped that this evening would be a good omen of their future together.

Richards felt sweat gather and trickle down his back, so much depended on this operation going smoothly. Keeping as still as possible, his dark eyes scanned the landscape, trying to pinpoint the location of his team members. When he couldn't, his heart rate surged then settled. If he couldn't spot them, neither could his enemy. They knew their job. They were the best. They were his men. More than once in the past, they had fought together. More than once, they had survived against impossible odds, simply because they were so well trained. He had called them out of retirement, from other jobs, from homes and family. They hadn't disappointed him. He knew these men better than anyone else. He had trained them.

They were his family. Except for his little sister, he had no one else. But he hadn't heard from her in three years, hadn't been able to notify her except through money transfers from the bureau and then only through a series of accounts so hidden that no one could possibly trace them. He could send her nothing personal. For her sake, he was as good as dead.

This last operation had severed their tenuous relationship. He didn't know if he would ever be able to make her understand the importance of his job, the importance of completing this task. She had begged him not to pursuit his plan. She needed him. But at the time, he had been so consumed with anger that he hadn't heard the desperation in her voice, hadn't really understood the price that she would have to pay for his neglect.

Now as the time had lengthened and he remained undercover, he realized the price that they had both paid. It was too late for second thoughts. The end was near, if everything went well today. Not if, he couldn't afford negativity. Sometimes the only thing left in a desperate situation was faith in the plan. He would be positive; he would win; he would be free—soon.

Richards could see the locals and the feds moving into position. They were good, but not the best. Still he had confidence that they could carry out their role. Graham had become obsessed with destroying his enemy. He had invested enormous amounts of his personal capital into eliminating them. Richards felt no qualms about helping him achieve his goals; they coincided with his own. To achieve his purpose everything would have to fall quickly in place. He needed the added confusion and uncertainty to make his scheme work.

At this same time all across the south, similar operations were taking place. This would be the largest drug bust in history, if they could pull it off. Richards had been in touch with operatives in other cities through third party intelligence. He knew if they could move quickly, before someone leaked the information, they could be successful. The time spent in organizing this scheme had not cooled Graham's fury, but it did lessen the impact of the first dire consequences for snitching.

The savage ferocity of first deaths associated with the drug cartels had lost it impact. People who needed a fix didn't remember or care just as long as they got the money or drugs they needed. They were consumed with the present; the past didn't matter to them; the future didn't exist, only the moment. Any advantage could be easily lost if someone became careless, if the wrong person talked.

Quickly, Richards glanced at his watch. It was time. He raised his weapon slowly and sighted his target as they approached from the far end of the street. Silence reigned, interrupted only by the soft footfalls nearing the contact point.

Men stepped from vantage points along the empty street and walked toward the group entering the target zone. No one would interfere; no one would get involved. The streets talked. Something big was going down. Richards sighted his man through his scope. His hand was steady. His pulse slowed. Voices floated up to him. He watched as the preliminary negotiations began a testing of strength, an assessment of determination, and a battle of wills. Moving only a fraction of an inch at a time, he sighted the main players in his scope, keeping his target always within range. Tension ruled. Richards could hear the raised voices of the men below. Lines were drawn. Then just as quickly, the negotiations ended. The powder was quickly analyzed, assessed, and approved. The exchange was made, money for powder. Motors idled softly at a distance; men waited anxiously, their hands strategically positioned at their sides; their eyes constantly scanned the perimeter.

The signal was given; vehicles began their approach, rumbling rudely in the quiet night. Suddenly, the surrounding buildings erupted with men and weapons; police and feds swarmed the group, weapons drawn. Shots filled the air. Confusion and chaos reigned. Vehicles were disabled, streets blocked, alleys cordoned off, doorways jammed, escape denied.

Targets fell as Richards' men zoned in, taking out the main force leaving little for the police to do as they rounded up men, seized merchandise, and loaded everything and everyone into waiting vehicles. Richards and his men faded from the scene. Their inside man would see that their targets were safely removed and taken to the assigned rendezvous spot.

Not everyone was critical; only key players would be held, an ultimatum given. What could they expect? Would they cooperate and face the consequences or choose to pay the price for their involvement? Either way the flow of drugs would be interrupted.

Their plan had been successful. Several important figures had been swept up in the raids and large quantities of merchandise had been seized. Moving the supposedly deceased targets from the morgue to isolated locations was a monumental undertaking. Richards just hoped that they could maintain their secrecy.

It hadn't been too difficult to arrange for tranquilizing drugs, and his contact in the Special Forces unit was able to make almost any type of necessary ammunition. His operatives had been well chosen. The challenge had been placing the shots effectively while making the victim appear fatally wounded. Their intent was to be able to question these men and, hopefully, bring in more suspects. Using the additional blood shots helped to disguise the injuries, making them appear fatal. The operation was a success, but Richards didn't feel safe, not yet. Too much could still go wrong.

He wanted the men in charge. He wanted to cripple their organizations to the point that they couldn't reorganize. He knew that was unrealistic. As long as one man fed off of the weaknesses of others, as long as people needed a fix, a temporary high, an escape, then drugs and those who provided them would always be a part of society, a part of everyday life for too many. Still, he had to try; he had to do his part.

A contingency plan—that was what Raul had demanded. He didn't trust anyone; he wanted insurance, something more to file away. He held the future of some of the world's most important leaders in his hand, but Raul wasn't stupid. He knew that it was better to quietly remind people of his power than to have to demonstrate it. No one won when he was forced to resort to extreme measures. To Raul, winning was everything. There was no other option.

Paul knew what he had to do. He wasn't sure that he liked it, but he didn't have a choice. Raul was probably right. Actually, Paul knew he was right. Most men who gained power eventually let that power rule them. That couldn't be allowed to happen—not now, not ever.

Paul liked Robert, but he also knew his limitations, his personality. Robert had the skills and the magnetic personality that drew people and, more importantly, that drew support from the right people. It was vital that they dominate all aspects of any election to have the success they envisioned. Paul would simply take out an insurance policy, one that would guarantee future success. Like Raul, Paul didn't like unexpected surprises. The next few days would help to eliminate any potential future problems.

Everything was arranged. Raul's people had been flown in several days in advance. A remote location had been chosen, one isolated from inquisitive neighbors and wandering passers-by. Robert had been advised to attend a private function with the idea of making future contacts from several Central and South American countries. It was never too early to develop diplomatic contacts or to begin laying the groundwork for potential economic and political discussions. The more people he knew, the more future influence he might have. Nothing could be left to chance.

With this thought in mind, Robert arrived at the well-attended function. The evening was soon under way. Dinner was a sumptuous affair. Afterwards, private talks began with drinks readily available, but Robert drank little; he wanted to keep a clear head. But as the night progressed, he began to drink more than he intended because his glass was continually refilled. He didn't want to appear rude or ungracious to his hosts, so he tried to drink slowly.

His hosts, however, began making toasts, and before long, Robert had become very effusive. He raised his glass often in pledges of camaraderie and good will. Before he realized what was taking place, the room was empty. He and one other man and his wife were the only people left. Robert rose to excuse himself but found that he couldn't stand. Instead of being concerned, he merely slumped back in a soft leather chair and blacked out. He wouldn't remember anything about the evening once the drugs kicked in, but they still had to hurry. It would take time to arrange everything suitably.

Robert was quickly transferred to another room. The bedroom had been prepared beforehand. Paul didn't want anyone to recognize where this evening had taken place. He wanted to keep as much distance between him and this evening's events as possible. With his contacts and his connections within the family, it was an easy task to have furnishings and staff brought in. Only trusted family members would take part in the set-up.

The young man was actually much older than he appeared. They were not corrupting the mind of an innocent child, although that would not have been a concern if the need had arisen. But this choice was much better because he was a member of the cartel. A child often forgot to be discreet, and a misplaced word could do irreparable damage or cause untold problems. Paul wanted neither. This night would not be mentioned, not by anyone involved. After the evening was over, everything would be returned to its original order as if nothing of consequence had taken place. The only reminder would be safely filed away with Raul.

The next day Robert woke to a massive hangover and a complete lack of memory about most of the night before. He wouldn't ask Paul anything; he didn't want Paul to know that he couldn't recall most of the evening. If he had blundered, Paul would tell him, and all hopes of having Paul's help with his political career would be lost. He wouldn't receive a second chance.

However, when Paul called later that day, he only asked if Robert had recovered from the night before. He didn't mention anything that had happened, nothing that might have gone wrong. Robert breathed a sigh of relief. Maybe he couldn't remember because he had been so tired. It had been a grueling week with long hours spent conferring with classmates, attending classes, and working with campus political groups. His schedule was loaded, but he had met a lot of influential people. Still, something about that night made him feel edgy, uncertain.

Maybe he just needed to see Caroline. She seemed to have the knack for relaxing him, making him take himself less seriously. She made him laugh, but he couldn't let her know that. She would kill him. He loved arguing with her; he even let her win sometimes just to keep her happy. But he was ready to graduate, ready to begin his life. He was tired of being a follower; he was ready to be a leader, and that time couldn't come soon enough. Having removed the last trace of doubt from his mind, he grabbed his phone to call her.

Paul was pleased with the outcome of the previous evening. Everything had gone as planned. All traces of his involvement had been carefully removed. He held the film and prints in his hands. The encrypted copies had been downloaded and secluded in Raul's private files.

Paul glanced at the photos. He held the end to a political career in his hands; he could end it before it ever began. Now that was real power. Knowing Robert, however, and his ability to persuade people, Paul didn't think that this one incident alone would be enough to influence him. Paul knew that something more was needed, but he could wait. He flicked a lighter open and lit the edge of the photos, watching them take on grotesque shapes as they flamed and burned. He needed to plan his next step carefully. His mind was already racing with ideas as the pictures turned to ash in his trash can. This would have to be something that Robert couldn't explain away, something that would be impossible to deny.

Richards had faded from the earlier scene like the ghost he portrayed, leaving nothing behind to denote his presence except devastation and death. Even though he had had accomplices for this last job, Graham would never know or care, just as long as the job was done and done to his satisfaction. After several days of isolation and interrogation, most of those taken had given up their confederates; evidently, loyalty wasn't something that money could buy, not from this group. Many of them had rolled over too quickly for Richards' peace of mind, though. He couldn't shake the idea that more was at play here than just their good luck.

Still, he would take what he could get. It appeased Graham who was bragging to anyone who would listen. In fact, he had become rather careless about what he said and to whom he said it. Richards was superstitious; he didn't believe in bragging too much. The pendulum of chance swung both ways, and he didn't want to tempt fate unnecessarily.

Richards melted back into the streets as though he had never left; no one commented; no one cared. All he needed now was a foolproof way to tie Graham into the distribution and manufacture of drugs by his organization. Richards knew that if he was patient, Graham would slip up; he had become careless, over confident. Graham had forgotten the first rule of illegal activity: trust no one.

Richards took a long, slow drag from his cigarette. He could wait—for a little while. He was bone-tired. He needed to end this operation soon. Mistakes were too easy to make, especially when his mind was consumed with worries he refused to acknowledge, but they always lurked just below the surface.

Where was she? No one had been able to locate her. He couldn't break cover and look for her himself, and he could only search indirectly through a series of contacts. He couldn't talk to anyone directly. He couldn't tell them how important it was to find her. It was too dangerous, but what had happened? Had someone made the connection between them? Were they planning to use her to draw him out? Guilt gnawed at him; he hadn't been there for her. Now it might be too late. He took another slow drag, his innate training taking over. It was second nature now. He had to break free soon to find her. The streets were consuming him.

His lungs burned, he forced himself to expel the acrid smoke and took a calming breath. The caustic smell of the streets did little to help. He focused on surveying his surroundings. Little had changed, but he carefully noted the subtle differences. Everything meant something out here, very little occurred by random coincidence. The ragged mass of humanity huddled across the alleyway seemed harmless, but he couldn't take anything for granted. Strong liked him even less after this last job. He wouldn't openly defy Graham, but if Richards went missing so much the better. Richards knew he was a dispensable commodity, maybe not easily replaced, but replaceable nevertheless. He tried never to assume too much; he knew he wasn't guaranteed his next breath. But in all honesty, who was? He just ran a greater risk than most.

The old man huddled under the bundle of clothing moved and cautiously stood. His stooped posture revealed a lifetime of suffering, his wrinkled face the visages of abuse, whether from alcohol or drugs, Richards couldn't say. He stumbled weakly, catching himself against the outer wall of the dingy building. His vacant stare caused Richards to recoil slightly. Was that how others perceived him? If so, he could understand their reticence toward him.

The old man hobbled slowly down the street and turned the corner, making his way toward the shelter located further on. He seemed harmless, but Richards would keep an eye on him just the same. Changes on the street always meant something. He would wait to see what this new addition revealed. Dropping the smoldering cigarette, he pushed away from the wall. He might just visit the shelter himself. The coffee was always hot even if the company wasn't.

If Caroline didn't know better, she would think that Robert was avoiding her. Even though he called frequently, he seemed distracted. She didn't like being an after-thought, and that was exactly how she was feeling. Paul had mentioned a small gathering that he was having. Nothing fancy, he had said. He hadn't mentioned Robert, and she would die before she asked. She hadn't planned to attend, but Robert didn't seem interested in making plans with her. She would go and see what the evening brought. At least, she could get out of the apartment.

She was tired of classes and studying and doing what was expected. Maybe she had become too complacent. Maybe it was time she showed Robert that she was a force not to be forgotten or ignored. She pushed aside the memory of the last time she had been defiant. Rafael wasn't in charge of her now, not directly. Paul was, and he had invited her. So if she had a good time, they couldn't blame her—not too much. She knew her limits, but she wanted to experience a little freedom. After all, Paul had promised her that.

Later that evening as she waltzed across her living room, Caroline reflected on her appearance. She loved that forgotten era, Grace Kelly-look. Muted shades of swirling fabric softly moved around her legs. She stopped before the wall mirror; she had good legs and she knew it. They drew men's attention, and tonight she wanted to be in the spotlight. Her hair was piled in a loose arrangement of cascading blonde curls, emphasizing her slender neck and accenting the glowing symmetry of her face. She was out to conquer. She wanted to wow them with her beauty and subjugate them with her brilliance. She wanted to shine, to sparkle, to leave them all speechless. She giggled at her own audacity. She just wanted to have fun. Grabbing her evening bag, she floated demurely through the door to the waiting car.

Paul sat behind the wheel. She caught her breath when she saw him. She hadn't expected him to come for her. He grinned as he climbed out to open her door. She swirled the silky fabric around her legs as she climbed in. Paul smiled; he knew those tricks. But he had to admit, she was a knockout. Robert just might wish that he had come after all.

Chapter 7

ROBERT GLANCED BEHIND HIM. He felt someone following him. Maybe it was his imagination, but every few minutes, he turned to double check. There was nothing. He was being paranoid. He slipped quietly into the entrance of a ramshackle building. His friend said that he would be waiting for him. Not his friend, he corrected, but someone he had heard about through someone else. None of his friends knew, and he wanted to keep it that way. Robert never revealed his real identity; he always paid in cash, nothing flashy. He wore slouchy clothes and tried not to speak unless he had to do so. He didn't like this arrangement, but it was the only way he wouldn't be seen.

The smell, the debris, the atmosphere made his skin to crawl, but he had a plausible excuse prepared if anyone recognized him. He was secretly inspecting slums for a project he was interested in. He worked on committees for almost everything. Why not use them to his advantage? The only drawback would be Paul; he wouldn't be so easily convinced.

He was involved in so many activities he couldn't keep them all straight. He had to have something to help him, something to take the edge off, to boost his energy. He wasn't worried about his grades or his work. He just needed a little breather. He wasn't addicted or anything.

There was Caroline, too. She was a beautiful girl; he really liked her. He just didn't have time for her, and he knew that she wasn't going to put up with that for long. He couldn't blame her. He didn't know how to put more hours in the day. He would have to set limits for himself, even if he had to eliminate some activities. He hated that thought. Tomorrow, he would begin. Tonight he had to have something, anything to help ease the stress, the fatigue.

The slight, nondescript figure waited patiently in the shadows, hidden from view, and watched as Robert entered the building. Minutes later, Robert left, walking quickly toward the sights and sounds of the city's center away from the destitution and decay of the lower side. The figure quietly blended into the late night traffic of pimps, prostitutes, and perverts. He had a report to make; he would be expected. This had definitely become a habit.

Robert hurried toward his apartment. He hated being part of that scene, but he had no choice. Maybe if he rested for a while, he could make it to Paul's tonight. He knew that Paul hadn't been happy when he had told him that he couldn't attend. But Paul had remained silent, not voicing any complaint. That was how Robert knew he wasn't pleased. He had learned early in their friendship that a silent Paul was a displeased Paul, and Robert needed him. By showing up, even late, Robert hoped to placate Paul and hopefully restore Paul's confidence in him.

Robert disliked needing anyone, but he knew that the future would definitely be easier with Paul's help than without. And there was Caroline. Robert understood the incentive she presented, but he didn't think it was a package deal. Partners in politics and friends in life, but Caroline might have something to say about any more than that. Robert picked up his pace. Now that he had a plan, he had to hurry. He was already feeling much better. As he took the stairs two at a time, he grinned; he liked this feeling. His blood raced through his veins; his heart thumped in his chest; he felt energetic, alive.

Paul recognized the number on his phone. He was definitely not pleased.

Robert made a mad dash for the elevator, just as the door was closing. He laughed out loud. That was close, but he had made it. As he pushed the button for Paul's floor, he smiled broadly. Paul would be impressed—he glanced at his watch—and almost on time. He felt great now. This hadn't been a bad idea after all, as long as no one found out. Even that thought didn't dim his euphoria. Nothing could daunt him tonight; he was on top of his game.

As he pushed the door bell, Robert could hear the soft strains of music emanating from Paul's apartment. A poker-faced butler of indeterminate age quietly opened the door and took Robert's coat as he stepped into the foyer. A passing waiter stopped briefly as Robert seized a slender flute of wine from the tray and quickly scanned the clustered guests, looking for Paul. He wanted to be sure that Paul knew that he had given up other activities to be here. Robert's smug smile slipped a little when he caught Caroline's reflection in the adjacent wall mirror. Even her reflected beauty put the others to shame; his heart beat a little faster as he watched her laughing and talking. He couldn't wait to talk to her.

Laughter and music swelled inside Robert's head as he walked across the crowded room. This was no small gathering as he had first imagined. The rooms were filled with Harvard's elite. Paul's parties were always well attended. Robert was glad that he had come.

Just before he reached Caroline, however, she slipped away and joined another group. She had seen his swaggering entrance. She wasn't catering to his whims. She didn't need him; it was the other way around. As far as she was concerned, he could be easily replaced. In fact, she almost considered asking Paul to choose someone else. They still had time. Although since her first meeting with Robert, she had done some investigating of her own and had learned just what a talented man he was. He would be the perfect political candidate, but probably not the best matrimonial candidate. She could handle him; he just didn't know it yet.

Unexpectedly, Paul moved to Caroline's side and assumed a rather proprietary stance. His hand moved to her waist and remained there. He had seen Robert enter and had noted the attention that his presence stirred. He was well known among many of the upper classmen; his reputation, until now, had been impeccable. Paul wasn't sure that would be the case for long. He didn't care about youthful indiscretions, but certain things were unacceptable. Robert had to learn to accept Paul's leadership if he wanted the future that they had discussed.

As Robert made his way across the crowded room, stopping to speak to friends along the way, Paul excused them from the group they were with and ushered Caroline toward the dining area. From there they made their way to the kitchen at the back of the apartment. Servants were busily emptying trays and refilling dishes. No one paid any undue attention.

These workers were trained *family* members. Nothing that happened here would ever be revealed, and no one would interfere with anything Paul chose to do. Everyone understood Paul's place in Raul's organization, and no one wanted to jeopardize their own life or future or that of their families' by being careless. They were well paid and well taken care of members of an elite force. More importantly, they knew their place. If they were ever dissatisfied, a quiet word to their superiors, and they would be reassigned. Raul knew that people often needed change to make life worth living, to add a little spice and adventure. He liked for everyone to know that they were appreciated for their work no matter what their jobs were. He treated them as valuable, respected members of his workforce. Because of this, he had their loyalty and devotion. Then there was always Rafael, if anyone made a poor choice. Those were few.

A quick nod to the chef and the room cleared instantly. Nothing needed to be said. Paul lifted a crystal glass from a nearby tray and swirled the blood-red liquid within. The overhead light shimmered across the swirling surface. Caroline hadn't asked any questions. He should have been surprised, but he wasn't. She seemed to read his moods rather well. He needed a moment to think. He didn't want to make a hasty decision.

"I need your help." Paul's voice had such a cold edge to it that when he spoke, Caroline actually shivered. She could feel the pent-up tension even though Paul did an admirable job of disguising it. She knew the men in the *family* too well not to realize that something ominous was about to happen. At first, she thought that she had inadvertently done something, but a quick glance at Paul reassured her that she didn't have to worry personally. But she had caught a glimpse of Robert as they left the party. He looked agitated, overly animated, certainly not his usual self. She was used to his being more reserved. She hadn't thought anything about it, until now. Maybe that was what had caused Paul to bring her in here.

Caroline watched Paul carefully as she spoke, "Certainly." There was no need to question him. He would tell her. She could almost see his mind working as he continued to turn the glass in his hand. He seemed almost mesmerized by the swirling red liquid.

"Can you get Robert to take you home? I need him out of here without a fuss."

Caroline laughed softly, "I can get him to do more than that if you need me to."

"No. Just take him to your place. I'll call you later." He turned to leave then stopped. "You can handle yourself, can't you? I can send someone with you if you need me to." His frown puzzled Caroline. Was he really concerned about her welfare?

"Have you forgotten who my father is? I've been trained by pros. There's no need to worry; besides I always have the "Rock." At his quizzical expression, Caroline laughed, "You've met her."

Suddenly Paul's expression cleared. He had indeed. No, he didn't need to worry about her. He nodded; laughter filled his voice, easing some of the tension, "Thanks. I'll send him in here. You can go out the back entrance and down the elevator. I'll have a car waiting." With those orders, he left the room.

Robert appeared almost instantly, making her wonder if he had been looking for her. Just as she was about to speak, a servant entered carrying her wrap. Caroline smiled her thanks. Robert helped her with her wrap, his hands settling on her shoulders as she turned to face him.

"Are you all right? Paul said that you needed to go home. Is anything wrong?" His concern for her welfare sounded genuine. Caroline couldn't quite look him in the eye. She wished she didn't have to deceive him.

Opting for the partial truth, she smiled. "I'm fine really. I just need to go home. It's getting late. I promised La Senora that I would take her shopping early tomorrow morning. I don't want to disappoint her." She moved aside, forcing Robert to drop his hands.

Caroline causally turned to walk away, "I told Paul that I could call a cab. There's no need for you to leave the party early on my account." She played her hand so well that Robert never knew he didn't stand a chance.

"Don't be silly. Of course I'll see you home. What type of gentlemen would I be, if I didn't?" He bowed slightly. "My mother would be extremely upset if she ever found out."

"Really," Caroline laughed. "I can't imagine your mother being upset with you about anything. I'll bet you could convince her that the sun comes up in the west, if you wanted to."

"Well," he hesitated, "to be honest, she's the one person who has never been swayed by my logic." Robert grinned boyishly, and for a moment Caroline could almost see him as a simple, rural farm boy running across the open fields. Then the moment was gone. She placed her hand through his arm as they left and listened half-heartedly as Robert extolled rural life.

The car was waiting as they stepped outside, and they were standing at her front door almost before she had time to devise a plan for keeping him in her apartment. She experienced a moment of panic when she remembered La Senora's stalwart presence, but hopefully she wouldn't cause a problem. Caroline had never had a man stay for any length of time before. Oh well, there was a first time for everything. She almost laughed when she considered how this report to Rafael would read—almost. She just hoped that Paul knew what he was doing.

La Senora opened the door and ushered them into the sitting area. She quietly took their coats and offered refreshments. Caroline was perplexed by her actions but decided not to question her good fortune. Robert seemed more agitated than earlier. Caroline had never seen him this way. She couldn't figure out what was wrong, but she knew something wasn't right.

As Robert wondered around commenting on the paintings and artwork, Caroline realized how out of focus he seemed to be. Finally, La Senora returned with their drinks; she offered Robert the first glass then Caroline. When she didn't leave, Caroline was confused.

Caroline lifted her glass and graciously thanked Robert for bringing her home. Covertly she watched him over the rim of her glass. He took a long drink as though he were extremely thirsty. Caroline's brow wrinkled. She motioned for him to be seated and was just about to question him when he stared directly at her. Then she knew. No wonder Paul was upset.

Carelessly Caroline plopped down on the couch. What was Robert thinking? Obviously, he didn't know who he was dealing with, but somehow Caroline knew that that was about to change. She filled the next few minutes with idle conversation, silently praying for Paul to call. Robert didn't seem to notice the brittle quality of her voice, and as she looked a closer at him, he appeared to be having trouble staying awake. Suddenly, his head fell back against the cushions; his empty glass slipped from his fingers. He had gone from agitated to comatose in a matter of minutes.

Caroline turned to see La Senora smiling broadly.

Paul didn't call; he arrived in person at her apartment. Within minutes, he and his driver loaded Robert's drugged body into Paul's waiting car and transported him across town. Caroline could sense the pent-up anger in Paul. She didn't know what was in store for Robert, but she wouldn't want to be him. She had never seen Paul angry, or Raul for that matter, but she had personally witnessed the terrifying cold remoteness of her father's anger. Just the thought sent chills racing down her spine. Somehow she didn't think Paul would react much differently. At least this explained why she hadn't seen much of Robert in the last few weeks. Surely he knew that everyone would know before long what he was doing.

Paul wouldn't have chosen him, if he had known about this little problem, so he couldn't have been playing for long. Maybe something had happened. It had better have been something life threatening, because it definitely was now.

Paul felt like slamming his fist in Robert's face, but he knew that wouldn't accomplish anything but a set of sore knuckles. Still it might release some of his frustration. He had Robert stashed safely in a remote apartment complex owned by one of Raul's holding companies. The manager was a direct family associate, so Paul didn't have to worry about any unforeseen complications with keeping him there. He would be taken care of, once he woke up, but he wouldn't be allowed to leave until Paul said so. Right now he was seriously considering never.

If this was going to become a problem, he had to come up with a solution and quick. Maybe he should just give him a good taste of what the future might hold. That could be the best medicine. A startling idea popped into Paul's mind. This could be that extra insurance that he wanted. All he needed was a little more enticement for Robert to be completely his. Lemons and lemonade, this was the time to make that work in his favor.

Paul knew who Robert's contact was; he made a quick call to an answering service. Within minutes a return call came in from a pay phone; of necessity the call would be short. A meeting was arranged. Within the hour, Robert's future had dramatically changed, and he still slept, peacefully unaware of the end result of his actions. Paul was pleased with his decision.

He tried to take in his surroundings, but he couldn't focus. He slumped back on the bed. He couldn't think. For the first time in his life, he couldn't logically analyze a problem and find a solution that would benefit him. He was screwed. He closed his eyes and let his mind drift. He couldn't concentrate; there was no point in trying.

The next time he awoke the sounds of music and laughter drifted into the room from beyond the closed door. Funny that he hadn't even considered trying the door before. He must have fallen asleep again. He knew several hours had passed because the room felt much darker. It was a sensation more than a fact, since there was no outside window. But he felt it was true. He set up and tried to get his bearings. He felt more clear-headed this time, his brain less muddled. But he needed two things—a bathroom and a drink—in that order.

Cautiously, he eased from the bed and walked toward what he hoped was a bathroom. He was much relieved to find that it was. He even laughed at his own weak pun. This was more like it. His brain was beginning to function again. He just needed something to drink. After checking his appearance in the mirror, he splashed cold water on his face and swallowed a mouthful to ease his parched throat. Straightening his clothes, he headed for the other door. The only way to find out anything would be to open the door and see what lay on the other side—the lady or the tiger? He smiled; he was feeling much better as he opened the door.

He just wasn't prepared for what he found.

Paul read the coded message and sighed. He would find out the details later. All that mattered was that the problem had been solved, that another set of encrypted files was safely stored away, a double insurance policy against future claims. Robert belonged to him now.

Robert had been his choice. He couldn't turn back now, but he was seriously considering finding a replacement, except nobody was as qualified as Robert was. That was the real issue. Of course, with the right amount of money almost anything could be achieved, any position bought. That was his other concern—almost wasn't good enough when Paul needed certainty. There was no room for uncertainty, not in this business, and ultimately this was a business, on a massive scale perhaps, but still a business. If there were problems, he would find a solution. He wasn't going to worry beforehand. It would accomplish nothing.

He needed a break. Caroline would take his mind off his worries. He liked looking at her; she read his moods, and she always said the right thing, well almost always. That was usually the funny part; she was so serious about being independent and proving herself that she didn't know how funny she was, especially when it came to understanding their future and their fathers' long range plans. That thought alone made him smile. He was feeling better already. Maybe he should invite her to dinner?

Caroline listened to Paul's message and wondered what it was really about. She hadn't seen him since the debacle at his party. She hadn't heard from Robert either. Maybe Paul was going to tell her what had happened. No, he rarely included her in his decisions even after the fact. He would simply say that things had been taken care of. Sometimes that really irked her.

Frustration was a feeling that she was becoming very familiar with, but she still didn't like it. She wanted to be part of the whole team, not just some fringe element. Between Robert who treated her like an after-thought and Paul who treated her like a little sister, she wasn't absolutely sure about her role in the grander scheme of things. But as the semester drew to a close, she knew that they were going to have to form a much stronger alliance.

Paul had mentioned sending resumes to various out-of-state firms. He seemed confident that it was only a formality and that there wouldn't be any difficulty in obtaining the positions they sought. Her role was, of course, contingent upon their acceptance. Even if she was hired by another firm, they would still maintain contact and having someone in a different office might actually be beneficial. She was good at encouraging people to support her causes, especially if they were men. She knew how to make the most of her attributes. If women were involved, she was often effective at logically persuading them to see her point of view. She wasn't always victorious, but she had a fairly good success rate.

A random memory flitted across her mind. One woman had gone so far as to offer her support for a proposal if Caroline wouldn't approach her husband. The lady had somewhat shamefacedly admitted that she didn't want to place too much temptation in his path. Caroline had had no intention of soliciting that particular man's aid, since his reputation often discouraged others from backing a project. That bit of information she, of course, withheld from the wife, who really was a sweet woman, if a little naïve about her husband. If his wife chose to turn a blind eye to his little indiscretions, that was her business, but in truth he would have chased a corpse, if he thought he could catch the hearse.

Caroline was still smiling when the phone rang. Her smile quickly disappeared.

Chapter 8

RICHARDS HAD SHADOWED THE haggard, old derelict for days. He seemed to follow the same routine, not varying his habits much any day. That was what made Richards suspicious. His routine seemed too contrived, almost too planned. Maybe Strong had finally hired someone with more brains than muscle. It would be a first, but in his line of work he couldn't afford to become complacent. One mistake was all it took. He watched from his usual spot as the man hugged a cheap bottle of wine close to his chest, rocking awkwardly to a remembered tune that only he could hear, his faint ramblings occasionally floating across the street. Richards tossed his cigarette butt in the filth that lined the alley. He had seen enough. He turned to leave just as he caught the faint echo of a familiar sound. He froze. Where had he heard that before? His heart raced as he tried to place the sound. A long forgotten memory pulled at him. Not what—who! He whirled back and had already taken the first step, when he saw the huddled figure quickly shake his head. The movement was so slight that at first Richards believed he had imagined it. He almost continued on until common sense warned him to stop. He had forgotten all of his training in a matter of seconds. His safety, the success of his operation, everything could have been lost in that one brief moment of total and irreversible stupidity.

He sagged against the wall as though he had been sucker punched. A cold sweat streamed down his face. Relief that he hadn't completely lost it and gratitude that he hadn't given himself away coursed equally through his body. Over three years of his life would have been wasted. He would have achieved nothing and lost everything. Now that he had caught his breath, he smiled to himself. So he had been played. At least it had been by the best, and he should know; he had trained him.

That just left the question of how to meet. Since they had both made a practice of frequenting the homeless shelter for a cup of coffee or occasionally a hot meal that would be the ideal place. But that would have to be tomorrow. They had already made their daily run. Richards' mind flooded with questions. Something big must have happened for him to be here. Why had he waited so long to make contact? Was he unsure of Richards? Was his loyalty in question?

All Richards had to do was to wait for twenty-four hours to find out what it was. He nodded slightly toward the slumped figure and turned back toward the outer door of his building. He could wait; he didn't have much choice. He might be jeopardizing more than just his life if he didn't.

That didn't make the wait any easier.

What had happened? Robert quickly looked around the room and sighed in relief. This was his apartment. He felt sick with overwhelming tension. He had been so sure when he awoke that something terrible had happened that he had been physically ill. Even now his stomach swirled in protest. What day was it? What had happened after he left for Paul's? Had he done anything irreparable? How could he find out without asking directly? He didn't want Paul to know how little he remembered or to think that this was a common occurrence.

He looked at the back of his hand. It was covered with scratches. His arm was scored with what appeared to be nail marks. What had he done?

He sprung from the bed, dragging the bedcovers with him as he tripped and fell, just making it to the bathroom before he vomited as he never had before. His whole body shook with violent tremors. His head pounded every time he wretched; his stomach muscles clenched. He clutched his head and tried in vain to stop the agony. He slid to the cold tile floor, shivering. He felt miserable and alone. He wanted to die. Living with this excruciating agony was too much for any normal man to bear, and he was definitely no superman, not today.

He crawled back to bed, dragging the bed clothes along with him, collapsing instantly into a semi-conscious state of denial. He refused to believe any of the memories that threatened his sanity. He lay there without moving for hours.

The incessant ringing of his phone finally woke him.

Now what should he do? Have Alberto solve the problem? Alberto had never liked him. Not that Alberto had ever said anything. It was a feeling Paul got every time he mentioned Robert's name, some flicker of disgust that emanated from Alberto's usually blank eyes. Like Rafael, Alberto was one of the few, trusted men in Raul's elite inner circle. He had proven himself. He was untouchable. No one dared go against him. Rafael had trained him, but like the others, he was also well-educated. When the need arose, he could be charming and witty, a good conversationalist, but to him that was all a game. He could be silent for days, weighing a situation carefully before acting. He had a special penchant for killing; his results were faultless. He was a true master of his art. He might be the only answer to Paul's dilemma.

It was odd that Paul had never feared him. Of course, that might have been because he was Raul's son, and Paul knew that no one would dare touch him. True enough, he had never given Alberto any cause to, and he certainly didn't plan to, ever. But it was nice to know that Alberto liked him. He had been the first member of the *family* that Paul had ever met. Paul still remembered the quiet man who had arrived in Aruba and had taken him to meet his real father in Bolivia. However, it had been the return flight that had sealed their friendship.

Alberto had sensed Paul's distress and had helped a frightened young boy accept his future. He had given Paul the strength to follow Raul's instructions, protecting himself and his family. He had shown Paul that he could accomplish all of things Raul demanded of him, that Paul could do what he had to do because he didn't have a choice. The sooner he accepted the inevitable, the easier his transition. The harder he worked, the greater his rewards. Mistakes were inevitable and expected at his age, but one result was never acceptable to Raul: failure.

Paul worked hard to prove himself and learned from his mistakes. If Raul expected one result, then Paul made certain that he achieved more. Soon Paul's personal expectations for himself far outreached anything Raul demanded. As a result, Raul was extremely pleased.

Although neither man ever revealed their true feelings, Paul could tell Alberto was pleased. By helping Paul fulfill his father's wishes, Alberto felt he was able to repay some of the debt he owed Raul. With each of his successes, Paul was shown more of the workings of Raul's operation. Even today, though, Paul realized he didn't know the true extinct of his father's businesses, but he had come to realize that Raul was possibly the most powerful man in Latin America, a very sobering thought.

Alberto, for his part, had given Paul his private phone number, telling him to use it when he needed to. On those rare occasions, Alberto had always appeared within hours, arriving on one of Raul's private jets, there to help Paul solve whatever problem he had. He never criticized Paul's mistakes but instead instructed him in how not to make them again, and he always fixed the problem. Paul never asked how. He had learned early not to ask too many questions.

Paul could laugh now at how naïve he had been. He didn't realize for years that Alberto had known about most of his troubles even before he had. Surveillance was not only maintained on the competition and potential future sources but also was an integral part of Paul's life; only he hadn't realized it at the time. Caroline's life, he felt sure, had been just as closely scrutinized. Raul didn't like surprises, and he definitely didn't like problems. The best way to insure against either was to closely supervise the lives of those of interest, whether a federal judge, a government official, a member of law enforcement, or his own son.

Paul soon recognized that most of the people who surrounded his life were part of the extended family, members of Raul's special-forces, which over the years had developed into an organization of worldwide importance. As he matured, Paul learned how to make the best use of these resources. He was able to manipulate situations and engineer outcomes to fit his personal agenda and arrange them for the desired results needed to snare many of his associates in less than admirable situations. All of which he was able to record in some fashion to use as leverage against them, if the need ever arose. Like his father, Paul enjoyed manipulating people and situations.

But he admired those who did not succumb to the usual human failings, who had strong morals and weren't afraid to be different, who didn't need the approval of others to feel confident in themselves, who knew the true value of family and friends. Those who never demanded favors of him, who never expected something from him, who appreciated him for who he was not what he had or what he could do for them, those were true friends. They numbered few, but even those could never become close friends, not in Paul's life.

Even from those earliest days, Alberto had been his closest friend and confidant. Paul knew that he owed much of his present success to Alberto, though his father had been the more demanding taskmaster. When Paul was at the compound, he would spend his days following his father, listening and learning how to deal with situations and people, but Alberto was the expert at solving problems. Between them, Paul's education in the psychology of dealing with the shortcomings of the human mind was overwhelming and exceedingly stressful.

There was so much to learn, to remember that many nights Paul couldn't sleep. His mind felt like a roller coaster looping out of control. Unlike his father who had grown up in the organization, Paul was trying to assimilate everything in a limited time. Even as young as he was at first, the business aspect intrigued him, but fear of displeasing his father made life miserable.

When he wasn't with his father, Paul spent hours with Ramon learning the fundamental workings of the organization, from surveillance techniques used to track individuals and vehicles, to tracing global shipments and surveying crop fields, to staffing residences around the world. He learned that legitimate sections of the business dealt with scientific research on improving the quality of the crops to developing better materials for shipping. Other departments specialized in reducing costs and in expanding shipping and distribution methods.

Paul studied every aspect of Raul's empire, yet he still didn't know all that he needed to in order to ever successfully assume Raul's role. At these times, he felt inadequate to even consider heading Raul's empire, but the thought that lurked just below the surface of his mind was whether he really wanted to do so. He didn't like doubt; he didn't like to question himself too closely; he didn't like the idea that he might not be the son Raul wanted him to be. What worried him most was that he didn't really have a choice. Refusal to carry out Raul's plan, even for him, was too frightening to even consider; yet the thought still plagued him.

Unlike other facets of the business, Paul had never been allowed access to Rafael's domain. Paul understood his role, but Raul preferred that Paul not be too involved in that aspect of their enterprise. Throughout Paul's extensive education in the organization, Alberto had become the middle man between Paul and Rafael. Anything Raul deemed necessary for Paul to learn about Rafael's affairs was delivered through Alberto. That was fine with Paul. He had heard the stories about Rafael and his father's takeover after Don Gonzales' death. At first he hadn't really believed them until he personally witnessed an event that altered his life and even now still haunted him.

Paul had no one to blame but himself for the events of that day. But it taught him exactly what Raul had been trying to tell him. His firsthand experience that day shaped the man he became. He never forgot how one careless action had unleashed a chain of events so horrific that, even years later, he had to fight against the overwhelming sense of guilt he felt for having endangered so many lives.

The memory flooded his mind. It all seemed innocent enough. He thought no one knew that he had taken the Jeep out that late afternoon. Of course, he realized later that it too carried a tracking device, and that the second he traveled beyond the limits of the compound, Rafael and his men had rushed after him. They had been tracking, through satellite imaging, the subversive movements of a band of marauding mercenaries who were known to be hiding in the nearby mountains. Rafael had seen instantly that Paul was headed directly toward them and had acted accordingly. Within minutes of his leaving the protection of the grounds, Rafael and his men had been in pursuit. They realized the danger these men posed and how defenseless Paul would be against them.

Of course, Paul knew nothing about any of this. He was letting his emotions rule his head. He was tired of restrictions, demands, limitations. He just wanted a few minutes of freedom. He had raced beyond the compound, not caring about the need for caution or what he had been told, not caring if he was endangering himself. He was caught up in a juvenile rebellion even he didn't understand. He just knew he had to break free, if only for a short time.

The hot, sultry air whipped through the open top of his old Jeep and sung in his ears. Adolescent temper heated his blood, making him quarrelsome and irritated with all those around. Only he had no one to argue with, no one to talk back to because he had to restrain his every thought, his every word. His family's and even his own life were at stake, but this day had been too much. He simply couldn't take any more. He felt as though he had no power over his future or his life. If he thought that he could, he would have run away, but he realized that would never work, not when his father practically owned the country and everyone in it.

Veering off the roadway onto a narrow path into the jungle, he drove his Jeep at break-neck speed. He halfway hoped he would just drive off a mountainside. He kept the gas pedal pressed to the floorboard. He couldn't go fast enough. Vines and limbs slapped at his face and hands through the open top. He didn't care; the pain felt good. It let him vent his anger.

Then just as suddenly as he had raced through the undergrowth, he plunged into a partial clearing. Immediately a barrage of men with automatic weapons stormed the area. Shots filled the air, slamming into the side of the jeep, hitting the tires, shattering the windshield. The Jeep bounced across the rough terrain, careening into a hidden embankment before it finally ground to a shuttering halt. Paul's head slammed into the steering wheel. Violent curses filled the air as armed men raced toward him. Shards of pain sliced into Paul's brain as he fought to stay conscious.

Before he could even speak, he was jerked from the Jeep and thrown to the ground, a rifle barrel shoved into the back of his head. He tried to turn to face his captors, but the rifle butt crashed against the side of his head. Pain shot through his body, blood coursed down his face. He didn't move again.

He could hear men moving around, examining the Jeep, and trying to decide what to do with him. He heard the word ransom and felt truly scared for the first time. He knew the common practice—a body part with a ransom demand. Right now even his stifling existence at the compound sounded good. He realized that he would give anything to be back safely there—with all his body parts intact.

Mentally he fought to make light of the situation; he tried to remember anything that Raul had taught him about negotiations, anything Alberto had taught him about solving problems, but his mind refused to work. His head throbbed with excruciating pain. No one knew where he was, when he had left, where he was going, nothing. He had broken every rule that Raul had insisted upon. He wanted to laugh hysterically at his own stupidity. All that he had proven by his reckless actions was how fast he could die. As the men argued loudly around him, he just prayed that he would die fast enough.

Then just as he was beginning to feel there was no hope, the clearing erupted with more gunfire. The man pointing the rifle at Paul's head was the first to fall. His body crumpled next to Paul, a huge hole in the side of his head, his brains spilling out through the shattered skull, his eyes staring sightlessly at Paul. The metallic scent of hot blood, the caustic burn of gunpowder, the pungent stench of sweat filled the air. Paul couldn't move, couldn't look away from the dead eyes. He couldn't let himself hope. He lay motionless, frozen with fear, paralyzed with shame, angry at his own stupidity.

The firing died down. Paul could hear shouts, voices raised in anger. Rafael's voice vibrated across the clearing, demanding that the men come and drop their weapons, assuring a peaceful ending to the confrontation. The rebels refused. Threats and counter-threats were issued. Paul was caught in the open, trapped beside the fallen body and his Jeep, unable to escape. The bitter taste of bile filled his mouth. His headed throbbed; his stomach churned.

Shots filled the air again, but in his direction. Dirt sprayed his body. Paul didn't dare raise his head. Bullets whistled by, clunking violently into the Jeep. He had become the target. He could hear bullets ricochet, the vibrating thud as others hit the dead body beside him, the sizzle of the engine as slugs sliced through the motor. He tried to prepare himself to die, but all he could think was that he wanted to live. Suddenly, silence filled the clearing; the only sounds the hiss of the motor and the slow trickle of fluid oozing from the crippled Jeep.

Paul couldn't move. Gradually he became aware of the shuffling of bodies as men were prodded into the open clearing, a scraggly, lawless band of mercenaries hardened to life in the jungles and honoring no man's laws but their own.

Rafael headed the men holding the group captive. His entire body radiated anger. His silence threatened greater violence than words. Paul tried to sit up, but he couldn't. He slumped against the battered side of the vehicle and tried not to look at the carnage around him. Bodies littered the clearing. The once green landscape was stained red with blood, the air filled with the stench of death.

Rafael spoke. Paul couldn't hear the words, but the menace in his voice pierced the air. The captured leader spat out a reply, lunging at Rafael. Rafael stepped to the side, embedding his knife in the man's stomach, twisting it violently, drawing it upward slicing through every vital organ in its path before shoving his dead body mercilessly to the ground. Then he processed methodically down the struggling line of captive men following the same process until he had killed every last man. Blood covered his hands and arms. His face was sweat-soaked and splattered with blood. The once white dress shirt he wore was soaked in crimson. His black leather shoes were drenched with gore, his tailored slacks, torn and dirty. He looked as out of place on this field of battle as any man could, until he turned to Paul.

Paul would never forget that look, la Cara del muerto, the face of death.

Anger visibly radiated from his body, shimmering like heat waves in the oppressive jungle atmosphere. His eyes blazed with blood lust. In that moment, Paul felt terrified, more frightened than he had ever felt. Rafael's body was covered with the hot, sticky smell of death; it permeated the air around him. Paul shrunk inside himself as Rafael's hand reached out, grabbing Paul by the shirt and dragging him to his feet. He slammed Paul hard against the side of the battered Jeep, barely restraining his anger, and only then did he check to see if Paul was injured. Satisfied that he wasn't badly hurt, he pulled Paul behind him all the way to his truck, hidden in the jungle growth farther down a narrow trail. He never spoke until he reached his vehicle. Jerking his phone from the console, he savagely punched out a series of numbers and spoke, "I have him." He said nothing more.

Only then did Paul see Alberto. Rafael shoved Paul toward him and climbed into his vehicle, tearing through the undergrowth as he sped away. Alberto guided Paul toward another vehicle and pushed him inside. Paul didn't seem able to move. He couldn't coordinate his thoughts or his actions. He felt numb. He felt dead inside, as dead as those men. He couldn't get the picture out of his mind. He couldn't forget the savagery of Rafael's anger. He couldn't understand his lack of feeling, of compassion, of mercy. He couldn't understand how Rafael had been able to do such a horrendous thing.

Paul knew that he should feel grateful to Rafael for saving his life, but he couldn't get beyond the horror of what he had witnessed. Then he remembered his father. His heart almost stopped.

The ride back to the compound was nothing like the one Paul had taken earlier. No one spoke. Paul knew that he was in disgrace. He had disobeyed a direct command of his father's and anyone else would have already paid the price for that disobedience. Paul had heard the stories, but now he knew they were true. Until today he had fooled himself into thinking that they were exaggerations. Now he was certain they were all too real.

His father stood waiting at the door. Alberto helped Paul out of the vehicle and walked beside him to face Raul. Blood oozed from the cut on his head. Dirt, grim, and blood from the dead man covered his clothes. He tried to stand tall and take his punishment like a man, but at the last moment, he blacked out. Alberto caught him as he started to fall and looked questioningly at Raul. He was surprised by Raul's show of emotion. Alberto had never witnessed that before. He was glad. He liked the boy, even if he was headstrong, but then so was his father. He was smart; he would survive this day's ordeal, and he would learn from it, especially if Rafael had anything to say about it.

Raul couldn't speak. He motioned for the men to carry his son upstairs. Alberto sent for the doctor. Raul hadn't until this moment realized how much his son meant to him. Now that the crisis had been averted, he would have to think of a suitable punishment, but at this moment, he only wanted to make certain that he was all right. This was an unexpected complication that he had never planned on. He disliked surprises.

For that reason, Alberto became a permanent fixture in Paul's life, always in the background, but never far from reach. Paul assumed Alberto was there to help him but also to protect him if the need arose. Paul was smart enough to know that Alberto's job was two-fold. He kept a close eye on Paul and reported to Raul as well. That wasn't a problem for Paul; he wouldn't have expected anything less. Paul was a major investment for Raul, and Raul always kept a close eye on his investments.

Paul would have been surprised if he knew the true reason.

Paul had never talked about what had happened that day—not to anyone. Most of the time, he forgot about the experience all together. But even years later, he could still envision the look on Rafael's face as he had turned to him. It would be with him always, and Paul never wanted to witness it again.

Even though Paul never spoke of his experiences, that didn't keep his father from making certain that he understood that nothing like that could ever happen again. Paul began a regime of training that would have benefited any military recruit. Rafael took over his life and he spared no mercy. His anger had abated, but in fact, in had never been directed toward Paul. In the heat of battle, it was hard for him to maintain an emotional distance when family was involved. He had warned the men, but they had refused to listen. He would have punished them for daring to touch a member of the family, but he would have spared their lives. They had made their choice, and they had died for it.

Rafael felt no remorse for the soldiers; he did regret their loss for their families. He had sent emissaries out into the jungle to make contact. The bodies had been returned and restitution had been made to those left behind. It was better to appease those in need than to let that need cause even greater problems. Rafael knew that desperation often caused people to make poor decisions; he didn't want difficulties with the marauding bands of rebels who hid out in the jungles. Their cause was not his, but he would destroy them if they became a problem. Most were smart enough to leave the compound and Raul and Rafael's private syndicate alone. Occasionally, there were minor difficulties. Rafael always tried to negotiate a peaceful settlement, but if force was needed, he spared no mercy.

After several days, Paul's injuries healed, and it was then that Rafael sent for him. Since his rescue, Paul had dodged any direct contact with Rafael. He was uncertain about confronting him, but he knew better than to refuse. He knew that any dictate from Rafael had his father's blessings; there was nothing he could do except face him. Paul was so afraid that he couldn't look at Rafael ever again and not envision that day that he was almost paralyzed with fear. But Rafael understood, and for that reason, he insisted that Paul meet him in his private apartment.

Raul's silence toward him had been difficult to endure, but facing Rafael was almost impossible. His hand actually shook as he raised it to knock on the door. He sucked in a deep breath and walked in to face his punishment, because he knew that was exactly what this was.

Rafael stood behind his desk, hands folded behind his back. Dressed in his usual white shirt and dark slacks, he looked anything but welcoming. He didn't speak; he didn't smile. Silence filled the room and threatened to suffocate Paul. He could feel himself begin to shake, but he refused to give in to his fear. He walked further into the room and stopped directly in front of Rafael's desk. He forced himself to look Rafael straight in the eyes. He almost collapsed with relief when all he saw was the man he had always known, the man who had saved his life. Paul was overwhelmed with gratitude for what Rafael had done and shame for the problems he had caused. He realized that he alone was responsible for the death of those men, not Rafael.

Rafael was as good at reading people as Raul, and he knew this young boy. He recognized the fear and the shame that he felt; he saw the remorse for the lives that had been lost. There was no need for lectures. Words were not what Paul needed. He needed to come to terms with his actions and learn from his mistakes, and Rafael had the perfect plan. He smiled.

At that moment, Paul knew he had been forgiven, but the way Rafael smiled told him that the punishment for his reckless disobedience would be greater than just the scar on the side of his head. But he was ready; he could take it; he knew he deserved it, whatever it was. He didn't have long to wait.

Rafael had pressed a button on the side of his desk as soon as Paul had faced him. He knew Paul was ready now to pay for his actions. Alberto had already been briefed. There would be no lenience, no reprieve, and no mercy. Rafael was proud of Paul. He hadn't given in to his fear. Rafael knew the stories that were told about him; they were true. He was not ashamed. He only did what he had to do. But Rafael had seen grown men whimper and beg when facing him for lesser grievances than Paul's willful disobedience. He was more like his father than he probably realized. It was that independence and willfulness that had gotten him into trouble, but now he would truly understand his position in the family, and after Alberto got through with him, he would be less likely to be such an innocent target.

When Alberto opened the door, Rafael smiled knowingly and Alberto laughed. Paul turned to face him and sighed. This was going to be interesting. He just hoped that he survived.

That summer Paul put on more muscle than he ever had at playing sports. He ran for miles over the mountainous terrain, learned how to survive in the jungle, and worked out daily with martial arts experts. Alberto took over his training in the use of weapons. He practiced loading, firing, cleaning every conceivable type of weapon. He learned how to use a knife and how to make simple but effective weapons from ordinary materials. He could protect himself.

But Paul's most daunting task came only after Alberto felt he had been successful in his weeks of training. Late one afternoon, Alberto cleared the indoor firing range of everyone with a quiet nod for them all to leave. They all knew that Paul hadn't really overcome that day's ordeal. He had hidden his feelings and braved his punishment, but he hadn't let himself think about what had happened. He hadn't internalized the need to protect himself.

After firing his last rounds, Paul automatically began breaking down his weapon, intending to clean it as usual. He looked up when Alberto approached; something was different. The room was too quiet. A quick glance told him that everyone had left. Paul waited.

"You've had plenty of practice. Now let's see how you handle yourself." Alberto picked up a rifle from a nearby table and quietly loaded it. Paul was confused, just what was this all about. Slowly, Alberto raised the rifle to Paul's head and pressed it against him, just like the soldier had done. Memories of that day flooded through Paul; he couldn't think; he couldn't shake free from the terror of that moment. Paul heard the click of the safety being released. What was he doing? Did he really plan to shoot him?

Alberto pressed the rifle harder into Paul's head. Pain shot through him, repressed memories of that day filled him, he yelled in rage as he swung his arm up forcing the rifle away from head. Alberto squeezed the trigger; the bullet roared by Paul. He slammed his fist into Alberto's face. Pain shot up his arm. It only enraged him further. He began savagely hitting Alberto. Alberto tossed the rifle aside, blocking most of the hits; Paul began fighting harder, throwing well-placed punches and kicks, his training finally taking over. Alberto grunted as more than one punch connected with his well-toned body. Paul had learned well.

Alberto let him continue until he worked off his rage and burned off his self-reproach. It was time for Paul to accept what had happened; he couldn't have done anything differently. He had survived. He had to quit blaming himself and get on with his life. If anything like that ever happened again, he would be better prepared. Alberto was going to have the bruises as proof. Finally, covered in sweat, physically and emotionally drained, Paul collapsed against his friend.

Paul shook his head to dispel the images that even after all these years still had the power to trouble him. Some memories never faded; some lessons were never forgotten.

Chapter 9

"BE AT MY APARTMENT in an hour." Paul slammed the receiver down, breaking the connection. He felt more like breaking Robert's neck. He hadn't bothered to acknowledge Robert's sluggish greeting. He was too angry. If Robert continued with this type of destructive behavior, Paul would be forced to take drastic measures. He paced back and forth, trying to decide the best approach to take.

Alberto smiled to himself. He could have saved Paul a lot of trouble, but he knew that it was better for him to learn on his own. There was still hope for Robert, but he would have to be watched closely. Alberto had already installed surveillance equipment in Robert's apartment. He knew that would be Paul's first response when he told him about the past weekend.

Robert had reacted rather strangely to the drugs. Alberto hadn't expected such a violent turn of events, but then everyone was different. He had only seen one other person respond with such aggressive behavior. He had been a local producer who got involved using his own product. Only a fool messed his mind up using powder. He had been quietly removed from his position of power and replaced with a more suitable family member. Using was strongly discouraged in the family. It was too easy to make mistakes when people started taking anything stronger than an occasional, good strong drink. They soon forgot their priorities, their responsibilities. They became a liability.

Of course, Alberto and his men were accustomed to taking care of liabilities. He rather enjoyed his work, but for the past several years he had been limited to assigning those tasks. When Paul had moved out of his home to go to Harvard, Raul had acquired an apartment building for his use, and Alberto had also become a permanent resident. Of course, he still made frequent trips to Bolivia, but he had assumed responsible for Paul's protection—not that Paul knew anything about it. But for the last few months, he had shadowed Paul's every move.

When Raul and Rafael had revealed the next phase of their plan to their children, their protection had become Alberto's domain. Caroline was watched as closely as Paul, but she had little understanding of such tactics. Paul, on the other hand, required more subversive measures to keep him from discovering Alberto's involvement. Of course, it was only a matter of time before Paul realized; he was too smart and too observant not to notice sooner or later. Alberto could only involve so many others in such a confidential task. He didn't believe in too many people having access to privileged information. Alberto wanted Paul's private life to remain just that—private.

Paul stopped pacing and turned to Alberto. "Who is this girl? Will there be a problem with her?"

Alberto shrugged. "Who can say, but it won't be anything that I can't handle." He smiled meaningfully. Paul had learned to accept Alberto's penchant for his job, but there were times that it still sent chills through him. He didn't like knowing too much about what he actually did. Alberto was his friend, and he had stood by him through some really rough times. Paul knew that Alberto was one of the few people that he could trust implicitly, one of the few people who would give his life for him if the need arose. Paul just hoped that he could do the same for him, if he ever needed to. Paul returned Alberto's smile, just having Alberto with him helped Paul to remain focused. Paul knew that he still had a lot to learn, and Alberto knew just about everything there was to know about Raul's influence outside of the family. It never hurt to have a second opinion.

Alberto had learned all there was to know about both girls. Through the older girl, Alberto knew the younger one had no money and few friends. She could easily disappear and no one would ever know or care. She wouldn't remember what had happened that night. The drugs they had given her would have seen to that, and the ecstasy in the drinks had more than produced the desired effect. Their uninhibited display had been beyond anything that Alberto had hoped for and had provided the perfect opportunity to gather additional leverage against Robert. If evidence of his actions that night wouldn't convince him, then nothing would. Alberto knew those pictures successfully sealed Robert's fate.

Robert rang the doorbell; its pealing sound vibrated through his skull. He felt as though he was about to jump out of his skin. He really wasn't up to this meeting, but he knew he had no choice. If Paul turned against him, it would ruin his chances of ever achieving his goal. He needed Paul's help, his money, and his influence. He tried to marshal his thoughts, but it was impossible. He had the jitters so badly that all he wanted was a little something to take the edge off, but he didn't dare risk going to get anything before he met with Paul. His tone on the phone had left little doubt that he would tolerate no delays in their meeting, and Robert certainly didn't want Alberto coming after him.

Alberto answered the door. Robert flinched slightly and forced himself not to back up a step when he saw him. Speak of the devil. He knew Alberto didn't like him though he had never said or done anything overtly; it was just a feeling that Robert had. There was something in his eyes that made Robert cringe whenever he was near. He forced himself to smile as he stepped into the room.

He did his best to sound sure of himself as he spoke, "Hi, Paul, did you need to see me about something?" His smile slipped a little when Paul turned to face him. Alberto grinned. Paul didn't know it but he had perfected Raul's glare. It usually reduced men to stammering excuses even before they knew what the problem was. It would be interesting to see how Robert reacted.

Alberto was impressed. Robert held his ground and waited for Paul to speak. Maybe he wasn't such a bad choice after all. The other problems could be dealt with.

Robert wasn't about to say anything, if he could help it, until he knew what this was all about. He just might reveal more by talking too quickly than if he waited for Paul to tell him. That didn't make it any easier to stand there waiting. This was turning into a mind game. Robert was usually good at those, except today his mind was not functioning at its fullest potential. And who could he blame for that, but himself.

Paul hadn't even asked him to sit down. This situation struck him as humorous, but he didn't dare smile; it actually reminded him of being called up before the principal. He knew better than to take anything for granted. He wouldn't just sit down. Paul might take offense at such a blatant assumption of familiarity. Even friendship had its bounds. Paul didn't look too friendly at the moment.

"Would you care to explain your recent behavior?" Paul's deadly calm tone grated on Robert's frayed nerves. He wanted to say that it was none of Paul's business, but they had formed an alliance. He couldn't go back on his part of the bargain now. Paul had a right to know, but it didn't make it any easier to answer to someone else about his private affairs. He glanced back at Alberto who remained standing behind him. He felt hemmed in, cornered like the proverbial rat.

Robert decided to be honest. He had a sinking feeling that he was lost either way. "To be quite frank, I don't know how." He shrugged and turned to walk toward the window looking out over an inner courtyard. The flowers along a pathway were beginning to bloom; their muted spring colors softening the harsh dead winter grass. Young leaves covered the slender branches of the surrounding trees just beginning to break free in their verdant foliage. His mind was wandering. He couldn't really concentrate.

"I don't really understand how it happened. I was feeling exhausted one day, really wiped out, and a friend offered me something that he said would help. He said that it wasn't addictive. I knew better, but I thought I could handle it. It was only going to be that one time."

He turned back to face Paul. "I liked how it made me feel. I could do everything that I needed to and still have energy for a little fun." He walked across the room and turned back to the window.

"I just needed it to help me through these last few weeks. I have so much going on that I can't think some days." He shoved his hands in his pockets to keep them from shaking, clenching his fists tightly. It didn't help. He could feel them jittering against his legs. He tried to force himself to remain calm. It was no use.

"Do you really think doing drugs will help you? If you don't mess up before graduation, you'll ruin your chances of a decent job afterward. Then what? How can you expect to have any type of political career if you have this cloud hanging over you? Someone always finds out; you know that."

Robert couldn't stand still; he paced back and forth across the room, clenching and unclenching his hands. Alberto knew what his problem was, but he didn't say anything. Paul would figure it out.

Paul's eyes narrowed. "Sit down!" he bellowed. "You're so strung out now that you can't focus. What were you thinking? Did you really think that I wouldn't find out? And if I can, so can anyone else!"

Paul nodded to Alberto. He knew that Alberto would know what to do.

"Alberto will see that you get enough to get you through the next couple of weeks until after graduation. Then you will get clean before we leave for Arkansas. I already have interviews setup with the law firms, and you will not disappoint me. Do you understand? If you mess up, I'll wash my hands of you and your political ambitions, and I'll make it my life's goal to see that you are never elected to any position anywhere, ever. Is that clear?"

Paul wasn't sure that Robert was actually listening. His legs were bouncing so quickly that his teeth were chattering.

All Robert really heard was that Alberto could help him. It had to be fast. He was going to be begging soon. He wasn't even sure how he had let himself reach this point. It hadn't seemed like a problem until just the last few weeks. He wanted to laugh; that was probably what they all said.

Robert almost cried in relief when Alberto returned to the apartment. It never occurred to him to wonder how he could get drugs that fast. He didn't care about anything but his all-consuming need.

Paul felt disgusted. To have the potential Robert did and to take the chance of throwing it all away on drugs was beyond his comprehension. Then the irony of the situation struck him. He almost laughed out loud. Sometimes he forgot who he really was. He finally just gave up and laughed. It felt good to release the tension that had been building. He was taking this way too seriously. He had accomplished his goal of getting more damaging evidence for his files, so what could he really complain about. For a moment he had become lost in his own lies. He laughed again. He felt better than he had in days. Alberto looked at him questioningly. Paul just shook his head and grinned.

Robert felt better. Alberto managed his needs. He didn't have to make any more trips to see his friend, and graduation was fast approaching. He wanted to see Caroline, but Paul refused to let him. Robert couldn't get the memory of that night out of his head. He thought if he saw her, he would know if it had been real or not.

But Paul wouldn't budge. He didn't want Caroline to know anything more about Robert's problem than she had already guessed. He knew she would have had to be blind not to know what had been wrong with Robert the night of his party, but he didn't want her exposed to his behavior until he got clean. Paul was responsible for her now, and he knew that Rafael would not appreciate his letting her associate with anyone on drugs. They might all make a living from them, but Raul and Rafael didn't want their children using them. That point had always been made crystal clear.

Robert wasn't good at dictates especially those that he felt were unreasonable. He had to see her. Maybe if he went through his friend, then he could arrange to meet her somewhere out of the way, somewhere Paul wouldn't find out about. He started to place the call from his apartment, but thought better of it at the last minute. When he left his apartment, just out of habit he began switching streets, appearing to walk aimlessly as though deep in thought. He caught a bus and rode across town then changed to another and rode back getting off several blocks from his intended destination. He didn't know why he thought that he was being followed, but something made him think it. It didn't hurt to be cautious.

When he neared his goal, he stopped at a pay phone and placed his call. The favor he needed had nothing to do with making a connection, at least not the usual kind. It didn't take long to find out who to call. A woman answered on the third ring. She knew the girl he was trying to contact and would be glad to talk to her. Robert only vaguely remembered that night. He thought that he had caught a glimpse of Alberto. He must have been mistaken.

He couldn't make sense of his memories. He must be going crazy. Maybe it was the drugs. He had been high most of the weekend, and he didn't really know what he had taken. At the time it hadn't mattered. There had to be some logical explanation for what he thought he remembered. If he could get her to meet him, then maybe she could help him find some answers. He paced outside the phone booth waiting for the return call. He didn't have to wait long. The night was cool, but he was actually sweating. He didn't understand his nervousness. He had already had enough to get by for the evening, but he had that jittery feeling he hated. It had to be nerves.

The woman gave him an address and asked him to meet them there in an hour. She didn't give her name and he didn't ask. Robert couldn't belief his luck. If she was willing to meet him, then things must be better than he thought. He arrived much too early, so he spent his time pacing back and forth outside the building. The time crawled by; he was so anxious he couldn't stand still.

Alberto was being too tight, too stingy; he needed a little more. But he didn't dare complain. His mind kept wandering. He didn't have this problem when he had enough. Paul should realize that he needed to function as he always had. He couldn't be slipping up now.

He paced down the broken sidewalk one more time. He couldn't help but notice that the neighborhood as well as the building was rundown, not the sort of place he would normally visit. Maybe she had something to hide herself. He liked a little mystery. He smiled. He was going to have to wear a brace on his wrist tomorrow; he had twisted it so many times to check his watch. He needed a drink; maybe that would help. Maybe she would have something.

He checked the time again. Thank goodness. He pushed open the outer door and walked up the dimly lit stairs. Certainly not what he expected, but right now he just needed to talk to her.

The woman who opened the door when he knocked was not who he expected to see. He glanced around the apartment. It was clean but by no means fashionable. It was simply furnished apparently with second-hand furniture; nothing seemed to match. The woman motioned for him to be seated.

She studied him for a minute. He was nice looking; it was just too bad his personality didn't match his looks. "Would you like a drink?" She had already placed a call. She knew what was expected of her. "Or something a little stronger?" she suggested.

Was he that obvious? He glanced around the room again. He wanted to say no, but he heard himself say, "Sure, why not?" Maybe she hadn't arrived yet. Maybe this woman was just trying to be friendly. She smiled at him as she left the room. She wasn't a bad looking girl, just not his type.

When she returned, she had his drink in one hand and a little pill in the other. His heart raced. He didn't recognize what it was, but he didn't really care. He was sure that it would take the edge off before he talked to her. He took the pill and washed it down with a long shallow of the drink. He began to feel better almost instantly. If only she would get here, but he could wait now. He already felt more in charge.

She watched as he slipped from edgy to mellow in a matter of minutes. It wouldn't be long now. She had already given her friend a little something special for this meeting. She sighed. She really hated keeping her doped up all the time. She had been such a sweet little thing when she arrived, but she needed the extra money. If she hadn't taken her in, someone else would have, and they might not have been as careful with her.

She didn't remember anything about that other night, and no one could tell anything had happened to her now. She looked just as pretty as ever. She had already helped her dress for this evening, but they wouldn't be going anywhere. She had gotten her orders. She refilled his glass. He smiled up at her.

She walked to the stereo and turned on a thumping melody, letting the volume fill the room. She could see him begin to move to the beat. He watched her as she walked slowly across the room. He rose and followed her, his heart beating to the music. He felt euphoric; he felt unstoppable.

Then he saw her, stretched out of the bed, dressed in a soft, filmy gown. It was her. He hadn't dreamed it. He went to her and she reached for his hand. The magic filled him. She was his again. Only with the rising sun did his overpowering need for her ease.

He had spent the night consumed by an insatiable desire that threatened to destroy them both with its violence. He couldn't suppress his need to inflict pain; he couldn't believe the power he felt when he did. He had soared to new heights this night. He looked at her bruised and battered body as she lay motionless and loathed himself for his actions. What would she say and who would she say it to?

He couldn't stay; he had people to meet. He needed to get to Alberto fast. He was getting jittery again. He had had too much last night. It left him needing more. He hated this feeling, but he needed the high. He glanced back at the girl. They hadn't talked at all. Should he wake her? He didn't have time.

He dressed and quickly left the apartment. His mind was plagued with questions. He couldn't think clearly. He had to find Alberto. He raced from the building never seeing the man who stepped out from the alley behind him.

Alberto had recognized the similarity in the girl's looks the first time he saw her. She even carried herself like Caroline. According to the woman, she was from some little place out west. He wasn't concerned. Right now she seemed to fill a need in Robert's life. As long as he was discreet, there should be no problem. He was a man after all. If she became a problem later, then that was easily remedied. Alberto had seen this before; it didn't last long. She would be a distant memory before Robert started his new life, a life that would involve Caroline. It was better that Robert get this out of his system now. That type of behavior wouldn't be tolerated later.

Alberto knew that Paul felt as he did. It was better to handle this now as part of a young man's initiation in life than to have it become an issue once he was established in a career.

Paul agreed to let Robert have free access to the girl as long as he kept to his bargain to stop using. Alberto would talk to him. Robert needed to know that the girl wasn't who he thought she was no matter how much they favored. If that was the appeal she had for him, then he would have to face the fact that she wasn't Caroline, but rather a drug-induced facsimile of Robert's mind. Alberto felt that as soon as he got clean, Robert would see the differences immediately. If it hadn't been bad luck the night they arranged the pictures, she wouldn't even be a second thought to him now. Alberto was intelligent enough to know how the mind worked under the influence of drugs, and Robert had fixated on the girl's looks. The ecstasy had only increased his desire beyond a normal range. Without it, he would be just an average man, and Alberto planned to see that he was without anything soon.

The woman almost felt sorry for the girl. But the money was too good. Besides she wouldn't remember anything about last night. As she slipped the needle into her arm, she knew she wouldn't care, and the bruises would heal. Life wasn't always what it seemed, but she wouldn't feel any pain.

Paul wasn't pleased with the choices Robert was making, but after talking to Alberto, he understood them a little better. In fact Paul almost felt responsible. It had been his idea to stage the last photo session. He should have realized that not everyone reacted the same way to stimulates. Raul would have thought this through better. Paul had learned from his mistake. He wouldn't make it again. He just hoped things improved quickly.

Alberto felt this was a good process for Robert to go through, so that if these tendencies developed later, they could be quickly handled. Robert had a chink in his armor. It was better to know about it beforehand. They would be prepared in the future. Raul always said, "Know your man then be prepared for disappointment." Paul knew exactly what he meant.

Caroline's days were filled with graduation preparations. Her parents would be arriving soon, friends and family gathering for the momentous occasion. Paul, Robert, and she had met with several potential law firms. The men were making the final decisions. They had all been offered rather prestigious positions. Of course, Caroline's wasn't quite as advantageous as the men's, but she was entering a "good ole boys" world. She understood the limitations of being a woman doing a man's job. It would never be about her qualifications or her ability to do a great job. It would always be about sex. It didn't matter how many laws they passed; equality was only on paper, and the paper in the copier was always placed there by a woman.

She was tough; she could handle anything a bunch of old men threw at her. She had survived her father's restrictions. After that, everything else would be a piece of cake, not that she would necessarily like the flavor. She laughed. Would Rafael be at graduation? He had never said and Paul hadn't mentioned Raul attending. She wasn't really sure how she felt about having both of her families together. It could be a memorable event of many levels. She left her apartment, smiling. It was going to be a glorious day!

Robert was so angry. They had all passed exams, graduation was eminent, their jobs were secured, his family would be arriving, and he was livid. He had been meeting her regularly; he was more addicted to her now than any drugs. He really didn't need them anymore. In fact he felt certain that Alberto had been cutting them for some time. He didn't care about any of that. He was angry at himself; he had known, but it was such a wonderful fantasy. He had known from the beginning that it couldn't be possible, but he had let himself believe. He could do anything when he was with her. She made him feel so powerful; he craved that feeling. It consumed him like paper in a flame. The more he had her, the more he wanted her. He knew that leaving her was going to be harder than giving up any drug.

He had finally realized when he stopped using. She was always wasted, high on something, but so loving, so sweet. She made him feel like a god. She didn't ask questions, she didn't demand anything from him, just him. The earlier furor had burned away, but the need was still there. How could he exist without her? He knew that he no longer had a choice.

They were leaving right after graduation, and he wouldn't see her again. The older woman had promised to take care of her, but he didn't like the way she looked. She had been sick a lot lately. He was concerned that it was the drugs; she didn't eat enough. She was so slender; she weighed nothing. She didn't sparkle like she used to do. She seemed so tired, but he couldn't do without her. He needed her.

Still he had to leave. It was over, a time when he felt larger than life, a time he had soared beyond the limits of mortals, a time that would never come again. He pulled the door closed on the apartment and on that chapter in his life. It was over. He was making a new beginning. Caroline was his future.

Paul sighed in relief when he got the call. Thank goodness.

Alberto didn't give Paul any of the details. He never did. What he did was his business and no one dared interfere. The roommate had already made plans to leave. He had sent someone along with her for insurance. He would drop her off across the state line at the local truck stop. She wouldn't have any trouble hitching from there, if she made it that far. There would be no connection between them. With no family and her few friends thinking that she had left the bright lights of the city for the quiet countryside, no one would even notice if they never heard from her again.

Her connection had sent her a special going away present, only to be used to celebrate her arrival at her final destination. The situation struck him as decidedly humorous. He knew she would use it as soon as she stopped for the night. But she would be a long way from the city when that happened. There would be no connection to any of them.

The younger girl wouldn't remember anything after tonight. He neatly folded the stack of bills and placed them in his pocket. He had business to transact. Sometimes he really liked his job. Tonight might prove to be different, but it was not his place to question.

Time passed quickly. With graduation and the bar exams behind her, Caroline soon located a suitable apartment in the capital city and moved into an exclusive, upscale neighborhood. In no time, she had become part of the bustling social and political scene. At work, she was busy filing briefs and arguing cases as a new associate with the prestigious law firm of Faulkner, Webster, and Street. Of course, they had her working with more experienced litigators, but at least they were keeping her busy.

Caroline was happier than she had ever been. She had freedom, she was independent, and she enjoyed her work, even if it was a little boring at times. She was meeting interesting and successful women, many who were involved in the political process of the capital city. Several recognized her father's name, but before long, she had convinced them of her own political insight. Before long her name was recognized not just as the new girl in town but as a woman on the move.

Paul let her have her freedom. He felt that she had earned it. He knew that she wouldn't do anything too foolish. Rafael still kept her on a tight leash and surveillance was more important now than ever, but Paul had convinced him that to allow her to become a vital part of the city's social scene would bring the necessary recognition they needed when she finally chose to settle down. Her good looks and vibrant personality had the men begging for dates, her sharp wit and intelligence had the courtroom buzzing. She was making a statement. She was making a name for herself.

She wasn't just going to be someone's wife. She had plans of her own. She intended to be the catch of the year, the woman to have at your side, the best choice that any man could make. When she had to marry, she planned to bring as much political clout to the marriage as her husband. She had a plan and she was working it. Let the men, beware. She would be no quiet little mouse, the woman behind the great man; she would be his equal, his partner, or she would be nothing. She had made up her mind, and unless Rafael stated otherwise, she was going to outshine every other star on the political horizon. She was happy for the first time. She was her own person. She knew that it couldn't last.

Robert and Paul accepted positions at a firm that they both felt would bring them the greatest success. Old and prestigious, the firm handled only the state's elite clientele. The litigation was unexceptional, but it kept them busy. They had access to the men of power and prestige in the capital. They became immersed in the social and political scene. They shared a typical bachelor apartment elegantly appointed and maintained by discreet family members. Paul didn't have to worry about anyone becoming too inquisitive about his personal affairs. His business remained private.

Like Caroline, they brought new life and excitement to a town searching for change. Making their way slowly through the maze of politics, teach the people to know, analyzing political platforms, and personal agendas kept them busy. Their positions in the firm occupied only a portion of their time. The rest was taken up in making them known, in being in the right places, seen with the right people, doing the right things. They became involved in every aspect of society in the capital city.

Intellectual, handsome, well mannered, and charming, they turned Little Rock upside down. Everyone wanted to be seen with them, everyone wanted to be a part of anything in which they were involved. Invitations poured in, seeking their presence whether at social, political, or community events. Their photos were a constant feature in the society pages of the *Gazette*, ranking second only to Caroline's.

Paul laughed every time he saw her at another gala event. She brought a completely new dimension to life in the capital city. Before long their names were linked with some of the most promising and prestigious families in the Land of Opportunity.

Paul had decided that at first, in order to establish themselves in the hierarchy of the city, they should see one another only occasionally. That was perfect for Caroline. She was enjoying her reign as the city's most eligible young woman. The joke around town was that men were breaking the law just to have her as their legal representative. Those she represented in court soon learned that they had the finest. She made sure that she was more than prepared and that she had thought of ever possible contingency before she entered the courtroom.

Judges respected her professionalism and recognized her determination. There were a few who tried to throw the occasional wrench in the works, who resented a woman being successful in a man's world, but she soon won most of them over. She wasn't her father's daughter for nothing.

A quiet word to Paul and she had access to personal information that she could subtly use to calm the fiercest opposition. When she made mistakes, and there were the occasional ones, she took it in stride and laughed, but she made sure that her clients never suffered from her incompetence. Though she might laugh about mistakes, she took them to heart and made certain that she didn't repeat them. Paul was amazed at the reputation she was developing. He and Robert were definitely going to have to step up their game if they planned to take the state by storm, because Caroline was creating a whirlwind all on her own.

That began a serious competition between Robert and her. Paul hadn't said anything to Robert about his earlier problem. He thought it best to let him forget about all that had happened. Somehow, Paul felt that Robert might be blaming Caroline for those events even though she had known nothing about them. He seemed to get extremely irritated every time Caroline's name was mentioned. Maybe subconsciously he held Caroline responsible in some way; it was an intriguing thought and one that Paul would have to give serious thought to.

Paul realized that Caroline wasn't even aware there was a competition, and Robert had never stated anything directly to him. It was more a feeling, an intuition, which caused Paul to step back and watch the interaction between the two more closely. He didn't know whether to laugh at them or shake them both. Paul realized that it wouldn't take very long for an observant person to notice the animosity that was developing between them. Their friendly rivalry would soon be making headlines and forcing them into a situation that Paul didn't think either of them was ready for, but he decided to wait and let fate play out its hand.

Alberto wasn't as sure of Robert's feelings as Paul. He wondered if Robert's reaction to Caroline's notoriety would cause him to revert to his destructive tendencies. Alberto placed a second guard on him and wired his apartment with additional surveillance cameras. He didn't plan to use them unless Caroline went there. Alberto was good at reading people. He didn't think Robert's feelings were friendly at all. Something wasn't quite right, but then he had known that ever since the night of the party. Sex and drugs were never a good combination—someone always got hurt. Robert, however, had taken it to a new level. Alberto meant to see that nothing like that happened to Caroline. He debated telling Paul about Robert's problem, but decided against it.

Robert appeared to feel slighted by the constant attention the press paid to Caroline. He felt his causes were stronger and more important for the state. This was his state, and he began to campaign for reform in the legislature, for change within the state, for improvements in education and the economy. He started volunteering at shelters, working with the jobless, seeking out opportunities to bring in new businesses to the state. With his phenomenal memory, he began reading everything about the state and its needs that he could find. In no time his apartment became a stock pile of folders, books, and research prospectus.

He became consumed by his need to best Caroline. He began struggling to keep up with all the demands on his time. Once again he had become involved in more activities than he had time for, and still he had to perform exceptional well at his job. He couldn't chance any blemish on his record. There were already hints that he should consider running in the upcoming election. The position of State Attorney General would become vacant at the end of the term, and even the partners in the firm had suggested that they would consider supporting his bid for office. They were pleased with his success in the firm and his contributions in the community. He had made a name for himself and represented the firm well. Helping him launch a successful political career would only add to their prestige.

Robert felt that same old, suffocating feeling begin to consume him. He just needed something to help him through the next few weeks; things would be less demanding by then. He would be careful. He hated making this call more than anything, but he didn't know who else could help him.

When Alberto got the call, he had known that it was just a matter of time. Paul spoke cautiously about a friend who needed their help with a personal problem. He asked Alberto if he could find a quiet retreat somewhere outside of the city, possibly a house, where discreet entertainment could be provided. Paul rarely used names in his conversations and was as vague as possible about details. He knew that Alberto would understand. Paul had always cautioned that if Raul could access someone's personal information, then others could too. Paul wanted to supply as few details about his life as possible. He valued his privacy. He trusted no one.

At last, Robert could breathe. He stretched out beneath the silk sheets and gazed out the windows. He liked this house. Its remote location appealed to his country-boy background, not that he ever planned to give up city life. No, he liked the bright lights and the bustling crowds. He just needed a break, a little relaxation. Thank goodness, Paul had understood. Alberto had everything waiting for them when they arrived. Robert still felt uneasy when he looked at Alberto, but he always had exactly what Robert needed. Robert reached for the pills on the bedside table quickly swallowing them.

Last evening had been unimaginably wonderful, almost as good as in college. He let his mind slip back to that earlier time. It had been nearly four years. It was good to let the memories go. He looked over at the girl lying beside him. She hadn't been bad at all. In fact, he reached out and turned her over to face him. He didn't remember her name; it didn't matter. All that mattered was now.

From that time on, the hide-away became his private sanctuary, a place where he could relax, unwind, and fulfill his every desire while Alberto's men quietly stood guard.

With Robert's bid for office, the demands on his time grew even greater. So the quite weekends away from the city whenever they could be enjoyed became essential to Robert. They revived him as nothing else could. He learned to experiment with drugs only during these times. It was vitally important that nothing he did now upset his future goals.

When it came time for the election, Robert with his impeccable credentials and charismatic personality won in a landslide vote. Arkansas' new Attorney General was the man to watch. He vowed to bring Arkansas into the twenty-first century and to bring prosperity to its people. One genteel, elderly lady was quoted as saying that he could charm the rattles off a rattlesnake. People flocked to be seen with him. He made friends where ever he went; he made promises impossible to keep, then he made people believe that he could keep them. He could take any issue and talk with such complete understanding of the topic that his audience was mesmerized. He brought doublespeak to a new level and people loved him for it.

Robert was happier than he had ever been. He was making a name for himself, he was gaining recognition, and he was working on issues necessary to improve the state. His weekends were wild celebrations filled with alcohol, drugs, and sex. He had the ideal bachelor life, and he loved every minute of it.

Chapter 10

ONCE ROBERT WAS SAFELY in office and his influence across the state was established. Paul felt that next phase of their plan could be implemented. Alberto already had a plan in place to take over the state's drug operation. During previous discussions with Raul and Rafael, Alberto devised a scheme to circumvent the local drug dealers. He quietly placed his own people in trade and negotiated positions of power where access to the city's elite users was assured. The word on the street was that a new syndicate was taking over; before long Alberto's forces held sway over the city and were branching out across the state. When individuals became problematic, the reports of their deaths convinced most to fall in line or leave the state entirely.

When word leaked out about the savagery involved in the deaths of rival drug lords, only the diehard users failed to take notice. Bolivian neckties were a reality, not a fantasy of the media. The media became reluctant to report the ferocity of the attacks between the rival factions, fearing retaliation from the gangs themselves. State police were overwhelmed by the violence and hard pressed to eliminate the problem. Many in power felt that it was best to let them kill one another off, then step in and try to bring order. Fighting had been limited to the gangs, and so far innocent lives had been spared. It would just be a matter of time before that changed. And when it did, something would have to be done. At the present time, however, local law enforcement was taking a wait and see approach.

Paul understood the steps necessary to take over an area, but he had never witnessed it before. He tried to remain detached from the violence, but even he shuttered at some of the more graphic details. Yet he was amazed at the efficiency of the process. Alberto was careful not to have any direct ties to the operation, although he actually headed the operation.

The takeover itself was handled through Rafael's agents and Raul's organizational forces brought in from out of state, keeping it all basically in the family. This eliminated internal power struggles as the operation grew. Nobody crossed Rafael and lived to enjoy his success. Those who were new to the family learned quickly. There was always enough for everyone. Greed was not tolerated. Death was the final equalizer.

When the opposition decided to relocate and order was established, Raul began the next phase of his take-over. He established a charter fishing and hunting service through one of his local travel agencies. Using legitimate holding companies, he had already purchased large tracts of land in the west central section of the state, a remote area secluded between low-lying mountain ranges. Using his own construction business, Raul began clearing the land and developing a private landing strip and aircraft hangar for his charter business. Pilots from across the country were trained to provide the personal service advertised by his agencies, specializing in fishing and hunting experiences throughout Central and South America.

Special guides were recruited and excursions from the most elaborate to the relatively simple were designed to enticed people from every level of society. The "Great South American Getaway" was devised, with trips given away to various exotic locations, to encourage people to explore the agency's travel options. Prices were reasonable; amenities were varied; options were plentiful. The agency touted, "Something for everyone," and tried to see that everyone received the most memorable vacation imaginable.

Word quickly spread about the exciting adventures which could be experienced through South American Travel. The agency was swamped with vacation requests. They had become the latest fad; the thing for the rich and idle; the hot topic in all the trade journals. They were an overnight success. Raul was pleased. He now had a legitimate base for bringing large quantities of cocaine into the States.

His crews busily outfitted special planes. His people mixed with legitimate travelers, making trips regularly to destinations all across South America, destinations chosen for their scenic beauty and their access to Raul's hidden warehouses. When the passengers and planes returned to the state, they disembarked in the remote splendor of Arkansas' rolling hills. Passengers praised the quality of their vacation experience while Raul's crews, under the guise of performing necessary maintenance on the planes, emptied the hidden cargo bays of their riches. This isolated section of the state soon became the crossroads for cocaine distribution, the Little Bolivia between Arkansas' low-lying mountains chains.

Caroline had been planning this trip to Hot Springs for weeks. She was determined to make it even if she had to drive herself. Paul had promised to take her, but he was having last minute problems with a client. Caroline flipped her long blonde hair over her shoulder. She shouldn't let his problem affect her so much, just because the client was a wealthy divorcee didn't mean that he was ditching her. She really should give him more credit than that. He had never failed her before, so she should give him the benefit of the doubt. The trouble was that she knew this particular woman and her problem wasn't legal; it was personal. She had made it perfectly clear that she intended to be the first Mrs. Paul Stevens.

Caroline had considered telling Paul but decided against it. Men could be so obstinate; he probably wouldn't believe her. He would just think she was jealous or something. Far be it from her to advise the mighty one. He thought he was above all of those petty machinations of women. She almost laughed. He was a man; therefore, someone's target, especially since he was handsome and wealthy. She sighed and shook her head, so foolish, so very, very foolish.

Judy had to admit she was a little scared. This wasn't what she had in mind when she first came up with the idea. Now it was too late; she couldn't turn back. She glanced around the room. She didn't know anyone here except her friend. Sherry smiled across the room at her. That little something that Sherry had insisted she take wasn't helping. She tried to smile back, but her face felt brittle. She could feel her heart thumping in her chest. The dress she was wearing was too revealing. She felt exposed. She shouldn't have listened to Sherry. She didn't really know anything about her.

They had only met a few days ago when she first arrived in town. But she had seemed so nice, so sincere. When she first met Sherry, she had been desperate. Standing alone on a street corner with her few possessions slung over her shoulder in an oversized bag, she had looked about as dejected as anyone could. The lead she had been following had proven false, and she had used almost all of her money just getting to the city. She didn't know anyone, and she didn't know where to go for help. She was afraid to go to the police. That could prove too dangerous. If her brother ever found out that she had left college to chase after a guy, he would murder her himself.

She had been standing there contemplating throwing herself in front of the next truck that passed. She ruled out a car because she wanted to make sure that there would be no regrets. She didn't want to wake up in a hospital paralyzed for life or disfigured somehow. If she was going to do this, she wanted it to be fatal, final, finished. That was when Sherry had tapped her on the shoulder, startling her so much that she almost fell in the path of an on-coming car. She had been so deep in thought that Sherry's touch had scared her silly. Her reaction to almost accidentally dying made her realize that she didn't really want to take her life, after all. She would figure something out. She always had before. She just had to have a little faith.

Maybe some good had come from all of this after all. The longer her search had taken the more she realized that maybe it wasn't her heart that had been involved as much as it was her need to escape. She had foolishly believed him when he said that he was going to take her with him. When he suddenly left without her, she had mistakenly thought that if she could just find him, talk to him, she could convince him that they were the perfect couple, that he needed her in his life. She was beginning to think that what he had really needed was her money, and when he found out that she didn't have any more, he had taken the fastest way out.

Sherry had offered her a place to stay until she found a job in return for cleaning the apartment and cooking. Since she had done that all her life, it was not difficult. She was a pretty good cook. In fact, Sherry had suggested that she might be able to find work at one of the dozens of restaurants in the city. She had to do something to bring in some cash; she couldn't even return home until she saved some money. Not that she wanted to return any time soon, but she didn't tell Sherry that.

Sherry had been so nice to her that when she suggested they attend the party together, she felt that she couldn't refuse. Besides, what harm could come from attending just one little party with Sherry's friends.

Now though, she wished she had asked a few more questions, found out a little more about those particular friends beforehand. All she really knew was that they were rich and from out of town. To Sherry, those were the only qualities necessary.

The actual reality of her situation left her feeling confused and scared. She hadn't thought her plan out well enough. At the time, it had seemed like such a good idea. Now she saw firsthand the problems. She was alone and in a city with no friends and very little money. Still, she needed to find him. She knew he had to be here somewhere. It was just a matter of time before she located him, but she didn't really have time. If it hadn't been for Sherry, she wouldn't have made it this long. She couldn't return home; she had burned that bridge and the flame had threatened to consume her as well. No, there would be no going back. She had made her choice, and she would have to live with the consequences.

She just needed more time. She knew if she walked the streets long enough, she would find him. He just had to be out there. She couldn't lose him, not after all she had endured. Just when she thought that she had put all that behind her, she felt the tears threaten, the dark cloud of depression pressing on her. She took a frosted glass from a tray setting near where she stood. False courage—anything that would help her last one more day.

If she could only find him, everything would be fine. That belief was all that she had left. There was no one else. He was out there; she had to find him. A few more days, she felt certain.

Sherry had offered to ask around, but she had refused her help. It would be too dangerous for him and for her. He had always emphasized that point to her. At first, she had thought that was the only reason he had left her behind. She had waited; she had been patient. Now she knew that all of it probably had been a lie. He had been using her, hiding out in her apartment from whomever or whatever was after him. Taking everything she had to offer and asking for more—more that she had gladly given without a single thought of the consequences.

Quickly she downed the sweet liquid. The coldness refreshed her, but she didn't really like the taste. Still, it helped her feel less nervous, or maybe it was that little something Sherry had given her before they had arrived. Either way, her panic was subsiding. She felt less anxious, stronger. She could do this. She smiled at Sherry. Sherry frowned and nodded toward the room full of men.

As she scanned the smiling faces, she realized she was extremely uncomfortable in a room full of strangers. She had heard several of the men speak English, but they always addressed one another in Spanish, and the way they looked at her when they spoke made her flesh crawl. It didn't take a mind reader to know that what they were saying wasn't complimentary. But she couldn't leave. For one thing she didn't have a clue where she was, and for another she didn't have any money on her. Sherry had insisted that they wouldn't need anything. In fact, a chauffeur driven limousine had picked them up and brought them here. Everything would be taken care of, she said, and if things went well tonight, this could become a permanent arrangement. She hadn't asked exactly what *this* was.

The idea of making money so she could continue her search had enticed her, lured her into thinking that this would be a simple social gathering. She realized now that she had wanted to believe Sherry. It would be the fastest way to raise the money she needed, and she had let herself be convinced. Now she wasn't so sure that she could follow through.

Sherry's friend had arranged everything. He said that all he needed were a couple of girls for an evening, girls who would show his friends a good time, but Sherry had insisted she wouldn't have to do anything that she didn't want to do. She had known before she came that that probably wasn't the truth, so she really had no one to blame but herself if things got out of hand. From the looks she was getting, someone had definitely failed to tell these men the same plan. Still, she would try to be friendly, but that was as far as it was going to go. If she had to, she would leave and just start walking. She would come to some place sooner or later. But what good would that do her? She didn't know anyone; she didn't have anyone she could call. For a moment she was so overwhelmed with desperation that she couldn't breathe.

She was panicking. Determinedly, she shook her head to clear the depressing thoughts, took a calming breath, and plastered a false smile on her face. Her soft blonde curls bounced around her face. Irritably, she shoved them back, just as a door on the far side of the room opened. The man who entered looked relaxed and friendly; something about him looked vaguely familiar. But before she could ponder that question, the thought skittered away as she realized that he wasn't Latino. She almost laughed. She wasn't sure why she thought that would do her any good, but somehow she felt better thinking it. As unobtrusively as she could, she began making her way across the room toward him.

Robert sucked in his breath. A quick scan of the room told him that several of Paul's friends were visiting. Then he saw her, walking provocatively toward him. This must be her first time here. He didn't remember her and somehow he felt this wasn't her usual type of entertainment. The music, the smoke, and the obvious party favors didn't fit with her innocent look. But then he didn't really know anything about her. He was just assuming she didn't go in for those types of things. She seemed too wholesome, even in that sexy body. He couldn't help grinning; he hoped she couldn't tell what he was thinking. With her body, wholesome probably didn't enter most people's minds. Maybe she wanted to appear sophisticated, experienced, uninhibited, instead of the innocent ingénue tonight.

Maybe he was wrong in his assessment of her. The closer she got; the more he liked what he saw. This wasn't some sweet little thing that needed to be sheltered and pampered. This was a woman out to have a good time if ever he had seen one. That was why he was here. He was feeling an overpowering need, and he knew just what it was. He wasn't going to disappoint her.

When she reached his side, she glanced at him uncertainly, her eyes soft and luminous. He didn't say anything at first; he was too busy trying to keep his eyes focused on her face and not her cleavage. She was beautiful and dressed so suggestively. And what a suggestion she was sending him. Before she could speak, he stammered, "I don't know about you, but I certainly could use a drink."

With that blunt statement, he grabbed her hand and led her to a makeshift bar, set up with an assortment of drinks. His grip on her hand was too tight, too possessive. He didn't care.

It probably wasn't the greatest opening line he had ever used, but it was honest. He was tired. It had been a grueling week. He glanced at her again; maybe he needed something stronger. He took a frosted glass of what looked to be some sort of fruit concoction and handed one to her. She took the drink and sipped at it tentatively. She didn't fool him. He reached behind the bar and grasped a small box. Taking three small pills from it and handed one to her. She shook her head, but he insisted.

"Go ahead. You'll like it. I promise. You won't believe how good you will feel." With that he swallowed two and emptied the drink he was holding. Tentatively, she swallowed hers.

She didn't really know what to say to him. He looked at her strangely. She was just relieved that he spoke English. She had become increasingly uncertain about the outcome of this evening before his arrival. At least Sherry had stopped giving her stern glances and nods to start mingling with the men. She seemed pleased now. But it was early; things could change.

His grip on her hand must be too possessive. She tugged at it, trying to break free. He smiled at her weak attempt. He loosened his hold but did not free her hand. Instead he lifted it to his lips and kissed it. Memories of an evening, years earlier, flitted through his mind. He planned for this evening to have an entirely different outcome.

She took another fortifying drink. It really was quite refreshing. She felt herself relax even more. It was a pleasant feeling. Things were definitely looking brighter. Her future seemed a long way off, and she felt rather euphoric as though something important was going to take place. The room took on a more vivid hue. The lights blazed brighter. She felt removed from her surroundings, yet so attuned to every movement that the room seemed to pulse around her.

When she looked at the man standing beside her and realized that his eyes were glued to her body, she mentally shrugged. What could she expect when she dressed this way? Too much body and not enough clothes, Sherry had insisted that she wear it, and she didn't really have a choice since she didn't have any other clothes to wear. With this outfit, though, she knew that she was asking for trouble; she just hoped that she hadn't found it. She took another long swallow, as he finished off his second drink and set his glass down.

Her skin prickled. She felt eyes watching her from across the room. She looked up. She could see the muscles, well-defined even through the expensive cut of his jacket; he was leaning negligently against the entrance to the dining area. Even with the width of the room between them, she knew that he had the coldest eyes she had ever seen, soulless. For a moment, she was utterly terrified.

Then she glanced back at the smiling man beside her; he looked calm, safe. And the moment passed. Actually, he was quite good-looking, and now that he was looking at her face, she could see that he had the kindest eyes. A person could trust someone with eyes like those, but then wasn't that what they had said about the Boston Strangler. His smile wasn't so bad either, a little quirk at one corner lending him a devil-may-care attitude. He arched one eyebrow questioningly and nodded toward the far side of the room. She smiled in return.

They seemed to be having a conversation without actually talking. That was all right with her. She had never been much of a talker. She much preferred to listen to what others had to say, but then she hadn't ever been allowed to say much either. Her opinions had never counted. It would have been pointless to argue. She sighed and let thoughts of the past fade from her mind. She was feeling too good to dwell on things that it was much too late to change.

The room seemed to be tilting. She giggled. She couldn't keep focused on any one thing. Her thoughts flitted around like hummingbirds seeking the sweet nectar of succulent flowers. For a moment she pondered why she was suddenly becoming poetic; then in the next, she realized she was fast becoming inebriated. But oh, how good it felt, as though she were a part of the room and yet not, removed somehow from this time and place, watching from some distant location.

Taking another swallow, she realized that her drink tasted much better now than it had earlier. She smiled at the strange man beside her; she had always liked the strong, silent type. Maybe she had had a little too much to drink, or maybe Sherry's little something had finally taken effect, or the one he had given her. For a moment she felt afraid. She had never taken so much before. But the moment passed. He looked safe, and she was feeling wonderful. She wanted to twirl around the room the way she had done as a little girl. She wanted to feel free and safe and loved, and she suddenly wanted to cry. What was wrong with her?

He didn't notice her sudden change of mood. He took her hand and pulled her toward a door on the far side of the room. It was hidden from the rest of the room by a screen and several exotic looking plants. The room was a little quieter, more secluded, a secret hideaway.

She didn't resist, but she glanced back at the other man. He was gone. No one was paying any attention to them. As they reached the door, he released her hand. She took another long drink and placed her empty glass on a nearby table. He pulled her into the room, and suddenly she was lying beside him on a sofa facing an empty fireplace, confused. The room seemed to take on a life of its own. Every sound seemed magnified, intensified, and more alive. She was floating, balanced on the brink of some great discovery, hovering on the edge of a death-defying precipice, ready to soar free. It was such a powerful, all-consuming feeling.

She could feel the air filling her lungs pressing her breasts again the fabric of her dress. She could feel the music thumping in her head, her blood rushing in her veins. Colors looked sharper, more intense. Her skin vibrated with feeling. She wanted him to touch her hand again, so she reached for his. His long fingers curled around hers, and he lifted her hand to his lips. They felt cool from his drink and a little shiver raced through her body. His eyes seemed to bore into hers; she felt mesmerized by his touch. She had never felt this way before. His other hand slid up her arm and cupped her face. She could feel the heat of his touch. He leaned toward her; she wanted to taste him, to feel him, all of him. She wanted him to touch every inch of her body. She was filled with insatiable need, an overwhelming hunger. She couldn't stop herself.

What was happening to her? Why was she acting this way? This was not like her. She didn't understand any of it, but she had to have him now, right now.

He must have felt the same. His hands were all over her body, and it felt so good, almost too good. But still it wasn't enough. She ran her hands over his chest, up his arms, through his hair. She could feel his muscles flexing. She could feel his breathe on her skin, the rasp of his beard, his teeth as he nipped her neck and throat, his tongue as he slid it across her heated skin. He felt so good. But it wasn't enough. She needed more. The room faded; the world ceased to exist.

The music soared in the other room; the beat pulsed through her. She felt herself slipping; colors and lights swirled in her head. She couldn't focus. Nothing mattered, but this need. She was stretched out next to him on the sofa. Her hand moved swiftly down the front of his slacks; she could felt the hard length of him pressed tightly against the fabric. She worked at the snap, the zipper. She couldn't free him fast enough.

He tugged at her dress, pulling it up to her waist. The straps fell easily, revealing the round perfection of her breasts to his touch. His lips and hand caressed one, molding and shaping it to his touch, as his other hand slipped into the fabric of her panties. She was so soft, so ready. He couldn't wait. It had to be now. His heart raced; his blood throbbed in his veins. This moment was all there was.

He felt himself surge free. He ripped the thin silk aside and thrust into her. Her sharp cry meant nothing to him. The music soared; lights flashed; the room spun. He didn't care about anything or anyone, just the moment. He couldn't believe she was so uninhibited, so passionate. He let the feelings consume him.

Quickly, he threw her to the floor and ripped the clothes from her body. With his hand at her throat, he pushed into her. She cried out. The sound surged through him. He liked the feeling; he couldn't get enough. Sweat poured from his body. She was slick with it. The music soared louder; lights swirled and flashed around him. Laughter echoed in his head. He couldn't think; he couldn't stop. It wasn't enough.

He could feel her struggling beneath him; he could hear her rasping screams. Her fingers dug into his hand; she clawed at his arm. Power surged through him; he couldn't stop, not now. His mind took up the litany, not now, not now. He pressed harder on her throat; the screams faded away. At last it was over. He fell against her body, gasping for breath. His sweat soaked clothes were cold against his heated skin. He felt disoriented, sick, completely exhausted. He felt powerful.

Alberto looked at the man sprawled on the bed. He was a fool.

After that night she and her friend became regulars at the secluded country estate. If she knew who Robert really was, she never said, but seemed satisfied to meet him on weekends and spend time together with him. She had quickly learned the advantage of mixing powder with ecstasy to achieve an incredible high, one that was indescribable. She loved how it made her feel; she loved how he made her feel, caught somewhere between heaven and hell.

Sherry warned her to be careful. She had never been much as a user, but after that first night she couldn't get enough; she had become a slave to the drugs, to the feeling they gave her, to him. She liked the world when she looked at it through a rainbow of lights and colors. She could forget everything. Even the pain meant nothing; it intensified the pleasure; it made her know she was alive. Only the moment mattered. All she needed was her next high, and he had an endless supply. She lived for the time they spent together and worried less and less. She no longer searched the streets. There was no need. He was the past. Robert was her future.

When she wasn't with him, she lazed around the apartment she shared with Sherry. He paid the bills. She didn't need to work; all she had to do was be available whenever he sent for her. She liked to think he needed her, cared about her, and cherished her.

For months they partied, safely hidden away most weekends in the seclusion of Paul's country estate, safe from prying eyes and wagging tongues, guarded by Alberto and his men. Life was easy; everything she needed was available, everything she wanted was provided. The only cloud on the horizon came when she realized that she was pregnant.

Robert didn't take the news well. He had seemed so happy when he arrived that she thought it would be the best time. Any happiness he had felt had evaporated with her news. Anger flashed in his eyes. He blamed her for the problem; he accused her of deliberately misleading him. She should have been careful; she should not have let this happen. He couldn't be responsible; he had a life; he had plans. They didn't include a child.

For the first time since she had arrived in the city, she was truly frightened. He changed right in front of her. He had never loved her; she had been a convenience, someone to fill a need, no one of importance, easily replaced. He would never want any child of hers. She was an addict, addicted to cocaine and pain; something would probably be wrong with it.

She couldn't believe the things he was saying, the hurt his words inflicted. He had given her the drugs; he had used them with her! How could he say those things to her? She had done everything he asked, taken every abuse, gladly. She had never complained. She had done it all for him. She didn't know what to do.

She was so stunned by his attitude that she couldn't speak, couldn't defend herself. Vaguely she heard him saying something about taking care of the problem, her problem. But this was his child nonetheless, yet it meant nothing to him. She wanted to laugh hysterically. Sherry had been right. She had been living in a fool's paradise of drugs and sex, and now she would have to pay the price, not him. He wanted nothing more to do with her.

Through a haze of humiliation and torment, she heard him phone someone. It would be taken care of, he told her. *It* would be taken care of—*it!* Not he or she, not a person, but a thing. As much as she had once loved him, now she hated him even more.

His callous behavior, his uncaring attitude drained the life from her. She had no one to turn to; she had no choice except to trust him. There was no one else. She sat on the sofa where they had first made love, paralyzed, unable to think, unable even to cry. Not love—what a joke that was. It was only sex to him; there was no love involved, not on his part. She had deluded herself into thinking that he loved her, would want to marry her, and would want to have this child. She couldn't have been more wrong.

Chapter 11

HE HAD LEFT MEMPHIS as soon as he could send word to Graham. He gave no details, no reasons, just that he would be gone for an indeterminate amount of time. He wasn't asking permission. He didn't care if Graham liked it or not, but he didn't want to completely alienate Graham, if he could help it. He still might be able to salvage something of the operation once he returned. Right now, none of that mattered. They weren't going anywhere, and he had to find her. That was all that was important.

It had taken him several weeks to get this close. She had left the university, and no one had seen or heard from her. No one seemed to know what had happened to cause her to leave. He tracked her to Little Rock, but there the trail ended. He couldn't find anyone who knew her, who had seen her, until this latest lead.

Richards waited as long as he dared. He didn't think he was being followed. He hoped Strong had taken his absence well. The weeks were slowly turning into months. Still, it never hurt to be careful. He was moving in some rough neighborhoods. The old hands didn't like to feel threatened. Cautiously, he moved down the back alley working stealthily around empty crates and piles of rotting garbage. The stifling stench of urine and decay burned his eyes and turned his stomach. It didn't matter, nothing mattered but making this connection.

Gradually, he worked his way through the maze of connecting allies, until the filth and decay was replaced with overturned trash cans and less cloying air. Still he moved cautiously, his training dictating his movements. Small patches of green heralded more upscale apartment buildings as he quietly slipped between buildings, moving outward from the city's center. Fenced in trash containers eliminated clutter and built-in security cameras provided a semblance of protection for middle class apartment dwellers. Finally, he could breathe more freely. Out of sight of the cameras, he pulled his cap lower and obscured his appearance as much as possible. He didn't want any evidence betraying his whereabouts.

For weeks he had followed the leads given to him by the old derelict, a message from his friend working out of state for a federal task force. He had to find her. The message said that it was urgent. She had been seen in the city months ago, recognized by his friend working undercover in a rough neighborhood, but she had virtually disappeared after that.

His friend had tried to locate her but hadn't been able to find her. So he had broken all the rules and tried to contact him. When the department couldn't or wouldn't tell him Richards' whereabouts, his friend knew that Richards was undercover, and he would have to resort to more deceptive means of contacting him. He also realized that to do so could jeopardize Richards' operation, but more importantly, endanger his life, so he had used one of their special-forces buddies to make the contact. It had taken time, but he was able to deliver the information without drawing undue attention to either of them. But more time had been spent in doing so. Richards was worried, not about himself. He could take care of himself, but her. He had promised to take care of her, and he had failed.

None of that mattered now. He had to find her. Something must have happened. He couldn't think what it could have possibly been. He just couldn't think. No, that was not right; he could think. He could think of all the horrible things that could have happened to her in this length of time; none of them were good. He was so worried about her. She couldn't survive on these streets, not for long, not by herself, and he couldn't think of anyone she might know. She didn't know this city. Why had she come here? It was hard to realize that she wasn't the dewy-eyed, little girl he remembered, but a woman. He would follow this lead and, with any luck, maybe learn something useful.

He slipped quietly in the back door of the building and eased up the stairs. They creaked in protest to his added weight. He kept moving steadily upward, out of habit checking for any signs of problems as he turned each corner. He stopped and took a calming breath when he located the apartment number he had been given. His knock echoed loudly down the narrow hallway. He could hear feet shuffling around inside the apartment. Someone was moving about. Automatically, Richards eased his hand behind his back. He didn't really know what to expect, but the white-haired, wrinkle-faced old lady who answered the door wasn't it.

She stared up at him blinking in the glare from the light in the hallway. She might look sweet, but the first words out of her mouth changed his mind abruptly.

"What do you want? Those girls don't live here no more, so go away and leave me alone!" She started to close the door, but he stuck his foot in the way. He had to talk to her. She must know something, if she knew the girls who had lived here. Maybe one of them knew where he could find her. Somebody had to know something. He pushed against the door, forcing it open again.

"I don't want to scare you. I just need some information. What do you know about the girls who used to live here? Where can I find them?"

She stared up at him, weighing his words with difficulty. "They'll do you no good." She turned from the door, moved across the room, and sat down in a faded, broken-down recliner. She stared at the television as though looking for answers. "Go now. I don't know anything. They're both gone. They were no good."

"You don't understand. I have to find them!" He knew his voice was revealing too much, but he couldn't reign in his emotions. He wanted to hit something, anything.

"You can find one at the morgue; the other left town. I don't know no more. Go away now." She continued to stare at the blank screen. He left.

He didn't care who saw him; he didn't care about caution. He walked like a blind man across the street through oncoming traffic, horns blared. He didn't stop. He knew before he got there what he would find. He knew the moment the old woman had spoken the word, that she was dead. She had been one of the girls. She had come to this city looking for something, but what? He had failed her.

When he finally entered the county morgue, at first, the attendant in charge didn't want to help him. He thought some derelict off the streets was trying to be funny, asking to see the unclaimed bodies. When Richards grabbed him by his collar and dragged him over the counter, he had second thoughts.

"We have several," he quickly informed him. "What description can you give?"

Richards had to think. All he remembered was a sweet-faced, little girl with a long, blonde ponytail. That wouldn't be how she looked now. It had been over three years. He had put his job above her needs and this was where it had ended. He knew before he even gave a description that he would find her here. He swallowed his anger and fell back on his training.

"Blonde, young, nineteen," he swallowed with difficulty. She would have just had a birthday. "No twenty, about five three, a hundred pounds or so—pretty," he finished the last in a whisper.

"I think I might have someone of that description. If you'll just wait right here, I'll bring the body out." He sounded so impersonal, so casual, as though the life of this person held no meaning to him, no importance.

Richards stood frozen to the spot. This was all formality. He knew that it would be her. If only he knew why? The squeak of the gurney wheels heralded the arrival of the cloth-draped body. White the color of innocence—the cover was pulled back and there was the face of an angel, so peaceful, so beautiful, and so lifeless. He could only stare at her. He could hear the man saying something to him, but he couldn't answer. Words seemed like a sacrilege before such innocent beauty. He touched her cold lips, brushed the hair off of her face, and placed her hand back under the sheet. She looked so peaceful. He prayed that she had not suffered. He pulled the cover over her face once again. She was gone from his life forever. He had failed her. He had broken his promise to her, and she had suffered for it. Someone had to pay, but whom?

He turned to the attendant. "I want to see the autopsy report." The stern tenor of his voice left the man in no doubt of his sincerity.

"I can't," he stammered, shuffling quickly behind the gurney. "Only official personnel can see it."

He tried to move the gurney back toward the morgue, but Richards stopped it easily. "I want to see the report, and I want to see it now!" His voice climbed a decibel, menace punctuating each word.

"I can't," the man pleaded with him to understand. "It's department policy."

"I am department!" Richards practically shouted. "Now let me see it before I do something that *you* will regret." He was in such a rage that his hands shook.

The attendant made the smart decision to ignore procedure and searched through his files for the report. Richards snatched it for his hands and opened the folder. After a minute, he sat down abruptly in a nearby chair. This couldn't be right! He slumped forward, his head in his hands. This couldn't be right! Not her, not ever! The folder slipped to the floor, spilling its contents across the hard, cold floor, the silent face of an angel staring up at Richards, accusingly.

As unobtrusively as possible, the attendant rolled the gurney back to the morgue, one wheel squeaking loudly in protest, and wisely left the grieving man alone.

It was proclaimed to be the most important event of the upcoming year. Everyone was vying for invitations. Proposed dates for mid-June were mentioned. The papers called it a whirlwind romance, since to outsiders at least no one knew that the couple had been seeing one another. Everybody loves a wedding; in this case everybody but the two people involved. The capital was rife with rumors. Elaborate plans were already underway for celebratory events to honor the union of two of the city's most eligible and outstanding young people.

The bride and groom were anything but happy. This was not the way this was supposed to happen. Once the furor of the announcement died down, Caroline and Robert were left to work out the details. Caroline was extremely upset. She had been forced into marrying him just because he made some stupid mistake, and Paul had decided they should announce their engagement to head off any damaging rumors. She didn't care about Robert's affairs, personal or otherwise. She had been enjoying her reign as the brightest and best Little Rock had to offer. Now that reign was at an end.

In public she glowed with radiance as any prospective bride-to-be should, but in private she ranted and raved against the injustice of it all. Then her father called. All it really took was a few brief words from Rafael to quell her anger. This was her chosen role; she would carry it out with the utmost dignity and grace as was befitting her station in life. She had to look at the grander scheme of things and remember that her star would soon be rising to unimagined heights and eclipsing any that had ever shone before. She wasn't happy, but she accepted the inevitable, and life for everyone around her became easier to bear.

Private arrangements were made for their families to come to the capital. A small chapel was reserved for a quiet ceremony. Family and close friends kept the well-guarded secret as plans were formulated for a small but stylish wedding ceremony. Before anyone knew, they were married and off on their honeymoon to a remote island paradise. Privacy was guaranteed because the island was owned by Raul and kept for his and Rafael's private use.

If Caroline's parents were shocked by the haste in which the arrangements were made and carried out, they refrained from voicing any opinions rather they seemed to be completely won over by Robert's charming manner toward them. Caroline for her part was just as successful with Robert's parents and friends. Most of the men considered Robert a very lucky man, and the women, once they took time to get to know more about her, actually liked her no-nonsense manner and her straightforward approach to life's little situations.

It might not be a marriage made in heaven, but it began amicably enough. Both of them felt that they had so much in common, that over time, any difficulties could be easily resolved. That was what they believed—at first.

The newly married couple had their first taste of life together as they landed on the secluded tropical island. Caroline was ready for a fun-filled few days of rest after the turbulent excitement of the wedding preparations. Robert wanted to get to know his new bride, and the quiet solitude of their bungalow appealed to his idea of togetherness.

When he refused to accompany her on a walk to view the scenery, she felt that he might be tired after the long plane trip and left him to recline on the over-sized sofa and sip at a perfectly chilled glass of wine, but when he adamantly opposed swimming in the crystal coolness of the nearby lagoon, she knew something was definitely wrong. This wasn't going exactly as she planned. She was used to having every minute filled with tasks, assignments, obligations, meetings, something. She never just lazed around doing absolutely nothing, never. She would go crazy. Where was all the drive and ambition that had marked him as the capital city's latest Man of the Year?

She had asked nicely, politely, sweetly, and still he refused. All he wanted was to lie around doing absolutely nothing—well almost. It was when she caught the glint in his eye that she realized exactly what he thought would be fun. She wasn't so sure. She went for the walk alone, trailed discreetly by Alberto who had boarded their plane at the last minute; she swam alone in the warm, crystal waters of the inlet; she stretched out alone on the warm sands for all of fifteen minutes before she felt the need to do something more exhilarating.

Robert watched everything as he reclined in his lounge chair and sipped at a frosted glass of mango-papaya delight. He smiled; the delight was in the nice little kick after you drank it. He quietly swirled the liquid in his glass as he watched Caroline's bikini-clad form race after her floppy hat as it was toppled off her head by the warm, sultry, island breeze blowing across the sand and danced precariously close to the water's edge. Laughing at its antics, Caroline caught it, splashing water and sand all over her in the battle for victory.

The sun had already left a faint pink tinge on her skin as she dashed back to their bungalow. She was starving and more than ready for an evening of dining and dancing. It would be nice to have a quiet evening without anyone around that she had to entertain.

"How was your swim?" Robert spoke as she neared the steps. She hadn't seen him there and his voice startled her slightly. She wasn't used to having a man around. This was definitely going to take some getting used to. "I see you finally caught your hat." He tipped his nearly empty glass toward the wayward accessory. Caroline slapped it lightly against her leg to dislodge any remaining sand and laughed.

"It did give me a good run for the money," she smiled, her eyes glinting with amusement.

"I'm starved. Are we going to the main house for dinner or dining in?" She hadn't meant the question to be provocative, but he seemed to take it that way.

He smiled, "I thought a quiet evening alone would be best after our long trip. It is our honeymoon, you know. No one expects to see much of us. We can do as we please for the next few days." He tipped his glass back and emptied its contents. His cheeks were slightly flushed. Caroline wandered just how many he had had before she arrived.

She swallowed back the questions she wanted to ask. "Sure. That sounds fine. Have you ordered or should I?" She walked toward the door as he rose to from his chair.

"It's all taken care of. Just make yourself beautiful. We'll dine in forty-five minutes, if that's all right with you?" He grinned. He knew she wanted more time than that. He was deliberately baiting her. He didn't really understand why he felt the need to do so, but it was almost a compulsion.

She never faltered as she made her way up the short staircase. She was a pro at this game. "That will be fine." She tossed the words over her shoulder as she sauntered toward her rooms at the far end of the landing, just barely keeping her temper. He was showing her who would be boss, she supposed. That didn't mean she had to like it. He could dictate all he wanted. If and when she decided it was worth a fight, he would see that he had met his match.

She left the room with five minutes to spare and had the privilege of seeing his eyes widen in disbelief as she floated down the stairs on a cloud of soft, flowing silk. It was the perfect cocktail dress, hugging her curves and emphasizing her slender legs. Of course, the five inch heels didn't hurt either. They did, however, make it rather dangerous to walk over uneven ground. She could only hope that dinner would be served indoors tonight, even though she could see torches burning brightly around an outdoor dining area. Well, what did she have a husband for if not to offer an obliging arm for support?

Robert reached for her hand as she stepped into the room. Gallantly he bowed to her beauty. Laughing, she remembered an earlier time that he had made the same gesture. "You seem to do that a lot." She couldn't help but be flattered; after all she was a woman.

"Only when someone is as breath-taking as you are." He lifted her hand and kissed the back, his eyes never leaving the beauty of her face. She felt a shiver of anticipation race down her spine.

He turned aside, breaking the spell. "Would you like a drink? I can wholeheartedly recommend the fruit drinks. They are rather addictive." He meant the words as a joke, but it fell flat as he recalled the last time he had used that word. What had become of her, of the baby?

He had never questioned Paul about any of the events after that evening. He had left her and never looked back, but there were moments that he felt haunted by the torment, the betrayal, the suffering he had seen in her trusting blue eyes. She hadn't said a word in her defense. She had just looked at him so sadly that it had angered him even more. He realized now that she had relied on him completely. She didn't care who he was; she only wanted to please him, and he had turned against her.

It had been the timing that had caused him to react so violently. He was so excited; he had planned an evening of celebration. He was on top of the world. The state's Democratic Party leaders had called a meeting to ask if he would be interested in running for governor. He was on his way up, and he couldn't let anything derail those plans. Too much work and sacrifice had already gone into the process. He couldn't let something like this become known, drag him down, and ruin his chances.

He turned back to his new bride. That was the reason for this rushed marriage, not love. Caroline was part of the package. Tied up in a pretty bow, he had to admit, but part of the deal nevertheless. Did that make her little better than a prostitute, selling herself for prestige and power? As first lady, she would command a great deal of authority whether as the governor's wife or as the President's. He watched her move across the room. Wherever she went she commanded attention. Whenever she spoke she drew support. A man would be crazy to fail to see that advantage of marriage to her, and he definitely was not crazy.

When she looked up at him and smiled that sweet, innocent, curving little smile she had perfected, he knew that she had not turned over the reins to him; he would have to fight her every step of the way. She liked things her way almost as much as he did his. At least theirs would not be a dull marriage. He smiled his own practiced smile, lifting one corner of his lips in a silent salute to the battle which had only just begun. She recognized his ploy and laughed.

When the private chef announced that dinner would be served at their pleasure, Robert escorted her to the dining room and pondered the question of who might be in command in the bedroom. Either way, he couldn't visualize himself as anything but the winner. He laughed aloud and tried to cover his amusement by coughing, but Caroline wasn't fooled. She knew adolescent behavior when she saw it, and Robert looked as guilty as sin. Men, she silently fumed, little boys in pin-stripe suits.

Alberto watched from his distant vantage point. Surveillance cameras followed each movement in the main rooms, only the bedroom suites were off limits. Even then no one but Alberto had access to the surveillance room. He didn't feel good about this marriage; he didn't trust Robert. He would not intrude on their privacy if things were going well, but he would if he felt the need. Robert had a dark side, a secret that even Paul didn't know about. Maybe he should have told him, but now it didn't matter. He would just have to watch and wait. He would slip inside after they retired for the night, just in case. All of the servants had orders to leave as soon as the evening meal was cleared to give them privacy, but she was his responsibility, and he never shirked his responsibilities. He only hoped that Robert's dangerous tendencies were a thing of the past.

After identifying himself to the local police, Richards was able to obtain a copy of the autopsy and investigating officer's police reports. He was puzzled by certain facts; it didn't make sense to him. On the surface everything looked aboveboard, but the more he thought about it, the more he was convinced that his sister's death hadn't been accidental or caused by drug use. The police report stated that the car his sister had been driving was a rental, leased under her name for six months, but Richards wasn't able to find the address listed on the lease contract and the phone number was no longer a working number. The more he checked into the circumstances of Judy's death, the more he believed that something wasn't quite right.

The autopsy report revealed marks on Judy's body, obvious bruises on her forehead where she had slammed into the steering wheel when her car impacted the embankment, but older deeper bruises on her neck and arms, bruises that seemed to be from a man's hands. The coroner reported that the bruises on her neck appeared to have been made in an earlier attempt to strangle the victim; those on her arms were most likely inflicted when she was being forcibly restrained.

The element in all of this that shook Richards the most was the unexpected fact that she had been pregnant. Whose baby was it? Was that the reason she had come to Little Rock? Had she been searching for someone or seeking help? He might never know now, but he intended to find out how she had gotten the drugs and who had supplied them to her, and if he could who the father of her baby was. The coroner had taken DNA samples; all he needed was to find the lucky donor—and he would.

Even the accident itself didn't make sense. Why would she be driving if she was as drugged as the toxicology report had revealed? In fact, how would she have even been able to drive with that amount of drugs in her? The more Richards found out the less he understood. Where was she living, and where was she getting her money or the drugs? He had to find the answers. But first he had to bury his sister.

Once Judy's body was released by the police, Richards flew back to Memphis with it. He had no family to contact, and he didn't know if she had any close friends at college. When he had been searching for answers, there had been no one who could help him, no one who knew why she had left. To him, they were all strangers, and he didn't feel like answering questions about what had happened to her or about her death. Until he had some answers of his own, he wasn't providing them for curiosity seekers. He made arrangements for a quiet burial in a plot next to their parents, and the next day Richards found himself standing solemnly by her graveside, promising to find whoever was responsible for her death. Another promise he wouldn't be able to keep? Could he ever forgive himself for failing her? All he could do now was try to find the answers to his questions.

As he turned from the grave, he tried to bury his emotions and once again assume his undercover persona, but his anger seemed to consume him as he went in search of Strong. He couldn't do anything more for Judy now; she was gone forever; all that remained was for him to find her killer, and he knew for a fact that there was one. Her death had been no accident, and he meant to prove it. If anyone could give him the inside information he needed, it would be Graham. To get to Graham, he needed Strong.

He found his quarry easily. Strong followed very predictable patterns. Today was the day he always played golf. He was a lousy player and he cheated. Richards had watched him on several occasions; he wasn't even good at cheating. Richards knew his partners had to know what he did but were just too intimidated to complain. Richards didn't care what he cheated on as long as Strong helped him contact Graham. He had a plan, one that even Graham might like.

As Strong left the club house, Richards was waiting for him. Strong pressed the keypad to unlock his car and Richards slipped into the passenger seat beside him. Strong started to object but one look at Richards' face silenced him. Without a word, Strong backed from his parking spot and headed for an isolated garage across town. When he reached the location, he used a remote control, opened the outer doors then pulled into the darkened interior, closing the doors behind them.

"This better be good," Strong growled as he switched on the interior light. "I've got more important things to do than be seen escorting you around town. What happened to you anyway? You've been gone for weeks and now you suddenly reappear. Do you think we need someone as unreliable as you?" Strong turned to face Richards, the soft leather upholstery squeaking in protest to Strong's weight. When he saw the ravaged look on Richards' face, he sucked in his breathe and waited. Strong was used to the blank stare, the unfeeling void that marked

Richards as a killer, but not this. There was so much anger burning in Richards' eyes that Strong could feel the heat. He broke out in a sweat. Perspiration trickled down his back.

Richards took a moment to quell the emotions raging inside him. "I want to see Graham." Strong was at a loss, floundering as how to proceed. He opted for cowardice. "He's out of town until tomorrow, but I can arrange something for the afternoon," he stammered slightly as he spoke. "Call in the morning and I'll give you the details," he tried to speak authoritatively but a telling tremor shook the last words. How he hated this man and what he made him feel!

Some day he would pay. That was a promise Strong had made to himself, and he meant to keep it. Strong almost smiled at his own brave thoughts; then wisdom made him reconsider. Richards had the uncanny ability to read his mind, and Strong didn't want to give his hand away this early. Besides, he was curious about what this was all about. He could wait a little longer—just not too long.

Without another thought for Strong, Richards climbed out of the vehicle and slammed the door. He didn't care where he was or how long it took him to return to his apartment. He had plans to make. He had to keep moving. If he stopped for too long, he began to remember too much, and he couldn't allow his feelings to interfere with his work. A plan was beginning to take shape in his mind. He just needed to work out the last details before he saw Graham.

He assumed the same ambling, uneven gait he had perfected; he did so without conscious thought. His years of military and civilian training dominated every aspect of his life when he was undercover. Even now when his mind was racing with possible scenarios, he kept to the same routine, back tracking, checking continually for anything unusual, out of place, passing in and out of buildings, stopping at unexpected locations; whatever it took to throw someone else off his trail or to protect his back, he did it. There were no second chances on the streets. The longer a person lived on them, the more he realized the price they always exacted was non-negotiable, irrevocable, and final.

By the time he reached his apartment, he knew what he had to do. It had already been months since Judy's death. It might be years before he finally had the information he needed, but he would find whoever was responsible for her death. He had a plan.

Paul was impressed with the way in which Robert settled into married life. He seemed more focused and ready to take on the challenge of running for the position of state governor. His political standing was at an all time high; he had brought success to the state through his work in the Attorney General's office, and the state's Democratic Party fully supported his bid. With his talent for debate and his expertise and confident demeanor, he was already the front runner, even before he had officially announced his candidacy.

Caroline, on the other hand, was another story. In private, she seemed unusually upset about something although she didn't allow her feelings to get in the way of her performance at work or in any of her numerous civic duties. In fact when Robert announced his intention to run for the governor's office, she wholeheartedly endorsed his effort. In public, she was the radiant bride of the Democratic Party's hottest political prodigy. In her interviews with the local press, she adamantly pledged her complete support for Robert's campaign and vowed to work diligently by his side to bring prosperity to the state.

Together, they were a charismatic couple, and everyone was caught up in the idea that with Robert's election, Arkansas would finally take its place in the world. They were viewed by many as the change that the state needed. Together they would revitalize the staid, old party and shake the aged bones of the state's legislators. Change was in the air, and progress became the byword.

Robert began a sweep across the state, which included every little town and backwater slough where he could gather an audience. He brought expertise, experience, and energy to his campaign and spoke on topics related to the people he addressed. He played on the fact that he understood Arkansas' needs, coming from a farming community himself. For her part, Caroline brought dignity, poise, and elegance. Together they drew people, they inspired reform, and they easily won the election. Arkansas was poised on the precipice of revolutionary change, and Robert meant to use his new position to develop a platform from which he would launch his presidential candidacy.

Arkansas' new governor sought every opportunity to bring financial prosperity and economic reform to the state. He fought for educational improvements and reorganization of the legislature. He became deeply immersed in the Southern Governor's Conference and soon won election as its president. With the power of this office, he began making himself known throughout the country. He became a force for change, a beacon of revolution, and an inspiration to all who met him. With his phenomenal memory, he could easily debate and discuss any issue and propose measures which became symbols of hope for people across the entire nation. Robert's name became synonymous with the future, with prosperity, with hope. All he needed now was just the right moment.

Richards had waited as long as he could outside the building. He used an entrance from the opposite side to gain entry then shuffled along the corridor to a vacant office on a lower floor where he waited for almost an hour before he cautiously made his way to Graham's office. He knew that he probably didn't need to be this careful, but habits were hard to break, especially after years of training. He hated to admit it, but he needed Graham. Graham had the information he would use to help find Judy's killer, and he meant to do that even if it cost him his own life.

After checking to make sure the outer office was vacant, Richards moved quietly to Graham's office door. He barely knocked before he slipped inside. Graham looked up from a hand full of papers he grasped and was stunned by the sight of Richards. He had visible aged; the once blank stare that Richards had used so well, had been replaced with a burning hatred that actually produced heat. Graham felt his skin warm as he dropped the papers back on his desk. Recognizing the danger Richards' posed, he spoke quickly, getting right to the point.

"I think I have the information you wanted. But before we get to that I need to know what this is all about. I don't want to stir up something that I can't handle. Just what is going on?" As he spoke he leaned forward toward Richards. He wasn't about to let Richards intimidate him. He was the one in charge, and he meant to keep it that way.

Graham's gruff question grated along Richards' skin. It was none of his business. But Richards' realized that he had to tell him something. Nothing said that it had to be the truth.

"A buddy of mine—a special friend—has a problem with some dust dealers. They messed up his old lady. He asked me to see what I could do. That's where I've been. It was really bad." He spoke slowly, letting his words trail off. Then he looked Graham directly in the eyes, "She was a friend of mine. She didn't deserve what they did to her." His words vibrated across the room, hatred punctuated each syllable. Graham was in no doubt as to Richards' sincerity. It was close enough to the truth that Richards could easily be convincing.

Graham interjected angrily, "That's what happens when you deal with outsiders. Our product is much better for everyone." His voice carried so much pride that Richards was momentarily stunned. How could anyone take pride in producing something so detrimental to a person's life? What kind of warped mind felt that way? He was amazed at how twisted Graham's logic was. But he had been on the streets long enough that his shouldn't have been shaken by anything Graham said. It must have been seeing Judy that had unearthed this moment of humanity, but he couldn't afford to let his real feelings show, not now. He had to stay on track until he had the man he was looking for, and he would find him, if it took the rest of his life. It was a promise he had made her, and this one he would keep, regardless of the price it exacted.

Graham silently watched the play of emotions on Richards' face. He had never seen him display any reaction to anything before this. Whatever had happened, it must have been unspeakable. He didn't have the nerve to ask though. He had seen Richards' work first-hand, and he didn't want to experience any of it himself.

"I can tell you who they are, but you'll have to find your own way in. Those boys don't trust anyone, and they don't leave anybody behind that gives them trouble." He studied Richards' face, watching for any reaction; when he saw none, he continued. "What's in this for me?" Graham held his breath waiting to see if he had pushed too hard. Richards only stared at him, silently weighing his options.

"What do you want?" It would be better for Graham to tell him than for him to offer more than he would have settled for. They could always bargain after that.

Graham recognized the tactic and smiled. "That all depends. What do you have to offer?" He was feeling much braver now. He leaned back in his chair; the upholstery creaked under his weight.

"If I can infiltrate their organization, we can talk. I think that has to be the first priority." He was stalling; he didn't want to do anything to help Graham, but he might have to.

Graham tapped his pen on his desk top as he considered his options, "That seems fair enough—for now. But just keep in mind that you owe me."

Richards nodded. He didn't trust himself to talk much; his anger still burned too strongly. He had to keep a grip on his emotions and for once he found that he couldn't disconnect. He was too close to this case, and he knew it, but he couldn't back off; he couldn't trust anyone else to handle this—this was his sister.

Graham sat quietly watching Richards for a few moments before he spoke. This could be a golden opportunity for him if Richards could pull it off, and if he didn't, well—he could be replaced—maybe not with anyone as skilled as Richards was at his job, but Graham was willing to take the chance. "Word is that they work out of a rural section of Arkansas. The powder is brought in then filtered and cut at distribution sites throughout the state. There's little interference from authorities. The cartel seems to own most of them. I'm hoping that we can come to the same arrangement if the opportunity presents itself." He let the sentence hang.

Richards got his meaning. This was the price he would exact. Who would ever expect a seemingly unimportant little southern state of holding such a crucial position in the drug trade? Of course, Richards knew that shipments were brought in through New Orleans and other Gulf coast cities. He also knew that the corridor for drugs through Mexico was rarely interrupted, regardless of how many fences, checkpoints, and inspection stations were added. As long as the demand remained high, then people were willing to sacrifice almost anything for the chance to make it rich.

The real losers in the cocaine process were the coca farmers. They earned just a few dollars for a kilo of coca paste, depending on its quality. They risked almost as much as the runners. The only protection they had came from the cartel leaders, *if* they chose to pay off the local officials.

Otherwise, their fields and cooking sheds had to remain well hidden in the far reaches of the jungle. Even that wasn't a guarantee that they wouldn't be discovered. Penalties could be severe; punishment often included burning everything the farmer owned as a deterrent to replanting, but life was harsh and little money could be made from farming crops. The year or more that it would take to replant and produce new coca leaves to make into paste were lean years that only encouraged farmers to continue with their illegal activity as they struggled to survive and make a better life for their families.

Families, they were the heart of everything. People would do almost anything for their family, just like him. Whatever it took to find Judy's killer, he was willing to do it—legal, illegal—it didn't matter, and he would succeed. Richards forced his thoughts back to the present.

"How can I make contact? Do you have anyone close to the operation, someone who won't be suspected?" Richards leaned forward toward

Graham as he spoke, his body language emphasizing his determination, his need.

Graham laughed quietly, "You must be joking. No one ever messes with those boys. Have you ever seen what they can do with a knife?" He shivered slightly to emphasize his meaning. "I wouldn't risk any of my men, but I can give you a name—someone who might be able to help you." He quickly scribbled the information on a note pad and ripped off the paper. He slid the paper across the desk top toward Richards. As Richards reached for the paper, Graham held on to it for a moment, "Don't forget our bargain. You won't do me any good dead." That was as close as he would come to telling Richards to be careful.

Chapter 12

THE MEDIA MADE MUCH of Robert's link to his earlier hometown of Hope. Hope became the symbol of his term in state office and the inspiration for his political future. As he had brought hope to the citizens of Arkansas, he pledged to bring hope to the nation as a whole. After consecutive election to the office of governor, the National Democratic Party recognized Robert's strength.

He had made quite a name for himself as the head of the Southern Governors Conference and had formed alliances with some of the nation's most influential political figures. His no-nonsense attitude and his quick repartee left any opposition to his programs for change running for cover. He was ambitious; he was charismatic; he was dynamite just waiting for the right moment to explode on the national scene. He had the political clout and the people's voice. He was the future of politics and only a few older, diehard conservatives refused to be swayed, but the Democratic Party recognized its destiny.

As the final term of the sitting President moved toward its close, the majority of the Party aligned its forces with Robert, but two other candidates made a bid for the position. The time had come for Robert to seriously consider forming his campaign staff. After lengthy debate about the qualifications of several potential recruits, Robert and Paul made their decisions. Robert was given the task of personally contacting their choices for the two most important positions, campaign manager and press secretary.

Robert had made the calls. Now he sat waiting behind his large, mahogany desk and restlessly tapped the gold fountain pen he held. He needed to make some critical decisions. He had met with most of the party's key people and had their full support for his bid. Now he had to create a campaign team that could handle any possible situation. Political campaigns were notorious for bringing out the worst in people and for shaking the skeletons from closets. He needed a team who could plan ahead, could stay one step ahead of the opposition, and knew how to spin a liability into an opportunity.

He needed a golden boy, a man of impeccable credentials, and a man who was willing to give up the next several months of his life for a twenty-four hour a day job that would demand his entire time until after the election. The upside was the position of power and prestige this person would assume during and after the election. Robert had contacted Vince Harris. Paul and he had agreed that Harris was the man for the job; now all Robert had to do was convince Harris that it was worth the personal investment he would have to make; money was no object; he would be paid well, and with a successful campaign, the benefits alone would be spectacular.

But Harris was a level-headed, seasoned veteran of political campaigns. He knew the toll they could take on not just the candidate, but also all those associated with him. Days were long on the campaign trail, and tempers became short. Rest became a luxury no one could afford, and time was tallied by split second decisions, thirty-second sound bites, and never-ending political polls.

Robert was waiting for Harris' decision. He knew that he should be glad that Harris was taking the time to consider all the angles of his offer before he committed to taking the position, but Robert had never been a patient man, and as the possibility of achieving his life-long dream came closer each day to becoming a reality, he found his patience was even less.

He had had better luck with his press secretary, a job almost as demanding as campaign manager. Robert and Paul had decided on Amanda Jeffery, a relatively young woman for the news business, but one who was well-respected by her colleagues for her hard-hitting coverage of the news, her zeal for the truth, and her unbiased reports. She had ruffled more than a few political feathers during her coverage of the last political conventions. When she immediately accepted Robert's offer, he didn't know whether to be honored that she supported his bid or concerned that she might have some hidden agenda. Either way, time would tell, and Paul would make certain that nothing she did would harm his campaign.

Paul kept a close eye on every aspect of the campaign, and Alberto kept a close eye on Robert. Robert smiled. Alberto made no secret of his position in Robert's life. In public, Alberto acted as Robert's personal body guard. In private, he was Robert's link to whatever he needed. They had spent so much time together by this point that Alberto knew what Robert needed even before he did. Robert didn't like being that easily read especially by someone like Alberto, but when he had to take the edge off or relieve the tension which sometimes threatened his sanity, Robert was glad for Alberto's silent understanding.

Although he never said anything; it was the look in his eyes that unnerved Robert. He would have liked it better if Alberto had been some nameless pusher or sleazy pimp, but Alberto was a well-educated, talented lawyer and businessman. Robert imagined Alberto's eyes were filled with contempt for his weakness and scorn for his needs. Alberto was concerned more about keeping him in line that actually helping him, but if Robert got what he wanted from Alberto without having to worry about being discovered, it was well worth his scorn. He had never liked Alberto, and Robert knew the feeling was mutual. He didn't lose sleep over it. When later the next day, Robert finally received a call from Harris accepting the position of campaign manager, they scheduled their first formal strategy meeting. Plans had to be implemented for their formal declaration to seek the Democratic Party bid for the presidency. Together with Paul, they quickly organized a staff, and the campaign began in earnest.

Opponents to Robert's bid struggled to find issues of contention and challenged his lack of experience. But after many heated debates, which only served to highlight Robert's ability to influence issues and dominate a forum, and grueling hours on the campaign trail with Caroline making her presence known as the woman behind-the-man, Robert pulled ahead in the primaries and solidified his bid as the Democratic candidate for the Presidency.

The Democratic Convention made an all-out effort to showcase the newlyweds. The media swarmed them at every opportunity. Privacy was impossible. Each moment of the day was spent shaping Robert's position on every issue and making his name the rallying cry of the nation. He pulled support from the young, the middle-class, all those who felt disenfranchised by the "good old boy" politics of the past generations.

Robert promised to give the nation back to the people. He promised the people whole-scale reform, not just a president who catered to the rich and influential, but a man of the people.

Robert had made quite a name for himself in the Democratic Party; everyone was eager to champion the rising star, anxious to be swept along on his fame and fortune. Congressional leaders within the Party scheduled private briefing and strategy sessions, offering their expertise, advice, and support—always for a price of course.

A veteran campaign leader was among the first, a woman from his home state, and a woman with influence and expertise who knew how to get results. She was also a woman with a private agenda. Robert's first meeting with her had gone well. She had pledged her support and offered to speak at an upcoming fundraiser on his behalf. As the session, held in her private offices drew to a close, she motioned for her assistants and Robert's campaign staff to leave, suggesting that they go ahead to lunch and that she and the Governor would soon follow, remarking that they just had a few final details to work out.

Margaret Franklin was a hardened professional. She knew politics better than most men. But she knew men even better than politics. As she ushered the others from the room and waved them on their way from the outer offices, she quietly closed the door and turned the lock. Robert had stood as the others made their way out of the room, shaking hands and offering appreciative remarks for their dedicated work on his behalf.

As he heard the lock click into place, he remained standing in front of Margaret's enormous oak desk, waiting to see just what was on her mind. He registered the slight smile on her lips and assumed that they were about to discuss exactly what her support was really going to cost him. He began mentally running through the offices, directorships, ambassadorships, cabinet posts that would soon be under his direction, trying to fathom what might be on her mind. She was still a good-looking woman. Striking, intelligent, hard-working, she had earned Robert's respect, and he grudgingly admitted to himself that she was almost as good as he was at persuading others to do what she wanted. As she slowly walked toward him, he waited for her to make the first move, but he wasn't really prepared for what that move was.

Margaret's silver blonde hair brushed her shoulders as she moved gracefully to stand in front of him. The hard veneer that usually cloaked her countenance had disappeared with the closing door. The dark red lips which often formed a hard line had softened into a warm and inviting curve. The strong hand that had gripped his at the opening of the meeting, now slid softly down the lapels of his suit jacket, tugging him gently toward her as she gradually continued downward to the front of his slacks. He was a man; she was a woman; his reaction to her unexpected attention was natural and almost instant. She had been right in her assessment of him. She knew a womanizer when she saw one, but she had to admit, she hadn't heard anything about him—yet. Obviously, he was being careful. She wondered if his wife knew, but it didn't matter. She had her own goals to achieve; he was merely another step.

As her hands slid over the slick fabric of his suit, one moving slowly up and down the lapels of his jacket, the other up and down the front of his slacks, she could feel him straining toward her, his chest pressing firmly against her left hand and his hardened length filling her right. With measured slowness, she gradually eased the zipper down and felt him shudder as she closed her hand over him. His hands gripped the carved oak behind him, his weight supported by the desk as he leaned back heavily against it.

She was trying his patience with each deliberately slow slide of her hands, testing his endurance, his manhood. His grip tightened on the desk. He tried not to move, not to moan, and not to force her down on the plush carpet. His jaw locked, but he forced his eyes to remain emotionless. It was the hardest thing he had ever done, not to give in to the pleasure. His heart pounded in his ears; his blood raced through his body; he could feel a flush cover his skin, but he refused to give in.

Suddenly she laughed; then she brushed her lips across the heated skin on his face and whispered in his ear. "You are good. Most men can't hold out that long. Would you like to finish what *I* started?" He didn't bother to answer. His lips covered hers in a savage assault meant to dominate. He could feel her laughter against his lips. She was letting him win the battle because she intended to win the war. It was the best sex he had had in months. Maybe there was something to be said for experience. She didn't look her age, and she certainly didn't act it. She was as ruthless and demanding as he was. He had met his match; she was all business, and she expected a pay off. He smiled.

They reached the sofa. She had made certain. She was a lady after all. He lay stretched out, wondering what exactly had just happened. She returned from the adjacent bathroom as immaculate as ever. Her silver blonde hair swung gracefully across the top of her shoulders; her makeup was flawless and left her skin softly luminous. Her lush red lips pouted prettily from his rough kisses, but nothing else betrayed their wild, rash behavior. She looked exactly like the leading woman in a Senate filled with chauvinistic men should—all business.

Personally, she didn't care about the moral ramifications of her actions. She knew what she wanted, and she knew how to get it. That was all that mattered to her. Publically, she could talk about ethical issues and convince anyone that she held strong moral beliefs. But she was a realist, and politics and morals were often mutually exclusive.

He moved to sit up, and she laughed that laugh he was beginning to recognize, the one that signaled she was up to something. He almost sighed, then caught himself, and smiled at her instead. "Okay, what is it?"

She studied him a minute before she answered, "The Attorney General's cabinet post when you win, and you will win. You can't find anybody better than me." With that obvious double entendre, she laughed again, a silky sound that slid across his senses, reminding him of other things. He was beginning to like that sound. "I like strong-willed men, and I'm beginning to think you might just be the best this Hill has seen in a long time. I'll give you my unqualified support, and you know it goes without saying that it includes a lot of added benefits."

Though her statement was deliberately vague, it was obvious what she meant. She began walking toward the locked door and then turned back at the last moment. "Do we have a deal?" She smiled; she already knew the answer. He smiled in return. She was right. He couldn't do better than her. Attorney General—she would make a good one.

With Caroline by his side, he continued to campaign, to promote family values, improved living standards, a better educational system, and a more equitable job market. He touted measures to encourage growth in the business sector and to increase trade with foreign countries. His plans included reducing the national debt, lowering taxes on the middle class, and limiting the United States' dependence on foreign oil. He included all Americans in the changes he foresaw and emphasized how Americans could empower themselves to help bring change to their lives, to transform the job market, to revolutionize the economy, and most of all to have hope in his ability as their next President to carry out his plans for the nation.

Dutifully, Caroline stood by Robert's side, smiling and encouraging people to see the promise in her husband, to see his vision for the nation, to recognize the potential of his dream, his hope for the nation. "A Man of Hope" became the rallying cry of the campaign trail as the Democratic and Republican Parties squared off for the final push to the polls.

In private, Caroline was unhappy. She hid her feelings well, but Paul could sense a storm brewing; he knew Caroline well enough to recognize the signs. He had to circumvent the problem before it had time to gain strength. Paul had already noticed that Robert was too self-involved to take note of Caroline's moods. Paul knew that if Robert had taken time to listen to her ideas, she would have been easily managed. Robert, however, got carried away by his own rhetoric and failed to see the warnings. Caroline needed to feel that she was an equal force in the campaign; Robert refused to accept that fact. It was a recipe for certain disaster.

Paul noted the change in her attitude toward Robert and began watching the couple more closely. If he could detect a problem, it would only be a matter of time before someone in the media did. They were at a very critical time in the elections. Even the slightest problem would be blown out of proportion by the rumor mills of the Republican Party. They couldn't afford a break in the solidarity of one of the strongest selling points of their campaign. The strength of the couple's marriage and their devotion and belief in one another was a priority. Caroline's unconditional support for Robert was crucial. Caroline knew this; Robert was about to learn. Paul just hoped she wouldn't do anything that would jeopardize their ultimate plans. Rafael would never forgive her if she did. That was a reminder that he had to give her and soon.

Paul would have to find a way to talk to her in private, away from Robert and the rest of the campaign members. That was an almost impossible task, but one that had to seem as though it was of no importance. A balancing act on a high wire would have been easier at this time in the election, but Paul would figure something out. He always did. He had his own father to consider if things went wrong. After all, he was in charge on this whole scheme. Caroline just needed a little friendly reminder. He prayed that was all it would take. She could be really headstrong when she chose to be, but then so could he.

Paul smiled as he watched Caroline walk across the patio. She was angry, he could almost feel the heat radiate across the distance. This wasn't exactly how he had planned to have this conversation, but there was no time like the present, and he really didn't think another time would be any better. Things had gotten progressively worse between the governor and his first lady, which was probably what was at the heart of the problem.

Alberto kept close tabs on everything that Robert did. Paul wasn't judging, but he knew that Robert had better tread softly, especially around Caroline. Her father might be old school, Spanish dominant, man chauvinist, but she didn't have to like it, and from what Paul knew about her, she didn't. Robert needed to remember that she was part of the plan also. Paul had a meeting scheduled with him later that day, but right now he had a bigger problem.

"Hello, Pandora, what's wrong today? You have a scowl on that pretty face that would scare off the meanest villain." Paul kept his smile in place, even though he could tell that she was really upset about something.

"Don't call me that," she snapped. "You know I don't like it. Nothing good came from opening Pandora's Box." Her blue eyes shone with unshed tears of frustration. Paul knew that something momentous had upset her for her to show this much emotion. She had been raised not to reveal anything to anyone. This had to be significant. He just didn't know what. She still hadn't looked at him directly. Her evasion was as telling as her tears.

"Okay, what gives? This isn't like you, so you might as well tell me what is going on. I've seen the tension between you and Robert. Has he done something that we need to talk about? Or is there something that I need to talk to *him* about?" Paul was beginning to think that Robert was definitely due for a good dressing down. He had become a little overbearing lately. Maybe he had forgotten who was making all of this possible. Maybe he had forgotten where the real money for his campaign came from. Paul knew from past experience that Robert had a high opinion of himself and his abilities, and rightly so, but those alone would never take him where he wanted to go—only substantial funds would defeat the more ardent campaigns launched by the Republican Party.

Paul grasped Caroline's hand firmly in his and turned her to face him. "You know I like to call you "Pandora," so why fight it? She was beautiful and even though she brought the world an awful lot of problems, she also brought hope. Did you know that? You are the hope for the future of this enterprise. Never forget that. You are crucial to our success. Our fathers are counting on both of us to make this happen. I can't do it by myself; I need you." As soon as the words left his mouth, Paul realized the truth behind them. He had never really thought about it until this moment, but he did need her. He had come to depend on her in so many subtle ways that he hadn't noticed how important she had become to him. He smiled at his own foolishness. Pandora was definitely a fitting name. What a mess this could turn out to be!

"*Hope* may be Robert's hot campaign word," he continued," but you are hope, not just for his success, but for mine and yours as well." His voice was so sincere that Caroline gazed up at him in stunned silence. He had never talked to her with such passion in his voice before. Always in the past it had been about their fathers' expectations, the campaign's demands, and Robert's needs—never about her.

"Hey, don't look so stunned. I can be a nice guy once in a while." He tried to play down the rush of emotions he was feeling. He knew he could hide anything that he needed to; he was a pro at masking his emotions, but for some odd reason he really didn't want to.

Caroline simply held on to his hand as she stared up at him. She was no dummy; she knew what she was feeling, and it certainly wasn't what she felt for her husband. Could it be possible that Paul felt the same? He had always been so remote and emotionless until today. What had changed? She couldn't figure it out, but she didn't really care as long as he felt the same way. She remembered the rush of feeling she had had the first time they met; she almost laughed. He had definitely put her in her place that day, but something was different. Maybe it was working together for so long, spending so many hours in planning for the campaign and working out their strategy for the operation that had brought about the change. She didn't care what had caused it as long as she was right about what she read in his eyes.

She didn't dare speak. She might break the spell, and like Pandora everything bad would rush in to consume her life again. Robert—she had begun to hate him. She had tried to understand his needs, tried to work with him, tried to placate his obsessive desires, but nothing she did was good enough, nothing was right, nothing was up to his standards. She couldn't believe his audacity. They had made him who he was, yet he seemed to have conveniently forgotten all of that.

She knew about the girls, the drugs. She didn't care; she had no feelings for him. She was forced into playing a role that was fast becoming unbearable. Her skin crawled every time he touched her. When they stood before the cameras and he placed his arm around her shoulders, it was all she could do not to flinch, to keep a loving smile plastered on her lips, to look adoringly up at him as he praised her for her devotion and hard work on his behalf. She was sick of the lies and the pretense. She didn't have anyone to talk to; there was no one who really understood what was involved in her life—except Paul, but they never had time to talk.

She and Robert were always on display; they had no privacy; there was never a spare moment even to breathe. She desperately needed someone who truly knew what was going on, someone she could confide in, someone she could trust. Even La Senora, who had remained in charge of Caroline's household staff, wasn't able to understand the pressure she felt, the anger she felt. She couldn't talk to any of her friends; after all, hers was supposed to be the fairy tale marriage, the happily-ever-after future. Who would believe her anyway? Who could she talk to about her father and the demands he made of her, his expectations, the less than subtle hints he had made lately about children?

There was only Paul, and she never saw him anymore, not where they could talk in private. It was too risky; it could cause problems for the campaign if there was any hint of impropriety between them, and simply meeting to talk could be misconstrued by a press just looking for anything to sell papers. The most innocent encounter could be blown out of proportion and cause untold damage to their political image. Even phone conversations were too risky. Paul was all she had, and he was effectively out of reach.

"Look, I know that this has been extremely stressful for you, but you have to hang in there. It won't be that much longer and you can relax a little. The presidential election will soon be over. Once that happens and the White House is your new home, there will be more time to talk." He tried to infuse his voice with optimism, but she wasn't fooled.

She laughed at him. "Okay, that was a miserable effort. We both know better. There isn't going to be a time in the next few years for anything remotely associated with privacy. You aren't fooling me. I know what to expect, but sometimes I become frustrated with no one to talk to, no one to trust. You realize that I only have you that I can truly confide in. Robert doesn't even know all the facts, and I wouldn't want him to. I don't trust him sometimes."

Paul arched one eyebrow at that confession. "What do you mean?" Did she know something that he didn't? Surely Robert wouldn't try anything foolish. He knew that Paul could easily end his bid for the presidency with just one phone call. No, it had to be something else that Caroline was referring to, but what?

Caroline looked at him for a moment before she spoke. "I know about the girls." She shrugged her shoulders. "They don't matter unless the press gets wind of them. I know that he uses occasionally. That isn't even a problem as long as he is careful. He is easier to live with when he has had a hit. He's mellower, less demanding. I'm sure Alberto takes care of everything." She didn't elaborate any further.

So what was the problem? Should he ask for more specific information? No, that seemed too much like an invasion of her privacy, at least what little she had. He would wait for her to tell him. Alberto was assigned as Robert's personal body guard. He would know anything that Paul needed to know. He kept Robert's apartment under surveillance, drawing a line at the bedroom, but everything else, Alberto felt obligated to monitor and record, probably under Raul's direction. Either way, he could find out what he needed to know from Alberto before his meeting with Robert. Maybe all she needed was a break from the campaign. He could suggest a weekend getaway for Robert and her, but somehow he felt that Robert was really who she needed to get away from.

"Let's take a trip? There's a two-day seminar in northern Arkansas on Educational Reform. Why don't we schedule you to appear at that and take a break from the campaign? You could speak one afternoon and take the rest of the time off just to relax, be by yourself, or whatever. How does that sound?" He still held her hand in his and lightly circled her palm with his thumb as he spoke. He could feel her relaxing and smiled.

She studied his face for a moment. "Actually that sounds good. I know the topic inside out, so I won't have to prepare anything new, and I can have my secretary write a speech this afternoon. I may not be as good as Robert at memorizing things, but I can have it ready by this evening. When do we leave?" She gave him a crooked little grin. It was a risk, challenging him to take her, but she needed to be with someone who knew the real her.

Paul grinned back. He recognized that she had successfully pushed him in a corner. He could easily give a valid excuse for not going, but why should he. He could use a little time off, and who else would he want to spend it with. Somewhere in the back of his mind, he recognized that he had been making excuses to himself for a very long time about how he felt. The fathers' plan left no room for personal feelings. They each had a role to play and they would, but nothing said they couldn't at least talk. He laughed out loud and squeezed her hand. Talking wasn't what he wanted, and he didn't think that was what she had in mind either.

After months of requests, the state police had finally released Judy's belongings. He was certain the only reason was because they had gotten sick of his questioning them about Judy's case. He wasn't sure what the hold-up had been; their excuse had been that her death had been suspicious, which didn't make sense with their determination that it had been an accident. Something was definitely suspicious all right, but he was beginning to think it had more to do with the authorities than anything else. He would probably never know for sure, but maybe something among her possessions would help him find what he needed to know. He didn't dare contact the police for information, not if he planned to infiltrate the local cartel. They would have people on the inside who would gladly sell him out, even if they knew he was law enforcement himself, or more likely, especially if they knew. Loyalty was a commodity now, easily bought and sold.

He turned her cell phone over in his hands. This was one of the last things she had touched. His heart physically hurt at the thought, but he couldn't let emotions get in his way. He plugged the phone into a charger and turned it on. He easily brought up her call list and sent it to his own phone. At least he had a starting point. Maybe someone would have the answers he needed.

The list was short. He recognized the first number as her apartment's. He still hadn't found her roommate. The landlord hadn't been able to give him any information, just that the rent was always paid in cash and on time. She hadn't left a forwarding address, and he wasn't good at keeping records. He didn't have any references or personal information on either girl. As long as they paid, he was happy. But that left Richards with no leads, and no one who lived in the building seemed to remember anything about either girl. They had kept to themselves and hadn't caused any problems. One lady remembered that they left together in a fancy car almost every weekend, but she couldn't remember anything about the car, only that it was dark and looked new. Dead ends, every where he looked for answers, that was all he found.

He scrolled through the list and three numbers kept coming up. He felt some hope and dialed the first. It was out of service. He tried the second and found it to be a local pizza joint. He smiled. Judy loved pizza; it didn't matter how bad it was; she would eat it anyway. She even liked the cheap frozen kind, the ones he called cardboard pizza. She would just laugh and gobble it up. Of course, the number could be a cover up for drug buys, too, just place a certain order, and it was delivered with the pizza. In his line of work, he had seen every kind of cover. Nothing shocked him anymore. He would have to investigate this one further.

He dialed the third number and was confused by the response he received. Surely he had dialed wrong. He hung up and tried again. When he got the same answer, he sat down and tried to make sense of the information. Why would she be calling this number repeatedly?

At first his mind went to his job, was she some type of informant, had she been recruited to help in some scheme, had someone known of their connection and drawn her into a drug bust, or had she been caught and forced to work undercover for some agency? His mind ran wild with conjecture, trying to make sense of the information. How could he find out? Was there anyone he knew on the force who might be able to get the information he needed? Mentally, he worked through the list of people he knew that he could trust. It didn't take long. He didn't trust or know anyone here, but he had to find out. The only other possibilities were too difficult to consider. He had to think she was an innocent pawn in someone else's game. He couldn't believe his sister would ever become mixed up with drugs intentionally. She knew that he had spent his career, his life, trying to help end the drug trade.

Without another thought he dialed his friend's number in Memphis. If anyone could find the information, he could. Their conversation was short and to the point, his friend already knew the details of Judy's death. He had been responsible for alerting Richards when he had first seen her in Little Rock, a twist of fate, since he wasn't supposed to be where he had been that day; otherwise, he would never have seen her walking down that street. He hadn't been able to save her, to find Richards in time to help her, but his chance sighting at least had allowed her body finally to be identified and claimed. She hadn't been placed in some nameless grave with no one to mourn her, no one to bring her killer to account.

Richards' guts twisted in anger. He deliberately slowed his breathing. He had to restrain himself. He couldn't change the past; all he could do was shape the future. To do that, he had to remain emotionless, ruthless, determined.

He left his shabby apartment with the intent of finding someone who could help him. His first stop was the offices of the Attorney General. The building was multilevel and held many of the state's higher level offices. He had changed his appearance to blend less conspicuously with business men and state officials. There was no good gained in presenting a disreputable front when he needed honest answers. His street appearance would put off most people; he didn't need to alienate them; he needed their cooperation.

As he stepped into the spacious, open lobby, he redialed the number from Judy's phone. When the receptionist answered, he asked to speak to the person in charge. The friendly-sounding woman asked if he could be more specific, remarking that their department housed over thirty separate offices. Richards hesitated for a moment then took the risk.

"Connect me with the Attorney General's office."

"Yes, Sir, one moment please." The ringing of the phone resonated in his ear. What did he do now? Who did he ask for, and what did he ask?

"Attorney General's office, how may I help you?" Was this the voice that Judy heard each time she called? He opted for the direct approach. What did he have to lose at this point?

"Hello, my name is Timothy Richards. I'm trying to contact anyone who might have known my sister, Judy Richards. Would you have any information? She called this number numerous times over the past fall." Richards heard a deep sigh vibrated over the link.

"I'm sorry, Sir. It would be impossible to identify one caller unless you have the times when the calls were placed. With those a possible cross-reference could be made. But, Sir, unless you have a court order for those records, it would impossible for you to get them. Couldn't you just ask your sister who she was calling? That would certainly be easier."

"Yes, it would, if she weren't dead. I need to know who she called and I need to know why. Do you have any ideas? Anything that might help me; it's very important." He could feel the burn of red hot anger building in him and fought to keep it from exploding. He gripped the phone so tightly that his knuckles turned white.

"I'm sorry for your loss. But the only information I can give you is that this number connects directly to the Attorney General's office and his personal secretary. I can connect you to her, if you wish." He heard the hesitation in her voice. "Yes, if you don't mind." Civility—pointless pandering to society's etiquette, but if it got him what he needed, then he would play the game.

Caroline glowed like a sparkling gem. Her blonde hair glistened in the glow of the chandelier hanging in the elegant ballroom. Her speech had been a blend of intellectual understanding and instinctual perception. She had held her audience spellbound with her passion and enthusiasm. Robert's speaking ability was incomparable, but Caroline could capture an audience just as well. Her impassioned plea for educational reform and restructuring of the state's educational system garnered a standing ovation.

Even after the dinner and speeches were concluded, she had taken time to speak personally with many of the leaders. Her personal touch was just the right note to conclude the evening; she had impressed many skeptics with her exceptional speaking ability and witty presentation. She won over those assuming that she was just window dressing for public appeal whose role was to help her husband gain election. Now they viewed her as a powerful influence, equal to her husband, and part of a team seeking to be the voice of a nation.

She had set out to prove a point to the public and her husband, and she had accomplished her goal. Her voice had been heard by the people; now her husband had better pay attention also. She would be his equal or she would be nothing. He had a choice to make and he would have to make it soon. She was tired of his condescending attitude and superior demeanor. She could break him easily, and it would almost be worth it just to see him fall. Almost—but not worth the price she would pay with her father. He was the only thing holding her back, but Robert didn't need to know that.

As she shook another hand in gratitude, she scanned the room for Paul. Her smile was becoming brittle and her face and hand hurt. She was more than ready to call the evening a success and return to her suite. Even her feet ached; something that rarely bothered her. But she had been going nonstop for weeks, and she recognized the signs of complete fatigue. She had been working on adrenaline for days. She really needed this break. Sometimes she didn't understand how Robert did it, but he fed off of the challenge, the demands for his time, the constant scheduling and rescheduling, the meetings and conferences. He loved it. To him, it was just one more step to his ultimate goal—the presidency.

Paul watched as Caroline worked the room. Good breeding and an excellent education always showed; she knew just how much attention to pay to everyone so that no one was excluded and everyone felt privileged to have met the state's "first lady." Whispers raced around the room; newspapers would carry reports of the Caroline's speech which had exemplified the grace, poise, and intelligence of the wife of the possible future President. Robert should be pleased, but somehow Paul didn't think that would be the case.

Inching his way across the crowded ballroom, Paul eased into position beside Caroline and graciously excused them from the group, praising those in charge for an excellent gathering and the opportunity for Governor Billing's wife to meet with the people of their home state and for the chance to address their needs. Governor Billings wanted the people of Arkansas to know that he hadn't forgotten them nor had he forgotten his desire to make Arkansas one of the best states in the nation.

Within minutes he had extricated them from the crowds and had propelled Caroline to their waiting car and toward their hotel. He had reserved the top floors of the hotel. Additional rooms were reserved for staff members and personal body guards. Their privacy was insured with limited access to these areas throughout their stay. No one was allowed on these floors without special clearance, and absolutely no one was allowed access to Caroline or Paul's private suites. Even with these security measures, Alberto had his own team members maintain surveillance and protection.

When Paul had mentioned his plan, Alberto had moved into action. He understood their need for privacy and a place to speak freely. He sent a team ahead to sweep the rooms and installed special equipment which would make it impossible to overhear, record, tape, or video anything said or done within their personal suites. Hotel monitoring of elevators and corridors on these floors was taken over by Alberto's team, and only that requested by Alberto himself was allowed. Like Raul, Alberto knew that if they could access information, so could others. Alberto eliminated that possibility.

This was nothing new to his team. They were experts at creating secure environments. Alberto made sure that all of Robert's meetings, conferences, and even his liaisons took place in just such places. The private jets and vehicles members of the family used were specially equipped and maintained by Raul's private companies. Security was taken care of by *family* owned and operated businesses. Nothing was left to chance, and no one would dare offend Raul by making mistakes. Special care was taken to insure excellence in anything associated with Paul or Caroline. Everyone knew that those who made mistakes were accountable to Alberto. Even in the States, everyone in the family knew what Alberto's job was, and he was not the man to disappoint or to anger.

Paul laughed when Caroline kicked off her high heels and sighed in relief as their car raced down the interstate. He reached down and grasped her feet. Placing them in his lap, he began to slowly massage them, pressing his thumbs into the soft arches, easing the ache and tension. Caroline leaned back against the plush cushions of the seat and closed her eyes, bliss, absolute and utter bliss. Had anything ever felt so good? She smiled and peeked up at Paul.

He sat watching her with a croaked little smile on his lips. He was a devil. He knew how good that felt, and she knew he was just waiting for her to make the first move. He had begun the dance, but he was going to let her lead. She remembered another time she had asked someone to let her lead, but he had refused. She didn't want to think about Robert; he had never understood her; he had never really tried. Everything was about him and his needs, his wants, his desires.

Paul could feel the tension fill her; he could see her eyes darken in anger. "Forget about him. He's just part of a plan. You don't have to live your life just to please him, not in private, not when you're with me." His fingers stopped moving, but his hands still clasped her feet. He was willing to let her decide what she wanted. He wouldn't rush her, push her. She was a grown woman with a mind of her own. He could wait until she was ready.

Pandora, it really did suit her. If they followed through on their feelings, would it unleash all the problems on their world that it had for her namesake's? Was he willing to risk it? He laughed out loud. That wasn't even worth asking.

Caroline looked at him with a puzzled frown. "Do I get to know what the joke is?" She smiled at him, her lush red lips just begging for him to kiss them.

"Nope, sorry, you'll just have to guess." His grin was infectious. She grinned back.

"Somehow I don't think I would ever be able to do it. What would it take for you just to tell me?" She lifted one arched brow provocatively as she looked at him.

Games—he was good at those. "I'll have to think about it." He lifted her feet from his lap and reached to slip her shoes back on for her. Their car had arrived at the hotel. Their conversation would have to continue later.

She sighed dramatically as the driver moved to open the car door. Waiting—that was all she seemed to do lately. She glanced in Paul's direction and smiled. It might be worth the wait.

The next morning, Caroline's staff received a message that she would be sleeping in that morning and that she was not to be disturbed. They all agreed that it was well deserved and took the opportunity themselves to relax before their hectic pace began again. When she made her appearance in the hotel foyer she seemed to radiate youthful well being, and for her part, Caroline felt better than she could ever remember. Of course, only she and Paul knew that sleeping didn't have anything to do with how she felt.

A smug little smile hovered on the edges of her lips, and her eyes sparkled in the noon day sunlight. It was their secret, and hopefully, it would remain so. Caroline was a realist; she knew that it would only be a matter of time before someone would find out. If nothing else, it would be impossible for her to remain this happy and for Robert not to notice. Eventually, he would pay enough attention to her to see the change. Even with his large ego, he would have to realize that it had nothing to do with him. She tolerated him only when she had no other choice, and he had no one else available. It was no secret to her that he preferred anyone else to her. She didn't care. They rarely slept together and then only enough to keep the staff from becoming curious about their private lives. They both realized their every move was scrutinized by others and a lack of husbandly attention was sure to start the rumors flying. Then it would only be a matter of time before someone dug deep enough to uncover Robert's proclivity for a variety of partners.

Whenever they were together, Caroline made certain that he used protection. She might have to share his bed, but she didn't want to share anything else with him. This morning, though, her mind was not on Robert or his campaign.

Paul walked discreetly behind her, smiling to himself. He would give up sleeping entirely for more of what they had shared last night. He hadn't realized how connected the two of them were. He didn't know if it was the secrets they shared or the feelings they had finally acknowledged, but everything was different with Caroline. What they would be able to do about it, he didn't really know, but he knew they would be together, somehow.

Chapter 13

COMMANDER REX DAY WAS at his naval office on the base when he received the call. The coded message was not what he needed to hear. He knew that he was late with the requested information, but he had been unable to retrieve it this time without drawing undue suspicion on himself. He had been forced to wait an unexpectedly long time before he could download the necessary schedules. Excuses were not acceptable. He should never have let things go this far. Now they owned him, and he could do nothing. His hands were tied figuratively, but he knew that if he messed up again they probably would be literally, and he would be found in some back alley cut into a thousand little pieces.

A highly decorated officer in the Marine Corp, and he had let the enemy infiltrate his country. He couldn't look himself in the face any more. He had never been a coward during any of his wartime deployments, but now as a silent and even more deadly war was being waged in his homeland, he found himself at the heart of the problem, unable to do anything. Day was savvy enough to know they he would easily be replaced if he failed in his job. His death would stop nothing, change nothing, but by staying in his position, maybe, just maybe, at some future date, he could do something to rectify his mistakes, to make amends for the problems he had brought to his country.

A lifetime of discipline took over as Day quickly walked toward the stately, old building which housed the office of a private mail service. The strains of jazz floated across the warm, humid air. He could picture the gaily dressed, street musicians playing for early morning tourists on the busy corners of Jackson Square, young boys, twisting and turning, gyrating energetically to the thumping beat. Further down in the French Quarter, the inhabitants would just be coming to life after the long Southern night of revelry and pleasure. The alleys would be filled with the previous day's litter and its usual number of drunks, addicts, and homeless. The acrid scent of sweat, booze, and bodies would slowly be replaced by the strong, hot smell of Louisiana coffee and the tantalizing aroma of sweet chocolate and freshly baked beignets.

Today, though, Day didn't have time to appreciate the old-world beauty of the city he had come to love. His mission was urgent. His life hung in the balance. All he could do was pray the information he had would be received soon enough. A lost shipment could mean his life.

More out of habit than concern, he glanced around as he pushed open the heavy glass door and moved down the short hallway, scanning the wall lined with numbered boxes. Finding the one he sought, he carefully unlocked it, slipped the disc containing the patrol schedules inside, and left without looking back.

Day knew he the service was a front; that was why he never worried about being seen. There were no security cameras, and the entrance was always empty. The building, set back from the hectic downtown of New Orleans, had recently been remodeled but still held a regal air of Southern charm and aloof isolation. Its remote location made it ideal to slip in and out of unnoticed by the regular patrons of New Orleans' back streets and side allies.

The Big Easy with its crowded docks, congested streets, and bustling populace was the perfect place to hide almost any activity. Illegal shipments were easy to slip into the busy New Orleans' port. He knew that it was an almost impossible task to scrutinize every vessel; smaller fishing boats moved unobtrusively in and out of the connecting waterways, while on a daily basis tons of cargo was loaded and unloaded to and from the mammoth holds of seafaring ships. Fishing boats often subsidized their poor catches with a few dozen especially prepared shipments. Port cities were busy places. The muddy waters churned with every conceivable type of craft. Ocean-going cargo ships vied for position at the busy docks, unloading everything from bananas and coffee to machine parts and textiles. Stacked two and three high, heavy metal cargo containers lined the docks waiting to be levered into the empty ships' holds. The pungent odor of fish permeated the air surrounding the large fishing trawlers, which emptied their catch into waiting containers at the cannery docks.

Private charter fishing boats eased into the quieter waters off the bays and docked at special births, unloading their clients and catch for the day. These local fishermen followed a set routine, shipping out at daybreak and returning at dusk. They made such a common sight easing across the horizon that their movements were seldom questioned. They could blend in among the larger ships and boats and get lost in the hectic activity surrounding the crowded docks, making them the perfect choice for an occasional extra cargo.

Random inspections of smaller vessels kept most captains and their crews honest, but a poor fishing season pushed many to chance being caught. With Day supplying patrol schedules, the chances of being detected carrying illegal contraband were greatly reduced, and the drug cartels had the means to deliver and nothing to stop their shipments from entering the States.

Day forced himself to act casual as he walked back toward his office, but the hair on the back of his neck prickled. He had known for some time that he was being watched, ever since he had failed to deliver the last information on time. All that kept him alive now was the time it would take for them to make a new contact. He was expendable, and he knew it. He was running out of time. He would have to act soon or not at all.

Graham stomped angrily back and forth across his office, the deep pile carpeting alone softening the harsh sound. He was extremely frustrated by the latest numbers he had received. His profits were continually declining. Reliable sources blamed a heavy influx of cocaine. City streets were flooded with a river of dust and crack. The ease with which it could be purchased had grown in equal proportions to the public demand. It was seen as the rich man's high; a snort at lunch and back to work, a sniff in the ladies' room and back to business. The strength of its desire lay in the fact that its use was not as readily noticeable as other drugs or even alcohol. The power brokers of the business world could safely return to shaping the future with little noticeable change in their behavior or their lives.

Graham didn't care how great cocaine was. He needed repeat business; he needed first time users. One hit was almost always all it took to be hooked on meth for life, trapped on a never ceasing treadmill, doomed to chase that first ultimate high, destined never to succeed, but always trying to regain that one, sublime moment, until there were no more moments left.

He didn't care what meth did to people, families; he didn't have any feelings about the broken lives or homes. All that he was concerned with were profits. He ran a business; businesses made profits are they were forced to close their doors. He refused to even consider that. His legitimate enterprises were successful, even profitable, but he wanted more. He needed some way to undermine cocaine distribution, some way to limit the cartel's success. He knew he could never stop the flow, but if he could slow it, he would be satisfied.

He stopped in front of his desk. "Get me Strong!" He bellowed the order so loudly that the intercom was really unnecessary. His secretary could easily hear him through the closed door. She shook her head as she dialed the number and thought to herself that it wouldn't be good if Strong weren't available.

Strong knew better than to argue when Graham was in a foul mood. Placating him with soothing words and vague promises of future profits wouldn't work. Graham wanted results. Strong knew how to instigate some drastic changes, which would most likely result in a reduction in the availability of cocaine, but he didn't like the odds that something could go wrong. He and Graham had discussed the possibility before, but Richards had been able to handle that situation successfully. As much as he hated to think about bringing him back, Strong realized that they needed Richards' expertise if they wanted any plot against the cartel to succeed and them to live long enough to profit from it.

Strong placed the call; all he could do now was hope that Richards would receive the message. There were no guarantees. Strong knew that Richards was on a personal mission. He might not be willing to help them; he might not be able to. Strong hadn't heard anything since Graham had given Richards the contact's name. Now that contact was their only link to Richards and the help they needed.

Richards thumped the folded slip of paper on the scarred surface of the table. Another rundown apartment, another sleazy neighborhood, another drug-riddled city, they were all beginning to look alike, and he was no closer to finding his sister's killer than before. Maybe this was a sign that he should move on, stop his aimless searching; he had found out a lot about cocaine trafficking, but he hadn't gotten even remotely close to anyone of influence. Graham had been right; they were tight, all family; no one from the outside was allowed in. Those who pushed too hard were usually found missing vital body parts. That was all they needed to discourage the remaining few, overly ambitious. He had hit a dead end in his search.

He laughed out loud, a harsh strident sound that echoed across the empty room, grating on his frayed nerves; ironic that he should have thought of that particular word and strangely fitting. He might as well return to Memphis and see what Strong wanted. He hadn't made any progress here, and he didn't feel that he would at this point.

His one lead had been to the Attorney General's office, but he hadn't been able to connect anyone in the office with Judy. All he could do at this point was focus on his undercover work and pray that something would turn up, some clue that might help him. He filed the names away in the back of his mind. At least one wouldn't be hard to remember; after all, he was making a bid for the Presidency. Still, it was all he had after weeks of work.

Robert slammed his speech on the desk top; he was irritated. He didn't see why Caroline had abandoned him at this critical time. He needed her with him as he made this final push through California and began yet another seemingly endless round of fund raising events. Money, everything hinged on having enough funds, and there never seemed to be enough, even with Paul's seemingly endless funds.

Most critical endorsements carried with them the understood benefit of additional campaign donations, but still there seemed to be a ceaseless round of expected events. For the most part, he enjoyed being the center of attention, and he could read an audience better than most people could read books. He knew what they wanted to hear and made sure they heard it. His charm and enthusiasm swept them along with his plans for change and his dream of becoming President. He made them all feel they were the deciding factor in his campaign and in his hope for the future of the country.

Even his success each day on the campaign trail had a hollow ring when Caroline wasn't there to witness it, and Paul had chosen to accompany her. That annoyed him as well. Although every aspect of the day was organized and orchestrated so well that all he had to do was follow Harris' directions and scan the list of names of those he would be meeting, he still felt slighted that Paul had chosen to accompany her, after all he and Paul had been friends for years. Paul had arranged for

Robert's bid for office, so he should be with him throughout the process, not trailing around behind Robert's wife.

Robert almost smiled; Paul had introduced Caroline to him and had encouraged their marriage. She was definitely a political asset, but Robert didn't have any real feelings for her. She met his needs, but that was all; he preferred younger, less sophisticated woman, women who knew how to have a good time. Maybe that was all he needed; he reached for his phone, dialed a private number, and placed a request. He didn't need either of them.

A short time later, his smile broadened as he opened his hotel door. Everything he needed stood on the threshold to his private suite of rooms. No one would dare disturb him. He could do just as he pleased, at least for the next few hours.

No one would ever be able to tell that he had indulged in a late night of wine and women, sex and sin. He could sniff a special little invigorating potion in the morning and carry out every task set before him with no one the wiser. He knew how to cover his tracks, hide his fun. He was becoming smug. There was danger in being overly confident.

He was good at deception, but without Alberto and his special team, he wouldn't have been able to do the things that he had. He had to give Alberto credit; they didn't like each other; neither one hid the fact; it was an unspoken reality. Yet Robert knew that Alberto would make sure that nothing was ever discovered about his amorous activities, his less than honorable habits, and his penchant for the perverse.

Alberto's loyalty to Paul insured Robert's privacy. But Robert was a realist; he knew that if Alberto ever chose, he could ruin him. Robert also believed that once he became President, he would be untouchable, that he would be able to command everyone and anyone who came into his life. In that, Robert was completely wrong.

Robert left the suite the next morning with a spring in his step and a smug little smile hovering around the edge of his lips. He had several important meetings today with key figures in the Democratic Party of California. His smile broadened as he remembered that evening's festivities. Toni Bradford, now there was a woman he wouldn't mind seeing more of. She was as beautiful in real life as she was in the movies—breathtaking—that would be an apt description. Caroline was beautiful, but her beauty drew more from an inner refinement. Toni's was the sculpted beauty of a Roman goddess.

The evening's fundraiser was being hosted by Toni and a few of her celebrity friends. Robert felt honored that they had chosen to back his campaign, and he hoped to encourage other well-known personalities to join forces also. Of course, he was a realist and knew that they expected a good return on their investment. Robert was good at making reasonable promises and appropriate concessions when necessary. He knew he would never be able to fulfill every promise, but he would worry about that later. Very few people would dare rebuke a President for failing to keep a campaign promise, and he knew that something suitable could be arranged when the time came. He was really looking forward to this evening.

The evening was a smash as Toni repeatedly told him. She had taken his arm early in the evening and had not relinquished it since, introducing him to the heads of studios, producers, directors, and a phalanx of actors. He was impressed by her understanding of the political process. She wasn't just another air-head actress who looked good in front of the camera. Beauty and brains, women were so much more intelligent than they had been in the past. He laughed. Caroline would have his head if he said anything like that out loud.

After a very successful evening with donations and pledges pouring in to bolster the lagging campaign fund, the party with its elite clientele came to a close. Toni graciously saw the last remaining few on their way and turned to Robert. Wrapping her arms around one of Robert's, she leaned in invitingly, "Let's go upstairs for a little private chat."

She smiled provocatively into his eyes, and just like any other red-blooded American male, he succumbed to her blatant charms. Robert was flattered; he hadn't made any overt attempt to pursue her. He had tried to keep the evening on a purely business level. But he was open to any negotiations she proposed. Robert was feeling confident in his success that night, in his ability to work a crowd which had ranged from hardened studio executives and often egotistical actors and actresses to unpredictable entertainers and musicians. Basking in the glow of his success, he was conceited enough to think that talk wasn't what Toni had in mind, but as it turned out that was exactly what Toni intended.

Robert was usually so good at reading people he had overlooked one important detail. Toni was always on display, always playing a role; she was the quintessential actress, and he had underestimated her ability. After leading him up a sweeping, spiral staircase that wound its way to her private apartments, for one brief moment, his stunned expression revealed his innermost thoughts. They had entered her rooms only to be met by several others, and he finally realized that she had been serious.

He hid his disappointment well as he greeted the group. Toni dropped his arm and began moving toward an enclosed bar across the room. Robert's eyes followed her. He forced himself to turn away, but her sultry voiced reeled him in again, "Would you care for a drink, or something a little stronger?" The question was spoken hesitantly, provocatively, softly, as though they were the only two in the room.

Robert knew what he really wanted, needed, but he wasn't fool enough to reveal that. "I'll have whatever you are."

She laughed a practiced sound that trickled across the senses like warm summer rain. "But you don't know what that is," she laughed impishly.

"I'll trust you," he laughed too, his own practiced, sexy sound meant to send shivers down the spine of the unsuspecting. She laughed again as she turned to pour their drinks. Nothing he could do would lure her into his trap unless she wanted to go. She recognized the swagger, the ego, the false charm. She had been in the business too long not to know the signs. Trust, they were about to see just how far his trust went.

"Have a seat," she lead him to an oversized sofa and placed her drink on the glass table in front of them. He sipped his tentatively. He realized that she was all business now. He felt a little uneasy; he wasn't sure what she really wanted from him. He glanced around at the group, two obviously gay men and apparently a couple of women of somewhat indiscriminate predilection. He had heard references to Toni's advocacy for gay rights, but nothing formal.

When he returned to campaign headquarters, they were going to hear about this. He had been left to swing in the breeze by the seat of his pants, and it wasn't a feeling he liked. He wasn't worried about handling the situation, but he hated not being completely prepared. Still, he knew enough about the issues to forestall any problems. He forced himself to relax.

Toni sat studying him for a few minutes, letting the time drag by, a method she often employed to force others to make the first move. Robert didn't bite; he knew the tactic well. He simply smiled and sipped his drink, waiting patiently for her to speak. He didn't mind gazing on beauty as exquisite as Toni's. He knew she would fold before he did. He tipped his glass to her in a silent toast and took another sip. He could see her begin to fidget. He almost laughed when she finally spoke. Caroline would have died before she would give in. That was one of her more admirable qualities. Strange that she should be on his mind so much lately.

"I'm sure you know that I have an avid interest in the gay rights movement. Many of my dearest friends are among those who have become disenfranchised by our present laws. I want to know where you stand on the subject and how you plan to address this issue when you become President." She turned more fully to face him, and he could see the defiant spark in her eyes. She meant to bring him to task. He would have to tread softly until he could fashion an acceptable response. He knew his usual rhetoric was not going to placate her or her friends.

The others had moved to sit with them, waiting for him to speak. "Exactly what did you have in mind? You know how I stand on the issue. I'm sure that you've heard my opinion before this." He stared directly in her eyes as he spoke, trying to gage her reaction.

"Yes, I have, but I'm more interested in what your *honest* opinion is. We all know that candidates say whatever they feel will get them elected. We want to have assurance of where you truly stand and exactly how far you will back us." As she spoke, one of the young men sat down beside Robert. Toni slid closer to Robert as the young man draped his arm along the length of the sofa behind Robert's shoulders. Robert remained passive, waiting.

Toni smiled at him, her eyes laughing at him as she slid her hand up the silky fabric of his pants leg.

"You do remember that I'm a married man." His voice vibrated with laughter at his use of Caroline to extricate himself from an amorous situation. It was ludicrous, the height of irony.

Toni laughed out right. "I'm sure that's a serious consideration for you, but we feel certain that we can work something out to satisfy your moral objections. A little demonstration of your serious commitment to our cause would be very advantageous for your political career. We have influence all across the nation, influence that can help you carry those states where your ideas have ruffled the feathers of the less liberal constituents." Her fingers slowly grazed up and down his leg, her nails lazily drawing lines in the fabric. The tension in him began to build, waiting, wondering what her next move would be.

"Just exactly what did you have in mind? I believe I can honestly say that I am a man of my word, and you can believe me when I say that I will do all that is in my power to support your cause and any legislation brought before Congress on your behave." Robert could feel the rhetoric building in his mind. He was on a roll. "I believe in just and fair treatment for all people whether the issue is color, disability, gender, or sexual preference; all Americans should have the same equal and guaranteed rights."

He had inched forward as he spoke, bringing a forceful resonance to his words. "I won't make promises that I can't keep. I can only say that I will do all I can to support your cause. But in reality, it will take time to sway public opinion. I can truthfully say that I have seen change taking place all across the nation, and I feel that greater change is on the horizon."

"That's just the problem; we want to see greater changes now, not at some time in the distant future. Our lives are impacted every day by the outdated laws and beliefs of a narrow-minded society stoked in the Puritanical teaching of the seventeenth century. We need a leader who isn't afraid of the establishment, a leader who will make a stand for us and for all people who are victimized by archaic ideals. We are your people; we are the future of this nation; we have rights!" Toni's voice shook with passion; she was vehement about this issue, more so than Robert had realized. This was no simple discussion group; she wanted action, results.

Robert had eased back against the sofa as Toni spoke. He felt a hand ease across his shoulders. He pretended not to notice, but as it continued to move down his arm, Robert turned to face him. What was going on? What were they expecting him to do? He had never had an encounter with another man, and he wasn't about to now. But how could he extricate himself from this situation without causing incredible problems and losing support that he badly needed?

Toni saw his hesitancy and nodded to the others as they slipped from the room. She reached over and pushed a concealed panel at the end of the sofa, dimming the lights as a slow, sultry undertone of music filled the room. Robert felt like a lifeless statue; he was emotionally removed from the situation, yet consciously trapped. He glanced around. He forgot the young man beside him, as Toni slid closer to him and began a foray of his face with her lush, red lips. Her hand moved up his leg and eased temptingly close. He felt himself surge against the restricting fabric. He sighed as her lips met his in a breath-taking kiss, her hand moving provocatively up and down, building the tension in his body. He closed his arms tightly around her as he deepened the kiss. His mind registered the zipper slowly moving down on his slacks. There was no turning back; he had to have her. It was too late. He didn't care, not now. Later, he would take care of any problems, repercussions—later.

After all, who would believe any of them? As President, he would deny any such action? He felt incredible satisfaction at having provided a logical defense for himself, at least in his own mind, and became totally engrossed in the moment, in the lush feel of Toni's body in his arms.

Toni ended the evening alone with Robert. He had gotten what he wanted, and he had only made vague promises in return. He felt revitalized at his ability to deceive and dissemble.

Much later, he climbed into his waiting car, smiling broadly; he hummed to himself as he sat alone on the back seat. He must have done something right last night; he thought back to the smug little smile of satisfaction that had curved Toni's lips when he slipped from her bed. That had turned out to be one very memorable evening—money and sex—could it get better?

He was returning to his hotel suite in the early morning hours, but he didn't worry. He knew that no record, no surveillance tapes would ever be found of his late return; no one would see or hear anything about his private affairs. Alberto saw to that.

Entering his suite, Robert took only a few minutes to shower and prepare for another whirlwind day on the campaign trail. It passed quickly and before the last rays of sunshine faded from the Golden State, Robert was aboard his private jet and taxiing toward his next destination. Safely on board, he studied his notes for the next day, while the campaign staff worked diligently to tally the donations from the previous evening's events.

The Federal Election Committee kept an eagle eye on their financial reports. Harris' staff was meticulous in its efforts. He wanted no black marks against their campaign for false reporting or discrepancies in accounting. As the final figures were recorded, they all celebrated, knowing that this had turned out to be a very successful trip.

On all these occasions, Alberto handled the loading of the luggage, along with specially marked briefcases. Only after everything was in order, did he allow the plane to leave.

As the jet taxied down the runway, Alberto's evening detail met with him in the privacy of his sound-proof room near the rear of the plane. The surveillance tech handed Alberto the miniature microphones, which had been placed on Robert's clothing. His rendezvous with Toni had been carefully recorded and appropriate action would be taken to insure none of Robert's evening activities were leaked to the press.

Alberto shook his head. He hadn't changed his feelings about Robert, and his actions the past evening only reinforced Alberto's belief.

Caroline had fallen back into her usual routine, following Robert around as he pushed to make campaign stops in every state. His speaking schedule was grueling and hers was almost as demanding. They were booked on every conceivable television talk show and radio network. Every issue imaginable was fair game, and Robert's quick thinking had saved them on more than one occasion.

Caroline was never forced to be as quick-witted. Her questions were usually related to women's issues and topics devoted to home life and family values. Silently, she fumed at the chauvinistic attitude of the media but refrained from any openly hostile remarks. At the end of the day, her face felt ready to break. Her muscles ached and her feet cramped from the long hours standing beside her husband shaking hands and greeting potential voters. The campaign staff counted the days left to the election; Caroline counted the hours left for campaigning.

She and Paul had been able to escape only on one other occasion. It had been brief and unexpected. Her mother had had a sudden heart attack, nothing critical, but scary none the less, and Caroline had felt justified in taking time from the campaign to visit her and assure herself that she was being well taken care of. Of course, Robert had seized the moment to benefit his campaign, making much of his love for his mother-in-law and Caroline's devotion to her well-being. It also gave him the perfect opportunity to lambast his opponent for his weak position on health care reform.

If Robert noticed any change in Caroline's behavior toward him on her return, he didn't say anything. In fact, he almost seemed to have missed her during her brief absence. Caroline was confused when he questioned her about her mother's condition in private, no camera to record his concern, no microphone to tape his reaction. He rarely took time to even note her presence, much less actually talk to her. She turned it aside, cynically thinking that he probably had some campaign angle that he was working on.

The campaign sweep of northern states was coming to a close when Caroline made a startling discovery. At first, she hadn't known exactly what to do. She had walked around in a fog for a few days before common sense finally took over.

Chapter 14

HER FIRST CALL WAS to Paul. "Paul," she whispered when he answered, unable to voice anything more. Now that she was about to acknowledge the fact out loud, she was terrified of his reaction. She didn't even know how she felt about this unexpected turn of events.

"I'm on my way," was all Caroline heard as she sat in stunned disbelief still clutching the phone in her hand. What would he think? What would he say? What did she want?

Paul dropped the phone and raced to her apartment as soon as he heard her say his name. He didn't need to hear any more than that; he knew from her voice that something terrible had happened. It wasn't safe to discuss anything over the phone. He made it there in record time. Before Caroline could organize her thoughts, he was standing in front of her and reaching for her ice cold hands.

He pulled Caroline to her feet and into his arms. They could talk later; he needed to hold her first and then he would ask what was wrong. He could see the shimmer of tears in her vivid blue eyes. He held her close and kissed her hair. It always smelled of some exotic fragrance, sunshine and spring rain. He felt her take a deep, shaky breath.

"I'm pregnant," she whispered quietly, but to his ears it sounded as though she had shouted. He sat down abruptly on the couch, drawing her with him and clasping her to his side.

Silence reigned. Then he laughed, not a soft mellow laugh, but a deep, rumbling laugh. It shook his body and trembled along Caroline's frayed nerves. It wasn't funny. She was about to push him away when he suddenly kissed her, not a soft little kiss, but a mind-blowing sizzler that curled Caroline's toes in her shoes; she knew in that moment that everything would be all right. At last, when common sense returned and his need for air forced him to release her, he hugged her so tightly that she feared her ribs might break. He was laughing again. She frowned up at him and was about to speak when he did.

"Just think the President of the United States is having a son! Only this son will be the grandson of Bolivia's greatest drug lord—no his will be the son of Bolivia's greatest drug lords." He continued to laugh and hug Caroline while she tried to see the humor.

Finally, she pushed away from him enough to breath, "What if it's a girl?"

"No way," he quipped. "I'll bet you anything you want to that it's a boy."

Caroline thought for a moment, "I'll take that bet, but I won't tell you what I want until the baby is born."

"Fair enough," he smiled broadly at her. "You can't imagine how happy I am." His arms closed tightly around her again. She could feel the love radiate from him, and she found inner peace for the first time in days. "Doesn't it bother you that I'm married to Robert and that this baby will be his legally?"

"We know differently, and that's all that matters. We will have to work out a way to convince him that it's his, at least until after the election." Paul frowned as he began thinking of possible problems.

"Don't worry. I'll just give him a due date that matches some of our time together. He won't know the difference, and he won't be concerned unless it affects him adversely." She couldn't hide her cynicism or the dislike she felt for Robert. Her words were laced with anger.

When Caroline finally decided to brave what she thought might turn into a full-blown argument with Robert, she scheduled a quiet dinner late one evening after Robert's last strategy meeting had ended. She had arranged with his campaign manager to have a rather early evening with her husband. Of course, the idea that Robert's wife wished to surprise her husband with an uninterrupted evening alone played right along with everyone's romantic idea of their marriage. She only smiled at Harris' less than subtle attempts to discover her reasons for a private dinner with her husband. His evenings were usually filled with special events, elaborate parties, private meetings, and not romantic dinners with his wife.

For Robert's part, he was irritated that Caroline had caused a rescheduling of his meetings. Of course, he realized to make a fuss about her request would raise a great many finely arched brows. He didn't need anyone wondering about their life together. Things worked well just as they were, at least from his perspective.

Playing the gallant and remarking to the staff about being an absentee husband of late, Robert left the campaign headquarters with a broad smile that faded the second he was out of sight of his staff. This evening was not one he looked forward to; Caroline had been less than accommodating recently, and he didn't feel like trying to appease her. He was, however, curious about her reason for this rather unexpected and unwarranted request. He had better at least pretend to be pleased, if he wanted the evening to end on any kind of peaceful note. Caroline's silences could be louder than most thunderstorms. He hated the fact that she could get on his nerves, get under his skin, with her adolescent behavior. She never even acknowledged his irritation with her. When the mood struck, she would act as though nothing untoward had happened, and life continued on as before.

Robert shook his head as he entered the apartment. He would never understand her, and he didn't really have the time or the inclination to try. She had better have a good reason for interrupting his schedule. On that sullen note, he walked into the living room and saw the embodiment of the woman he had first met and admired years ago.

Caroline had gone all out. She was dressed in a shimmering gown of iridescent blues and greens that flowed softly around her. Her silky blonde hair was swept up in a cascade of curls that draped the slender curve of her neck. Diamonds glittered brightly at her ears and throat, a wedding gift from her father. She was stunning and he was confused.

Caroline floated toward him on a cloud of shimmering silk and alluring scent, all woman, all his. Then he caught himself and almost laughed. That type of thinking was bound to lead to disaster. She never saw things the way he did. He sometimes thought she liked being perverse just to irritate him. He waited for her to speak. Any other evening, she would have let him stand there until he spoke first.

It was a crazy game they had begun playing, and she didn't even know how it had started. She realized that to him it was an issue of power; he wanted to make sure that she knew he was in charge. She just wanted him to care enough to want to speak to her as an equal, not someone he needed to dominate.

At one time, they had worked together, but that time had passed, the closer the election, the greater the distance between them. Only their unspoken desire to keep others from realizing the true state of their marriage kept them sharing a bed at least on occasion, and now Caroline was grateful that they had. It would be easy enough to convince him that his protection had failed and that was the reason for their unexpected evening together.

Caroline smiled sweetly as she handed him his favorite drink. He took a fortifying swallow and felt the burn ease down his throat to his stomach. His blood warmed and he felt some of the tension leave. She had deliberately made it strong. His eyes widened as he sipped the drink. He wouldn't care what she wanted if he continued to drink this. He laughed.

"Okay, if we were the usual couple, I would think about now that you had wrecked the family car or something. So just what has happened that I would need such a strong drink before you told me?" The alcohol was quickly relaxing him. He hadn't eaten much during the day, and he could feel the heat racing through him. He sat down across from her and waited.

She smiled that provocative, little witch smile that she had that always made him want her, made him think that she was up to something diabolical. Oh, yes, she was definitely up to something. He just wondered how long she would make him wait to find out. He laughed again.

"You know you look beautiful tonight. I feel honored. Should I go and change before dinner?" Now she would have to talk just to answer his question. He hadn't planned to force her hand, but he had unintentionally nevertheless. He felt rather pleased with himself.

"It's not necessary. I just wanted to look nice. I'm glad that you approve." She tried to keep the sarcasm from her voice. "There's something that I need to talk to you about. Would you rather eat first?" She felt that she would choke if she had to eat now, but she was trying to placate him. She didn't need to stir the waters before she knew where the ship was headed.

"No, I'll admit that you have my curiosity—aroused." He hesitated suggestively. "This is a rather unexpected, but not unappreciated, surprise." He gave her his most charming smile. With all this preparation and fanfare, she had his undivided attention.

"In that case, I'll get right to the matter at hand." She took a calming breath and looked him straight in the eye. "I'm pregnant."

He sat stunned, speechless. "Well, that was rather direct." He stood and began pacing the room. He turned back to face her. "Are you sure?"

She laughed softly, "Yes, I went to the doctor yesterday." She wasn't telling him anything more until she knew how he felt.

"Well," he started then stopped and began pacing again. "I supposed there's no point in me asking how this happened. I realize that the type of protection we were using was less than foolproof. Still," he stopped again. "You're sure?"

"Yes, Robert, I'm certain!" Her temper was beginning to rise. "Are you pleased or not? If you had rather not have anything to do with this baby, then I can certainly make arrangements to see that you have nothing to do with it—ever." She was becoming agitated. The doctor had warned her that she was likely to experience an emotional roller coaster ride for a while. She could already see how she was less able to maintain her composure.

He stopped, turned to her, and took her cold hands in his. "Of course, I want this baby. I'm just stunned; that's all. You'll have to give me a little time to adjust. This is wonderful news. Just wait until the press gets hold of this." He squeezed her hands before he dropped them and began pacing again.

She stared at him, her mouth open in astonishment. She snapped it closed. "Is that your primary concern? The press? What they will think?" She whirled around and started to leave the room. Let him starve. She wasn't about to go in to dinner with him.

"Of course not!" he raced across the room, whirled her around, and kissed her surprised lips. "But you have to admit, this is going to be an added bonus for the campaign. Just think of all the votes this could get us. A President with a new baby in the White House what could be more newsworthy?" He stopped suddenly. "When is it due?" She was so slender; she didn't look as though she was going to have a baby any time soon. How would this affect the campaign? She wouldn't be able to travel with him for long. But he could use that to his advantage.

This was the moment of truth. She took a deep breath. She had prepared her answer beforehand. All she had to do was be convincing. "Not for some time. The doctor thinks that I'm possibly two months, maybe a week or two more. He can't be sure until the ultrasound is done. But that won't be for several weeks yet." She wanted to wring her hands in frustration but managed to keep a smile on her lips. Selfish pig! All he was really interested in was his election. But why was she letting his reaction upset her. Paul was the real father, not this egotistical womanizer. Thank God for that!

"You'll have to excuse me. I need to lie down. Dinner is ready. Please enjoy your meal. I had them prepare your favorites." She turned and walked to her rooms without looking back. He didn't attempt to stop her. He had a lot to think about. This could definitely work in their favor. He entered the dining room and sat down to a very pleasant meal. His mind was filled with ideas by the time he finished his dessert. Yes, he could definitely make this work for him. He didn't really give any thought to the child—his child. Children had never held any place in his life before; he saw no reason to be troubled now.

Caroline had called it; she knew him well. The only thing that would bother him would be how well this would work to his advantage, and she knew that he would find every opportunity to make this new development work in his favor. She almost wanted to tell him that the child wasn't his, just to see his reaction. Then she realized that he really wouldn't care. As long as his name wasn't attached to some scandal, he wouldn't even be concerned. In fact, he would probably applaud her for giving him such a golden opportunity to swing another section of voters in his favor.

Caroline slipped out of her dress, removed the carefully applied makeup, changed into comfortable pajamas, and fell instantly asleep. She would worry about the future tomorrow.

The hastily called press conference was attended by every available media. Rumors were rife, conjectures filled the hallways. What could this be about? Every conceivable scenario was addressed as the press waited anxiously for Robert to make his appearance. No one had considered the real reason for this unusual event.

When Robert made his entrance, most conjectures were eliminated by the broad smile on his face and the noticeable spring in his step. Others fell to the wayside when Caroline walked graciously beside him, basking in a radiant glow. When no one else joined them, the remaining few suppositions were erased. Everyone sat in silence wondering what was about to take place. Only one rather aged woman correspondent for a popular ladies' magazine guessed the truth. She began quietly taking notes, a knowing smile on her face.

Robert stepped to the podium and drew Caroline to his side. He gazed lovingly at her for a moment before he turned back to his audience. "Ladies and Gentlemen, I know that this conference was called rather hastily, but we—," he hesitated, took Caroline's hand and drew it to his lips for a kiss then turned back to the microphone, "I—couldn't wait a minute longer to share this unexpected and wonderful blessing. Caroline and I are expecting a baby." The room lit up with flashes at that announcement. Robert paused meaningfully, giving them time to make this moment memorable for his campaign. Questions were already being shouted at them when he held up his hand for silence and continued. "I know that you have questions, but my most important concern is for the well-being of my wife and child, so Caroline will only be continuing with the campaign as long as the doctors consider it advisable. I can't express how delighted I am by this unexpected news, but I'm sure you fathers know just how I feel." He beamed proudly for the cameras.

Caroline longed to slap his smug face, but she played her part to perfection. She knew how to work an audience as well as Robert. When he drew her to the podium to answer questions, she handled the session with poise and dignity, using a balance of expertise and humor to answer the more personal questions, leaving them all laughing when she ended the conference by remarking that after the election they **had** planned to get a dog, but now they wouldn't need to.

As the smiling couple moved back from the podium, waving to everyone as they left the room, Amanda Jeffery stepped forward and began fielding the more serious concerns. Yes, they were delighted by the news. No, the pregnancy had not been planned to bolster Robert's campaign. Yes, Robert planned to be a hands-on father as much as his time allowed. No, there would be no changes in their campaign schedule, unless something unexpected developed. Yes, they would receive updates as those were made available to her.

Amanda wrapped up the conference as soon as she could. Her phone had not stopped vibrating at her side since the news had hit the airways. She almost dreaded the next few days, chaos would reign, and there was no stopping it. But the upside would most likely be a surge in support. Voters, who saw Robert as an inexperienced, Southern liberal, would reconsider in the face of this news. Fatherhood was an amazing equalizer in people's eyes. Decisions made by a President, who was also a father, were deemed better because he would have the best interest, not only of the American people at heart, but also his own children. The American psyche was a strange thing.

Amanda handed out press releases, containing all of the pertinent details at the end of the conference then made her way back to the staff offices. Phones were ringing faster than people could answer them. She just shook her head and grabbed a cup of coffee as she headed to her private office. At least in here, it was slightly quieter. She scrolled through her messages and decided her best option was a blanket text message and e-mail response. Otherwise, she would never get anything accomplished. She quickly composed a brief text message and sent it to her call list, wrote a similar e-mailed version and sent it, then updated the campaign's website.

The phones gradually rang less as the news spread, and after a few hours, the staff was actually able to work on campaign issues. Amanda couldn't help but wonder if this had been planned. Robert was so determined to win this election, she wouldn't put anything passed him, but Caroline was a different story. The more Amanda was around them as a couple, the more she felt that something just wasn't quite right. There was nothing obvious, but it was a feeling that she got every time. Her grandmother would accuse her of letting her sixth sense rule her good senses. Her grandmother also knew that Amanda had a special gift for some things, an unexplainable instinct, and she was rarely wrong, but Amanda hoped she was wrong this time.

Paul had not informed anyone of Caroline's news. He felt that it was her place to tell her father when she was ready, and to the world this was Robert's child, even their fathers wouldn't know the real truth. Paul and Caroline had decided that this was a secret that had to remain between the two of them. Of course, after seeing the morning news, Paul knew that Caroline would be forced to contact her father. He would know before the day was out anyway, so she might as well notify him. The letter she sent by Alberto was short and definitive. She knew Rafael would be pleased. After all, he had been advocating just such a move for months. This just placed them all closer to their goal.

Alberto boarded the jet in its private hangar at the airport. He didn't like to be seen leaving the country any more than necessary. This jet was scheduled for a trip to one of the remote Caribbean islands. From there, he would board another to complete the trip to Bolivia. This tactic made the trip a little more time consuming, but obscuring his destination provided a better cover for his movements when he had to enter or leave the States unexpectedly.

Today, he needed to meet privately with Raul and Rafael. He also had a very important letter to deliver. He wasn't happy that Caroline was carrying Robert's baby, but maybe Rafael's blood would prove stronger, and the child wouldn't have any of Robert's proclivities. Some things were beyond even Raul and Rafael's power. For a moment, Alberto wondered how Raul would feel about this news. Would he be concerned that the child was of Rafael's lineage and not his? It was an interesting question, but one he didn't have time to ponder at the moment.

When he finally arrived at his destination, his meeting with the men went well. They were equally pleased and concerned by Caroline's news. Of course, no expense was to be spared in protecting and providing for her. They instructed Alberto to consider her his prime objective and to assign others to Robert's detail. Alberto didn't reveal how close he had already been shadowing Caroline, and even Paul. Their fathers didn't need to know everything.

Plans were also put into place to advise several of their key political associates that now was the time to declare full support for Robert's election. They were to offer both political and financial support funneled, of course, through the cartel to them. Their unconditional support was guaranteed by Raul's intelligence and surveillance systems, very little happened in the lives of key figures in both politics and finance that Raul didn't know about almost as quickly as the participants themselves. His comprehensive documentation kept anyone he needed in line and insured their support. If they chose to follow another path, Raul easily accommodated them, and their lives, with all its sordid details, became an open book for the world to read. Any hint of scandal in the lives of influential figures drew public interest like sharks to the scent of blood, and they devoured it just as aggressively.

Alberto boarded his return flight within a few hours of their meeting. He didn't trust anyone to do his job. Even though his men were the best, he was too much like Rafael; he needed to be there.

Strong was stepping high. He had received some very important news, news that would give Graham the push he needed to strike against the cocaine trade. The Columbian cartel was moving large shipments through a special underground system from Mexico to the States. Strong had firsthand information that identified the route and the time for the next shipment. With Richards as his backup, Strong met with Graham to finalize their plans.

Richards was to take a force and create a disturbance that would draw attention to the area where the shipment would be brought through. Timing had to be perfect, but Richards had given enough details to his friend at the DEA for them to unwittingly assist in Graham's scheme. More importantly, Richards had organized his own special squad to back him up. He didn't trust Strong not to take him down when he least expected it.

Graham was concerned about retaliation. Richards told him that he had that covered but for him to be prepared to sacrifice a few men during the operation. If they weren't lost in the crossfire, they might find themselves swept up by the DEA. Graham wasn't concerned about anyone. He just wanted results. He would provide for his men. They were loyal to him, and they knew that he would take care of them. Graham was delighted that Richards had found a way to leak information to a well known snitch, providing a way to involve the DEA. With them on the scene, the Columbians were less likely to assign blame to any other drug organization for their takedown. It seemed like a foolproof plan, but Richards knew not to depend on everything going right.

When the time came, their plan went off without a hitch. The DEA moved in and Richards and his men slipped away, leaving the cartel's men caught illegally crossing the border. Richards didn't know whether he should be relieved or concerned. Strong was suddenly a man with all the answers.

Richards slipped away from Strong at the first opportunity. He had to cover his trail just as furtively as always. Strong still tried to have him followed, but the newer ones were never any smarter than the ones who had tried it before. At least, it kept his skills sharp. He didn't need to get careless at this point.

Richards had to make a special contact. Strong had a lead on a critical distribution center in Chicago. If Strong's Intel was right, they could all profit from this takedown. Richards used his secret apartment to make contact. Through coded messaging, he relayed the information to a friend in the DEA. After several hours, Richards received the news he needed. A recent bust by state troopers on the interstate had uncovered a heavy weight package on its way to Chicago. The DEA had some scanty information, but they needed more substantiation before they could make a move. They were able to supply enough details from their contacts to verify Strong's information. Richards felt sure they could act on what they knew and would most likely get the results they needed. If they were careful, they could do some real damage.

Locking up the hidden section in the empty apartment he used for official work, Richards memorized the number he had received, wiped the phone's memory clean, removed the SIM card, and crushed it beneath his foot. It was overkill, but he felt better for using extreme caution. Taking the disabled phone, he melted back into life on the streets; he wiped all traces off of the phone's surfaces, and made his way furtively along the back alleys and side streets of the city toward the churning shores of the Big Muddy.

From a remote overlook, he tossed the phone into the murky depths and watched as it faded from sight, one less worry. He stood there for a few minutes watching as the waters rolled endlessly onward, pondering the many secrets hidden in the depths below. Turning aside, he walked toward the noisy center of the city. At a corner newsstand, he stopped and waited for several minutes studying the people who passed, watching those who hid in the shadows. When he felt reassured that no one was following him, he slipped into a small neighborhood store and purchased a disposable phone, a reoccurring expense in his life, but necessary. Keeping his identity safe was vital if he wanted to remain living. Richards knew that in his line of work, he was as disposable as his phone and just as easy to get rid of.

Richards worked on a plan as he walked back toward his apartment, but he was puzzled. The information Strong had given him had proven to be accurate, in fact, too accurate. Richards couldn't figure out how he had gotten it. Strong wasn't that good at deception. Who did he have on the take that would risk revealing so many details about the cartel's business? Richards couldn't believe anyone in the organization would chance being discovered. If they were found out, their death would be extremely disagreeable and meant to set an example. Even he, as hardened as he was, had had to turn away from some of the crime scene photos he had been shown. Those found guilty of betraying the cartel would not be given a quick or a pleasant death. In fact, he was sure they would beg for death many times over before they received it.

The location Strong gave them was a secluded, back lot in the Chicago warehouse district. Trucks loaded and unloaded every conceivable type of merchandise from the warehouses, moving in and out of the district almost continually. The constant flow of goods and materials made it the perfect spot to conceal illegal movements. Richards saw only one element in their favor. The warehouse under question was slightly removed from the others. Although this would help by separating them from others working in the area, it also made surveillance difficult and dangerous.

Richards became even more suspicious of Strong when he brought in sophisticated surveillance equipment, linked to a satellite, and accessible through remote computer uplinks. Richards was no fool; there was no way that Strong had come up with this type of planned operation on his own. Graham might be footing the bill, but Richards knew that he had no idea exactly what Strong was up to. All Graham wanted was results. How he and Strong achieved those didn't matter to Graham in the least. Richards was more concerned about who was at the back of this setup. He wasn't sure that Strong was smart enough to really understand who he might be dealing with and the consequences if he chose the wrong group to back him.

Richards kept his thoughts to himself but made a mental note to check out Strong's recent activities and place a tail on him. Something was definitely wrong. Richards didn't want to get caught in a sell-out, not where the cartel was involved. Strong might not realize it, but his position, his money, and his ego meant nothing to these men. They always played for keeps, and they didn't play nice.

With Strong's men helping, they used one of Graham's trucks and set up into a rented warehouse positioned at an angle to their target, which appeared to be used for maintenance. After two days, Richards was beginning to wonder if Strong had been fed false information. Even Strong was getting antsy, constantly asking when something was going to happen.

Richards wasn't sure why Strong wanted to be in on this raid; it was out of character for him. Lawyer types usually tried to remain safely in the background, protected by their legal rights and fat bank accounts, not involved in anything that could tie them directly to illegal activity. Ever since Richards had returned to work for Graham, Strong had been directly involved in all of the operations. He didn't just supply men, funds, and information as before, but he had assumed a hands-on approach that left Richards completely baffled. Something had happened while he had been gone. Someone had gotten to Strong. Richards just didn't know who it was or what their reason was. The more he thought about it, the more he felt that Strong was being used by someone with a lot of power.

It was the third in another long, uneventful day when late in the afternoon, a man driving a pickup and wearing a mechanic's uniform arrived, unlocked the double doors to the warehouse and drove inside. By using highly sophisticated heat imaging, Richards was able to track the man's movements inside the building. Apparently he was checking invoices or other paperwork in an office. He made one phone call, which they intercepted, ordering maintenance on a truck, identifying it by serial numbers. It seemed aboveboard, but Richards knew something wasn't quite right. He just couldn't figure it out.

As the man locked up to leave, Richards was about to turn off the link to the heat-sensors when a glimmer in the back of the building caught his eye. At first it was faint, a slight smudge of detail, nothing positive. Richards signaled for one of the men to follow the mechanic and report back when he reached his destination. Keeping his eye on the computer screen, Richards watched as the image grew in clarity and strength. Where had it come from? Then just as it became visible on the screen, the image appeared to move back to the rear of the building and slowly fade. Turning off the imaging device, Richards didn't say anything. Maybe he had imagined it. He was tried after long days of inactivity. Yet he couldn't just let it go.

Instructing the men to notify him immediately if anything happened, Richards slipped out of the warehouse and edged his way toward the building. He didn't know what he expected to find, but he had to check. His left hand automatically slipped under the dark jacket he wore to the 38 in the back of his jeans. The feel of cold steel, he felt better just knowing it was there.

A single side door at the back of the building enabled Richards to gain entry. He easily disarmed the alarm system and now began a furtive exploration along the side aisle of compartments. An assortment of crates and boxes filled the sections, but the center aisle was empty and cleared of material. Richards saw the faint impression of tire marks in the soft dirt covering the floor. Richards frowned; unusual, most warehouses were built on slabs. To his left, he saw bays filled with mechanics tools and maintenance equipment. That fit with the mechanic's maintenance order for the semi.

Everything seemed normal, so why was the hair on the back of his neck standing on end? Then he heard it again, soft at first, but clearly a faint sound, muffled by something. Where was it coming from? Keeping as quiet as possible, he moved slowly toward the center of the room. He tried to follow the tread marks, but the skylights had long ago been crusted over with dirt and grime, and sunlight, barely visibly at the best of times, was negligible by the late afternoon. All Richards had to go on were his instincts, and they were already on alert.

Richards felt his way further into the warehouse, moving slowly, cautiously. Then he heard it again, a slight shuffling sound like feet dragging slightly under weight of some type. As he bent to look under a stack of pallets piled in a recess along the far wall, the sound was more distinct. Then it all fell into place, the dirt on the floor, the disappearing image, the indistinct sounds—a tunnel. That was what he had almost literally stumbled on.

Unsuccessfully, he tried to envision the outlying buildings. It had to be fairly close, yet somehow removed. He needed to get back and find an aerial map of the warehouses. Several of those to the rear were accessed by another roadway. That might explain how they had remained undetected. Shipments brought in at one point were taken out at another, while safely hidden underground in the meantime if anyone did get suspicious. It was a well thought out operation, and obviously lucrative.

Most likely, trucks brought in for maintenance had secluded compartments containing special shipments. One was being brought in some time this evening, supposedly after completing its scheduled run. If he could determine where access to the tunnel originated, they could close in from both sides and catch them with the drugs in hand. Strong wanted to take the haul himself, but that could be risky. He didn't want to give the game away, but if all went well, the DEA would be waiting for his signal, and he and Strong would have to clear out quickly if they didn't want to be arrested.

Richards had enlisted his friend's help, and the DEA had been advised of Richards' undercover operation. They would allow his men to escape when they closed in on the operation, but that had been before Richards discovered the tunnel. Richards and his contact had planned for their escape through the back roads; now that might be exactly where the cartel's men would be. He would just have to improvise. Richards knew he couldn't trust Strong or Graham to help him if he was arrested, and he couldn't trust anyone else with his real identity. He would have to watch his back tonight.

He slipped from the building and made his way cautiously back to where Strong and his men waited. Entering the rear of the building, he shook his head in disbelief. Some surveillance team he had; ignoring the monitors, the men played cards on an up-turned crate. Strong sat kicked back in a chair, flipping through his messages. Richards sighed in disbelief. No one took pride in their work anymore, not even the criminals. They were either completely indifferent to their job or on someone else's payroll. Where had Strong recruited them anyway? He just hoped they could follow orders. He wouldn't have long to wait and see. The camera positioned on the road to the warehouse showed a semi moving slowly toward them. He only had a few minutes to decide where the tunnel ended before the entire operation blew up in their faces.

He grabbed the computer and clicked on a special link hidden within another screen. Anything he typed would be transmitted secretly to the DEA. He pulled up an aerial view of the district and drew a line from the warehouse they were watching to one a short distance further back and facing an adjacent road. He was almost certain it had to be that one. It would be too difficult to dig a tunnel much further than that.

He typed the word *tunnel* in white text across the bottom of the screen. It didn't show on his monitor but would be visible on the recipient's. He prayed they had enough time to close in from both areas and not give away their plan. If they couldn't carry out the operation quickly, the workers could easily dispose of the merchandise or escape with it. Everything would be lost.

Richards wanted to bring down the main players, but he knew that probably would never happen. All he could hope for was crippling their business, slowing public access to cocaine. This would be a major step in that direction, if they could pull it off.

The air brakes on the semi barked and screeched as the driver pulled to a stop. A man jumped down from the passenger side and unlocked the double doors to the warehouse, pushing them aside for the truck to enter, and then closing them behind it. Richards watched as the sensors picked up heat from the engine and the two men moving about inside. The driver had pulled to the back of the warehouse. Then both men appeared to climb into another vehicle. Sensors picked up the heat from a smaller engine. The doors slid open, and a pickup pulled out. After closing the doors behind them, the two men drove off.

Richards signaled for his men to move out. As they gathered at the rear of the building, he sent one group to enter the first warehouse from the front, another from the rear, and the last group went with him to move in on the second warehouse. They had the element of surprise with them only if they could coordinate their efforts. They were to move in on his command. He warned them that they were probably going to face some heavy opposition once the doors opened. There was no need to worry about security systems; they were forcing their way into the buildings without warning, using the element of surprise to catch their targets off guard. From what Richards had already observed, he felt that one reason this operation was so successful was because they limited the personnel involved. Too many people moving in and out of an area would definitely cause questions. That played in their favor by limiting the manpower available to stop them.

When he and his men reached their destination, he gave the signal, and they entered both warehouses simultaneously. Surprise may have been with them, but they met intense resistance once they broke in. Both entrances to the tunnel lay open and men were hurriedly removing packages from the first truck and depositing them in the tunnel.

On the other end, men in the process of taking packages from the tunnel grabbed for nearby weapons and opened fire. After several intense minutes of combat, the firing slowed and Richards and his men were able to seize both buildings. The vastly outnumbered guards had quickly fallen and left the tunnel unprotected. Chaos reigned inside. The men were trapped by Richards' forces, which now held both entrances to the tunnel and both warehouses. They had to move quickly. If he didn't signal the DEA soon, they would move in on their own. Gesturing to some of his men to take the cocaine in the trucks and scattered in the buildings back to Strong, he then ordered the men trapped in the tunnel to come out or risk being blown up inside.

He had no way to carry out his threat, but they didn't know that. He was hoping that the workers were illegal or, at least, unwilling to die needlessly. As the few men remaining filed out, Richards ordered them locked up the storage rooms at the back of the building. It was pointless to kill them. Richards and his men couldn't be recognized. They wore protective gear, which disguised their features and head sets, which allowed them to communicate. The men taken captive would never talk anyway. Retaliation was part of their lives; they wouldn't risk it.

Moving quickly, Richards sent his remaining men back and rushed through the exposed tunnel. It was dangerous; someone could still be hiding inside, but it was a risk he had to take. What he saw amazed him.

He found a reinforced room big enough to take the cocaine, cut it, and repackage it for distribution. Somebody had put a great deal of thought into this operation. Richards wondered if he would ever know who that person was, but he didn't have time to investigate. Nothing he could find could be traced to those running the cartel. He was certain.

Exiting the warehouse at a dead run, he signaled the DEA to move in and rushed to join Strong and his men. They had loaded the surveillance equipment into the semi along with the cocaine they had taken by the time Richards raced through the door. He jumped into the passenger seat, and they eased the big rig onto the side road and pulled away.

Richards glanced into the side mirror and watched as covert operatives poured into the vacated buildings and began rounding up people and seizing the remaining drugs. The operation would be dismantled, the people arrested, interrogated, and either jailed or deported. Either way, the cost to the cartel for this evening's raid would be substantial, even more so because Graham now had most of the cocaine.

With the raid on the border crossing and the hit on this major distribution center, the Columbian cartel would be effectively hurt, at least for a while, and that was all Graham wanted—time to get his product back on the market and increase his profit margin again.

As they eased into the flow of traffic and blended into the evening, Richards finally felt that he could breath. Up until that moment, he hadn't really known how this evening would end. They had achieved their goal and lost very few men in the process. They had taken a large quantity of cocaine and crippled the cartel. Would this be enough to satisfy his need to avenge his sister's death? Could he finally find the peace he sought? He just didn't know.

When they returned to Graham with an accounting of the week's activity, Graham was so impressed that he made Richards an unexpected offer.

"I want you to come to work for me full time. Get to know the operation. Strong needs someone he can rely on. I want someone I can trust. I think you're just the man." Graham looked so smug that Richards wanted to laugh, but he was so shocked and completely unprepared with an answer that it left him speechless for a moment. Luckily, Graham was used to his reticence, so he thought nothing of Richards' reaction. It was the perfect opportunity to obtain the much needed detailed information about Graham's organization that he had been working to learn. He couldn't seem too eager, but he couldn't be too indecisive either.

"Just what exactly do you have in mind?"

"I want you to continue our campaign against the cartel. I want them crippled. I would love to say eliminated, but I have to be realistic. Strong has some reliable sources of information. We can use those to undermine their operations and, at least, play havoc with their plans." Graham didn't expect him to refuse, but Richards had to seem reluctant.

"I'm not sure. I prefer working alone and choosing my own jobs. What kind of assurance do I have that I will still be in charge?" Graham barked a laugh.

"In charge? I'm in charge, but I guess you will still be making all the decisions for your part of the operation. I've never told you how to do your job before, so I won't start now, but you will have to make some changes." He eyed Richards closely, weighing his words carefully before he spoke.

"Now don't take this wrong, but I think you ought to fix yourself up a little. I'll pay the bill. Get yourself some proper clothes and all. I'll need you around more, and I don't want you scaring off the office staff." He looked Richards up and down. "Maybe get a haircut or something."

Richards made as if he were about to stand. Graham put up his hand to stop him. "Hold on. I know a man has the right to look anyway he wants, but I have an image to maintain with my trucking business, so you have to fit in, if you see what I mean." He stood and walked around to where Richards sat.

"I'll give you a more than adequate salary, a starting bonus to get up set up, and a bonus for every successful job. It will be much more lucrative than our present arrangement. You will have to make yourself available to me on a regular basis. None of that nine to five stuff, but whenever I need you. How does that sound?" He looked the part of the benevolent despot. Obviously, he thought the offer lacked nothing and should be readily accepted.

Richards had worked alone for too long. This offer made him nervous, and he was never nervous. Why now? Why him? What didn't he know? This had to have something to do with Strong and his new found source of information, but what? The only way he would be able to find the answers would be to walk further into the lion's den and pray that he didn't get eaten.

Richards sighed. "When do I start?"

"That's what I like to hear! Take your time; get whatever you need, just be here first thing next week. We've already received some new information. I want to get started." He acted as though he might be ready to take part himself. Of course, Richards knew better.

Maybe he could find out who Strong's source was or at least more details about Graham's contacts. Richards knew he had some very important and influential people in his pay, but he needed facts. His files on Graham's organization were sketchy; even after four or so years undercover, he didn't have enough. Now he had the chance to obtain names, dates, amounts, real evidence, and it had to be quick.

He wanted out of this business. He felt suffocated by the double life he led, smothered by all the lies, strangled by the deception. He needed his real life back, and he needed it soon.

When Monday arrived, Richards walked into Graham's outer office and introduced himself to Graham's secretary. He would need assistance in obtaining the evidence he was seeking, and he needed to know just how involved other members of Graham's staff were. If they were innocent pawns used to cover his illegal business dealings, then Richards needed to find out as soon as possible. If they weren't, then he might be able to use them himself to help close down Graham's operation.

Richards followed Graham's advice, not that he needed it. He had longed to revert to his former self; this just gave him the perfect opportunity. As he sat with one hip on the edge of her desk, he flirted half-heartedly with the little brunette. She was polite, but not overly friendly. She was all business when Graham walked into the room and frowned at Richards. He was about to ask him what his business was, when it dawned on him who Richards was.

Walking over, he slapped Richards on the back. "Well, I'll be. I didn't recognize you at first." He laughed. "Come on in. Jeanie, bring us some coffee. Strong will be here in a few minutes. You know lawyers. They're always running behind." He pushed open his office door and motioned for Richards to follow.

Graham shuffled papers around on his desk for a few minutes until Jeanie brought in the coffee. Then he sent her on an errand and waited until the outer office door closed behind her.

"Nice girl," he stated flatly, then cleared his throat. "Now, Strong has some information that I think will help us really heat things up.

We are going to hit them in as many places as we can. I'm willing to invest whatever it takes and call in a few favors on the West Coast. See if you can figure out a way to get the authorities involved. Let them take credit and keep the pressure off us. I know enough about these Coca boys to respect them. I don't want them breathing down my neck, not if I can send them in another direction." He thumped a stack of papers together. "Did you see what they did to that guy in Mexico City? Just like the *Godfather*, only it wasn't a horse's head, it was the guy's. Sick, I'm telling you, real sick."

Chapter 15

As ROBERT'S CAMPAIGN WOUND through the states, he worked the crowds, listening to concerns, addressing issues. He made a point of focusing on as many little towns and out-of-the-way locations as he could. He was building his campaign around the people, and he needed to be seen meeting with as many as possible, a common man reaching out to the common people, not just the elite, the rich, and the powerful. It was a bold idea, and it made for extremely long hours getting from the necessary city sweeps to the byways of America. But Robert was determined to do it, and Caroline stayed by his side.

In her glowing condition, she brought a touch of nostalgia and tenderness to the most hardened and disheartened voters. She swept through a high school gymnasium or a fair ground exhibition hall as though it were an everyday occurrence. She put people at ease with her down to earth charm and her respectful attitude. She asked advice from matrons and shared concerns with young mothers; she added the special heart that Robert's campaign needed. She made news wherever she went, and Robert began to resent it.

Caroline was at her best when she was alone, when she was not eclipsed by Robert's shadow. People crowded around, eager to hear what she had to say. She became the woman behind the man in the press, and to women across the country she became the woman beside the man. They were ready for equality on more than paper; they wanted to see it in action. Women's magazines featured stories in just that frame. Reporters began questioning Robert about what his wife's role in the White House would be after the election. Of course, Robert joking responded that her first concern would be the baby, and hopefully, then him. But he was quickly feeling as though she were stealing his show.

Caroline only laughed. She was just playing his game, making the most of her unexpected condition. She was doing her best to help her husband get elected, and she loved every minute of watching Robert squirm. Of course, no one else knew how he really felt, but she knew Robert, and in private he was furious with the press, the public, and with her. Campaigning was agony most days, but she would suffer through it. After all, he had said that she would be by his side until the doctors advised against it. Some days, she didn't know if it was worth it; she was so tired. Then he would make some snide remark, and she was set again to prove him wrong.

As the first primaries drew to a close, Robert forged ahead of the conservative candidate by such a large margin that he quickly withdrew and pledged his support to Robert. With a final push through the North, Robert pulled out in front of the two remaining candidates. He had the necessary votes to claim the Democratic Party's nomination at last, and for a few days they could relax.

Caroline was so relieved that she didn't even care that he hadn't bothered to thank her for her support. Of course, she couldn't help but laugh too; she had been really awful those last few weeks. She knew how he liked everything to be about him, and she had truly enjoyed forcing him to share the stage with her and the baby. He'd better get used to it. This baby was going to be a real part of their lives, and people would be interested in every aspect of its life.

All she wanted to do now was sleep. Robert had other plans, but thankfully they didn't involve Caroline. She left him in Harris' hands as they began the search for Robert's running mate. Their selection would set the tone of the election. A misstep now and everything could be lost. Harris had already compiled a short list. The qualifications had to offset any deficiencies people felt that Robert had. Their choice had to balance the ticket and be a recognized force in his own right without overshadowing Robert's qualities as the Presidential candidate.

It was a difficult task, and one that required much consideration and discussion. After several days, Harris began the arduous task of contacting people, sending out feelers, testing the waters, to see who might be interested. The position was not one that everybody wanted; a Vice President always held second position, and many times he was never able to move beyond that in voters' minds. If he aligned himself with a President who failed in his role, then the Vice President was often considered to be as badly qualified. His chance of ever becoming President many times was lost.

Robert was not really concerned; he felt that he could win the election on his own merit and that he would just be bringing his running mate along for the ride. Harris had to admire Robert's faith in his abilities, and he would have considered it to be conceited on Robert's part except he was beginning to think Robert could actually do it.

Harris was amazed at Robert's ability to focus on so many things at once and never forget anything. Harris had lists that had lists and still he needed an assistant to help him manage everything. Robert was like a whirlwind that sweep through an area and left everything fresh and pristine. He lifted the spirits of all those around and inspired them to believe in the future. Harris laughed as his placed another call. He was beginning to believe his own hype.

Privately and after many long hours of debate and consultation, they had made their decision but waited until the convention to reveal their choice. The public loved a good story, so they played to the press, revealing little snippets of information as the days drew closer. Harris was pleased with their man.

They had hit every target. An astute businessman, who headed a successful cooperation with no overseas ties, a graduate of the Air Force Academy, a decorated soldier who had received the Distinguished Flying Cross for his valiant efforts in saving a group of Marines pinned down in battle, a veteran of the Vietnam War who had risen to the rank of full colonel, he was their man. Alexander Chambers was a conservative, family man with a wife of thirty-two years and two happily married children. He was solid; he was stable; he was respected. When he gave his word, people knew he would keep it. He had integrity, he was honest to a fault, and he wanted to serve his country. That was all Robert needed to hear. He knew that he couldn't find a better man. They were unbeatable. Robert refused to think otherwise, and no one dared to disagree.

Robert's acceptance speech, after the final roll call vote and his unanimous selection as the Democratic Party's candidate, was the best he had ever given. With a radiantly glowing Caroline at his side, he spoke passionately about his vision for the country and his desire to unite all parties to forge a path for the people of the United States to follow, one that encompassed all races, colors, and creeds, one that didn't distinguish between people based on gender, economic level, or education. His sincere desire to be a President of the people rang clear through his words and touched the hearts of the American public.

Raul listened to the speech and knew that Paul had been right. Billings might not be perfect, but he was definitely going to be hard to beat. Raul smiled. His plan was soon going to succeed beyond even his imaging, and now there was to be a child, Rafael's blood. Raul thought about that for a moment; it went without saying; he would be godfather, of course.

The campaign was grueling beyond belief. Weeks of passionate speeches, intense public forums, arduous debates, taxing late night talk shows, demanding interviews, and uncompromising critical reviews left everyone's nerves stretched like fine wires. Tempers flared at the least provocation, and sleep became a luxury no one could afford.

The Republican candidate was hopelessly outclassed, outmaneuvered, and outwitted. Even though he was a well-known member of Congress with an impressive Senatorial record and years of legislative experience, he came from old money, the privileged upper-class, a blue-blood Bostonian. Political cartoonists had a field day revering him as the old man on his way to the grave and Robert as the young man plowing ground for a new future, a future that swept the American public right along with it.

Robert fought a tough battle, but in the last hours of the election, he pulled the win from the Republican's grasp by taking Florida and Ohio. Other states fell like dominoes once the first major state conceded. Before the witching hour, Robert had secured the number of votes needed in the Electoral College to guarantee his win. The landslide popular vote in his favor added the bubbles to his champagne.

When their hopes were finally verified beyond any doubt, and Robert and his staff watched and listened as the Republican candidate conceded the election, Robert was ecstatic, and for one fleeting moment speechless. Standing at his side, Caroline laughed in satisfaction and relief. She had never seen him beyond words, and it was actually quite touching. She raised her hand to his face and turned him to face her.

He was shocked that all his dreams and hopes and all their hard work had really been successful. He had never doubted, but still he couldn't quite believe either. He cupped his hand over Caroline's and drew it to his lips. He held it tenderly and kissed it as he stared into her radiant blue eyes. For one brief moment, the spark of passion they had once shared flared between them.

Then the roar of the room intruded on them and it was lost. Robert became the newly elected President of the United States, and his time and life from that moment on was no longer his. He glanced back at Caroline as he was being drawn into the excited chaos of his staff and smiled a sad little smile that revealed regret that their lives had not turned out to be what they had hoped, that they seemed to be taking divergent paths, that they were no longer the fairytale couple. Then he shrugged, turned from her, and became the stranger once more that she shared her life with.

Caroline slipped from the room. She would be by his side for the final events of the evening, but now she needed time alone. Time to reconcile the feeling of loss that the brief moment they had shared had caused her. She felt depressingly sad, unsettled, everything but what she should be feeling on this momentous occasion.

Alberto nodded to Paul as he walked beside Caroline, letting him know that he would be with her. Robert was never concerned for her well-being. He was already engrossed in his success. Flanked by Alberto and a team of Secret Service agents, she left the campaign headquarters by a side entrance and returned to her hotel suite. She laid her head back on the car seat and slept until they reached the hotel. She was exhausted, beyond talking. Alberto followed her inside where La Senora was waiting. She helped Caroline quickly undress and climb into bed. She would think about everything tomorrow. She fell asleep almost instantly.

Alberto left as soon as Caroline was asleep. He wanted to keep an eye on Robert. Now that Robert was President, Alberto would have to relinquish some of his control to the Secret Service, but he could get around them any time he wanted. He already had plans in place.

Now that the election was over, it would have been nice if things could have settled down a little, but as Amanda Jeffery was quickly learning there was no rest connected with her job. Robert had asked her to stay on as Press Secretary for the White House. The short amount of time between the election and the inauguration didn't allow for rest. She needed to organize her staff and begin the daily task of presenting the news from around the world in a concise and thorough form to the President, organizing media events and press conferences, and disseminating the dozens of press briefs associated with any presidential activity.

Then there was the inauguration itself. The scope and magnitude of the event required countless hours of planning. Every time Robert stepped out in public, she had to be prepared with responses to questions and solutions to problems. She was the liaison between Robert, his staff, and the public. She was responsible for the public's view of Robert and any actions he took as President and as a husband and as a soon-to-be father. Amanda was a pro at *spin*. Just give her anything, and she could make something good out of it; at least she had always been able to in the past.

The staff's layover in Memphis was a Godsend to Amanda. She had hardly had time to talk to her parents since she had joined Robert's campaign staff. Now as the Presidential Press Secretary, she had even less. The staff was staying at the Peabody, so they had available conference space. Meetings throughout the day were a necessity; time off the clock was a luxury. Amanda was exalting in a few precious minutes of solitude. She had left the others finishing the final details for the day and was rushing across the lobby toward the elevators when she ran into a solid mass of muscle and bounced precariously back.

Strong hands steadied her as she struggled to gain her composure. Rarely did she falter in such a manner. She was used to tight situations and mass chaos. Press rooms were dens of confusion. But she was tired and hadn't really been paying attention. As the hands steadying her dropped from her arms, she glanced up into a pair of laughing brown eyes.

"I'm sorry. I didn't mean to mow you down like that." Laughter sparkled in the dark depths.

"No, it's my fault entirely. I really wasn't paying attention." Amanda smiled up at him. He wasn't bad looking, but she didn't have time for strangers. She glanced down at her watch.

"Excuse me. I really have to run."

He stepped aside and watched as her hurried to the elevators. Of course, he had recognized her. How could he fail to when she was constantly standing in front of a room full of television cameras? She seemed rather normal, not the sophisticated elitist he had expected. He would have thought a woman in her position would be more reserved. It was a pleasant surprise. As she pushed the elevator button for her floor, she glanced back in his direction. He was still standing there watching her; she smiled and he lifted his hand in farewell, a slight smile curving his lips. Somehow his day seemed a little brighter.

When Amanda stepped into the elevator much later that evening, she was surprised to see it already occupied. At this late hour, most patrons were already fast asleep even in a city as busy as Memphis. She smiled tiredly at the occupant and turned, reaching for the button to her floor.

"You look beat." It was said matter-of-factly. "Tough day?"

She glanced in his direction, "I'm afraid from now on they will all be not tough exactly, just long." She looked at her watch. Two in the morning didn't seem like the time to be talking to a stranger in an elevator. She almost asked him what he was doing up so late, and then thought better of it. That was the journalist in her, always asking impertinent questions.

She really didn't know if she should continue the conversation. She was usually so preoccupied with work that she didn't have time to converse with anyone, in an elevator or anywhere else. Her job dominated all of her waking thoughts, but she was finished for a few blissful hours, and she could join the human race again.

"I know that you're probably wondering if you should be talking to a strange man in an elevator this late at night, but I just wanted to congratulate you on the victory. It was a hard fought campaign. You did a good job of getting your position on the issues out there for the public to see. I admire that. So many times, all the voters get are vague promises and unreal expectations. The President seems as though he will really try to bring the change our country needs." She had turned to face him as he spoke, and she stood smiling up at him.

"Sorry. I don't usually speak my mind so openly." He actually felt rather embarrassed by his little speech. He was so accustomed to keeping his thoughts to himself that he was amazed at his actions.

"Your secret is safe with me. I'm off the clock and thanks. It's always nice to hear what others think. Too often people say what they think you want to hear. In my line of work, I need honesty." She put her hand out to him. "I'm Amanda Jeffery. It's nice to see you again."

He took her hand in his. "It's my pleasure. My name is Richards," he hesitated, "Tim Richards." For a moment he had reverted to his usual last name. In his line of work, last names kept everything all business, less personal.

The elevator dinged, signaling her floor. He glanced up at the red number. "Listen, I know it may sound crazy, but would you want to meet me for a drink tomorrow. We can stay in the hotel lounge, if you like."

"I would like to, but I don't know when I'll be free. Mine isn't the usual nine to five job," she laughed a light, carefree sound, "unless you mean five in the morning."

She looked steadily at him for a minute; he didn't flinch. He was used to being scrutinized by some real pros. He almost wanted to laugh as she tried to decide if he could be trusted. He gave her all the time she needed to make up her mind. He really wanted to see her again and preferable not in an elevator, well not in one that had a security camera at least.

"Why don't you give me your number, and if I can get away, I'll give you a call?" That was a pretty good maneuver. She could check him out before she committed to anything. Smart move, smart girl. He liked her more by the minute.

"That sounds good." He pulled a card from his pocket and wrote out the number. "I'll wait to hear from you." The elevator door began to close, and he put out his hand to stop it. "Have a good night." She smiled at him and stepped into the hallway.

She glanced back as the doors moved to close, "You too."

How did she feel about him? Did she have time for a friendship that was destined to be short-lived? She was leaving for Washington in a few days. What then? She unlocked her door; she was too tired to think tonight. Tomorrow, she would find out what she could then decide.

Tim laughed as the elevator doors closed. He could see her mind working. The first thing she would do when she had time would be to check him out. She wouldn't find anything, but that still might not be enough to get her to call. He would just have to make a contingency plan. He hadn't felt this way about anybody in a long time; he was determined to see her again.

The next morning started off in a flurry of activity. Amanda rushed from one meeting to the next. She barely had time to check her email let alone make a request of the Secret Service. She smiled; then she took a sip of her lukewarm coffee and wrinkled her nose. She had a sad feeling that she might soon grow accustomed to cold coffee, but at least the job had a few perks. Her request had been expedited rather quickly and without the backlog of paperwork that usually accompanied any such favor. She was impressed by the information she had been given. Even though she had to make sure, she had already decided that he could be trusted.

After a brief rap on the closed door, her assistant stuck her head in. "Amanda, there's a man in the outer office who says that you have to sign for a delivery personally. What do you want me to tell him?" She had a knowing little smile on her face as she peered at Amanda.

Amanda frowned. She hadn't placed any order, and why couldn't someone else sign for it? She had better things to do. She was tired and ready to leave for the day. "I'll take care of it," she sighed. "I'm leaving now anyway. See you tomorrow—early. Just give me a minute."

Her assistant laughed, "Sure thing," then raised one eyebrow suggestively, a smug little grin patently obvious, as she closed the door.

What was going on? Emily was acting crazy, but Amanda was just too tired to care.

She cleared her desk, grabbed her jacket, and opened her office door. She took one step into the outer office and froze. There stood Tim, leaning nonchalantly against a desk. She hadn't called; she hadn't had time all day. She tried to smile; a half-hearted effort was all she could manage. He was determined; she had to give him credit for that. She headed across the room.

He held up a hand as she approached him. "I know, you were supposed to call, but I figured you wouldn't have time. So, how about a quick drink, before you call it a night? I promise not to keep you long." He gave her his best smile, one guaranteed to get results.

Amanda grinned up at him. He was so obvious, but she had to give him credit for not giving up. Most men would have written her off without a second thought. "All right, but just one," she emphasized the number.

"It's a deal." Taking her arm, he guided her toward the door. As they stepped into the waiting elevator, he couldn't resist asking, "Okay, how did I check out?"

She moved away from him and looked him directly in the eyes. "Just how do you know I did that?" She seemed a little affronted by his question. He frowned. Maybe he was wrong.

"If I were you, I would. You work for the President now. You can't afford to take chances. I could be anybody trying to find out information or a way to get close to the President. It seemed logical to me. I didn't mean to offend you, though." He shrugged.

She studied him for a few seconds. He was almost too good to be true. Most men would be angry if they found out that she had had the Secret Service run a check on them. He was right. She couldn't afford any mistakes in her line of work; more than her job depended on who she let in her life now.

"You're right, of course. I guess it surprised me that you would understand; most men don't."

"If they don't have anything to hide, why would they mind?"

"I don't know, but the next time someone does, I'll ask."

They entered the lounge and sat in a booth, slightly removed from the others. They could easily see who entered and who sat nearby. Privacy wasn't essential, but Tim could tell she didn't want anyone to overhear their conversation. He didn't mind; he liked that about her; he was a private person too. They ordered drinks and sat discussing the election, her job, and their families. Then gradually the conversation shifted to more personal things and before she realized, the time had flown by, and they had been there over an hour.

Amanda was amazed, and for the first time in weeks, she had actually relaxed and enjoyed the evening. She hadn't tried to impress Tim, and she didn't try to watch every word she spoke. Amanda looked at Tim and without thinking of the consequences, she spoke from her heart.

"I can't remember when I have had a better evening."

Tim laughed, "What was in your drink?" He tipped her empty glass toward him and peered inside.

Before he could continue, she added, "I'm serious. This has been wonderful. I feel like I already know you." She smiled so sweetly that Tim felt a moment of regret. She didn't really know him, and he couldn't tell her anything about his life, not yet. It wouldn't be safe for either of them, but soon.

Tim reached across the table and took her hand in his. "I know what you mean."

She sighed then squeezed his hand. "You know that I have to leave for Washington in two days. After that my time will not be my own for months. The first major hurtle will be the inauguration; then there will be decisions about cabinet posts, appointments, staffing, the list goes on and on. The press is involved with all of these plus the President's daily activities; it can be mind boggling." He squeezed her fingers and began lazily drawing circles on the back of her hand with his thumb.

"Hey, don't worry. I'm a patient guy. I don't mind waiting until you have some free time. I knew who you were the moment I saw you. I didn't have to stake out that elevator for half the night just to see you again." Her eyes flew to his. "Don't be so shocked. I told the Secret Service guys beforehand. I didn't want to get taken down for stalking you." He laughed at her stunned expression. "Hasn't anyone ever told you that you are definitely worth waiting for?"

She thought for a minute and shook her head. "No, I can honestly say no one ever has." She grinned at him. He had to be crazy. Who did anything like that these days? But she had to admit, she was impressed. Then she really laughed; she knew enough about him already to know that was just what he wanted her to be. For once her weird sixth sense wasn't warning her to steer clear, for once she felt good about a man. She just prayed that she wasn't fooling herself. Time would tell because this was not going to be a close friendship. He would remain in Memphis, and she was headed for Washington.

"I really have to go. I have to be up early, and I hate being late." She was thinking about her coworkers and that little smirk she had seen on Emily's face. She would have some explaining to do if she planned to get anything done tomorrow. Emily was tenacious if nothing else; the staff hadn't secretly nicknamed her "Bulldog" without good reason.

They exchanged email addresses and private telephone numbers. Tim was risking a lot by giving her his. He would have to keep the same number, or she might get suspicious. He would just have to be careful. He already knew before the evening was over that she would be worth any investment he made, even his life.

The kiss they shared at her door was more sweet than romantic, but somehow it felt right. He didn't want to rush her, and she appreciated his reserve. It only made her like him more, but she was beginning to realize, she wouldn't need any extra help liking him.

For the first time in years, Tim sauntered back to his room, whistling. He didn't care who heard him. He wasn't trying to hide or slip by unseen; he was a free man for a little while, and he was in love. It struck him as absurd that after only a couple of days, he could know for sure how he felt about Amanda, but it was true, and there was no denying it. Somehow it just felt right, and as he thought about his sister, he hoped that she would have been happy for him.

The days leading to the Presidential Inauguration were filled with activity. Plans had to be coordinated so that the President and First Lady could attend as many of the celebratory balls given that night after the swearing-in ceremony as possible. Amanda knew that Caroline wouldn't be able to attend every one with Robert. She had been looking extremely tired for several days. Even under the carefully applied makeup, the dark smudges around her eyes could still be seen. No one expected her to be there for all of them, but Amanda was trying to work out a schedule that would allow them to attend most of them together.

Amanda knew that the President would be happy to attend without Caroline, but she was trying to forestall any such obvious plan because she didn't want any rumors starting this early about their marriage. Amanda still had an uncomfortable feeling whenever she was around them. Sometimes she felt it interfered with her work, but it was her job to foresee problems and prevent them from happening. She was already working on a strategy for this possible problem. If nothing ever happened, she could always scrap it, but if it did, she would be prepared. An ounce of caution and all that stuff, her grandmother would say.

Late at night or rather early in the morning when Amanda was finished for the day, she would text Tim, most often just a brief note saying that she was home and going to bed. On rare occasions she was able to talk to him on the phone, but those were precious moments and much too few. She had made arrangements for Tim to accompany her to the inauguration balls. She had reserved a suite at an elegant hotel in the city. Her apartment was on the outskirts and would be too difficult to reach with Washington's streets gridlocked with traffic for this special event. She would meet Tim at the hotel, where she would change, and together they would make the round of the evening's special celebrations. Of course, her schedule would match the President's; she would need to see to it that nothing unexpected happened and that he and the First Lady were seen in the very best light. Amanda didn't want anything to diminish the couples' celebration of Robert's long, hard-fought battle to victory.

Amanda had even arranged for a backup plan in case the First Lady was taken ill. She had gone so far as to place nearby hospitals on standby, just as a precaution, and they were more than happy to accommodate her wishes. The public seemed to identify with Caroline and looked forward to the birth almost as much as Caroline herself. A baby in the White House was exciting news, and Amanda had already been inundated with gifts sent to the expecting couple from all across the States. She could only imagine the chaos that would surround the birth.

As the evening of the inauguration came to a close in the early morning hours, Robert and Caroline had attended almost all of the balls on Amanda's list. Those few remaining ones were informed that the First Lady had been forced to halt the evening a little earlier than previously planned. In fact they had made appearances at all of the most important party celebrations, and those of key political figures as well as several lesser ones. Robert was flying so high on success that he could have had gone on all night and the next day too, but Amanda discretely reminded him that his public would expect him to accompany his wife back to the Presidential residence. His first concern had to appear to be for her and the baby's welfare.

Robert would have objected, but he could just see the headlines on his first official morning in office. "President abandons pregnant wife to party all night!" He wasn't that stupid. He knew that there would be plenty of opportunities for the press to grill him over the next few months. He didn't want to give them the advantage this early. Besides, they had been to the most socially elite balls and the most politically advantageous for him.

After helping Caroline into their waiting car, he settled back in the seat and thought about the day's events. Everything had gone so well. He was pleased. Caroline had looked beautiful. He glanced at her as she sat with her head back against the leather seat, her eyes closed. He was proud of her, but even he could tell the day had taken its toll. She looked exhausted now that they didn't have to pose for anyone, now that they could let their guard down for a moment. Their life together would never be the same after today. He wasn't sure how they would deal with it, but he was determined to keep their private life private. He sighed. They would have to talk and soon. The baby was due in a few weeks. That had to resolve their differences and discuss their future, but not tonight. Tonight he wanted nothing but happy memories and good thoughts for them both. Besides, he wanted to be up early his first day in the White House.

He might as well start out the way he meant to continue. He wanted to leave a legacy of determination and hard work. He wanted his tenure in office to be remembered by all for the things he accomplished, the goals he meet, the promises he kept, and the changes he made. When he finally reached his bed, Robert went to sleep a very happy man. Caroline just went to sleep.

Amanda and Tim had followed behind the Presidential couple throughout the evening. Amanda was so beautiful to Tim that he had trouble keeping his eyes off of her. She might be spending the evening dancing and dining with Washington's most impressive people, but she still had a job to do, she still had to make sure that everything went as scheduled.

Tim was relieved when the First Lady finally had to call a halt to the celebration. She suggested that the President continue without her, but Amanda quietly stepped in and advised him to reconsider. He didn't really want that image plastered across America's newspapers the next day. Tim realized that Billings had had to think about it before he agreed with her.

Tim was beginning to see a very different side to Billings' personality; he wasn't sure that he liked it, but he didn't say anything to Amanda. Billings was her boss, and he knew Amanda well enough to know she would be loyal to Billings and wouldn't appreciate his opinions, at least not yet. He could be wrong, but he doubted it. Men in power were almost always the same.

Tim was just glad that the evening was over and that he could spend a few minutes with Amanda without having to share her attention with someone else. She had thanked him for being so understanding, for letting her do her job, and for not making her feel any guiltier that she already did.

Amanda felt she was being selfish by asking him to accompany her; she had a handsome escort, and she didn't have to worry about drawing undue attention to herself. To be honest, he made her feel protected. She liked that feeling, not that she had ever been frightened while she lived in the city—cautious, definitely, careful, assuredly—but afraid, never. Still, it was reassuring to have a strong arm to lean on. She glanced in Tim's direction. He definitely had strong arms and a sexy smile. She smiled in return and took his arm in hers.

Together they left for their hotel suite. It was the early morning hours, but for once she didn't have any responsibilities. After tonight, she would be free for the next three days. She quickly wrote press releases as their car crawled through the heavy traffic and emailed them to her office. Her assistant had already been briefed. Photos of the inauguration, the

Presidential couple, and the evening's galas had already been uploaded to Amanda's computer and phone. She had screened and selected the White House's official photo documentation of the great event and those had been made available to the press services.

Of course, free was a relative term. She wouldn't be in her office unless some official crisis arose, but she would be in contact with those she left in charge. Everything still had to be scrutinized and approved by her. After all, it was her responsibility to prepare all of the official press releases from the White House and to preserve the President's good image in the media.

No one in the city slept; the streets were crowded even at this hour. A feeling of excitement still clung to the early morning mists, which swirled through the air. Amanda felt the tension of the evening slip from her as she finally sent her last text and closed her phone.

She let her head fall back against the plush leather seat as they finally reached their destination and wondered if Tim was hungry. Suddenly, she was starved. She hadn't had an opportunity to eat much during the evening, and now she was ravenous. Would he think it was too unladylike to mention food? Did he prefer the picky little salad eaters or the meat and potato girls? At this moment, she didn't really care; he would have to take her as she was or not at all.

"Okay, we finally made it. Thanks for letting me get the work out of the way. Now I can relax and enjoy the last few minutes of this evening."

"No problem. I enjoyed watching you work. You're really good at your job. I liked the way you slanted those comments made by the President to give him just the right amount of concern for the issue. I didn't realize how informed you had to be to handle this position. I'm impressed." He had stepped from the car and reached back for her hand. As she stood beside him, she looked directly into those gorgeous brown eyes. Was he being sincere? She hated flattery. She opted for sincerity and the benefit of the doubt. She would trust her instincts and him. She gave him a broad smile.

"Thanks, but all this work has made me hungry. How about an extra-large pizza with everything? My treat—we can order in and at least have a little time to talk. We haven't been able to do much of that tonight."

He smiled back, "Food, I should have known. I thought that was the way to a man's heart."

"Haven't you heard of equal rights? None of this sexist rhetoric. Food right now would thrill my little heart." Laughing at his supposedly shocked expression, she grabbed his hand and headed through the hotel lobby. Room service better be quick. She had a few other things on her mind besides food.

He followed her gladly. She had been so serious most of the night that it thrilled him to see her relaxed and having fun. He would give anything to be able to spend the rest of his life making her smile, but he knew that would have to be much later. He had things to complete before he could really be free to ask someone else to share his life. He let her pull him along behind her. He didn't plan to waste any time wrapping up his other life. He was ready to start a new life one that he hoped included Amanda.

He pulled against her, and she turned and smiled at him. He loved her smile, sexy and sweet, innocent and alluring—contrasts that described her completely. He laughed as she hauled him into the elevator. He was hungry too; the little smirk that twitched his lips revealed that food might not be the sustenance he sought. He glanced at the elevator camera and rolled his eyes; Amanda giggled at his absurd expression. He felt like a kid again. He hadn't felt this way in such a long time that it almost scared him. Every time things went too well in life, there was always disaster waiting just around the corner. He prayed this time would be different.

Holding hands like teenagers, they fled the empty elevator and raced to their suite, laughing at nothing and everything. As they reached the door, Tim pulled her into his arms and kissed her soundly. Rather breathless from laughing, Amanda wasn't quite prepared for his unexpected action. She melted into his arms and clung to him as he deepened the kiss, pressing her against the door of their suite.

He released her rather suddenly. "Sorry. I couldn't wait another minute. I've wanted to do that all night." With a slightly trembling hand, he pushed the hair back from his forehead and reached around her to open the door. He wasn't used to revealing his feelings. He laughed and glanced down the corridor to the discretely placed camera. Oh well. He wouldn't take it back even if he could. Cameras, be damned!

Once inside, Amanda began dropping articles of clothing as she walked to her bedroom, first one shoe, then another, her wrap trailed behind her for a moment and slipped to the floor. When she glanced back over her shoulder, she smiled that bewitching little smile that filled him with a slow burn; then she eased one strap of her evening gown slowly off her shoulder. Tim didn't wait to see just how far this little demonstration was going. He reached for her, turned her to face him, and pulled her in his arms as he covered her smiling lips with his. She made him forget himself, forget everything. He could lose himself in her arms and die a happy man, but life was never that simple.

Their time together was limited. They understood that, but understanding didn't make it easier. The morning sunlight slipped around the edges of the blinds as he watched her sleep. They had spent the last few hours of morning indulging in some of his nicer fantasies. She had made him forget the horror of the last few years; she left him cleansed of the pain and suffering he had witnessed. She made him feel reborn, ready to start a new life, a new life with her.

Hours before they had first indulged in more amorous pursuits then finally took time to indulge in the food. Between bites of hot, gooey pizza and sips of Amanda's favorite red wine, they planned a brief excursion to the coast. Tim had friends with a condo in Hilton Head, and in no time they had made arrangements. With no set time to leave, Tim let her sleep for a while longer. He liked the feel of her in his arms, the soft silkiness of her skin, the subtle fragrance of her hair, the warmth of her body against his. Yes, it was definitely time to wake her or their morning would be spent in bed and not on the road to their vacation spot.

Chapter 16

JOE MORALES WAS A heavy set man of Latino origins, but as solid as a brick wall and as patriotic as George Washington. He was one of the elite forces of men chosen to protect the President of the United States. It was deemed an honor to serve in this capacity. Morales understood this and served the President with integrity and loyalty. He would give his life, if need be, to protect and to defend. If asked, he would swear on his life that these ideals were standards by which he lived and carried out his duties, and he would be right.

His parents had brought him up to set his goals high and to always seek to achieve them. Their pride in him was a tangible element that filled their simple lives with pleasure and joy. He had achieved a position in the government of the country they had chosen to call home.

It was beyond their thinking that a black mark should ever be found against their son. It was beyond his thinking that he would ever fail in his duties in such a way that he would receive such a disgraceful stain on his reputation.

In a perfect world, integrity and honor are easy to achieve and maintain. In the real world, deception and disillusionment often break the strongest will. Against Raul and the power of his cartel, Joe Morales was helpless. Before he even knew, he had forfeited his life and was indebted to the enemy. Raul's takeover was insidious, creeping in when Morales was unaware, establishing a foothold in his life before he even realized.

Through his contacts within the government, Raul had easily found the weak link he needed in the Secret Service forces. Out of necessity

Morales had begun working extra hours to help provide for his parents. His father's long fight against cancer and his extensive treatment and hospitalization had resulted in astronomical medical bills. Morales felt honor bound to ease their burden and had assumed the debts as his own. He had quickly used all of his savings helping them survive until his father could return to work part time, but even then Morales was left with a staggering burden.

When Raul had discovered Morales' dilemma, he used a third party source, a bogus charity, and paid off the debts and had them instruct Morales that a philanthropic benefactor had chosen him to receive this special gift and wanted nothing in return. To have such a weight lifted was more than Morales could ever hope to receive, and he readily accepted the charity's money and explanation. Being an honorable man, Morales failed to consider that anything might be inappropriate about the gift or its source. To him, it was an answered prayer, and he was able to sleep well for the first time in months.

To Raul, it was an investment in the future. He was extremely pleased.

Soft music playing in the background, slow strolls hand in hand along the beach, sultry breezes blowing off the warm waters, all led to a memorable three days. Tim couldn't have asked for more. Lazy mornings and passionate evenings, he was revived and resolute. He had confessed everything about his life, Judy's death, and the job he still had to do. He wanted a fresh start with Amanda, but he wanted her to know what his life had been like before her.

He had to admit, she always surprised him. She sat quietly watching him as he told her about his past. She didn't interrupt; she just let him ramble until he felt there was nothing left to say.

He had told no one about his life before. A few friends knew some of it, but not all. He told Amanda everything. He didn't want something to blindside them later. He wanted a clean slate, a fresh start, and all the other crazy clichés that he could think of. But most of all, he wanted Amanda, heart and soul, and that was what he was trying to give her, a glimpse into his soul. Without her to fill the emptiness, the dark void, he would be nothing, have nothing. Without her, he would have no future; he would be just another lost soul aimlessly wandering the Earth. Tim was so sure of that fact, that it actually scared him, and nothing ever scared him.

Amanda watched as he forced himself to talk about a life filled with death, destruction, and loss. Working under cover, hiding out, slipping through life, yet never a part of it, had taken a toll on him. Amanda could see the pain etched in the lines of his face, the sacrifice hidden in the depths of his eyes, the integrity buried deep within his soul. He was a man who had chosen to forfeit his life in order to help others, others who often didn't even want to be helped. He had persevered, but he had suffered for it. She could tell he was worried that what he revealed would change her feelings for him, but his life had shaped the man he was, the man she loved.

She watched him for a moment after he stopped talking. How had he been able to give up so much? She stood and walked over to where he sat. He didn't look at her. She smiled, grasped his chin firmly in her hand, and turned him to face her.

"I hope you didn't think I would let you out of this relationship that easily." She kissed him softly, molding his face with her hands. Then she straightened. Her eyes filled with compassion and understanding.

"Finish your job. Do what you have to. Then come back to me. I'll be waiting, however long it takes. We will start from there." She eased into his arms and sat on his lap, covering his face with kisses until he took possession of her lips, firing her blood with a burning passion that only he could quench.

As he lifted her in his arms and walked toward the bedroom, she whispered softly in his ear. "I'll always be waiting." They never made their dinner reservation.

When Tim returned to Memphis, he was determined to find Judy's killer and finish his undercover work as quickly as he could. Graham laughed when he saw him. "What's her name?"

"I don't know what you mean." He tried to play innocent, not reveal anything, but Graham only laughed harder. Tim realized just how difficult his job had now become. Never before had he had any problem remaining emotionless. That was what had kept him safe on the streets.

"Okay, I get it. It's none of my business. So we'll just get to mine. I have some new information about a couple of places that it might pay us to check out. Get with Strong; he has the details. See what you think. I'd like to clean out the southwest, at least. The market has already improved, but I want a better share." He was shuffling papers on his desk as he spoke.

"All right, but I need a little time when we go through the South. I want to check out something for a friend. I won't let it interfere with our plans." He didn't like to ask, but if Strong was with him, he would need to make different arrangements.

Something kept nagging him; something he had missed. It lay just beyond his grasp, and it was driving him crazy. He had to get back to Little Rock. The numbers he had been given were etched in his memory. Somehow they were connected to Judy's death; he was certain.

Graham looked up. He studied Richards for a minute before he answered. He had changed. Something was different. He would bet it was a woman. He nodded his head knowingly, "I don't see a problem. I'm more than satisfied with the results of our little campaign so far; take all the time you need. Just let Strong know how to reach you."

Strong was eyeing a leggy brunette who sat across the bar. He swirled his drink in time to the music, trying to act nonchalant. It wasn't working. Sweat beaded his brow, and he kept glancing at the door. He didn't like meeting here. All these Latino types made him uneasy. He jumped when a heavy hand fell on his shoulder.

"Follow me." The voice behind him didn't sound inviting, but Strong had no choice. He had risked everything when he hooked up with this bunch of boys. The payoff was worth the risk only if Graham didn't find out. When they had first approached him, Strong had been impressed. It was a daring plan, but the upfront money had been the clincher. Strong had run up a sizeable gambling debt. Graham didn't know anything about it, but somehow these boys had. They had offered to clear his debts and include a bonus if he would arrange for their rivals to be taken out of business.

Strong couldn't help but smile as he followed the man to a back room. He was getting paid twice to do the same job. His mercenary little heart skipped a beat at the mere thought of what he had done. Richards thought he was a fool, but he planned to show him just what he could do. Before this was over, he intended to get these boys to take care of Richards. They weren't like the inept bumblers Graham had on his payroll. Strong would give a cut of his money just to see Richards taken down. A smug smile cloaked Strong's face until he entered the well-lit back room, and his bravado failed.

Anxiously, Strong glanced around. This wasn't the stereotypical clandestine meeting. No bulging jackets, no whiskey filled glasses, no cigar smoke, just a room full of businessmen, but sweat was pouring down the sides of his face, his knees were weak, and he felt sick because he knew what type of business these men were in. They carried with them the aura of death.

Strong took the proffered seat, relieved that his knees had held. He slipped a handkerchief from his pocket and mopped at his sweating brow. The man in charge gave Strong a moment to compose himself. He disliked men who allowed their weakness to show, but he had a mission to carry out. Strong's compliance would make his job easier, so he would disregard his failings. He signaled for one of the men to bring Strong a drink and waited until he had taken a swallow before he began. He wanted to be sure that Strong completely understood what was expected of him. He didn't want any problems.

Robert's first weeks in office were hectic. The transition from one President to another went smoothly with Robert patiently listening to the former President's words of advice. But each minute afterward was filled with decisions. Paul stood at Robert's side; his expertise in governmental affairs was essential to safeguarding Robert's role. Paul wanted no blunders at this juncture. With Robert's personal staff in place, cabinet posts became the first priority. Vince Harris and Amanda Jeffery worked all the angles on the proposed candidates for each position. Then Paul researched each one himself with the help of governmental data bases. In addition, he had Raul run checks on each. His files would turn up any discrepancies that might be missed by governmental sources.

Concessions had to be made for campaign promises, but at least with the Attorney General's post, Robert felt sure they couldn't find a better qualified person than Margaret Franklin. Her legal expertise was legendary. When the memory of their interlude flitted across his mind, Robert smiled. Paul looked at him questioningly, but refrained from comment.

After much consideration and discussion, Robert's cabinet was in place and his staff assembled. Daily activities became regulated and interruptions were handled in an orderly fashion. The office of the President could never become routine, but Robert felt that they had an understanding of the procedures now and some order was established.

Amanda established an excellent rapport between the White House and the press. She kept them apprised of anything that was newsworthy and everything important for the public to know. She included a daily briefing on the First Lady and her limited activities as she prepared for the birth of her child. Office pools became a pastime activity all across the nation as friendly wagers on the baby's date of birth, weight, sex, and even possible names were placed. Even the White House staff had one. America was caught up in the idea of having a baby in the White House.

The public's approval rating of the President in his first few weeks in office was high, but the rating for the First Couple was even higher. America was engrossed in the idea of the First Couple living the American dream, America's version of Camelot.

In private, Caroline just wanted the baby to arrive safely and soon. She couldn't rest and she couldn't do anything. She was irritable and short-tempered, especially with Robert. In public, she gritted her teeth and played her role to perfection, the soon-to-be mother with an adoring husband and a perfect life.

Robert, too, played for the cameras and the press. He used every opportunity to mention the baby, Caroline's plans, anything that he thought would gain him good press and public support. His tenure in office so far had been uneventful. But the numerous campaign promises he had made began to haunt him.

It was left to Paul to sort out the problems and find amicable solutions. Raul's personal files became a vital asset. Some of the older, resolute, party members were adamant about the positions they felt were due them. Alberto quietly insured their cooperation. A visit from a family member, a photocopied file, a video recording, any of these would bring about the desired results and the involved party would quietly accept any post or position the White House felt he deserved. Political figures were all the same; they would do anything to stay in power, to remain in office, or to gain in position. They were, for the most part, a self-serving and avaricious breed. These characteristics allowed Paul to manipulate them and the decisions they made.

Late one cold winter night in February, Caroline delivered Robert Billings, II. Soon nicknamed Robbie by the press, he was hailed as the President's greatest personal achievement to date. Minute by minute updates were given on the internet and scrolled across the bottom of every television channel. Videos of the loving couple adoring their newborn son were broadcast over the airways and photos showing the proud parents were splashed across the front page of every newspaper. Robbie was an instant hit.

Caroline wanted to scream. She didn't want Robert taking credit for anything connected to her or her baby. Paul quietly reminded her of the grander scheme, but the large diamond and emerald necklace Alberto brought to her and the personal note she received from Rafael sealed her silence. To anyone who might have noticed, she brushed her moodiness aside and passed it off as an imbalance in hormones and acted the loving wife and devoted mother.

Robert, holding his son, posed and preened for the cameras. He was in his element; he could have continued for hours, but Robbie had other ideas. When he began fussing loudly, Robert quickly relinquished him to his mother. At that point, Paul adroitly removed the news personnel from the hospital suite and promised them that Amanda would hold a press conference shortly to supply all the relevant details and answer any questions they might have.

Although the rooms were packed with exotic plants, with exotic plants arrangements, and innumerable plush animals, it was a somber and moody group Amanda encountered when she walked into the First Lady's hospital suite. A private nurse was busily tending the baby, Caroline was lying with her eyes closed looking pale and drawn, Robert was busily studying a brief for a later meeting, Paul was talking quietly on his phone, and the tension in the room was so strong that you could actually feel it. This wasn't the picture that the world saw. This was the reality.

She signaled Paul so she wouldn't disturb Caroline or the baby and walked into the adjacent room. She could only hope that the tension was the result of stress and anxiety from the baby's delivery. Now that both mother and baby were resting peacefully, she could only pray that in the future joy and happiness would fill their lives.

Then Amanda looked back at Robert. Somehow she doubted that would be the case.

With the birth of his son safely behind him and his cabinet posts filled, Robert began work first on his economic reforms. Paul, as his chief of staff, arranged for meeting with heads of the labor unions and economic advisors. Robert wanted to create an economic incentive that would aid present programs and expand business growth. He wanted better job security for America's work force and was promoting the idea of build-here stay-here for big businesses. He was shopping for support for a big business makeover. He wanted to encourage the growth of businesses here and promote the idea of keeping the production and manufacture of products in the U.S., thereby, insuring a growing job market for American citizens.

He wanted to call an economic summit to meet with the heads of all the major businesses, which now shipped their jobs overseas. He wanted to find a solution to the loss of jobs and encourage fueling the economy by returning American jobs to American soil. Robert had mentioned the idea of an American led trade embargo against its own companies.

Paul reminded him that many of his own party had overseas connections and had made significant campaign contributions and would not be pleased with even the hint of such a plan by the man they had helped elect. Robert realized that, of course, but he still wanted something that would create shock value, something that would capture the heart of the people.

It was a gutsy idea; no one had ever said Robert didn't have nerve. Paul considered it unrealistic, but it would certainly garner him good press if it leaked out, and it would push the problem of the ailing economy square in the laps of the Republican-lead business moguls.

When Robert realized that the summit he wanted to attend was to be held in California, he decided that he had better work on another campaign issue he had promised to address. Gay Rights was a hot topic, but there was never a good time to bring it before Congress. Robert had no feeling one way or the other, but he knew that much of his West Coast donations had been tied to his promise to work for equal rights for gays. The recognition of marriage between gays was the issue which gay rights advocates were determined to pursue.

He met with his staff and asked them to gather the necessary materials he would need to study in order to present his idea to Congress. He wanted to be able to tie the issue to something else in hopes that he could get the measure passed.

When he made his plans known to several key congressional figures, they dismissed the idea flat. They had fought against the Christian Coalition for years and knew they didn't have the votes to pass any measure without their support, and they were adamantly against any such proposal. After days of meetings and discussions with key congressional figures, Robert felt that he had fulfilled his promise by having tried to get the measure passed and turned his attention to other matters. With that issue settled, Robert felt ready to tackle his next project.

Paul knew Robert needed an issue that would bring him notice in the press and grasp the public's attention. He had the perfect plan. Most of the issues brought before the President were doomed from the first, but Paul recognized an opportunity when he saw it. Now was the perfect time to draw attention to the problem of drugs. States were struggling to find funding to fight drug production and distribution, especially chemically produced drugs like meth.

With a little encouragement and direction from Paul, Robert focused his attention on the anti-drug effort and creation of a special task force in the Drug Enforcement Agency to oversee the problem of meth production and the illegal sale of prescription drugs. Amanda and her team were scrambling to find all of the relevant material on the problem and present it to Robert. With his ability to read, remember, and disseminate, he was always pressing for more facts. Amanda was amazed at the sheer amount of information he could instantly recall.

Working for him was a daily challenge, and Amanda gained new respect for his ability as President, though she reserved judgment on his qualities as a husband. Whenever he was around his wife and child, he seemed absent-minded and unfeeling, unless the press or others, outside his inner circle, were present. Then he came to life and assumed the persona of the loving husband and devoted father.

Amanda could tell that Caroline resented his behavior more and more, although the men probably never noticed. She began running various scenarios through her mind to explain his attitude in case anyone else were to notice and ask questions. Maybe it was the reporter in her that made her see the little things that didn't quite fit the picture. Maybe it was her overactive imagination. Maybe, but she doubted it.

When Robert felt he had a clear picture of the drug problem across the States, he authorized Paul to contact the DEA. Their role was to first create a plan of action and report back to the President. From there, he and Paul would determine their next course of action.

With information from Strong's contacts, Richards and he were able to make a sweep of several large cities. Using some of Graham's own men to lure dealers into their traps, they were able to cripple the dealers and distributors in cocaine and seriously interrupt flow of powder into the South West. At the same time, coca flowing into the United States from the Gulf States diminished, seriously limiting the availability of powder on the streets. The result was that buyers and dealers searched for alternatives, and customers experimented with the cheaper substitute, meth.

Graham was ecstatic. His business was booming, and his profits soared. Richards seized the opportunity and asked for an indefinite leave with the possibility of not returning to work for Graham. Graham was so pleased with the results of their operation that he willing allowed Richards to leave and even gave him a large bonus for exceeding even his expectations. Strong was irritated that Graham would let him leave and warned that Richards could be a liability to them. Graham only laughed and asked how he could be when Richards was responsible for most of their results. Strong wasn't as easily convinced, but he remained silent and vowed to talk to his own contacts.

Richards left without looking back, taking Graham's money gladly. He had earned every penny. He laughed as he left the building, for the last time he hoped. He had enough information on Graham's operation to close it down permanently. Graham and Strong might have influence with a lot of people, and Graham had a legion of people in power on his payroll, but Richards had enough on all of them now to derail any assistance they might try to give Graham. Names, dates, places, amounts, Richards had it all. Over four years of his life and the lost of his sister was a high price to pay, but he felt good about being able to close Graham down at last.

When Richards was at last free to rejoin his own force, he felt isolated from the men. He had been undercover so long that he had no bond with anyone. After weeks of debriefing and hours spent writing detailed reports, Richards was at last ready to return to a normal job. He was considering asking for a transfer so he could start fresh somewhere else with no memories, no ties, and no regrets when he was approached by the Chief of Police and asked to meet with special agents from the DEA. Richards was skeptical about what their reason might be for asking to see him, but he went along just the same.

He had seriously considered asking for a desk job, but he hadn't wanted to until he knew how things were going to work out. When the special agent in charge of the meeting noted what a distinguished career he had had and how grateful they were for his undercover work and all that he had accomplished, Richards began to frown. He knew that a build up like this was going to lead to a request, and he wasn't sure that he would want to comply. He had more to consider that he had five years ago. He had sacrificed enough of his life. Now he wanted to start living.

He was just about to hold up his hand to stop the agent, when he finally made his plan clear. The DEA wanted him to oversee a special branch, an office dedicated to the meth problem, and since Richards knew firsthand about the distribution and sell of meth, he was the perfect man for the job. If he agreed to head the office, he would need to prepare and present a plan for the DEA to approve. The agent emphasized that this directive came from the President and that whatever Richards needed to implement his plan would be provided.

Richards was stunned. This was almost too good. He would have his own men and develop his own strategy. With adequate funding, maybe they could make a difference in the meth trade. As he considered the possibilities, Richards felt a thrill of excitement. He readily agreed that he would undertake the assignment and stood to shake hands with the agents as they prepared to leave. He would begin tomorrow. Now he could finally have a life.

Richards arrived early the next day at the office set aside for him and his team. His first order of business was to request the manpower he needed. He petitioned each state's field office to provide one agent to work with his team and to be the liaison between the state and his task force. He didn't want any power struggles or adolescent glory hounds to foil their operation. After placing several calls, Richards had his own personal squad, men that he knew he could trust, who knew the streets, who he could count on if things went wrong, men he had worked with before. They were few in number, but great in experience. Several of them had trained and served with Richards in the Special Forces. Released from their other duties, they began arriving later that day. With his team in place and with their expertise, Richards began developing a plan, operation "Slam Shut."

Their first objective was to establish a centralized information center in the DEA. All pertinent information would be channeled through this center along with any new intelligence as it became available. Richards wanted a select team of experts to work fulltime compiling the data and projecting possible avenues of attack. Richards requested a presidential directive be issued to all local, state, and federal agencies requiring them to forward all information they had available to the center and to give their complete cooperation to Richards' special task force. With DEA approval and the President's sanction, Richards' team began operation. He warned everyone that this would not be a simple or easy task, nor would it be accomplished quickly. But with perseverance and determination, he felt that they could and would make a difference. Operation "Slam Shut" was underway.

Robert was making a personal appearance at the Labor Union Convention in California. Strong supporters of Robert's presidency, they expected a return on their money. They wanted his support for legislation in Congress, which would allow them to form unions in any company. Robert was set to disappoint them, although he would do his best to appease them first. To gain such legislation, he felt they needed a bargaining chip. It was his contention that if they proposed changes in union benefits to make workers more competitive with those in other countries, then he would be able to garner greater support for their cause in Congress. Likewise, he believed these changes would be the first step in getting American based companies to bring their manufacturing and production jobs back to the American labor force. Robert felt it was necessary for both parties to make concessions in order to move forward.

Robert had his speech for that evening ready well before the plane landed in Los Angeles. His only appointment that afternoon was with Toni Bradford. He had received a personal phone call from Toni earlier requesting an appointment with him. Robert didn't have any problem seeing Toni. He had made an honest attempt to fulfill his obligation, and he was more than capable of making her see why it was impossible at this time to obtain the support that type of legislation needed in Congress. This was a sensitive issue and one that might take years to address. Gay Rights and abortion were two issues which invariably drew a line in the sand.

After a leisurely lunch in the Presidential suite of his hotel and a short conference with his staff, Robert and Paul discussed the report they had received from the drug task force. Paul was impressed with Richards' work and decided that he should contact Raul when he had time.

Every day for the President was a busy day, and Robert had just dismissed the staff for the afternoon when Toni was announced. He stepped around his desk to take her hand and lead her to a large sofa in the sitting area. This was to be an informal conversation between friends. At least that was what Robert thought. It didn't take long for him to realize that Toni wasn't in a friendly mood. She got right to the point.

"How kind of you to take time to see me. I know how very busy you must be, so I'll come directly to the point." She glanced back at Paul who sat slightly behind her. "However, I would rather speak to you in private."

Robert frowned. "Whatever you have to say, you can say in front of my chief of staff."

"Are you certain?" Now she was frowning. She would prefer to talk to him alone.

"I have nothing to hide." He responded adamantly. She almost laughed.

"In that case, I would like to know what has been done to pass legislation on the issue of same sex marriage. We gave you our full support. The donations you received through our efforts on your behave were monumental, and as far as I can tell, you have not followed through on your promise to us. Care to explain why?" She had leaned toward him as she spoke, allowing a splendid view of her décolletage.

Robert held her eyes instead. She was playing for keeps, but he was not so easily influenced. Maybe she needed to know just who she was addressing. He was no longer a mere governor seeking election. He was the President of the United States. She should be grateful that he had even taken time to see her. But he was tempted; he smiled.

"Toni, as I told you before in the letter I sent, it's impossible at this time to get the votes necessary to pass the legislation. I'm working on a plan to reintroduce it to Congress next session. I hope to have enough votes by then to insure our success. In the meantime, I have to ask you to be patient. I haven't forgotten my promise or the support that you gave me. I will do everything in my power to expedite the legislation when I know that it can pass." He had reached for her hand as he spoke and held it in his. He wanted to impress her with his sincerity, but he forgot that she was an actress, who recognized a play when she saw one.

Toni deftly removed her hand from his and reached inside her purse. Paul had already risen from his seat and started toward her when she withdrew a manila envelope and handed it to Robert. "I think that you might want to expedite that plan a little faster after you take a look at these. I didn't think you would be any better than the others. You're not a man of the people. You're just another man who says whatever he thinks will get him what he wants." She sat back on the sofa giving him a minute to withdraw the contents.

Robert was almost afraid to see what lay inside. His future could be in ruins if she had anything scandalous on him. He struggled to remember that evening, and when he did, he wanted to kill her. He had been a fool, and she had been an excellent actress. He slowly withdrew a series of photos. He had played right into her hands. It was Paul's fault. If he had been with him, this wouldn't have happened.

When the color drained from Robert's face, Paul stepped in front of him, took the photos and crammed them back into the envelope. "Are you threatening to blackmail the President with these? They can easily be staged, and as an actress, you know how easy it is to get someone to pose for such pictures and swear to their authenticity." He tossed the envelope back to Toni.

Toni stood up. "Don't think this is the last you'll hear from me. I'm sure the press would be very interested in the President's amorous liaisons." She was face to face with Paul and wasn't giving an inch.

"What do you think we can do that hasn't already been done? The President has made an honest and honorable attempt to fulfill his promise. He will need time to build a strong base in Congress. Give him the time he needs and you will see results. You're smart enough to know that nothing in Washington moves fast. Keep your photos and give us a little more time. I promise you that you will see results." Paul had spoken so convincingly that Toni actually believed he might be telling the truth. She snatched the envelope from where it had fallen in the chair. What did she have to lose? She could afford to wait and see. Nothing was going to be done otherwise.

"All right, but keep me informed. I don't want to ruin a good political ally unnecessarily, but keep this is mind too, there will come a time when you will want to be re-elected." She had spoken directly to Robert. Always the consummate actress, she turned regally and swept from the room, leaving an alluring scent and a dead silence in her wake.

Paul stepped to the outer door of the suite and canceled the rest of Robert's afternoon meetings. When he turned to face Robert, he was angrier than he had ever been. He knew Robert had problems, but Paul had actually thought he had learned his lesson after the Little Rock incident. All that Paul could do was pray that Alberto would know how to handle this latest situation.

For Robert's part, he just sat with his head in his hands. The photos had brought it all back. That evening in her apartment, the people, the drinks, the sex, it was all true. The photos weren't faked, and Toni knew that he would know.

Paul went to a sidebar and poured himself a strong drink. He rarely drank during the day, but right now he needed something to help him keep his hands off of Robert. Was it treason to beat the crap out of the President? That's what he wanted to do. Instead he tossed back the drink, took a deep breath as it burned its way down his throat, picked up his private phone, and dialed Alberto's number.

The conversation was short by necessity. Paul didn't take unnecessary chances. Obviously, he could leave that to Robert. There was no point in worrying until he had time to talk to Alberto and find out what could be done. He had bought them time, but he didn't know how much or if she could be trusted at all. Paul turned back to Robert.

"Get a drink. Take a shower, and get ready for your speech. This evening will be long enough without you alienating the unions, so be prepared. I'll take care of this. Harris can accompany you tonight. I have a meeting. If I can, I'll join you at the conference. Otherwise, I'll see you back here." Paul's anger had punctuated each word. Robert heard his commanding tone and inwardly bristled, but he didn't dare speak his mind. His future now lay in Paul's hands and his ability to contain a very volatile situation.

Paul left the suite after instructing the staff on their duties for the evening and detailing the men accompanying Robert. Harris would take care of Robert tonight. The Secret Service would protect him, and hopefully Paul could save him, or at least his political career.

Paul drove quickly through the traffic burning off some of his anger as he negotiated around slower moving vehicles. He entered an underground garage, parked his car, walked to an upper level, took the elevator to another floor, and knocked quietly on a door. The room had been chosen for its isolated location. Alberto was always discreet.

When he opened the door to Paul, he shook his head. "I tried to warn you. He'll never change. It's in his blood. I've seen too many like him."

Paul laughed. "You don't even know what he has done." He walked across the room and sat down on the sofa. He already felt better just having Alberto to talk to, to advise him.

Alberto poured them both a drink and handed one to Paul. "Okay, so tell me." Paul explained what had taken place that afternoon then waited for Alberto to say something. No one rushed Alberto. He emphasized making decisions, and he always made the right one.

"It may not be as bad as you think. Give me a little time, and I'll see what we need to do." He was already punching numbers in his phone. "I'll get back to you."

Paul was dismissed. He almost laughed. Alberto still treated him like an adolescent, but he headed for the door without another word just the same. Paul could almost see Alberto's mind working. He would have an answer to the problem in a few hours, Paul felt sure.

Now all Paul needed to do was stay away from Robert for a little while so he wouldn't be tempted to physically hurt him. If Robert fouled up, Raul would be furious, but not at Robert. Paul shrugged as he made his way back to his car. He couldn't do anything about it at this late date. He would just have to ride the wave and see what washed ashore.

He just wished Caroline wasn't tangled up in all this. He didn't want to see her publically humiliated. If Toni followed through on her threat, then that was a very distinct possibility. Alberto had to find an answer before Toni called their bluff, and that was exactly what Paul had been doing. He just hoped that she hadn't recognized it.

Alberto mentally ran through his options. Some were less pleasing than others, some more likely to garner the results they wanted. Alberto quickly downloaded the files he had requested from Raul to his phone. He had always known that she would be a problem. He had known she was up to something. Now he had the facts as he listened to a recording of Robert's amorous adventure with Toni and her friends the night of her party. The phone call she slipped from bed to make later that night gave Alberto the information he was after. Now he would have the leverage he wanted.

Alberto would take care of Toni himself, but he needed a couple of trusted associates to help carry out part of the plan. He placed a call, left a coded message, and waited for the return call. Within minutes, Alberto had the means to control or destroy Toni, whichever she chose. Alberto shrugged philosophically; he had the way to make Robert's problem disappear, at least until the next time, and Alberto knew there would always be a next time with Robert.

A short time later, he slipped passed the security guard and entered Toni's building; he knew that the information he had would make his job easy. He didn't feel any regret in using it or actually carrying through with his plan if he had to. Toni had made the rules when she tried to blackmail Robert. He felt no remorse; he would show no leniency.

He had the security code to Toni's apartment and entered without her even being aware that someone was there. He stood inside the entry watching as she moved around in the back dining area. She walked toward him carrying a drink in a glass. When she finally realized that she wasn't alone, she dropped the glass. The contents spilled across the carpet, leaving a rosy stain. Her hand flew to her mouth in an attempt to stifle her scream, but she had lost the battle already by showing her fear. She wouldn't be able to conquer her emotions now. Her innate fear only made his job that much more enjoyable.

Alberto smiled, a cold heartless smile, his eyes an empty, unfeeling void. The face of death—no one wanted to witness its devastation in person. Toni almost dropped to the floor. Alberto was well aware that when he wanted he had a look that could terrify the strongest soul, and Toni was extremely vulnerable. He had caught her off guard and that left her easy prey.

"Why don't we sit down?" His voice was calm, quiet, and deadly. Toni wasn't able to move, but when Alberto started to assist her, she shivered convulsively, clutched her arms around her middle, and stumbled to the sofa unaided.

"What do you want?" Toni almost stammered, afraid to hear just what it was.

Alberto smiled. He gave Toni time to truly absorb the full effect before he spoke calmly. He was in no hurry. No one was coming to rescue her. She had no way to protect herself. He knew her routine. This late at night, if she was at home, she would either be entertaining a large group, or she would be alone. She rarely had lone guests. That just made his job easier.

"Earlier today you paid a visit. You made certain people aware of the existence of some rather damaging photos. You insisted specific concessions be made on your behalf, or you would make those photos public." He stopped, giving her time to assess his statements.

"Yes," she stammered, "but I gave them time. There's no rush. I agreed to give them time. He promised he would take care of it, and I gave him more time. Didn't he tell you that?" She was becoming so agitated that she was incoherent; she was truly panicking.

"The point is you thought that you could hold the President hostage with your little scheme, a scheme that is as old as time. Did you really think it would be successful?" He shook his head, regretfully. "I want to know what you plan to do."

Toni tried to brave it out. "Look, it won't do you any good to kill me. I have arranged for those photos to be made public if anything happens to me." She was feeling stronger as she spoke. She sat straighter and even dared to lean forward toward Alberto. She thought she had him now. Then he smiled again.

"That's nice to know. With whom did you leave them?" He arched a brow questioningly.

Toni tried to think quickly. "My lawyer, of course, I told him that if anything happened to me he should take the photos to the press. They would know what to do." She wanted to smile as she leaned back against the sofa. She felt a surge of confidence fill her.

"Is there anyone else who knows of their existence, your guests that night, for instance? Would any of them pose a problem?" Toni laughed. She was back to her old self.

"You can't be serious. They don't remember yesterday much less months ago at one of my parties. That was just an average night for them. I always have people of interest, exciting newsworthy people. They are not easily impressed by position and power. They just want to have a good time. After a few hits, who is here doesn't even enter their minds. By the morning, they've forgotten everything." She did smile this time.

Alberto spoke calmly, deadly. "That's nice to know. Do you mind getting all of those photos and the negatives, please? It's rather late and I have another appointment."

"You can't be serious. You want me to just hand them over to you. Besides, like I said, my lawyer has a set at his office." A slight tremor filled her voice. She didn't feel quite so confident. A cold, clammy sweat coated her skin, and she clinched her hands together to stop the shaking.

He took his time, emphasizing each point distinctly. "I think that you aren't being completely honest with me. I think that you have the photos. I think that you didn't give any of them to anyone else, and I think you should get them, now." His voice vibrated along her nerve endings, leaving her frayed nerves tingling with fear.

What would he do if she refused, if she swore that what she said was the truth? Did she want to find out? She stared at him intently, trying to weigh her options, trying to overcome the terror his deadly calm was creating.

"Like I said, I don't have them all. My lawyer has a set."

"In that case, I think you should take a look at this." He stood and approached where she sat and handed her his phone.

She didn't want to take it, to touch anything he had held, but she put out her hand anyway. When she turned the screen to look at it, she stifled a scream. Her hand flying to her mouth, her eyes shot to his face.

"Please, I'll do anything you ask." She begged him, no longer afraid for herself. "Please."

"I've already told you what I want. Now do it." It was a command, laced with steel. He had wasted enough time on her. She was beneath his contempt.

"What will you do? You won't hurt him, will you? He's just a little boy." There were actual tears in her eyes, but Alberto wasn't sure that they were real. He didn't trust her.

"Nothing will happen to him as long as you keep your part of the bargain."

"What bargain?" She tried to think if he had mentioned any type of agreement earlier.

"The one we are about to make. Now get the photos and the negatives."

This time he reached down and jerked her to her feet. She needed to know he meant business. She stumbled in her haste to get away from him, but she left the room and headed down a corridor on one side of the apartment. Alberto was no simpleton. He followed in her wake. He wasn't going to give her the opportunity to call someone from another room. Even though he didn't think she would. People had been known to do less intelligent things. They just hadn't lived to regret it.

It had been so long since he had actual killed anyone that the urge was great to finish her as soon as she gave him the photos. He would probably be doing the world a favor. He smiled again as she fumbled with the safe combination. The safe, secluded behind a photo on one wall of her bedroom, was so cliché that Alberto wanted to laugh. Hollywood types, their whole lives were spent living roles so much that they didn't even have any imagination left.

He growled in irritation when she fumbled the combination again. She shot him a frightened look. She didn't know how thin the ice was under her feet. She had better tread lightly if she wanted to live to see tomorrow. He didn't feel any sympathy for her. She had probably played this little game before. He actually pitied the child to have her for his mother.

She turned to him with a large manila envelope. It shook in her hand. He let her hold it out to him for a minute before he spoke. "I think you know that if you want to insure that **your** little secret remains so, that you won't speak of this evening to anyone ever, that you will forget the demands you were making, and that you will forget that your evening with the President ever took place. It wouldn't pay you to do otherwise." He paused. "He's a cute little boy, about two, isn't he? I hear the father doesn't know about him. I would hate to see anything unpleasant happen to him or his mother. Likewise, I'm sure that you would hate to see any harm come to the President or his son." He jerked the envelope from her shaking hand. "Are you certain there are no more copies?" She nodded her head. She didn't trust herself to speak; she was afraid to breathe even.

"I'm going to make you a promise, and I never forget a promise." He stopped and stared coldly at her. "I promise that if anyone is ever made aware of this incident, then you and your son won't live to see another day. Now, you will promise to keep your word."

She swallowed nervously. "I promise," she whispered. "What will you do with my son? Please don't hurt him."

"That decision is in your hands. For now, he will be returned safely to his nurse. We will check on him from time to time. However, you don't want us to ever have to visit you. That pretty face wouldn't look very good after our chemical peel." He laughed at his own absurd joke. Strange, what crazy thoughts entered one's mind at these moments?

Without another word, Alberto turned, left the room, walked through the apartment, out the door, and from the building, never looking back. He didn't think she would be a problem again, but he would make sure that she knew she was being watched. He would insure that little reminders were sent regularly. He sighed. He almost wished she had refused him.

Toni grabbed her phone. As soon as she verified her son was back at his home safely, she stumbled to the bathroom and vomited violently. She had been lucky, and she knew it.

Paul was relieved when he received Alberto's call later. He knew that Alberto would take care of everything. Still, Paul wondered if someday he might not be able to. Alberto was right about one thing, of course. Robert would never change.

Chapter 17

CAROLINE WAS TOTALLY IN love. He was the best thing that had ever happened to her. She couldn't imagine her life without him, and whenever she was around him, she made no effort to hide her feelings. She just wished she could have more time with him but that seemed to be a luxury she no longer had.

Her days were filled with the necessary duties of the First Lady. Her personal assistant tried to keep a few hours free each day, but as Robert's presidency gained momentum, she was required to spend more and more time attending functions, events, meetings, and a myriad of other activities on everything from education to child care. Being a new mother, she was constantly inundated with requests to speak to various family oriented groups.

Motherhood had gained her entry into a previously closed section of voters, and Robert wanted her to make the most of this opportunity. He wanted her involved in anything that would help gain his reelection in three years.

She had to give him credit, he was always looking forward. If he ever regretted or worried about anything in the past, she didn't know about it. Sometimes, she wondered if he had any feelings at all. He seemed so remote, so isolated, but, of course, that was only with her.

To the rest of the world, he appeared to be the most loving of husbands and fathers, the most concerned for the welfare of the American public. His public persona cloaked a darker side few had ever seen. If they only knew they hadn't elected a god, only a man with faults and failings. People didn't want to know that; they wanted someone to admire, to hold to a higher standard, someone who could raise them above the mediocrity of their own lives. How the mighty would fall if they ever discovered the true man.

She didn't want to think about Robert. Her precious minutes were reserved for the man in her life, and she grabbed him from his nurse and snuggled him in her arms, tickling him lightly until he squealed in delight. He was a happy, chubby little darling, and she loved him beyond reason. Her only regret was that Paul couldn't be the father he so desperately needed.

Robert didn't have time for him, nor was he interested in taking time, unless he had an ulterior motive. Caroline had learned to recognize the signs whenever he had a plan to exploit her son. She wouldn't have minded if he had any true feelings for Robbie, but it was obvious to anyone who spent much time around them that he didn't.

Caroline had seen Amanda looking at Robert questioningly, searching for some little sign that he cared for his son. There wasn't any. Caroline had known that it was just a matter of time before others would realize what she already knew. She just didn't know what to do about it.

She needed to talk to Paul, but even that seemed impossible these days. They hadn't spent any time together since before Robbie's birth. She longed to have a few private minutes to talk to him, to let him know how she still felt about him.

In public she remained the aloof First Lady rarely voicing her opinions in the presence of her husband, never going against his wishes, feeding his gigantic ego with adoring smiles and loving glances.

Even in private, when the three of them were together, she refrained from drawing attention to herself. Robert didn't like to have her gainsay him in anything. Even though she had been part of the plan from the beginning, in Robert's eyes she was window dressing, nothing more. He had conveniently forgotten her role in helping him gain the presidency, the strength she had brought to his governorship, the power she had added to his job as Attorney General. All he remembered were his contributions, his strengths, his abilities—it was all about him.

Paul saw what was happening and tried to warn Robert that others would soon notice if he didn't make a better pretense, at least, of caring for his family. Robert didn't want to listen to anything Paul had to say about his personal life and told him so. Paul had to remind Robert of the circumstances of his rise to power, but Robert seemed to think that as

President Paul no longer had any power over him, and to a certain point that was true. Paul had accomplished the first step in Raul's masterful scheme and was quickly moving to complete his latest directives, but Robert could be eliminated at any time; he just didn't realize it. It was a card that Paul would play later, if necessary. He hoped that time would never come.

Paul had always admired Robert's abilities, and he knew that, beneath the swagger and posturing, Robert was a decent man. However, he was a man that had to be held in check. So far, Paul had been able to appeal to his logic and make him see what he had to do, but Paul had seen a shift in Robert's attitude ever since the incident with Toni Bradford. He couldn't figure out what had changed, but something had. He needed to talk to Alberto and see if he had any ideas. It was puzzling; life around Robert was always demanding.

Maybe Caroline had been right in her assessment. He shouldn't think of her as Pandora because the evils of the world seemed to have been unleashed on them since they had met. The questions, always at the corners of his mind, never left him for long, yet they probably would remain unanswered. Had their fathers ever cared about them? Had they meant anything to them other than the means to an end? Remorse was a difficult emotion to deal with. It led to questions that could never be answered. He had been taught to remain emotionless, to never show feelings, but unlike his father, there were times Paul found that very difficult. When he was around Caroline it became almost impossible. Yes, he smiled, Pandora was the right name. One mistake on their part now could unleash an avalanche of problems unlike any the world had ever seen before. Sometimes unknowingly, Robert tempted him to reveal his true feelings and let the consequences be damned, but then logic would reign, and he knew the ones to suffer most would be Caroline and Robbie.

Paul knew that Alberto had tried to make him see a caring side to Raul, but Paul had failed to find it. He was a tool his father used, and if he failed to perform, Paul felt that he would be just as easily discarded and replaced. On one hand, he couldn't help but have feelings for the man who had shaped his life, who had given him everything that he had. On the other, he couldn't help but resent the man who had taken him from his family, who had forced him to become what he was, who had never really explained who his real mother was.

Paul always came back to that question. Who was she and what had happened to her? Alberto refused to talk about it, telling him to ask his father. Paul wasn't that brave, and he couldn't question anyone else in the family. Loyalty to Raul was absolute. They would never reveal anything without his consent, and if they didn't know, Paul knew no one would dare question Raul about his actions, not even his son.

When he walked into the private residence in the White House, he found Caroline sprawled carelessly on the carpet, playing with Robbie who was giggling and cooing at her antics. It was such a domestic picture that it hurt him to see it. He wanted to be a part of their lives, but he was doomed to play a second role, the friend, the godfather, always on the edges, never at the center. The saddest part was that the leading man didn't want the role himself.

Paul stopped short watching them silently. "Well, I can see that you two are having fun." He moved into the room and sat down on the blanket beside Robbie. He picked him up and held him for a minute. Robbie looked at him for a second then giggled. Paul smiled and kissed his chubby cheek. Rules could be damned; this was his son. "Hey, Buddy, what have you and Mommy been doing?" he tickled his tummy as he lay him back on the blanket. He didn't want to monopolize his time. He knew Caroline had little free time to spend with her son, their son.

His dark eyes went to Caroline's face searching for answers to unspoken questions. She smiled sadly. She looked tired. Paul knew her life with Robert was trying. But there was nothing he could do. Their fathers held the strings. They were just the puppets in this little side show. But the way Paul figured it, they only had to wait seven more years at most—a lifetime.

He looked steadily at Caroline hoping she could tell how he felt, hoping she could feel the love he had for her and their son. Their son—he hated that Robert had any connection to Robbie. He had been unrealistic when Caroline had reminded him that Robert would be Robbie's legal father. Now that he was in their lives, Paul wanted the world to know that Robbie was his son.

He swallowed his anger and reached for Caroline's hand. She pulled it away just as the nurse entered the room ready to take Robbie. Caroline picked him up and hugged him. He was so precious, a special gift from the man she loved. She refused to look at Paul until the nurse left the room. She knew that she was too emotional. A blind man could see her feelings. Since Robbie's birth, she had been unable to control her emotions, a cardinal sin in her father's eyes.

She grimaced. She had received a letter from Rafael through Alberto asking about her welfare and the baby's, and of course hinting at her duties. She knew that he knew every detail of her life, so the letter seemed unnecessary, but maybe it was his way of letting her know he did care about her. She couldn't help but wonder. Stranger things had happened.

She wasn't sure exactly how she felt about him. He was a severe task master and an absolute disciplinarian. Still she had developed feelings for him over the years. She wasn't sure that they were love, but she did care about him. She would never understand him, but she did care. He was Robbie's grandfather, and though she would like to deny it, he was her father.

Caroline had followed the nurse's departure from the room with sad eyes. Paul saw the glimmer of tears and knew that he had to do something to lighten the mood. He reached for her hand and helped her to her feet. She brushed at her skirt, self-consciously. He was Raul's son; emotions were unheard of, but when she glanced at Paul, she saw compassion and understanding, and she wanted to curl up in his arms and spend the rest of her life. He lifted his hand to her face and just stared in her eyes. Neither spoke; words were not necessary; they knew how they felt, and they knew the futility of those feelings.

"Someday," Paul whispered then dropped his hand.

"I know." She smiled sadly and turned to sit on the sofa. She took a deep breath and put on her business face. "What can I do for you?" she spoke lightheartedly when Paul knew she felt anything but happy, but he went along with her anyway. They couldn't risk speaking of anything else.

"I just dropped by to see my godson and ask if you wanted to attend the conference in Dallas with the President next week. It would means three days away from Robbie, but I know that there are several women's groups that would love to have you speak to them. You could drop in on your parents too. I know they were just here a few weeks ago, but you could work that in if you wanted to.

"I'm not sure they would want to see me without Robbie. He absolutely captivated them. I'm afraid they forgot about me all together." She laughed as she spoke, letting him know she wasn't displeased by their reaction. "I'll check my calendar and let you know. Have you talked to Robert about my going?" She frowned as she waited for his reply.

He was so easily provoked these days. She didn't want to set him off again. She had had to wear long sleeves for a week after the last time. Eventually the bruises had faded, but the memory hadn't. He had been furious about something she had said at dinner, and the minute the staff left for the evening, he had grabbed her wrist and dragged her into the bedroom. The shaking he had given her had made her teeth rattle, and her arms had grown numb before his tirade eased. The sex had been forced and rough, meant to prove his dominance and his lack of feeling for her. She got the message. She steered clear of him after that, and she didn't dare voice an opinion even in private. That didn't keep her from having them, and she made certain that he was never alone with Robbie.

She would bide her time. Someday she would see that he paid for every mark and every remark. She was too much like her father to take his abuse. She knew that one word to Alberto, and Robert would die a slow and painful death, but she cared too much for Alberto to tangle him up in her affairs. He would be left to deal with Rafael; she would never want that for him. No, she would never tell anyone; this was her problem, and she would handle it. Besides, she didn't want to bring the wrath of her father down on her head either. There would come a day when she would have the opportunity she needed, and she would take it.

Paul watched the play of emotions on her face and wondered what had caused such strong feelings. Then he saw her blink, and she was the consummate First Lady again. Maybe he had imagined it. He answered her question, "I have and he thought it would be a good opportunity for you to be seen together away from the White House and Washington. The idea of family friendly press always excites him." Paul laughed.

It was meant as a joke, but Caroline didn't even smile. Now he was really worried. Something had happened. He wanted to ask, but he knew her well enough to know she wouldn't tell him. He would check with Alberto. Maybe he knew something. But it was a fine wire he walked; he couldn't reveal too much interest without giving his feelings away. He would just have to wait. Maybe they would have time on the trip to talk, maybe, but he doubted it.

"I'll get back to you on the details." He stood as her secretary came in the room with the afternoon's agenda. She smiled sadly as she watched him leave. "Someday," she whispered softly.

Four days later, just as Caroline was packing for their trip, the nurse came in and advised her to call the doctor. Robbie had begun running a high fever, which she couldn't account for. She told Caroline it was probably nothing, just a virus or something of that nature, but it was better to be safe. Caroline, of course, panicked as first time mothers often do. She called the doctor, then her mother, who reassured her that babies always ran high fevers. But Caroline was a nervous wreck by the time the doctor arrived. Just as the nurse had predicted, the doctor diagnosed a virus which would run its course in a few days. He prescribed a fever medication and patience. Viruses had to run their course and very little could be done to alter that fact. Even though Caroline was relieved, she didn't want to leave Robbie in the care of the nurse. She dreaded facing Robert with the news, but her son came first; she would just suffer the consequences of her decision.

She dialed Robert's private line in the oval office and asked to speak to him. His secretary hesitated then put the call through. He had been in a foul mood all day, and she hated to interrupt him. She just hoped this was really important or her head would be on a platter.

"Yes," Robert snapped, trying to conceal his anger but failing miserably.

The secretary made it short, "Your wife, Sir," and made the connection. Let them sort it out. Maybe she would be out of the line of fire. When she didn't hear shouting, she surmised that things were better. She would have been wrong if she had listened to the call.

"Robert, the baby is sick, and I'm going to have to cancel my trip." She tried to sound all business. She wasn't asking his permission; she was telling him her decision.

"What do you mean by not going? You have commitments." His voice was laced with anger. She heard it clearly. It didn't matter.

"You heard me. My son is sick and I won't be going on this trip. I'll reschedule for a later date." Her voice was adamant. He recognized the anger and decided to back off. He still needed her even if he didn't like the fact.

"Very well, have Amanda get out a press release and have your secretary make the necessary calls. Play up the worried Mother angle.

That should create some sympathy, especially in those women's groups. This could be in our favor."

"It's already been taken care of." Did he think she needed him to tell her what to do? The conceit of the man, he was impossible. She refrained from slamming the phone just barely; after all she had to remember she was a lady, even if he had forgotten how to be a gentleman.

She turned and took her sick baby from the nurse. As she cuddled him to her and worried about his fever, she wished she could call his real father to be with them. He wouldn't see this as an opportunity to gain support. He would be concerned about the welfare of his son. She almost called him, but sanity prevailed.

Paul was just entering Robert's office and heard the end of the call. "Anything wrong?"

"It was just Caroline. Apparently the baby is sick and she is canceling her trip to Dallas." He sounded more disgusted than worried.

"Why don't you go up and check on them. I can handle the office for a few minutes. I'll just give the keys to Chambers if a crisis occurs." He laughed knowing that Robert hated the idea of anyone usurping his power.

Robert never blinked. He just went back to studying the papers in his hand. "There's no need. It's just one of those kid things, nothing to worry about."

Obviously Caroline didn't see it that way, or she wouldn't have canceled her plans. He stared at Robert amazed. He had about as much feeling for his son as a dead mouse. Paul was quickly coming to the conclusion that he knew what Caroline's problem was. It wasn't any mouse but a real live rat, and she was caught in the trap with him. The phrase "'til death do us part" kept running through his mind. Robert didn't have a clue who he was messing with. If Caroline was anything like her father, Robert might one day regret his rash decisions and lack of concern. He made a sudden decision. He didn't take time to think first.

"You don't mind if I check on them, do you? After all, Robbie is my godson." He wasn't really asking his permission. He planned to go with or without it, but it would look better if Robert approved first. "I'll tell her that you asked about them." He started toward the door before he even finished talking. Robert was obliged to give his consent or face an argument with his secretary listening. Paul had already opened the door and was walking away.

"Tell her to be sure and call me if she needs me." He was almost shouting at Paul as he continued on his way. As an afterthought, he added, "Give her my love."

He would choke first. If he gave her anything, it wouldn't be Robert's love, but his own.

He had built up a great deal of righteous indignation by the time he arrived as the private residence. He knocked lightly on the door then entered quietly. He didn't want to disturb them if the baby was sleeping. What he saw broke his heart. Caroline was walking Robbie back and forth across the nursery, singing softly to him. He was fretting and crying, fighting against the fever that raged through his little body. His face was bright red and his eyes were glazed. It was easy to see that he was inconsolable and that his mother was fast approaching desperation. Tears were streaming down her face, and she didn't even notice Paul.

The nurse spoke to him from the corner of the room where she was changing sheets on Robbie's bed. She was a *family* member, carefully vetted by the Secret Service, but like La Senora there would be nothing to find. No one would ever connect them to Raul in any way. These positions were elite in Raul's eyes and well endowed by him. They were his personal links to the front lines of the action. Ms. Martin, the baby's nurse, knew more about the lives of those around her than she would ever reveal. Even Senor Contreras didn't need to know everything. The First Lady needed some privacy, but she had lost much of the respect she had once had for the President.

She had been raised in a male dominant society, but she didn't always agree with the idea. Women had rights; men just didn't like to think they did. She respected the First Lady for trying to protect her husband's image, even though she was beginning to think he didn't deserve her loyalty. "I've tried to get her to let me hold him for a while, so she can rest, but she refuses. Maybe you can make her see that she'll wear herself out if she keeps this up. His fever will break soon. It just takes time." She smiled at Paul as though she thought he would be the answer to her prayers. "You talk to her and I'll fix her a cup of tea."

Left alone, Paul walked over to Caroline and wrapped his arms around her and the baby. She dissolved into tears, her whole body shaking with the force of her emotions. Paul had enough sense to know that this was more than a sick baby, but he didn't question her. After holding her briefly, he stepped back. He couldn't afford for anyone to see them, even a family member, no especially a family member.

"Here, give him to me." His voice had just enough authority to force Caroline to relinquish Robbie to his care. She could trust Paul. Robbie quieted almost instantly. He was reassured by Paul's calm voice and his soothing words. He had picked up on Caroline's emotional state and had been reacting to it. Now he calmed down and sucked on his fat little fingers.

Caroline didn't know if she should be happy or mad. Then she sat down in the rocker and smiled to see father and son together. They had so few moments that to her they were golden. Robbie soon fell asleep against Paul's shoulder, and he continued to hold him, patting his back and talking softly to him, saying all the things he couldn't when others were around. Paul liked to think that Robbie understood him and someday would know that he was his father, a father who loved and adored him.

Caroline closed her eyes against the pain the picture of the two of them made. She regretted so many decisions in her life, but her time with Paul was not one of them. She dreamed of a day when they could be a family, not some part of someone else's plan or someone else's ambition. Just a simple family filled with love and happiness that was all she wanted. She never knew when she fell asleep.

Paul walked the baby until his fever broke; then with a kiss on his soft curls, he gave him to his nurse to put to bed. He turned to Caroline, slumped against the back of the rocker. He started to wake her, but the nurse stopped him.

"She hasn't been sleeping. She wouldn't want me to tell you, but she is exhausted. Let her sleep. I'll watch the baby and take care of her."

"I have a better idea." He bent and scooped Caroline up in his arms and carried her toward her bedroom. The nurse quickly entered and pulled back the bedcovers. Paul laid her down. She weighed nothing. She had lost weight since the baby, too much. He eased the covers over her. Robbie began fussing in the next room and the nurse returned to him. Paul stood for a minute just watching Caroline sleep. She would hate to know he had done that. He didn't care. He could look all he wanted for a minute at least. Robert was such a fool, but he had always thought that. As smart as Robert was, he was always reaching for more and didn't even see what he was throwing away. Paul bent and kissed Caroline's cheek. She whispered his name, "Paul?"

"Go back to sleep. Everything is fine." He turned and left the room to check on Robbie once more. When he was assured that Robbie's fever had broken and that he would rest for a few hours, Paul returned to his office. The nurse had promised to call him if there was any change. He sat for a long time trying to piece together a future. It was impossible. Like Caroline, he would have to learn to be patient, but he was not a patient man. Alberto could attest to that.

He smiled when he remembered some of the antics of his youth and picked up the phone to dial his friend. Maybe Alberto had some answers. If he wasn't careful, they would all know how he felt about Caroline, and it wouldn't take them long to figure out that Paul was Robbie's father. He was amazed someone hadn't already figured it out.

When he received the phone call later that evening, he didn't know who to thank, but he started with the appropriate source. The fact that he was a key figure in the negotiations had been a taxing experience so far, but after today he would consider it a stroke of genius. He knocked briefly on Robert's office door then entered. He had to force himself not to be exuberant at the thought of the possibilities.

Robert looked up. "What now?" He sounded irritated. Paul was beginning to think that he might know what Robert's problem was. It had been a long time since he had made any special requests of Alberto, but maybe he should suggest it. Then he felt guilty. Was he trying to get Robert out of the way, just for his own benefit? Was it so wrong? Robert had never felt constrained by his marriage vows. That was probably the hardest thing for Paul to accept about him. How he could fail to see the special qualities of his own wife was a puzzle to Paul.

"I've got a problem with the trade negotiations. I won't be able to travel with you to Dallas. I'll let Harris know. Alberto can run interference for you if need be. I'll send him along. Do you have any special requests? Let him know beforehand, so he can work out the logistics. I don't want any more surprises like the last one." He raised one brow in inquiry.

Robert thought for a minute. "I'll get back to you on that. Can you get the negotiations wrapped up before the next Congressional session? I'd like to start off with some good news." Paul saw his eyes dart around the room. He was having trouble concentrating. Paul was right. He would speak to Alberto. He might as well be prepared. Paul knew that look too well. It was only a matter of time before Robert called anyway. It was sad really to think of the brilliance of the man, and the weakness he was chained to. Choices, everything was about making choices. Paul just prayed his own were better than Robert's had been.

Robert left early the next day and most of the White House stall used the opportunity to catch up on the back log of work that seemed to be the rule not the exception. Paul worked his committee twice as hard as usual, emphasizing the President's desire to have good news when he returned.

Of course, he had other motives, but those were secondary to his job. He would always be a professional. His work meant something to him. He really wanted Robert's legacy to be an accurate representation of the good he had accomplished during his Presidency. Paul knew that he was probably being naïve, but he still believed in good men doing good things for others without self-serving interests involved.

Paul had called the residence twice yesterday to check on Robbie and again the first thing this morning. His fever had returned during the night, but they had been able to reduce it much faster. This morning he was beginning to take more liquids and had even played for a few minutes before falling asleep again. Paul had insisted that Caroline rest whenever Robbie did and he called to check with the nurse to see if she was following his orders.

As soon as the meeting adjourned, Paul called the residence to see if he could come to check on them in person. The nurse informed him that both mother and son were feeling much better this evening, and the First Lady was insisting that she take the evening off, but she didn't like leaving her alone just in case the baby got worse again. Paul told her that he would be glad to keep them company for the evening, so she could go ahead with her plans.

Paul could hardly believe his luck. The staff was used to him being in the residence. They all asked about the baby when he spoke to them and were glad to hear that Robbie was better.

The First Lady was well-liked by both the staff and personnel in the White House. Most of them were withholding their opinion about the President. He was not as outgoing as his wife, but they gave him credit for doing a good job so far. Since he was officially their boss, they didn't offer their opinions to others. They liked their jobs and wanted to keep them.

Paul was good at reading people, and he knew that most of them had reservations about Robert. They were waiting to see how he managed the long haul. It was too early to have an accurate assessment, and these people were seasoned staff. They would take care not to offend and always keep their opinions to themselves. They would know soon enough.

When Paul entered the residence, Ms. Martin left for an evening with friends, but she left her personal number with Paul just in case they needed her. He smiled at her dedication. Family, even in this removed instance, was important. It was nice to know that Caroline had her to rely on.

After seeing the nurse off, Paul turned his attention to the two people he loved most in the world. He just stood and watched them playing on a blanket on the floor. Robbie still had a slight fever. His eyes were overly bright, but other than that, he seemed much better. He giggled and swatted at the stuffed animal Caroline was teasing him with. She was laughing as well. The sound of their laughter made his heart soar. Happiness from such simple things, he would never have guessed it as a young man. He had never met anyone like Caroline. She made his heart sing and life worth living. He laughed at himself and sat down to join them.

If the staff thought anything about his presence alone with the First Lady, they said nothing. Most of them felt it was good to hear her laugh again. The last few weeks an aura of gloom had settled on the residence, and it was easy for them to tell something wasn't right. Most of them credited it to the stress of the position. Adjustments had to be made in any marriage when one held such a demanding responsibility, and a new baby added even more stress. The kitchen staff prepared an outstanding meal with added treats meant to entice the First Lady. They had seen the dishes returned uneaten for weeks. They were beginning to worry that her health would be affected. This was an evening they could focus on her and not just the tastes of the President.

Paul and Caroline played with Robbie until time for his bath. Then they bathed him together, laughing as he splashed water all over them both. After his bottle, he went fast to sleep, exhausted from his evening of playing and laughing. Now that he wasn't between them, they had time to talk. When dinner was served they were still talking about the President and the events of the past few weeks.

They discussed Caroline's involvement in women's rights and education and health care reform. She was fast become the spokeswoman for the underprivileged. She didn't mind, but it took so much time away from Robbie that she was feeling guilty. Paul made suggestions about how she could limit her involvement and still satisfy Robert. The more they talked, the more he got the feeling that Robert had become very demanding. Now he was wondering just how demanding. Paul had no right to pry in her private life with Robert, but he desperately wanted to do so.

When dinner was finished and dessert eaten, Caroline realized that she had really enjoyed the meal for the first time in weeks. Robert usually spent the time criticizing her and belittling her efforts. She hadn't realized how much he was affecting her until tonight. She looked at her empty gold-trimmed plate and knew that she had let him take over her life. She had forfeited her self-respect, her sense of self-worth, but no longer. He was trying to break her, her confidence in her abilities, her strength of purpose.

She glanced at Paul. He had stopped talking when a strange look had come over her. It was a look of discovery, a look of wonder. He couldn't explain it, but something had changed. She smiled at him, not the superficial smile that she had given everyone for days, but a soul searching, heartbreaking smile that stole his breath. Whatever had happened, she had worked through it, and she had prevailed.

He reached for her, pulling her into his arms and kissing her until they were both breathless. Laughing at the absurdity of the situation, he hugged her to him. He could feel her heart beating against his chest, and he knew that his was beating just as fast. He stood, letting her slip from his arms. Together they walked back to Robbie's room to check on him. He was sleeping soundly. Every few minutes he sucked noisily on the fat, little fist he had stuck in his mouth. They laughed softly. Paul hugged her to him as they stood watching their baby sleep, relieved that he was getting well.

Caroline turned in Paul's arms and stood on tiptoe to kiss his smiling lips. He gathered her in his arms and deepened the kiss hungrily. He didn't think he would ever get enough of her. She stole his breath and gave him the reason for breathing all at the same time. She took his hand and led him to the guest bedroom further down the hall. She didn't want to taint her love for Paul with the anger associated with nights spent meeting Robert's demands. The longer they were married the more she realized he didn't care about her at all. He didn't even make a pretense of it any more. She was a convenience when no one else was available.

During his term in office, she knew he was limited in his escapades. He liked his image, so he would be careful, but there were times he used Caroline. Those times he treated her like some paid prostitute, some meaningless encounter, not a cherished wife. Now she understood that his intention had been to degrade her. She felt no compunction at anything she did now. Paul's love had set her free, and tonight had made her realize just how browbeaten she had become. No more. She was a new woman. When he got back, he was in for a few surprises.

Paul locked the door and watched as Caroline slipped her dress off her shoulders and held her hands out to him. He wasted no time in joining her. They hadn't been together in months, but nothing had changed. They loved each other, but they realized it would only be stolen moments for years possibly. That only made the love they shared that much sweeter.

After a hurried breakfast, Robert had boarded his jet and had flown straight back to Washington in time to attend a meeting with the head of the DEA and the newly appointed director of their new task force. He was pleased with the proposals made to help restrict the meth problem. He was impressed with the task force leader, Tim Richards. He was a hardened veteran of the streets and his first-hand experience left Robert feeling secure that their plan would be successful.

Robert stood and shook hands with the men, something he rarely did. Paul realized Robert was impressed by Richards and made a note to send him a personal message acknowledging the President's support for his operation. Paul wondered if Robert ever felt as though he were fighting against himself. Maybe he didn't consider his casual drug use a detriment to society or a problem for concern. It was an interesting concept.

Paul had spoken very little to Robert and only when absolutely necessary. He sent his assistant in his place whenever he could. He didn't trust himself alone with Robert, but it had been necessary for him to attend the meeting with the DEA. Paul left immediately afterward with a cool good night to Robert and a smile on his lips knowing that Caroline was happy once more. She was his Caroline again, the one that didn't take any crap from others, but said it in such a ladylike manner that it cut the ground from under their feet before they realized it.

Robert was in for a shock, and he dared him to touch her ever again. Rafael wouldn't have a chance to get to Robert if he ever laid another hand on her. Paul would suffer the wrath of both Raul and Rafael, if need be, to protect her and Robbie.

It had been Ms. Martin that let it slip about the bruises she had seen on Caroline's arms. Now Paul understood the weight loss, the haggard look, and the tears. He had held her in his arms and let her cry after he made her confess the secrets she had tried to hide. She had felt so degraded, so unworthy from Robert's cruel treatment that she was almost inconsolable. But she assured him that she had made a promise to herself the night before. She would never let him treat her that way again. She was his wife, not his possession. She would show him the honor due a husband in public, but in private, their life was over. There would be no more nights together while he berated her every action, no more threats of retaliation for imagined wrongs, no more slurs against her for slights he perceived. She would stand by him as long as he was President, but after that they were finished.

Paul whistled as he left the building. Everyone wondered who the woman in his life was. They had never seen him act in such a way before. He didn't care. He and Caroline might not be together, but she wouldn't belong to Robert again, ever. That thought made him sublimely happy. He had never let himself think about Caroline with Robert, but now he realized just how much he had hated the idea. She was his; she had always been his; he just hadn't realized it. No one could take her from him now, not even their fathers.

Chapter 18

RICHARDS WAS IMPRESSED. OPERATION Slam Shut was starting off with a bang. Information was pouring in from the field operatives in each state. The data was being compiled and connections all across the country were being tapped for leads. The operation had the President's endorsement and inter-departmental cooperation was better than he had ever imagined gaining. But he was confused.

When he met with the President's committee and the DEA, he had expected the President to be less informed about the drug problem. He had been astounded when Billings had quoted statistics that he had only recently learned himself. He had continued by expressing his desire for complete disruption of the drug highway from the northern states to California and the elimination of distribution routes. Billing also mentioned Chicago and Philadelphia as cities of concern. Never before had a President taken such personal interest in drug activity. Billings reiterated his strong commitment to eradicating this new plague on American society.

Richards was truly impressed, but he couldn't shake the feeling that something wasn't quite right. Billings had looked him squarely in the eye when they shook hands, and Richards had known instantly that he was hiding something. He had lived on the streets too long not to know some things instinctually. He trusted his feelings; they had saved him more than once over the years, and he knew Billings had some dark secret.

Richards started to ask Amanda about him but decided against it. It wouldn't be fair to her to ask about her boss. That would be asking her to be disloyal, and Amanda was a stickler for loyalty and honesty. In her chosen profession, there was little of either. But in a way she did help him reach a decision. She inadvertently mentioned a change in the First Lady since Billings had returned from Dallas.

She seemed to have regained her energy at last after having the baby and from being in constant demand. The kitchen staff reported that she had begun eating again and had complimented them on their menu selections. She was seen taking the baby out in the afternoons for strolls in the gardens and leisurely visits with the staff. Everyone loved seeing them make their way down one of the numerous hallways with her telling Robbie all about the history of the White House as they strolled along.

The President was seen in his office much later than usual. The staff was instructed to schedule meetings as late as five and through dinner if necessary. He had undertaken a major work load and seemed determined to accomplish all of his campaign goals in his first term.

Richards didn't understand the working of the presidential staff, but he knew enough to realize that the more the President worked, the more his staff had to. It wouldn't be long before tempers raveled and nerves frayed, not ideal for a long term working relationship. He would withhold judgment until he had something substantial to go on. Still, he could make a few discreet inquiries. He had friends in the Secret Service who might be able to shed some light on the problem. The more he thought about it, the more he felt something was wrong.

Paul just laughed when he heard and scheduled more work. If he couldn't have her, he was glad that Robert couldn't either. They could both work themselves to death, just as long as Caroline and Robbie were safe and happy, nothing else really mattered.

He was dog tired most days, but he left whistling every time.

Richards didn't have time to worry about the President for long. His job took on a life of its own. Meth production was soon tracked to four major distributors. Graham was at the head of their list. Richards had known that as soon as Graham found out his true identity, his life would be forfeited. He knew the risk when he took the job, but he really felt he could make a difference. He knew Graham's operation inside out, even better than Graham did.

His first concern was for Amanda. She deserved to know what she was risking by staying with him. He couldn't imagine life without her, but it had to be her decision. He was asking a lot and giving little in return. He was just a worn out narcotics agent, a street punk, a retired special services officer, and the man who loved her to distraction. But he wouldn't say those things until she had time to make up her mind without interference from him.

Later that night when he told Amanda about the risk she would be taking by staying with him, she laughed. "Didn't you think I was smart enough to figure that out before now? I had you checked out remember. I knew who you had been and I know who you are. I'll be just as safe with you as without. I don't want to lose you. I plan for us to have a family someday soon. So don't worry about me, just see that nothing happens to you." She hugged him so tight, he almost lost his breath, but he didn't care. She meant the world to him, and she was talking about spending her life with him. What could be better than that? After sharing a toe-curling kiss, she slipped from his arms and walked across the room.

"Now, I need to tell you something." She turned to face him. As he frowned, she quickly replied, "No, it's nothing bad. Well, not about us anyway. Most people don't know about it, and it's the reason I want to help you make a difference in the meth trade." She paced back and forth as she spoke, fighting back her emotions. "My little brother— just nineteen—was killed in a drug war last year in Kansas City. Two rival factions decided to fight it out, and he got caught in the middle. Dumb wasn't it?" She hesitated, holding back the tears. "He didn't realize what he was getting into. He couldn't shake his addiction. He tried, but it sucked him right back in until he didn't care anymore. I tried to talk to him, tried to make him see what it was doing to him, but he couldn't see it. It only made him mad when I wouldn't give him any more money. He finally quit calling." She stopped pacing and took a deep breath. Remorse filled her voice. "The last time I saw him was stretched out on a gurney in the morgue. I didn't even recognize him. He was so wasted, so changed. I don't want anyone else to experience that. Someone has to do something. I think you're the person to make a difference, and I want to be with you when you do." She brushed the tears from her face and tried to smile. He took her in his arms; he understood the pain, the desire to hide from the truth, to keep the memory alive without the drugs, the death, the loss. He understood. He loved her even more for sharing her pain, for encouraging him to work to break the stranglehold meth had on society.

When news of the President's drug task force finally hit the newspapers, Graham was livid. Blood vessels protruded along the side of his head; his hands were clenched so tightly his knuckles were white. The face staring up at him from the newspaper was a man he had trusted, a man he had given special treatment, a man he had raised up in his organization to a position of power. His trust had been totally misplaced, and it was completely Strong's fault.

Strong had brought him in, had praised his abilities. Strong was responsible for this debacle. He was going to clean up this mess and rid Graham of the one man who could bring down his whole operation. Richards knew almost everything—names, dates, places, routes. Graham would lose his empire. He had to move fast, if he wanted to survive. There was only one option, but Richards was tough. It wouldn't be easy. It might not even be possible, but Graham had to try; he had no other choice.

Strong had been expecting Graham's summons. When Strong saw the morning's paper, his heart had sunk like a lead weight to the pit of his stomach. He knew Graham would hold him responsible. Facing Graham would be almost as bad as confronting Richards. He might as well face the lion; the most he could do was eat him alive, but Graham needed him if he wanted Richards taken out. Graham didn't believe in doing his own jobs. Strong's lips curled in disgust. He had taken on the task of cutting out the cocaine trade and had been right there on the spot, risking his life for Graham. Graham needed to remember that. He should be grateful.

With his own blood simmering from Graham's curt phone call, Strong left for his office. He wasn't taking anything from Graham; he had done his job, and Graham better recognize that fact. He would take care of Richards. That was all Graham needed to know. Strong had already arranged a meeting with his associates. They would know how to get the job done.

Strong entered Graham's office with a confident smile. He let Graham vent his anger and sat unresponsive to his attack. His attitude completely deflated Graham's rage, and instead of another hour wasted with accusations and recriminations, they were able to develop a defensive strategy and arrange corrective procedures to handle the government's new drug operation. Forewarned is forearmed. They weren't going down without a fight, and Graham had influence in places Richards knew nothing about. Graham was almost excited about the idea of taking down the DEA's new boy and "slamming" his operation back in his face.

Strong told Graham he would take care of Richards. He had a personal score to settle. Graham agreed as long as he got the job done right and soon. He didn't want any foul ups.

Strong left Graham's office on an upbeat note, but it fell flat later that afternoon when he met with his new associates. They had ideas of their own, and Strong wasn't about to argue. Death in three piece suits—that was the picture in Strong's mind every time he dealt with them. He had defended some really tough characters in his career, but these boys set an all time high. It was all he could do to sit still and pay attention. Still, he had a job, and they expected him to do it. Unlike Graham there were no second chances. Do or die was their credo.

When Strong left the back room of the restaurant, he sank into the seat of his car. His heart was beating so fast that he thought it might burst out of his chest. How people could deal with this constant pressure, he didn't know. He would be thankful when it was all over. He had some serious thinking to do. If he was going to make this work, he had to be prepared.

He didn't have a choice now. He had hooked up with the Bolivian cartel. Their leaders were notorious for setting examples of those who failed them. Everybody knew about the Columbians, but these Bolivians were incomparable. They took death to a new level, and they carried it with them wherever they went. It surrounded them with an aura of darkness, a void made more sinister by its total lack of emotion. These were hardened criminals, men of death, dealing in drugs and destruction.

Their plan actually might save him if he could carry it out. To repay his debt to them, he had to bring down Graham. They wanted the meth rings broken and cocaine to become the drug of choice in the American market. Their plan was feasible, if nothing went wrong.

Strong laughed a harsh barking sound. Richards always said that it was impossible for everything to go right in any plan. The difference in good leaders and great ones—great ones could make a plan work even after things went wrong. Odd that he was remembering what the man he was going to shoot had said. The Bolivians were going to back him up, but he had to do the initial shooting; after that it would be up to him to take care of himself. He had his instructions. He knew his job. He would succeed. What other choice did he have?

Graham wasn't waiting on Strong. After he calmed down, he realized it would take time to plan a hit, but he had a plan of his own. While Strong was hitting the DEA operation on one side, Graham planned a different point of attack. He was going after the leader, someone whose death would bring the whole operation to its knees.

Weeks earlier Graham had placed a call to an attorney in Washington and had him notify General Moreland that he needed to contact his friend. The attorney recognized Graham's voice, but refrained from saying anything. It was better to know less not more when dealing with some clients. He placed the call, wondering how a well respected general had gotten mixed up with Graham. He reasoned it could be a legitimate enterprise but not likely.

General Roger "Rocky" Moreland was a highly decorated and respected leader in the military. His current command placed him at Andrews Air Force Base, his job to oversee the President's air transportation. He felt uneasy when he returned Grahams' call until Graham asked if he would help secure a position for a friend. Graham gave him the Air Force captain's name, and Moreland told Graham he would be glad to have the orders put through. Moreland exhaled loudly as he hung up the phone, thankful that his request had not been for anything more. His dealings with Graham left him feeling decidedly uncomfortable.

It was hard to believe that he, a highly decorated veteran, a test pilot, and a career officer could have fallen in with a man like Graham, but that was exactly what had happened. Graham had never done anything to make Moreland distrust him, but he knew some of Graham's dealings bordered on illegal. It was too late for second thoughts now. He was Graham's man, and nothing could change it.

Moreland dropped his head in his hands, rubbing his brow in frustration, as he remembered their first meeting. They had met at a lounge in Florida. Graham had spotted him getting drunk and rowdy as usual. He started buying him drinks and talking. Moreland mistook Graham's attention and in his drunken stupor hit on Graham. Graham brushed the incident aside and even agreed to stay in touch.

Months later, they met in a casino in Tunica, Mississippi. It didn't take Graham long to realize that Moreland had more than one vice. He knew his failings; he was an incurable gambler, and that night had run up astronomical debts at the tables, gambling, he realized later, against odds a blind man wouldn't take. Graham paid his debts and finally ushered him from the floor after securing the favors of a young man for the night.

Unknown to Moreland, Graham used his phone to video a few of the more intimate details as a souvenir of his visit to the Magnolia State. Graham left the next day but promised to stay in touch. When Moreland found out later about the video, it was too late for him to save his reputation or his career. His only choice was to do favors for a man who held his future in his hands, a man he didn't trust.

Graham had never liked the new President, too much change for his peace of mind. Graham liked things just the way they were. The idea had occurred to him after he inadvertently found out about a subversive group of radicals. They were a group of religious extremists, an underground splinter group claiming to be advocates of the Islamic faith. Through an intermediary, Graham contacted the group with a plan to make them heroes in the Muslim world. After much discussion and negotiation, they finally agreed. Graham would supply the weapons and everything to carry out the plan. In return for their services, they would receive a substantial reward and positions in his organization later, if they chose. As a good faith offering, Graham agreed to safely relocate them and meet all their needs until time for the strike. Once the details were finalized, Graham stationed his men with them to insure no one leaked any information beforehand.

When Graham contacted Moreland at his home some weeks later and asked for a copy of the President's flight schedule, Moreland was not surprised. He tried to explain that the procedure for transporting the President was complex. Three helicopters were used. Routes were not given until the last minute and differed for each helicopter. The craft carrying the President was chosen at the last minute and designated as Marine One only after the President was safely on board. It was impossible to identify the Presidential aircraft beforehand.

Graham instructed Moreland to supply all the information he had about the routes and to make certain that Captain Newman was assigned to pilot one of the helicopters. He informed Moreland that Newman would take care of the situational logistics when the time came.

Moreland made the arrangements. He didn't have any other choice. He hadn't asked what Graham's plan was, but it was obvious. Now all Moreland could do was pray that the Secret Service was prepared for the situation. Moreland feared they were about to be tested.

Graham had been patient for weeks. He felt vindicated in his actions. The President had brought this on himself by authorizing this new drug operation. Billings was scheduled to leave Camp David the following Sunday morning. Graham's men had everything in place. Anti-aircraft missiles were easy to obtain if money was no object, and Graham was willing to pay. The three teams, now fully equipped, positioned themselves at designated vantage points miles from Camp David and awaited Graham's final instructions. If they received no verification, then they were to take out any aircraft which flew in range. They were willing to sacrifice themselves on the altar of religious zeal to bring about the downfall of America, their despised enemy.

Moreland had warned Graham that it was practically impossible to identify the President's craft before departure. Graham told him that Captain Newman would take charge from his position on the squad and for Moreland to forget he had ever heard anything about Graham. Moreland was more than happy to agree.

As the morning approached, Moreland prayed that someone would intervene, but he refrained from doing anything to stop the impending strike. As the helicopter with the President's aides was being boarded, the President received an urgent message, and he was recalled to the compound. The helicopter lifted off without him and began the trip back to Washington. Within minutes, the craft reached the first strike zone, and the radicals fired, thinking it held the President. Their missile hit the tail of the craft, and the helicopter spun out of control, crashing into the dense trees below, instantly killing several of the crew and passengers, one of which was Captain Newman whose last minute message to Graham about the change had not been received.

Air Force jets accompanying the individual aircraft were instantly relayed satellite images pin pointing the missile's launch site and retaliated immediately by firing on the radical's position. Within seconds of the strike, the remaining helicopters were told to stand down. The President was rushed by car to a nearby airfield where he was flown by a circuitous route back to Washington.

Camp David for miles around was cordoned off. Military and civilian forces began a sweep of the adjacent area. The remaining radicals were quickly apprehended and, still fervently swearing death to all Americans, immediately incarcerated. Graham's plan had failed. His last hope for survival now lay with Strong.

The Secret Service began an all out campaign to find the source of the information given to the radicals. After hours of investigation searching through phone records and duty rotation schedules, the most likely sources were narrowed down to a handful of personnel. Eventually one disgruntled subordinate following lengthy interrogation gave them Moreland's name. When questioned, Moreland refused to answer anything or take a lie detector test and requested immediate representation from the Judge Advocate General's office.

Moreland now faced the charge of treason and plotting with terrorists to assassinate the President of the United States. He was in total disgrace, his military career ruined by lust and greed and stupidity. Realizing there was no hope for him, no reduction of charges, no extenuating circumstances which would ever appease the crimes he had commit, he calmly and quietly revealed to the board of inquiry his association with a man who had blackmailed him. He refused to give Graham's name believing that Graham might retaliate against his family. He knew the FBI would soon find Graham's connection to him, and justice would be served.

With the shame and disgrace of his actions now known, he asked for time to talk with his family before matters were made public. A decorated officer and veteran who had fought admirably in the service of his country, Moreland was left with few alternatives. As he marched from the interrogation room to his holding cell, he overpowered the young soldier detailed to accompany him, grabbed his side arm, and calmly blew off the top of his skull.

Following the investigation, transportation for the President was revamped and security measures tightened. President Billings praised the Secret Service and Armed Forces for their swift and decisive retaliatory actions and their increased security measures. He spoke to the American public about the need for continued safety measures for all citizens both at home and abroad, and he adamantly refused to let one incident affect the way he carried out his duties or to undermine his belief in the rights of all Americans to protect themselves and their families.

Gun Rights advocates began taking a closer look at the President's policies with the aim of backing him in his re-election.

Caroline just shook her head in disbelief. They could have been killed and Robert viewed the incident as a political windfall. She would never understand his thinking. No, she understood his thinking. It was his feelings that were lacking. He had none where she or the baby was concerned. He focused solely on his Presidency and his future re-election.

Slam Shut was one of the most successful operations ever undertaken by the DEA. With cooperation from other agencies, they were hitting labs, breaking up distribution routes, seizing trucks, drugs, and equipment. Ring leaders were arrested and sentenced to lengthy convictions. Prior records forced the courts to declare many habitual offenders and incarcerate them in maximum security facilities. Lawyers were raking in the money just trying to make a defense for their clients. Richards' men had irrefutable proof, in most cases, and coupled with previous arrest records convicted meth dealers and their associates were placing a heavy burden on the federal prison system. For once, that was an indisputably good thing.

Strong laughed when he heard about Graham's latest loss. He knew the Bolivians were behind much of the intelligence being funneled into Richards' operation. He was biding his time. He would have to strike at a moment's notice, but he was ready. Through his Bolivian contacts, Strong had arranged for a utility van to be prepared and placed in a hangar at the airport. Richards was most vulnerable when he was boarding or exiting a plane. The plan was to shoot him, incapacitating, but not killing him.

Later that day when Graham finally reached Strong, he was livid. His plan had failed and he was left relying on Strong. He didn't bother with greetings; he was practically screaming. "Why haven't you done something about Richards? I'm losing everything! Who's going to pay your fat fees if I'm in jail?" He pounded his desk, emphasizing his anger.

Strong mopped at the sweat running down his face. The weeks it had taken to get everything in place had cost Graham a fortune, and Strong knew it. "Calm down. You want this done right, don't you? I won't get a second chance." He assumed his most authoritative voice. "Look, I've been getting men and vehicles in place. Everything takes time unless you want to raise suspicion." He paused. He could hear Graham's labored breathing over the phone. He was going to have a heart attack if he didn't relax. He grinned. That wouldn't be so bad, and it sure would solve a lot of his problems. "I have the perfect plan in place and the men to carry it out. Everything is set. He leaves for Cleveland in the morning. Just watch the news."

Graham could hear the arrogance in his voice. Strong had gotten cocky lately, and Graham wasn't impressed. There was nothing to be smug about. His whole operation was going south faster than he could think. A deadly calm filled his voice. "I will. There had just better be something for me to see."

The menace in his tone sent a shiver down Strong's spine. The Bolivians weren't the only ones Strong had to please, but he didn't take kindly to threats, not from Graham. It was going to be a pleasure to see him fall.

Strong reloaded his rifle. He was going to do the hit himself. He wasn't a bad shot, but he wasn't the greatest either. If he had anyone else do the job, there would be too many questions, and he couldn't afford for people to start asking questions now. He definitely didn't want anybody noising around in his business. His dealings with the Bolivians had to remain secret; revealing anything about them to anyone would bring an excruciating death sentence. He couldn't afford for Graham to find out either. If he did, Strong knew the Bolivians wouldn't help him. He would be forced to face Graham on his own.

He took a calming breath, sighted the target, and gently squeezed the trigger. The bullet sliced through the outer portion of the outlined leg. Not bad. He had gained some valuable first-hand experience tagging along with Richards on their earlier operations. It was finally about to pay off.

Strong laughed to himself. He was becoming quite adept at working both sides of the fence. He was a very, very rich man now, and all that stood between him and his future was this last assignment for the Bolivians. He lifted the rifle to his shoulder again.

Early the next morning, Strong lay secluded in the back of a dark, airport utility van; his driver had orders to cover him while he made the hit. A second vehicle would act as a decoy for them to get away. If they acted quickly, they could make the hit and be out of the airport before security could react. The second vehicle would draw airport security's attention giving them time to escape. That was the plan that he had given his men. It was a good plan, but different from Strong's. He wasn't worried. These men were being paid well enough that they were willing to take the chance of being caught. They wouldn't talk; Graham would see to that.

Much too early to Amanda's way of thinking, Tim climbed out of bed and got ready for work. Today he was flying to Cleveland for a scheduled afternoon meeting with their local task force. He left the apartment at a run, a little later than usual. It always seemed to take longer to say a proper goodbye these days. His car finally pulled to a stop a short distance from his plane. He thanked his driver, grabbed his briefcase, and started toward the airplane.

The white hot pain that seared his thigh slammed him to the ground just before he heard the rifle's report. He had been stupid. He had forgotten the first rule of the streets. He had underestimated his enemy. He lay crumpled on the pavement beside his car while the vehicle and driver were sprayed with bullets. Shattered glass fell over him and bullets ricocheted in every direction. He couldn't move. He was pinned down and unarmed. He heard his driver moan as the barrage continued. The firing stopped; tires screamed as his attackers fled the scene. Within minutes, the sound of sirens filled the air. Airport security and emergency vehicles swarmed the area, careening to a stop beside his car.

Paramedics rushed to attend him, but he insisted they see about his driver first. They returned and shook their heads when he looked up. It could just have easily been him. He had been lucky. He fought against the pain as they applied pressure to the wound to stop the blood loss and secured it tightly. They placed him in an ambulance, but he refused to leave until the scene was secured and his men could arrive. He identified himself to airport security and requested special clearance for his team. They arrived within minutes of the attack.

The airport had gone into immediate lock down; no flights were taking off or landing. Passenger planes taxied to the far side of the tarmac. Those in the air circled in holding patterns. The airport was at a standstill. The second vehicle, which had assisted Strong in his escape, was caught behind the fence at the outer perimeter. The two men inside quickly gave up. They believed it would only be a matter of time before they were released and could flee the country. The job paid well for any inconvenience or extra time involved with its completion. Even if it meant prison time, they would be well provided for, so there was no need to risk dying. They just needed to make their excuses convincing.

By using two identical vehicles, Strong and his driver managed to escape from the airfield but were caught in a road block at the outskirts of the airport. Strong had shoved his assault rifle in a tool box in the back of the van. Police dogs, searching all suspicious vehicles, immediately hit on the scent of gunpowder. When the tool box was opened, police armed with assault rifles surrounded them. Strong and his driver were seized and taken into custody.

After Richards' team arrived to oversee the investigation, he allowed the medics to take him to a nearby hospital where his wound could be treated. It had been more superficial than critical, but against doctor's orders, Richards returned to police headquarters to interrogate the men taken into custody.

When Richards saw Strong on the other side of the two-way glass, he wasn't surprised. He had known it would be just a matter of time. For Strong to be personally involved, Graham must be running scared.

Strong was relieved when Richards finally walked into the interrogation room. It was vital that Richards survive the day's attack. Strong wasn't much of an actor, but his life depended on his ability to convince Richards of the reason for his actions.

Richards walked stiffly toward the table and eased down in a chair opposite Strong. A betraying grimace crossed his face before he could hide it. Determination etched his brow as he stared at Strong. He let the silence lengthen, giving Strong the opportunity to start his explanation. He wasn't in any hurry; he had waited years to bring this operation down. He wasn't going to make any false steps or bungle any civil rights at this late date. He had hammered his men with lectures on following correct procedure in handling evidence and interrogating suspects. In many cases, they would only have one opportunity to make their case, and all their work, hours of investigation, could be lost by a simple procedural error.

Strong finally spoke. "Look, you don't have anything on me. I just happened to be in the wrong place. That's all. I was meeting a client who was flying in from out of town." Strong knew that his excuse was flimsy; he wasn't really trying to make it too believable.

"Sure, then where did the rifle come from?" Richards didn't act impressed by Strong's obvious stalling.

"Hey, I told you I was meeting a client. I didn't know that was in there. It must have been someone else's." He raised his voice to emphasize his innocence.

"How do you explain the fact that the rifle had been recently fired? Or that your hands have gunpowder residue on them?" Richards tossed the forensic report on the table. Papers slid across the scarred surface. Strong didn't even bother looking.

"That doesn't prove anything. You know I'm a sports shooter. I went to the range recently. If you check, I'll bet you'll find that I went late yesterday afternoon." Strong leaned back in the chair with a smug look on his face. He had to be convincing but not overly so.

"I bet I'll find someone who will swear that you were there. I bet I'll find a record of your scores and everything, but we both know you're lying." Richards didn't take his eyes off Strong. He knew Strong was lying, at least about the shooting. Just like he knew that the evidence he was talking about would actually be there. But he was still lying.

"Let's get real. You were found at the scene, with the weapon in your possession, and gunpowder residue on your hands. It can't get much better than that. First degree murder, attempted murder, assault on a federal officer, destruction of public property, endangering the public, possessing firearms in a restricted area—do I need to go on?" Richards was tired of his dancing around the subject. Strong was guilty, and they both knew it.

"You've got nothing solid against me. Someone else could just have easily fired that gun, and I can account for the rest." Strong tried to appear calm, but he was getting a little nervous. He needed Richards to offer him a deal, something. He had to continue his bluff.

Richards pushed back his chair and stood stiffly, slowly easing his weight onto his injured leg. White-hot fire raced up his spine. He gritted his teeth against the pain and turned to leave. "Think about a nice long prison sentence while I'm gone. See if your memory improves. Maybe you'll have something better to offer tomorrow after a night in jail. The accommodations may not be to your usual high standards." He reached the door and left without looking back. He would give Strong time to enjoy his solitude and then talk to him again.

He needed to get home. His leg was on fire, and he didn't want to take the painkillers until he could lie down. The doctor warned him that they could take down an elephant, and right now, his leg felt about that size.

When Amanda received the call from Tim's office that he had been injured, her heart stopped. She hadn't really considered the possibility before; now it was a reality, and she was panic-stricken. She knew that once she saw him, she would be fine, but as she raced through the late afternoon traffic, she was anything but the level-headed, dispassionate reporter.

She arrived just minutes after him, but he had already taken the prescription from the doctor. He could tell that it was beginning to take the edge off, so he could put on a brave face without completely giving too much away. For her sake, he would down play the day's events. All he could do was hope that she didn't get hold of the police reports. He would have a lot more explaining to do if she did.

The first thing she did was wrap her arms around him until the shaking inside her lessened. Then she made a frontal attack that he wasn't expecting. "Where are your jeans?" She pointed to the jogging pants he was wearing. "These aren't quite your style."

He shrugged as though it was not important. "They cut them off at the hospital." He reached for her hand. "Why? Don't you think these are sexy?" He was beginning to feel really good, kind of like he was floating. He tried to smile, but it turned into a silly grin. As a narcotics agent he saw firsthand the devastating effects of drugs on people; he made it a personal rule never to take anything stronger than aspirin, if he could help it. Today was an exception.

"What did they give you?" She could see that his eyes were dilated and his head seemed too heavy for him to hold up.

He felt good, but he couldn't focus on her questions. He could see how this could become addictive, but no one ever achieved that elusive first high a second time. That was what created the perpetual circle of dependency.

"I don't know, but it's really nice." He slumped back against the couch and just lay there with his eyes closed. Maybe getting shot wasn't so bad after all. He could hear himself talking, but he didn't really know what he was saying.

Amanda pushed him down on the couch and covered him with a blanket. He was asleep before she could straighten up. Now the tears fell, coursing down her face in an endless stream. She didn't try to stop; she knew it was just reaction to her fear, relief that he wasn't killed this time. He was right; she didn't really know how stressful his job would be, for both of them. She kissed his cheek, and he reached for her in his sleep. She slipped out of his arms and stood studying him as he lay there. She loved him to distraction, so she better learn to toughen up if they were going to make this relationship work. Then she went and poured herself a stiff drink.

Richards was tough but every step on his injured leg the next day sent a searing pain racing up his body. He would have to block it if was he going to get anything accomplished. He certainly couldn't take the pain medication they had given him the day before and remain upright. He hadn't slept that soundly in years, but he felt groggy this morning. The steaming cup of black coffee clutched in his hand should help that problem. Now all he needed was for Strong to roll over on Graham and his day would be off to a good start.

Richards had the leverage he needed. He had detailed records of Strong's activities over the past three years, everything he needed to put him away for years. He would be spending time with some of the very men he hadn't successfully represented. Richards wondered how many of them would be glad to get up close and personal with Strong if the opportunity presented itself. He might just have to remind him of that.

He had to stop himself from grinning when he entered the room. Strong looked up and swallowed hard, his throat desperately dry. He didn't like the scowl on Richards' face.

"I heard you wanted to see me, so don't waste my time. If you have something to say, say it." He set the steaming coffee on the scarred table and eased into the chair across from Strong.

"I'll get right to the point. I can help you get Graham. I'll testify for you and with the information I'm sure you already have, we can present an air tight case." Strong felt that he could persuade Richards to make a deal. He sat back in the hard chair and waited.

"I'm not taking any chances. Right now it's just your word against his. He could simply deny the accusations and pass the blame on to someone else, deny culpability. I want solid, irrefutable evidence. Can you get me that?"

Strong hesitated. "I don't know. What did you have in mind?" He didn't want to chance a confrontation with Graham, but that was what it sounded like Richards wanted.

"I'll get you released. You arrange a meeting with Graham. I want an ironclad confession. I don't care what you have to do, but get it. If you don't, you'll grow very old before you get out of prison. Don't think you'll be alone when you meet with him; I'll be right there with you, listening to every word. If you try to double cross me, I'll take you down. Understood?"

Cold dark eyes stared directly at Strong; he could feel the intensity underlying every word Richards spoke. He had seen Richards in action; he didn't want to be the recipient of any retaliation. "Can you be sure that he won't find out that we've talked?" Strong's brave front was slipping. If Graham thought for a minute that he had made a deal, Richards wouldn't have time to save him. Strong felt like a clown in the circus juggling three time bombs all set to explode: Richards, Graham, and the Bolivian cartel. He had to make this work. His life depended on a successful juggling act.

"No one knows about your arrest. The driver has been held in isolation, since his paperwork accidently got lost." Richards smirked. He wasn't above bending the law a little when it was necessary. "He hasn't had the opportunity to talk to or contact anyone. You should be safe on that score. All you'll need is a good reason to have escaped from the airport." He leaned back, his next words laced with irony. "I'm sure a fine lawyer like you can come up with something believable." He waited for a minute, letting Strong weigh his options. There weren't many. "Do we have a deal?"

Strong laughed a humorless sound that bounced harshly off the concrete walls. "Sure what choice do I have?"

Richards stood. He didn't feel any pity for him. "You always have choices. You just might not like them. I'll get back to you." With that, he left the room. Strong wanted to sigh in relief, but he knew that he had to come up with a convincing story for Graham. He hadn't counted on Richards wanting more than his testimony, but he could make this work.

When Strong telephoned Graham in Memphis later that day to arrange a meeting, he told Graham he didn't want to talk on the phone but would explain everything in person. He told him that he would need a new identity and a passport. He wanted to get out of the country fast. Graham didn't sound pleased but agreed, and they arranged to meet in two days in an abandoned warehouse near the docks of the Mississippi

River. It was reasonably remote, which would hopefully give Graham an added sense of security.

Richards wanted him to talk, and the only way he would do that was if he thought he was safe. Richards' team worked all-out to get the surveillance equipment in place and to be out of the area a full day before the planned meeting. Richards figured Graham would send someone to check out the area before he risked coming down. They wouldn't find anything. The sophisticated electronics Richards' team used weren't easily detected, and they hadn't activated anything yet. Anyone doing a sweep wouldn't find them. When Graham arrived they would set everything in motion. Now all they needed was for Strong to do his part. He was a wild card. He could be convincing, but Graham was no fool. Strong better be at his best.

Strong was early; he wanted to arrive before Graham. Richards might be able to protect him and he might not. Strong didn't want Graham setting a trap set for him. His footsteps echoed down the empty building and bounced off the rafters. He felt like he was about to jump out of his skin. He had to get a grip. If he could face the Bolivians, he could face Graham.

A car engine whined around the corner and echoed through the entrance; Strong turned to see Graham's SUV pull up. Graham climbed out; he walked quickly to the door but hesitated before entering. He wasn't any braver than Strong. Neither one of them trusted the other.

"Come on in. I want to get this over as fast as possible. I don't feel safe out in the opening. I don't know if the DEA has any hard evidence to connect me to anything or not, but I don't want to wait around and see." He had moved toward Graham as he spoke, lessening the need to raise his voice.

"Just how did you pull that off and not get caught?" Graham set his briefcase down beside him.

Strong smiled. "I consider that a stroke of genius. I had a new car flown in from out of state and stored in a nearby hangar until I could pick it up. After I fired my shot, I tossed the rifle and gloves in the van and slipped away while the others had everyone pinned down. I shoved my jacket in a trash barrel and jumped in my car. Later when I was stopped by airport security, they had no reason to suspect me of anything. I had my paperwork ready and off I went." He laughed. "It was almost too easy."

"I heard that a DEA officer was killed in the attack. Is it true?" Graham eyes narrowed.

"What do you think? That's why I need to get out of here fast. Besides, we both know that you've already had that checked out. So why waste my time. I did what you told me. I took care of Richards. Now I want to start a new life somewhere warm. Did you bring everything?"

"What about the others? Can they tie anything to me?"

"No, they were hired through a third party. They knew the score. Just make sure that they are taken care of and there won't be any problems. I've already arranged for a lawyer, and since the only death can be attributed to me. They shouldn't face too much time." Strong looked directly at Graham. "Keep your word. They'll keep theirs." He frowned. He didn't like the look on Graham's face. "Once I'm gone, you shouldn't have any more problems."

Graham laughed, "my thoughts exactly." He bent to open his briefcase and strengthened holding a 38 pistol, equipped with a silencer. "Ironic, wouldn't you say. With you gone, my problems will be over. You didn't really think that I would have you kill Richards and then be stupid enough to let you live. What would happen when your money ran out? I would never know a minute's rest." He raised the revolver.

Strong began easing back. Where was Richards? He wanted to raise his hand to ward of the shot; he wanted to beg. He could feel his knees getting weak. Graham took aim. It would be hard to miss at this range.

Then the room exploded with sounds. Strong could hear Graham's high pitched scream as his own knees crumpled and he fell to the ground expecting to feel the agony of the bullet any second. Suddenly Strong was jerked to his feet and pushed aside.

Graham lay writhing from the impact of the 50,000 volts from the stun gun. His revolver was now in the hands of the SWAT team. Richards couldn't ask for more. It had been dangerous to risk Strong, but Richards felt he was justified. He had waited that extra few minutes and Graham had added attempted murder to his long list of other felonies. With conspiracy to commit murder, attempted murder, racketeering, and all the related crimes, Graham didn't have a prayer. Even with their evidence in order, the hardest part would be waiting for the trial.

After weeks of delays, Graham's trial was finally underway. His lawyers had tried everything to buy more time, to subvert the evidence, to suborn the witnesses, but when Richards walked into the courtroom,

Graham visibly paled. At that moment he knew all was lost. Strong was being held in custody in the courtroom, and Graham turned in his seat to face him. The look he gave Strong was chilling. Strong knew that if he lived through this trial, he had better have his plans in place. The witness protection program was just a front for him until the trial was over. He had already arranged with the cartel to make Bolivia his new home. They were pleased with the results he had obtained for them.

Graham's death sentence for the shooting of Richards' driver and for being implicitly tied to multiple other murders shook the drug world. Richards only wished he could have taken Strong down with him, but Strong was a marked man. One false move and he would reap his just reward. Richards could only hope.

Raul opened the latest report from Alberto whose reports along with satellite news programs kept Raul apprised on the progress of Graham's trial. He felt pleased that everything was going so smoothly. By supplying the American drug task force with information on the meth trade, he was able to eliminate his biggest competitors without having to wage all out war. Wars of any kind were messy, and everybody got hurt. This way was a little slower but well worth the investment of time and money. He was very pleased with the results.

After reading Alberto's message, Raul sat down at his desk and punched in a code on his computer opening a recessed panel on the opposite wall. Multiple computer and surveillance screens were displayed. He studied the screens. The crops were flourishing and almost ready for harvest. He repositioned the satellite, and the aerial photos showed hundreds of fields lush with green foliage. They would be ready for processing and shipment at just the right time.

He was indeed a happy man, and with the unwitting help of the DEA, he could now pursue the downfall of the meth dealers in the southwest, thus insuring the demand for cocaine for years to come. Paul had done well. He was extremely proud of his son.

Chapter 19

PAUL WAS EDGY. IT wasn't like him to feel that way. His work kept him busy, but he needed more than that; still, it was becoming increasingly difficult to find even a few minutes to talk to Caroline much less actually spend time together alone. Robert, on the other hand, had it made. He wasn't really bothered by Caroline's dismissal of him from her bed. With one phone call, Robert could have anything he wanted. Paul sighed dramatically. He still had a job to do. He might as well get busy.

Robert had lost all true feelings for Caroline. Unless she was needed to bolster his public image or endorse his political efforts, she remained a fact of his life, but not a part. He couldn't fault her display of public support and admiration for his work. In return, he admired her loyalty to his presidency but was unconcerned by her latest dictates. Besides, being banned from her bed was no hardship. Alberto always found older, more experienced or younger, more enthusiastic political supporters willing to discreetly contribute their time and personal attention to meet the President's needs.

Alberto was amazed at how foolish women of all ages could sometimes be. They vowed to keep their liaisons secret until their dying day, assuming quite falsely that they were the only ones on whom the President bestowed his favors. Alberto would have laughed if it hadn't been important that they truly keep their actions secret. Of course, a few discreet photos and a little background information was all he really needed to influence any situation. He honestly felt that his skills were being wasted most days.

Caroline's schedule was becoming increasingly demanding. She was finding it harder and harder to schedule even a few minutes with her son. When her secretary mentioned her upcoming trip to Phoenix, Caroline wanted to scream. Then she had a wonderful idea. She would take the baby and stop off in Texas to visit her parents. She had her secretary begin making the necessary arrangements as she returned to the residence to inform Ms. Martin that she and Robbie would be accompanying her.

It never crossed her mind to ask Robert first. She no longer considered him a part of her life, and as far as she could tell, he felt the same way. It made her sad sometimes to think of their earlier friendship and the fun they had had in those early days. Now there was nothing; they didn't hate each other; they didn't love each other. There were no feelings at all, such an empty wasteland in which to raise a child.

The message Paul received simply stated that the President needed to talk to him. One secretary to another, not friend to friend, those days were gone for the most part. Now it was President to personal advisor. Paul frowned. Was Robert concerned about Caroline's upcoming trip? That seemed unlikely, but with Robert it was difficult to tell. Paul knew that Alberto was handling most of Robert's personal requests, so that probably wasn't the problem either. He would just have to wait and see. He drew the meeting to a close and headed for the Oval Office.

Robert sat behind his desk, tapping his gold fountain pen on a stack of papers awaiting his signature. He had been advised of Caroline's change in plans. He was not overly concerned about how her parents perceived their personal relationship, but he did worry that if they felt something was amiss between them that it might translate into less support for his political future. Texas money followed Texas money, and Robert didn't want to lose a penny of it.

Robert sat deep in thought. Just like Caroline believed, he was always thinking of the future. His presidency had not faced any dire threats, nothing to put Robert's expertise in the spotlight, to make his presidency memorable. He had made steady and consistent progress on his campaign promises. He had carried out his duties as President honorably and admirably. He had upheld the dignity of the country in his dealings with foreign dignitaries, but Robert realized that wasn't enough. He needed something to capture the hearts and imagination of the American people if he wanted to be sure of his reelection. He glanced at the folder on his desk and smiled to himself; he had a plan, one that he felt certain would insure his success.

Paul knocked briefly then entered the office. Robert sat staring at the papers in front of him. He looked up rather absently.

"Hey, I got your message. You look a little dazed. Anything I can help with?" Paul sat on the edge of the desk and waited.

Robert thought for a minute before he spoke. "Actually, I think you can. I don't want Caroline and the baby traveling alone, especially since they will be visiting her parents. Can you clear a few days to go with them?"

Paul didn't want his pleasure to show. He made a pretense of thinking for a minute. "I think I can arrange it. I'll check with her secretary and make the arrangements. Anything else?"

"As a matter of fact, there is. Have a seat. I want to talk to you about a plan that I think will bring a windfall of support for us." He tapped the folder on his desk. "This is a final report from Tim Richards and the DEA's special task force outlining the progress that has been made in limiting the production and distribution of meth in the United States." He stopped then glanced at Paul.

"Yes, I have a copy. From what I've read so far, their operation has achieved remarkable results. How does that figure in your plan?" Paul's earlier excitement had waned. He was beginning to get the feeling things were about to take a turn for the worse.

"I want to propose an all-out effort to combat the cocaine trade in the States." He sat back with a smug look on his face, waiting for Paul's reaction. He obviously thought Paul would approve.

Paul was stunned. Robert had to be crazy if he thought he could ever be allowed to pursue such an idea. "Don't you think that might make it a little hard on you?" He couldn't keep the cynicism from his tone. "Or do you think they would make a special dispensation for the President?" Paul was beginning to let his anger affect his judgment. He had to tread carefully. Robert didn't know the true involvement he had with cocaine.

Robert frowned. He didn't like Paul reminding him of his occasional, special needs. Many brilliant people had little idiosyncrasies. That was one of the things that made them exceptional. "No. But there's no reason the widespread trafficking and use can't be curtailed. Think of the press such an effort will elicit." He sounded like an excited little school boy.

"Think of the scandal it will make if anyone ever finds out about your use." Paul had to make him see reason.

"That won't happen. Alberto will see to that, besides I rarely need that anymore." He really was pleased with himself.

"Is that going to be your argument if someone does?" Paul stood leaning over his desk.

"It won't come to that and you know it."

"I know nothing of the sort. Anything can happen. It only takes one slip, one disgruntled person, to bring an army to its knees. What makes you think you're any different? That it couldn't happen to you? Just think how many people would love to bring this presidency to an end. Do you really want to hand them the ammunition for the gun?" He slapped his hands against the hard surface of the desk. Some days he wondered if he would survive Robert's presidency without strangling him.

Robert was actually excited about the idea. Paul was speechless. He didn't even know how to begin arguing against the idea. He needed time to think, but he had to keep Robert from discussing his idea with anyone else.

"Look, let me have a few days to think about this and then we'll talk. When I get back from Phoenix, I'll have something definite for you. In the meantime, concentrate on that bill we have before Congress. See if you can swing some of those undecided voters in our favor. Use that persuasive genius you have for our good while I'm gone."

"All right, but I want to pursue this before the end of the year. We can extend the authority already mandated for the meth effort and the tenure of the members of the special task force. Richards did a good job. I'd like to see him head this operation also." Robert had assumed his authoritative voice, and Paul knew when to accept defeat gracefully in order to fight another day.

Let him think that his plan would work. Paul would dissuade him from implementing it later, if necessary. He might just have his work cut out for him, though. Robert could be very tenacious sometimes, especially when he thought he had a great idea, and from the zealous gleam in his eyes, Robert thought he had a brilliant plan.

Paul left Robert's office running his hand through his hair. He felt like pulling it out. Robert could really foul things up if he insisted on this course of action. Paul needed this trip more than ever now. Maybe Caroline would have an idea about how to handle this latest development. Just when things seemed to be going so well—this!

Caroline stepped from the limousine to board the plane with Robbie in her arms. She turned at the top flight of stairs and waved to the gathered crowd. Everyone laughed and applauded, and cameras flashed when Robbie raised his chubby little arm to wave, too. Caroline laughed at his antics. Newspaper articles the next morning featured photos of the laughing mother and smiling child, dubbed by the press as the White House Darlings, the Pride of the President.

Robert always liked good press, but these photos irritated him. If he had been better at analyzing his own feelings, he would have realized like everyone else around him did that he was simply jealous. When he snapped at his secretary for dropping a file, she knew that it was going to be a long week with the First Lady gone, especially if she gained much press at the conference. She sighed mightily as she returned to her desk and reached for the bottle of aspirin she kept handy in her desk drawer.

Later that afternoon when the President requested his personal line, she knew that his temper hadn't improved. He only used that line for conferences with a personal advisor not on staff in the White House. People speculated about who this person might be, but no one dared ask questions. Obviously, he wasn't being kept secret since both the First Lady and the Chief of Staff knew him and had made reference to him in conversations, but if anyone had ever seen him they didn't know it. His identity added a sense of mystery to the White House, much like the spiritual advisors and numerologists other Presidents were said to have conferred with.

Robert, of course, knew nothing of his staff's speculations nor would he have appreciated their interest in his personal affairs. He was President, and he could do almost anything he wanted. Right now he wanted Alberto to bring him someone young and willing, someone who wouldn't ask questions or expect favors, someone who would show him the respect he deserved. He slammed his fist on the desk, anyone but Caroline.

After two days of meetings and speeches on the pollution of underground water tables, contamination of above ground water sources, pesticides in foods, and the harmful effects of genetically engineered products, Caroline was ready for some home grown beef barbeque, Texas style with a house full of friends and neighbors and more food than a small army could eat. She didn't want to discuss politics, polls, papers, or husbands either. She wanted a few days of peace and quiet and solitude.

What she would get was the first on a grand scale, the second on a national scale, and the third not at all. But she would settle for the change in atmosphere, and knowing that she and Robbie were loved and appreciated, by her family at least.

When they boarded the plane for the flight to Texas, Robbie began fussing. When the nurse couldn't settle him, Caroline tried and was alarmed to see that he had begun to develop a slight fever. By the time their flight arrived, he was running a high fever; his little face was flushed, and his eyes were glazed. At first Caroline passed it off as another virus that he had picked up, but she arranged for the family doctor to meet them at her parent's home as soon as they landed. The nurse had given him fever medication, but it didn't appear to be helping. Caroline was being much braver this time after having survived the first incident, but she was really worried. Paul stayed by her side as they rushed through traffic to reach her parent's.

When the doctor examined Robbie, he seemed unconcerned, but decided to take a throat swab and blood sample back to the hospital just as a precaution. He spoke confidently of high fevers being typical in small children and gave Robbie a stronger dosage of fever medication, advising them to give him as much liquid as he would take. He would return later that evening to check on his progress and let them know if he found anything unusual. When Robbie lay impassive during the examination, Caroline knew something worse was wrong.

Caroline was rocking Robbie in her arms, singing softly to him as he lay half asleep when she received the call from the doctor. An ambulance had already been dispatched, and it was vital that Robbie be brought in as quickly as possible. Caroline couldn't think; she simply stared at the phone as though it were a strange object from another world. Paul grabbed the receiver and had the doctor repeat his information. Paul hung up the phone and put his arms around Caroline and Robbie. He held them close without speaking until the sirens sounded outside the estate. Paul nodded to the nurse to quickly gather the essentials as he walked Caroline and Robbie down the stairs from the nursery to the waiting ambulance.

When the paramedic started to tell them they couldn't ride in the back with the baby, Paul's scowl silenced him immediately. When he reached to take the baby, Paul turned and faced him and without a word spoken, the young man returned to his seat. They boarded together with Robbie still clutched in Caroline's arms. She would not relinquish him until they reached the hospital and the doctor insisted that she must. Paul gently eased him from her. She hadn't spoken; she hadn't cried. Now she simply folded like a paper doll. Paul caught her and led her to a private suite of rooms where they waited until the doctors made their diagnosis.

War might be hell, but waiting to hear the fate of a loved one was unbearable torture, an indescribable mental anguish, an agonizing physical torment that went even beyond pain. Caroline was numbed with fear. Paul was almost as frightened for her as he was Robbie. He could have handled hysterics, tears, anger, but deadly silence was impossible to fight. He clutched her ice cold hands, trying to warm them with his. He didn't care who saw or what they thought. They belonged to him. He would do whatever was necessary to protect them. He just didn't know how. Robbie's grandfathers were two of the richest and most powerful men in the world and there was nothing even they could do to help their grandson, even if they knew.

The doctors were concerned that Robbie's high fever was a symptom of something much worse, some internal irregularity. As a precaution they were asking for the parents to give blood only as a safety measure should surgery be required. Apparently, Robbie had a rather rare blood type, but Caroline's blood type didn't match. When Paul heard this, he sat frozen in place. This would be difficult to explain and impossible to keep secret if he didn't handle it the right way.

Paul asked to speak to the doctor in private and suggested that he be allowed to contact the President and make arrangements for the blood to be drawn by the White House physician and flown to the hospital. He assured the doctor that everything would be done expeditiously, and that as a means to insure the First Family's privacy, he would take charge of the necessary details. Anything that the doctor's required should be addressed to him since the First Lady was obviously extremely distraught with her son's illness, and as the child's godfather, he would assume the father's role in the absence of the President.

The doctor agreed that their paramount concern was receiving the necessary blood as quickly as possible. Insuring the family's privacy was also important to them, and anyone working with the doctors or involved in any way on Robbie's case would use the utmost discretion and maintain the strictest confidentiality. Paul prayed that would be the case.

He assured the doctor that he would personally keep the President up-to-date on Robbie's condition and that he would have transportation on standby should the need arise for the President to fly to Dallas. As it was the President was meeting with the Peruvian President and his trade minister and was in the process of negotiating a critical trade agreement between the two countries. Paul assured him that the President would fly out at a moment's notice if necessary. The doctor promised that if Robbie's condition worsened even the in slightest, he would immediately alert Paul so he could notify the President personally.

When the doctor left, Paul went to Caroline and told her that he would take care of everything. She was to only concern herself with praying for Robbie's quick recovery. He assured her that Robbie would be fine because he refused to think otherwise. He kissed her cheek and left her in the capable hands of Ms. Martin, who promised Paul that she would take care of Caroline until he made arrangements with the President.

Paul stepped into the adjoining room of the hospital suite and began punching Alberto's number in his phone. He would need Alberto's clear thinking if he expected to pull this off.

Paul explained the situation with Robbie quickly; then took a deep breath and told Alberto that Robbie wasn't Robert's son. There was no need for Paul to tell or Alberto to ask who the real father was. Alberto could hear the anguish of a father for his son in Paul's voice. Paul waited in silence for Alberto to speak. After a lengthy pause, Alberto offered him a workable solution to the problem.

Paul would contact Robert, have the White House physician draw the necessary blood, and give it to Alberto to transport to Dallas. Paul would have to have his own blood drawn by someone whom they could trust in Dallas while Alberto was in transit. When Alberto arrived, he would meet with Paul's doctor and an exchange would be made. No one would be the wiser, and Robbie would be safe.

Alberto told Paul to give him a few minutes, and he would have someone they could trust ready. In the meantime, Paul was to call

Robert and explain the situation and make arrangements to carry out his part of the plan in Washington.

Paul called the White House physician and had him beginning gathering the necessary materials to draw Robert's blood at the White House residence and safely store it for transport. Then he called Robert in his residence. For once he was alone. Robert realized there was a problem as soon as he heard Paul's voice. Paul's tone was laced with steel; he would brook no refusal on Robert's part, but Robert readily agreed to his instructions and even went so far as to ask if he should fly down in person. Paul assured him that he shouldn't because his unexpected departure would cause an avalanche of questions, and they would find themselves swarmed by curiosity seekers and reporters. Paul promised to keep Robert apprised of any changes and would direct the staff to have Air Force One placed on standby. Paul ended the call as Robert's personal physician and his nurse were admitted to the Presidential residence.

Paul had refrained from mentioning that the baby's blood was a rare type. Instead he told Robert that Caroline was insistent because she wanted to insure that the blood given to Robbie would be safe. If Robert himself hadn't been shocked by the events, he might have wondered at the plausibility of that reasoning. At the time, he didn't think anything about it.

Paul alerted the President's transportation officer to prepare a special flight for Alberto, the fastest available, and then he requested stand-by status for the President's plane. He emphasized the need for complete secrecy.

When he returned to the room, Caroline hadn't moved. He sat down next to her, waiting, hoping to hear from Alberto soon. Paul's phone vibrated slightly; he jumped and hurried into the adjacent room. Everything was arranged. Paul would be taken by car to a nearby residence where his blood would be drawn and prepared for transport. The doctor would meet Alberto at the airport and bring the container to the hospital. During transport, he would make the exchange, and no one would know the difference.

Paul didn't usually show his nerves, but this situation was like nothing he had ever faced before. It was too close to his heart, and he couldn't seem to detach himself from the situation enough to make wise decisions. Thank goodness he had Alberto; his level head and cool composure had come up with a feasible solution. All Paul could think about at first was just telling Robert the truth and letting the consequences be damned. Now he saw how foolhardy than would have been. Raul certainly wouldn't have been pleased when he found out.

Paul looked at Caroline, hunched over with her arms folded tightly around her middle. She looked as if she was in physical pain, but Paul knew that she wasn't. This was so much worse. He wanted to hold her in his arms. She looked so fragile, but she shook her head when he started to move toward her. She was right; they still had to maintain a physical distance if not emotional. She smiled at him sadly, so close yet so far away.

Paul took a breath and mouthed the name, Rafael. Caroline thought for a minute then shook her head. There was nothing he could do, not now. Afterward, she would contact him, earlier if she thought there was anything he could do, but not right now. Her parents were beside themselves with worry and would be here soon. That was enough. She didn't want to talk to anybody else.

When his phone vibrated again, Paul knew it was time for him to leave. He leaned toward Caroline. "I have to leave for a few minutes, but I'll be back soon. They have my number if anything changes." He frowned. How did he tell her what he had to do without anyone else knowing? "I have to arrange for transport from the plane to the hospital. Robert was adamant; in fact, he insisted that I take care of this—personally." He emphasized the last word. His eyes begged her to understand what he was trying to tell her.

Caroline looked at him blankly for a minute, then her eyes flared wider. Robert wouldn't care who handled the problem as long as it didn't adversely affect him. What was Paul talking about? Then it hit her. What had she been thinking? Now, she understood. What a mess this was! She nodded her head for him to leave then grabbed his hand and squeezed it tightly. She couldn't trust herself to speak.

Paul returned the pressure then smiled slightly, his dark eyes mirroring the pain she felt. "Everything will be all right. I promise." He turned then and raced from the room.

Caroline knew that the men in Paul's *family* didn't make promises that they couldn't keep. They learned that at a very early age. Someone's life might hang in the balance. In this case, it was their son's. Paul would keep his promise. Caroline took a deep breath, the first one that she had taken in hours.

Paul recognized *family* without conscious thought, even before the man stepped from the waiting car. There was an aura that the men of the family carried with them, a confidence that whatever they needed was theirs to have. It wasn't the flashy, old world gangster look or the tough guy, mafia swagger. It was more than that; it was a solitary aloofness, a detached reserve that separated and defined them. The main figures in the family were all sophisticated, educated intellectuals, wise in the workings of whatever world they had chosen to make their own, yet steeped in the world that had formed them. They were here to help him, and there would never be any fear of betrayal.

The man stepped forward and reached to take Paul's hand. "I'm Dr. Alvarez; I hear we have a little problem, nothing that we can't handle, of course. Just come with me, and we will have everything taken care of and awaiting the plane's arrival before you know it." He turned and ushered Paul into the car, and they quickly sped away. Paul didn't really want to talk. He needed a moment to process everything. His mind was working at warp speed and his heart was racing. So much could happen; so much could go wrong.

Dr. Alvarez, a middle-aged man not many years older than Paul, said nothing further as they raced across town to his clinic. He had recognized the first son instantly. He carried his father's handsome features but somewhat softened, no doubt by the mother's influence. The man destined one day to rule one of the world's greatest, yet little known, empires sat beside him steeped in thought, obviously deeply worried about his son.

Nunez had said that nothing most be spoken of about this meeting, not to Raul or Rafael nor anyone else. Nunez told him that he would personally take care of everything; all Alvarez had to do was follow his instructions and then forget everything about this evening. It went without saying, if Alberto Nunez asked a favor, no one would dare deny him, and no one would repeat anything considered private. Anything concerning the family was off limits for idle discussion. Of course anyone of importance in Raul's world knew who Paul was and how far he had come in the political circles of the United States' government. Raul was extremely proud though he never spoke of it. Still, it remained a recognized fact.

After parking in the private entrance to his clinic, Dr. Alvarez left Paul in the vehicle while he went inside and disabled the security and video surveillance systems. Nunez wanted no record of any kind of this evening's proceedings. Once he had taken care of those, he ushered Paul into the clinic and within half an hour had the required blood bagged and safely prepared for transport. Paul lay reclined on a sofa in Alvarez's office trying to drink the juice that the doctor had insisted he have while he finished up the last details. They left the office and the doctor returned Paul to the hospital; then he went to the airport to await Alberto's arrival with the President's blood.

Flanked by a Secret Service detail, Alberto exited the jet and headed purposefully to the private car waiting a short distance from the plane. Alberto had already secured special clearance for it and all that remained was to make the switch while in transit to the hospital. He motioned for the other men to follow in the second car as he climbed inside with Dr. Alvarez and they hurriedly headed out. There would be no special escort or anything that might draw attention to their actions. A low profile was essential if this evening's actions were to remain private. Alberto slowly drew a deep breath. All was going as planned. Alvarez made the switch, replacing Robert's container with Paul's, and adhered the appropriate label to it.

He quietly assured Alberto that everything had been carried out without any difficulties and without any type of documentation or record of the events. Alberto nodded his thanks and asked that the doctor complete his task without delay once he left the hospital. Robert's blood had to be destroyed without anyone becoming aware of a duplicate container.

Alberto entered the hospital through a side door instead of through the emergency entrance. No one paid any special attention to the refrigerated bag he carried. He entered the first available elevator and sped to the floor of private suites set aside for the hospital's special patrons. He had phoned Paul as the car arrived and the doctor was waiting for him as he stepped out of the elevator. He thanks Alberto and rushed to carry the blood to the staff and insure that everything was in order.

At the moment Robbie's condition seemed to have stabilized. Specialists had been called in, and they had ruled out many of their first concerns. With each passing hour, their hopes that Robbie had simply fallen victim to some unusual and unexplained virus were growing. His temperature had finally begun falling, although he was listless and unresponsive in his normal way. He had begun to whimper slightly and the doctors felt this was a good indication that he was improving.

When Caroline had finally been allowed to see him, she maintained her composure and softly rubbed his little arm, talking quietly to him. He tried to reach for her, so she leaned over him and placed her cheek next to his. She remained in that position until he quieted again. Paul knew her back had to be hurting from the awkward position she was in, but he also knew she didn't really feel it. All that mattered to her was her son—their son.

Tubes and monitoring devices were attached to every conceivable inch of his tiny frame. While the thoroughness of the doctors was on one level reassuring, on another it was frightening. Robbie looked like a tiny science experiment, and all Paul wanted to do was to hold him in his arms again and protect him from whatever was tormenting his little body. The fact that there was nothing more that he could do was nerve-racking.

No one would guess the distress Caroline and Paul were both enduring. Each behaved as was expected of the First Lady and her son's godfather and the President's chief of staff. There were no dramatic scenes, no hysterics, no impossible demands just the quiet composure of people who realized everything was being done to safeguard the trust they had placed in the doctors, hospital, and staff who diligently worked to find an answer. Admiration for the First Lady grew as she accepted the directions of the doctors and gave them the necessary space they needed to work. She would leave Robbie whenever she had to, but she returned to him the second they allowed her.

As more time passed and his condition gradually improved, doctors began extensive blood analysis, searching for an explanation. When Robbie's fever finally broke, and he began drinking small amounts of fluids, the doctor's hopes, for his recovery, rose. By the next morning, Robbie was asking for his mommy, and the doctors could find no other reason to hold him. After exhaustive discussions with specialists and review of all the various tests and screenings, the doctors finally decided to release Robbie.

By late afternoon, Caroline was holding her son and boarding a private jet for home. Alberto had usurped the Secret Service plans and had secured his own plane. Her parents were as relieved as she and promised to visit as soon as Caroline and Robbie had both fully recovered from his illness. Robbie would be closely supervised in the following weeks to determine if anything had been overlooked or if any other anomaly presented itself. Otherwise, he was pronounced fit and capable of resuming his usual activities. At the moment those only included clinging to his mother and hugging his favorite little soft, brown plush puppy, a gift from his adoring godfather. Robbie didn't want to be separated from his mother, and even as he napped he held tightly to her. No matter how much Paul wanted to hold him just a few minutes, he wouldn't ask. They both needed the reassurance that nothing was going to separate them. He could wait. Just seeing them both safe would do for now.

As the jet taxied to a stop at the Washington airport, a waiting car pulled up beside the plane and Alberto escorted them back to the residence. He allowed no one to intercede or ask questions. The only comment Caroline heard as she hurried passed some of the staff in the halls was simply, "Welcome home." There had been concern for the baby, but nothing had been officially stated, so no one commented directly. With Alberto walking at her side, no one would dare anyway. He had a way of looking at people which let them know without words that they didn't want to cross him in any way.

On the rare occasions when Alberto's presence was required at the White House, no one ever questioned his authority or his right to command those around him. His attitude brooked no discussion, and the staff had learned early that he was the silent, third man in the line of authority after the President and his Chief of Staff. They would have been surprised to know that Alberto often had more authority than the President if it pertained to the private lives of his family. Caroline, Paul, and Robbie were his responsibility, and as well as he could he meant to protect them at all costs.

He would assist Robert with his needs only as long as it benefited Paul and Caroline. If the time ever came that he had to take sides, Robert would lose. Alberto knew that Robert realized this fact but chose to ignore it, just as Robert knew how Alberto truly felt about him and his weaknesses. Alberto shook his head; for some people, ignorance was bliss, he supposed.

For once Robert was waiting for Caroline's arrival. But no one really cared. He made a big production of taking the baby and asking all the right questions. He played the role of the concerned father to perfection; no one was fooled, not even Ms. Martin. She quietly slipped to the nursery and began preparing Robbie's bed.

Robbie fussed and struggled in Robert's arms, unaccustomed to his presence, and stretched his chubby little arms out for his mother.

Caroline finally had enough and took Robbie from him. He quieted instantly and laid his head on her shoulder. Caroline answered all of Robert's questions, but she was bone tired, and as usual Robert didn't even see it. He was too concerned with putting on a good front.

As he turned to thank Paul and Alberto for their assistance, Caroline slipped to the nursery with Robbie. Why was Robert making such a display? She didn't trust him. It was almost as though he were practicing. She didn't doubt that he would find some political angle to Robbie's illness. Right now, she didn't care,

She sat down in her favorite rocker and after a few rocks back and forth, both mother and child were sound asleep. Ms. Martin eased the chair into a reclining position and covered them both with a light blanket. Rest was what they needed more than anything. She felt no compunction in telling the President that when he entered the nursery a few minutes later.

Paul smiled to himself. Caroline had a strong advocate in Ms. Martin. He was glad Raul had sent her. He would rest better knowing that she was present.

Ms. Martin knew trouble when she saw it, and the President for all his brilliance was just that. She also knew other things better kept private; she had seen the looks pass between them. She knew how things were, and when she glanced at Alberto as he started to leave the apartment, he nodded to her. They both knew, but they would protect their secret.

Robert was no fool. He was a lot of things and even he would admit some of them weren't too admirable but he wasn't lacking in intelligence. Something had happened when Robbie got sick. He wasn't sure exactly what that was, but he knew that it was something. Robert knew that Caroline was head-over-heels for the little boy, but he just couldn't seem to find any real affection for him. He was cute; he was reasonably well-behaved; everybody loved him—but Robert. He couldn't explain it. He didn't dislike him. They just didn't have a connection. Something was missing.

Robert couldn't shake the feeling that Caroline was keeping something from him. Maybe there was more wrong with Robbie than she had wanted him to know. Maybe there was some type of physical problem, some type of disability that she hadn't told him about. What if she was keeping something bad from him? She knew how he hated to think of children with disabilities, deformities, learning disorders. He was so gifted that it never occurred to him to wonder if his son would be, or to be concerned that he might have some type of problem. Could that be it? Had she learned something from Robbie's tests that she didn't want him to know?

As soon as Robert could clear a few minutes in his schedule the next morning, he called his secretary and asked her to connect him to the White House physician. Within an hour Robert had Robbie's medical records on his desk in front of him, and Dr. Lynn Weinstein sat across from him ready to answer his questions. Robert flipped through the records unsure of exactly what he was looking for, so he asked the question weighing most heavily on his mind.

"Is there anything in Robbie's records to indicate that he might have some type of physical or mental disability? I know it sounds crazy, but I've been so worried about him. I just want to be sure that he is receiving the best care possible."

Dr. Weinstein smiled. She was used to overly anxious parents. "No, there's absolutely no reason to think that Robbie has any problems. His illness was just one of those ailments that babies occasionally get where there is no real explanation for the problem. Nine times out of ten nothing like that will ever present itself again." She laughed. "In fact, I would say that he is in exceptionally good health. I was just telling Mr. Steven's the same thing when he asked about Robbie after his check up yesterday."

Robert had been feeling much better about Robbie's condition. At the doctor's last statement his smile frozen in place. "Yes, Paul takes his duties as godfather very seriously. I think we should be looking for a wife for him so he can have a few children of his own." He laughed and tried to turn his anger aside. "I want to thank you for taking time to put my mind at ease and for the trouble I've put you to. I hope you don't mind if I ask you not to mention our conversation to the First Lady. I don't want to worry her needlessly."

"Certainly, Mr. President, it's been my pleasure. I also want to assure you that the blood we took has been carefully stored should there ever be an occasion for its need. It can sometimes be difficult for Robbie's particular blood type to be found in short notice, and since his isn't compatible with his mother's, I just wanted to set your mind at rest, knowing of your impending trip overseas."

Robert was shocked, but he hid it well as he circled the desk to shake hands with the doctor and walk her to the door. "I truly appreciate all that you have done for us. You and your staff have been most helpful."

Now Dr. Weinstein laughed. "Those were the exact words Mr. Stevens used." She turned back and smiled at Robert. "The way he plays with Robbie is such a wonderful thing to see. They seem to really love one another. I know how proud you must be; Robbie is such a remarkable child. Everyone adores him."

With that parting bit of information, the doctor left and Robert returned to his desk and picked up Robbie's file. Robert's blood type was O; there was nothing in the least rare about it. What was really going on?

After reading Robbie's file for the second time, Robert dismissed the idea of asking Caroline directly and embarked on another plan of action.

Robert's secretary placed the call. Agent Joe Morales had been part of the President's personal protection staff since his election. Robert had always liked him. He did his job and discreetly looked the other way if Robert had any special guests visit his office or late night meetings with younger interns, political devotees, or female volunteers on his staff. Robert spoke directly to the head of his security force and asked him to send Morales to his office.

Morales was honored that the President had requested to see him personally, but he couldn't think of any reason to explain the request. He hurried through the hallway leading to the Oval Office. He would know soon enough.

Morales was shown into the President's office as soon as he arrived. Robert stood, walked around his desk, and extended his hand as he greeted him. "Thank you for your quick response. I appreciate the excellent job that you do here for me." Robert put his arm around Morales' shoulder and began walking toward the open French doors. "Let's take a walk. I need a breath of fresh air." He dropped his arm and stepped through the doors. Morales followed and walked beside him.

Robert began without preamble. "The truth is I need to ask you a personal favor, and I'd rather that this conversation remained just between the two of us." He stopped and turned to face Morales. Robert gave him his most sincere smile, meant to put him at ease and yet elicit his help.

Morales was confused but more than willing to aid the President. "I'll do my best, Mr. President, and you can rest assured that no one will hear anything from me."

Robert reached out and clasped his shoulder. "Thank you. That means a lot to me." He hesitated as though reluctant to continue. "This is a delicate matter. I'm not sure exactly how to begin...." He hesitated again as if torn between whether to speak or not. If Morales had known Robert better he would have recognized this ploy as a way to lure him in, to gain his confidence.

"There has been as incident concerning the First Lady. She seemed unduly distraught about something. I'm just afraid someone has said or done something that has upset her. She insists that there is nothing, but I'm worried. I don't want anything happening to upset her especially since little Robbie has been so sick." He frowned, playing up the concerned father and husband act, and paced a step or two away from Morales as though overcome with emotion.

"We were all pleased to hear that your son is doing well, Sir." He spoke from the heart.

Robert turned as though touched by the sincerity of his words. "Thank you. I can't tell you how worried we were." He took a few more steps then turned back to face Morales. "That's why this incident is so upsetting. It probably is nothing just like she said, but I would be grateful if you would oversee her protection from now on. I'll arrange it with the department head. You won't need to say anything about it to anyone." He moved closer again as though speaking in strictest confidence man to man, not President to civil servant. "If you could just keep a record of who goes and comes from the residence, especially when I'm gone, it would put my mind at rest. If you would just note who visits the First Lady, I'll be able to eliminate those who have a reason to be there and identify anyone who might have some other agenda in mind, who might be upsetting the First Lady in some way. I know you wouldn't want that to happen any more than I do." Robert knew how much the staff liked Caroline.

He clasped Morales' shoulder again. "I know you understand the needs of a man and the pressure of the job. I wouldn't want anything that happens in the Oval Office to cause distress or displeasure to the First Lady. She's a wonderful woman, the best any man could ever hope to have. I'm a very lucky man." His hand tightened slightly on Morales' shoulder. "You can see why I wouldn't want anything or *anyone* to upset her, can't you?" He emphasized the word, implying that one of his amorous liaisons might have found a way to cause problems.

Robert continued with what he thought might solidify his reasoning. "I know that I haven't been as careful as I should and I may have unwittingly allowed someone to assume too much. I truly hope that isn't the problem, but I just want to do this as a precaution. I want to protect my wife and family. I know you understand that. I can tell you are a man of the world, that you've been around, and you understand a man's need, needs that he might not feel right about imposing on his cherished wife, the mother of his child." He stopped and stared directly in Morales' eyes. He could tell he was pondering this blatant admission, but he was too well trained to ever question the morality of the situation. He was there for protection, not judgment. Morales nodded his understanding.

Robert continued. "I don't think anyone would dare telephone especially since all calls are recorded. That's why I feel, if there is a problem, it might be from someone visiting the residence. I know that you are just the man to help me with this and keep it confidential. You can make your report to me personally once a week or earlier if you feel the need. I sincerely hope that there really isn't a problem that it's just my overactive imagination, but I would be eternally grateful if you can see fit to help me, to lift this burden from my mind." He smiled confidently.

"It would be an honor to serve you in any capacity that I can, Mr. President."

Robert reached out and shook his hand firmly. "I knew I could count on you." He turned with Morales and walked back toward the French doors. "I would like you to start with this evening's shift, if that can be arranged."

"Certainly, Mr. President," Morales replied.

As Morales walked down the hall and back to his office, he quietly pondered all that he had been told. It didn't seem to fit with the image he had of the President, but maybe he did love his wife, maybe he really was concerned about her, maybe he had gone too far with one of his political assistants, and she wanted a little revenge. It wouldn't be the first time. It wouldn't be a hard request to document who all entered and left the residence. Morales just couldn't figure anyone being brave enough to try something like that. But like the President said, it could all be his imagination. Morales thought more likely it was a good case of guilt.

The President really did have a wonderful wife; he should appreciate her more. But then it wasn't his place to offer advice or share an opinion.

He had seen the way the younger political aides threw themselves at the President. It would take a strong man not to give into all of that temptation, and obviously, in that aspect, the President wasn't strong at all. Morales shook his head and gathered the material he would need. He would keep a voice recording during the evening and transpose that to a written account to present to the President. That way he wouldn't forget anything or anyone. Some days a lot of people came and went. He didn't want to make any mistakes. This was a Presidential request; they didn't come any greater than that.

Residential surveillance wasn't as boring as he first feared. He remained out of the line of vision as much as possible, but anyone part of the White House staff was used to seeing Secret Service men stationed all over. Most staff and family were all who entered regularly. The First Lady had a busy schedule and wasn't in residence much during the day. On those days, Morales took time off since she was escorted by several others. In the evenings he stationed himself outside the entrance and made notes on everything that transpired.

He hadn't noted anything suspicious or unusual until the President made a state visit to Venezuela. During his absence, the chief of staff made several visits to the residence and remained through dinner, leaving sometime after midnight. Morales didn't think anything about it since it was a well-known fact that he was a long-time family friend and the baby's godfather and Robbie's nurse was also in residence. Still he documented the visits as instructed.

When the President returned, Morales presented him with the written documentation. Robert thanked him for doing a good job as he scanned the list of names. Just as he thought, he smiled at Morales and told him that he didn't see any reason to be concerned and that he would no longer need him for this special duty. He told him he would clear it for him to take a few days off; then he could return to his regular schedule.

"I have to admit, I feel rather foolish. It must have been my imagination. Caroline said that nothing was wrong, that I was imagining her upset. She told me that she was just tired and not fully recovered from Robbie's ordeal. I should have listened to her. She has never told me anything but the truth. I made a lot of additional work for you, but I can't thank you enough for doing this favor for me. It has put my mind at ease." He stepped forward and grasped Morales' hand. "I would never intentionally hurt my wife. I think you know that. I'll be more careful in the future." He gave Morales that cocky little grin that said men-will-be-men as he walked him to the door. He was treating Morales as a personal friend.

"You can call on me any time, Mr. President." The President shook his hand as he left the office. Morales hadn't seen anything that would have caused the First Lady concern. Besides, she had Mr. Stevens with her most evenings. Surely she would have been safe with him. Morales frowned then left to check in with his supervisor. A few days off would be nice.

Robert tapped the folder on his desk top. It made sense, more than any other explanation. Still, he couldn't really believe it. It would be easy enough to check. He just needed a good excuse for asking for the records.

What was he thinking? He didn't need an excuse for anything; he was the President. But who could he ask?

Obviously, he couldn't ask Paul; so who could he make curious enough to do his work for him. He laughed. There was nothing like having an investigative reporter on staff. He might as well make the most of her talents.

It had been easy enough to get Morales to do his bidding, but it would be another story with Amanda. She wouldn't be so easy; she had never fallen for his charm. She seemed to be laughing at him at times, but she did an excellent job handling the press. That was it!

He had a way to hook her interest, Robbie. It was almost laughable. Women!

He buzzed his secretary and made his request. Amanda was in his office in just a few minutes. He stood as she entered and motioned toward a chair. "Have a seat." He waited for her to sit before he began. "I have a request that may sound strange, but I feel that it might cause problems if we don't address it beforehand. One of the medical staff brought it to my attention; otherwise, I wouldn't have known." He slid Robbie's medical report across the desk to her. Amanda looked a little confused but took the file and opened it. She didn't really know what she was supposed to be looking for. She studied the information for a few minutes then looked up.

"What exactly am I looking for?"

"That was my thought at first also. I didn't see any problem, but I found a typed note attached to the file that stated a discrepancy in the blood types." He slid the typed note across to her. There were no identifying backgrounds, headings, or signatures, just the typed words on a white sheet of note paper. How odd.

Amanda looked at the note then back at the file. Now she saw what she should have noticed the first time. Neither Caroline nor the President had the same blood type as Robbie. Robbie had to have one of his parent's blood types, didn't he? What did this mean?

"Exactly what is the problem? Was there a mix up in identifying Robbie's blood type, or was there just a misprint on the document?"

Robert leaned back in his chair and sighed. "That's what I want you to find out. I don't want to cause the First Lady any embarrassment by asking her myself. My involvement would only make matters worse if I start asking questions, and if word leaked out that there was a problem, what a scandal it would make." He shook his head. "No, I need someone who can investigate this as quietly as possible and find out exactly what is going on." He stared at Amanda, giving her his most concerned husband look. "This is a private matter; I don't want anyone else learning of it. Can you do it?"

"I would need your permission to access your families' personal medical files, but yes, I think I can come up with some excuse for requesting them that won't raise any suspicions. What do you want me to do once my investigation is complete?"

"Report back to me, and we will decide how to continue once we know the facts." He rose and handed her a typed paper authorizing her access to his files. Amanda couldn't help but think that he had given this quite a bit of thought if he already had the authorization ready.

"I can't thank you enough for handling this for me. I know you will be discreet. I will wait to hear from you."

She was dismissed. She didn't know what to think, what to make of these crazy events, but she had better find out what was really going on before the press did. She was certain of that much. Still, she couldn't shake the feeling that the President was hiding something, that he might be using her as a decoy. Maybe he thought if she couldn't unearth his secret, if there was one, then no one else could either. That could be a very dangerous game to play.

The other side of the coin was that he might have a secret that he wanted her to reveal so that she could be the scapegoat, if it caused much damage. Either way, she knew she was being used for more than he indicated. Now it was up to her to find out what it was and how to proceed with the information. She knew for a fact there was something to be found, but what?

When Amanda returned home later that evening, she was so distracted that Tim couldn't help but wonder what the problem was. "Do you want to talk about it? I'm pretty good at keeping secrets." He smiled, a devilish little grin, knowing she would laugh at that remark. His whole life had been a secret. She turned and looked at him, and he could see that she was really bothered by something. "A burden is always lighter when the load is shared. Let me help you. Sometimes just talking about something helps."

He put his arms around her and held her tightly. She laid her head on his chest. It would be so easy to confide in him, but did she have the right? She looked into his eyes and considered what the best thing to do would be. Maybe he was right; maybe he could help her see through the maze of conflicting information to the heart of the problem, maybe.

"Okay, but this is going to sound crazy, and from what I've learned so far, there's probably more to this than I know right now." She smiled. He looked as confused as she felt.

"What if I told you that I don't think the President's son is his? What if I told you that I can only come up with one possible alternative?" She was serious. He hadn't expected that type of bombshell. The fallout from that bit of news would wreck havoc on Billings' entire political future. Maybe his first question should be, who did she think was the father? He frowned. If he was a betting man, he would lay odds on the family friend, but he didn't voice his thoughts.

"Well, I guess I would want to know what the facts are first then go from there." He took her hand, led her to the sofa, and pulled her down onto his lap. This might take time. He might as well enjoy it.

He wasn't playing fair and he knew it. She laughed. "This is serious. You have to pay attention."

"I will." He lifted his right hand. "Scouts honor." He didn't say what he would be paying attention to. He grinned at her disbelieving frown.

"Billings called me into his office today and asked me to do a little investigating for him. He had some story about his son's blood type being mislabeled on his hospital records or mistakenly identified.

But it didn't add up. He could have placed a few tactful calls and had everything he needed, so why involve me? I think there's more to it, and he wants me to reveal whatever it is so he won't get caught up in any political fireworks."

"Are you saying that you think he knows that he isn't the father and knows who is, but wants you to reveal the fact. What would be the point? What could he hope to gain? Couldn't he just tell his wife and the would-be father that he knows?" He was frowning for real. This was a mess. He tried to figure out what Billings had to gain by having Amanda reveal the facts. "Do you think that he just wants to play the wronged husband and gain sympathy from the voters because his wife cheated on him? I might be more likely to think he was a fool for not seeing what was going on in his own backyard." She leaned her head against him.

"I told you this was a mess." They sat holding each other and quietly thinking for several minutes. "I know he has to know. Look at the absent way he treats Robbie. I don't think any father would be that cool toward his son. He says all the right things, but everyone knows he doesn't really have any feelings for him." She stopped and sat up. "I don't think he loves his wife either. I know during the campaign they were the perfect couple, but away from the press and the meetings and parties, they just didn't seem close, connected. Do you know what I mean?"

"Sure I do. When I see you, I feel like my whole world is right. When you're gone, there's something missing, a piece of me, a piece of my heart." She hugged him so suddenly. He jumped. "What? Didn't you think I would understand or that I wouldn't know how to be romantic?" He laughed a deep rumbling sound. "You're right. I'm not romantic, but I do know how you make me feel, and I've never had the feeling that Billings felt that way about his wife." He sighed, wishing he were wrong but knowing he was right. But something else was nagging at him. Maybe there was a connection, maybe this had something to do with the time Billings had spent in Arkansas politics. He needed to think about all this before he brought that up.

Still, he was certain about a few things. "If you ask a man, he'll tell you that Billings has a roving eye and a traveling hand. I knew it the first time I saw him in person. He's been lucky so far, but I'll bet you any amount of my hard earned money that there have been women on the side. I wouldn't put up with that if I was a woman, but the First Lady has responsibilities to the country just like her husband. Bringing disgrace and dishonor to him now wouldn't be the right way to handle the situation. Maybe he wants to see what others might have guessed?"

He was really frowning now. What could Billings possibly hope to gain by having his suspicions investigated? What did he expect Amanda to do with the information? He could see why she was worried.

They lapsed into silence again, each weighing the information and trying to reach some type of logical conclusion.

Having finally decided Tim took a deep breath then exhaled slowly. It was still hard for him to talk about Judy's death. "Maybe I have something that might help."

Amanda looked at him and grinned. "All that will help is you. That's not the answer to everything, you know." He was stunned and then elated. They had come a long way. Then he started laughing, and the more he thought about it, the more he laughed. He laughed so hard that he almost dropped her. She clutched his arms in desperation.

"I can't believe you even thought of that." He was trying frantically to catch his breath. "It's a great idea, but I had something else in mind, information."

She punched his arm with remarkable strength. He had forgotten she could pack a mean wallop. "Okay, smart guy. What is it and it better be good after laughing at me like that."

"Sorry, I was just shocked that's all. What a naughty little mind you have. But I don't mind in the least and as soon as we get this conundrum sorted out, I'll do my best to fulfill your every fantasy."

"That might take some time, you know." She smiled seductively, and he almost forgot what he wanted to tell her.

"We have all of our lives to work on them." He pulled her to him and kissed her soundly before releasing her. He touched his forehead to hers then sighed.

"I hate talking about this, but I think it might be important. You remember that I told you about my sister. I think her death might be connected to Billings' time in the Attorney General's office when he was in Arkansas. I traced her phone records, and she had repeatedly called his office. The only other person with access to his private office number was his secretary, and I checked her out. She didn't know Judy, and I couldn't find any connection. She did remember answering several calls for Billings when he wasn't available. All she remembered was that the girl sounded young and occasionally high or drunk, but she wasn't sure. The girl never gave her name and would only ask her to tell Billings that his informant had called. She couldn't make sense of it because she knew Billings didn't deal directly with informants, but she figured that it still might have something to do with his work and never questioned him." He was absently stroking her arm as he spoke.

"I think that it was just their personal way of relaying messages. I think that he was supplying her with drugs and that he was responsible for her death. I just can't prove it."

"Why don't you tell me what you do know and let me see what I can find out?"

"That's just it. I don't know much. I have some suspicions, but they're not facts. I know she called his office a lot. I know that she had unaccounted for bruises on her arms and neck, old bruises. I know her body was full of drugs, and I know that she was pregnant, and more importantly, I know she didn't deserve to die like that." He stopped. His voice had taken on a hard edge, and Amanda could feel the tension building in his body.

"A woman in her apartment building said that most weekends, she and her roommate were picked up in a dark luxury sedan and brought back late Sunday night or Monday morning. She didn't think that either girl worked, but they never talked to anyone or seemed to have friends over. She said they were quiet and didn't bother anyone." He looked so sad. "How do you put that on a headstone?"

Amanda hugged him and gave him a minute before she spoke. "Listen, I might not be able to find out anything either, but I have different sources than you. Maybe I can come up with some answers." She looked so adamant that he was frightened for a moment.

"This isn't some little money laundering scheme we're talking about. Someone killed Judy, either because she was pregnant or because she knew too much. You have to be careful. I can't lose you too. I don't want you taking any chances, so," he hesitated, "I'll go with you, and we'll do this together." He tried to smile, but it didn't quite reach his eyes.

"How does tomorrow sound?" she asked hugging him tightly to her.

"What time?" He hugged her back. They had a plan and maybe this time he could find the answers he needed. While she sat pondering the logistics of their plan, he made a plan of his own. Tomorrow was out of the question, they both knew, but as soon as they could, they would go in search of answers together.

"About that earlier suggestion?" he arched one brow in question then stood up with her in his arms and headed for the bedroom. Dinner and everything else would just have to wait. He had other appetites to satisfy first. She was unbuttoning his shirt and giggling before he reached the bedroom door.

Robert just wouldn't listen to reason. Paul was at his wits' end. He really wanted to slug him, but he didn't think even that would make him change his mind. They had gone over and over this until Paul was ready to scream in frustration or beat Robert's head against the wall. He was very tempted to call Alberto, but he didn't dare. Paul knew how Alberto felt about Robert. It wouldn't take much for Alberto to end Paul's headache permanently. Paul didn't know what Raul would do if that happened, but then he didn't know what he was going to do when Raul heard this last bit of news either.

Raul had already heard. He was as angry as Paul and much less forgiving. He wanted an end put to the DEA's crackdown on cocaine and he wanted it now. He called Paul personally.

When Paul heard his father's voice on the line, he knew that things had to be taken care of immediately. If Paul couldn't make it work, then Raul would take over, and the United States would be plunged into a war that it couldn't possible win. Raul influenced more of Congress than either party, and if he started calling in favors, Robert was doomed. He would never see the end of his term. He would be out of office, if he was lucky, or dead if he wasn't. But either way Raul would win. Paul was more certain of that fact than he was that the sun would rise the next day.

Chapter 20

THE DEA WAS MAKING a strong push against the cocaine rings. The smaller traffickers were more than willing to sell out their competitors if their necks were in the noose. Most information was reliable, other not so much, but Richards knew how to find out what he needed to know. When it came to interrogation, Richards was the best. By the time he finished, suspects were almost begging to tell him more. His cold demeanor and hardened attitude could shake the strongest man. He had finally found a benefit to living on the streets for so long.

The DEA had acquired important information from several sources which led to the tracking of shipments being smuggled in from Mexico. The Norte were shipping it across the border faster than drug dogs could sniff, but Richards got an even bigger break when one of the Bolivian cartel's informants turned state's evidence. Richards had followed a lead to New Orleans hoping to discover how the cartel always seemed to be one step ahead of the coastal patrols, but even he couldn't believe this bit of luck.

The guy had signed his own death warrant. At one time, the DEA had considered him a suspect, but they didn't have any hard evidence against him. When the tall, distinguished man walked into the regional office in New Orleans and gave himself up before they could even figure out who he was, Richards had been searching for anything they might have missed in the stacks of reports. Day's eyes met Richards' across the littered desk, the bustling noise and chaos of the office receded, and Richards knew this was the break they had been looking for. Day calmly laid the Coast Guard and Louisiana State Water Patrol schedules for the next month on the desk in front of him.

Richards slumped down in his worn desk chair. It creaked in protest. He couldn't believe what he was seeing. With this information, they had scored a major hit against the cartel. They now knew when and where the cartel would most likely run a shipment. It was only a matter of time now before they could make a major strike and cripple another supply route.

Richards motioned for Day to take a seat, signaled for his partner to join them, and turned on the room's audio and visual recording system. He immediately began hammering Day with questions, almost afraid to believe their luck. Day unemotionally explained how he had become entangled with the Bolivians and his role in their organization. Once Commander Rex Day finished his debriefing with the DEA, Richards asked for a few minutes alone with him. They had his sworn testimony, taped interviews detailing his involvement, the actual papers he had copied for the cartel, the drop location, and his contact number. They had everything but an actual shipment in their hands. This was a major accomplishment. Success was no longer possible, but probable. It now lay within their reach. Richards was almost afraid to breathe.

There was an undercurrent of anticipation and excitement running through the department, but nobody wanted to jinx it. Success would not be celebrated until they had the supplier and his cargo in their possession. The men knew from hard experience there was no such thing as an airtight case. The possibility of unforeseen complications was always in the back of their minds. Life held no guarantees.

Day looked up when Richards closed the office door. His haggard face revealed the extent of his emotional suffering. This was a man who had reached a conclusion that was certain to end his career and inevitably his life. He knew what he had done to his country and he accepted the responsibility for his actions. What he was trying to do was right a wrong, before it was too late. What he had done was sentence himself to a life of fear and uncertainty.

The deal he had struck with the DEA would require relocation, a new identity, a new life. But what they couldn't give him was peace of mind. They couldn't guarantee his safety, and Day realized his life was over. It was only a matter of time before the cartel tracked him down, and they would. To men like them, it was a matter of honor. They would spend any amount of time and money until they achieved their goal. Fear of reprisal was a key element in their ability to dominate others. They couldn't allow anyone to escape punishment for turning on them.

Richards pulled out a chair and sat. "I guess I don't have to tell you that it will be almost impossible to insure your future safety." Richards studied the man in front of him. Rugged, weathered, he had seen the horrors of the world firsthand, an honored veteran who had risked his life to protect and defend the United States and who had risen in the ranks to a position of power and prestige, only to throw it all away.

Day didn't speak; he was out of words. He simply nodded. He knew; he knew too well. When he felt assured that he had repaired some of the wrongs he had committed, he would quietly slip away. No witness protection program could save him now. His life was over. He had made peace with his decision. All that remained was to survive long enough to testify in court. To help insure that he would make a difference regardless, he had videoed and recorded all of his information. He had sworn affidavits detailing his involvement. He had done everything that he could to rectify his mistake. Now it was just a matter of time—of survival.

"Is there anything I can do, anyone I should contact, in case?" He asked the question out of respect for the man Day had once been, for the man who was fighting to correct his error in judgment. Richards knew how the cartel worked. He understood the hold they could get on a person's life. Graham was tough with his men, but he was an amateur compared to the drug cartels who had surveillance systems and technological equipment at their disposal that the DEA only dreamed of having. Money bought power, and the cartels were extremely wealthy.

Day shrugged; he was exhausted. He had been talking for hours. He didn't know if he would have tomorrow or not. He wanted to get it all taken care of today. Once he walked out of this building, he might never take another breath. "No. I took care of everything before I came. I'm ready." He spoke with finality. "Thanks, I know that I don't deserve any consideration, but I appreciate it."

Richards nodded. "I've worked too long in this not to understand the stranglehold they can get on someone. Most just never get a chance to correct their mistakes." Richards stood and held out his hand to Day.

Day stumbled as he pushed his chair back and stood. He was dog tired. "I wish you well, Commander." Day stared at Richards trying to decide if he was being sarcastic then realized he was sincere.

Day could barely speak. After talking for hours, his throat was raw. He reached for the glass of water and took a drink. "Thanks." They shook and Richards left, signaling the men at the door that he was finished. That would most likely be the last time he saw Day. He hoped that he would be wrong, but his chances were slim. Even in the jails and prisons, the cartel ran the show. Death was an almost certain fact, even if he was placed in isolation. There were always ways and always someone willing to take the risk for the right amount of money. If it did come, Richards hoped that it would be fast for Day's sake.

Richards picked up a transcript of Day's testimony and as he scanned the last page, he noted that Day had only made one special request to be allowed to keep his favorite writing pen. Richards studied the request for a few minutes then signed off on it. He knew that Day didn't plan to write to anyone. He had already taken care of that, and he hadn't asked for paper. No, the pen he wanted was necessary for his peace of mind. Richards had carried similar devices on subversive missions for the military. He hoped, if the time came, Day would have time to use it.

With disruption of the shipping lanes in the Gulf and dismantling of the Mexican coca highway, the DEA was ramping up its push against cocaine all across the States. Richards felt confident enough to ask for a few days leave. He and Amanda planned to travel to Arkansas and investigate the few, sketchy details he had and see if they could uncover anything new. He felt more confident since she seemed to think that she would be able to contact different sources than he could. It was probably a waste of time, but he was willing, and so was she.

Amanda had arranged to take a short leave of absence. Everything was running smoothly and she planned to stay in constant contact with her staff. She was only a text message away and video conferences were already set up to keep her apprised of daily events. It wasn't ideal, but it was workable. Besides the President had instructed her to follow the leads she uncovered, and that was exactly what she was doing. The most that could happen would be that she lost her job. She wasn't worried, at least not about that.

They left for Little Rock the next morning. After the short flight, they register at the Peabody and had a quick lunch. Amanda was going to the county clerk's office to see if she could find any record of land or homes purchased by Billings. Tim was headed to the Attorney General's office to follow the trail from there. Neither felt overly confident, but Amanda assured Tim that she had uncovered important facts about people years after the fact before.

Paul left his apartment and went straight to Robert's. If he couldn't talk some sense into him now, it would be too late. He was going to have to come clean and let the game play itself out. But first he wanted to reason with him although he had become very obstinate lately. Paul frowned as he pushed the office door open.

Robert sat behind his desk reading a file. He glanced up but returned to what he was reading. Paul knew he was deliberately snubbing him. He wasn't about to put up with that kind of behavior. It was late and he was tired. He had had a grueling evening. Conversations with Raul were always tense and never pleasant.

"Put the papers down. We have to talk, and you have to listen." Robert set the papers aside and leaned back in his chair. He crossed his hands on top of the desk. He stared at Paul without saying a word. "This campaign you've instigated against drugs has served its purpose. You have established a strong base of credit, you have broken up the largest meth rings, and you have disabled the cocaine trade. Now it's time to focus on a new issue, something that will capture the public's interest." He leaned forward as he spoke and flattened his hands on the desk trying with difficulty to restrain his anger.

"I think that it's time to focus on health reform and education. We need improvements in both areas. Let's plan a strategy that will force both parties to join with us and set the stage for your re-election." Paul straightened, waiting for Robert's response. Robert only stared at him. Paul leaned forward again, letting his anger show. "What's wrong with you? Didn't you hear what I said?"

Robert stood and leaned forward, putting his hands on the desk top too. They were equally matched in stature, and they were mere inches apart in fact; both were angry. "Give me one good reason why I should desist from my present course of action." They were almost shouting. Thank goodness Robert's secretary had already left.

Paul started to hedge then opted for the truth. "If you don't, you won't live to be re-elected." His eyes flared with temper.

"Are you threatening me?" Robert was shocked, but he didn't give an inch.

"Would it help?" Paul almost snarled the words.

"What makes you think that anyone could kill me?" He was confident in his security.

"What makes you think they can't?" He practically growled the words. Then he relented and broke the stalemate, stepping back from the desk, running his hand through his hair, a habit he had when he was deeply troubled. Robert frowned; very little ever troubled Paul.

Paul spoke slowly, "Possibly because it has been done before." He let his words sink in. "You can't anger the people that you have and expect to just go about your merry way." He was ridiculing Robert and Robert knew it.

"What makes you think this might happen? Do you have some type of inside information?" Robert was being snide. Paul ignored it.

"The horse's mouth, as they say." Let him make what he would from that. Paul didn't really care at this point. "Look, Robert, I like you, I always have. I don't agree with some of the decisions you have made, but I have supported you in everything that you have done. Now I'm telling you. End this before it's too late." He casually leaned one hip on the desk, trying to bring some sense of balance back to their confrontation. "I promise you that no one will ever be the wiser. They will see the change in strategy as a financial decision. This whole operation has cost the taxpayers a small fortune. Now it's time to move on to something that benefits a greater majority of the general public—of the voters."

Robert sat back down. Paul made sense, but why had he threatened him. No one threatened the President, not even his friend. Robert suddenly laughed, some friend. Well, maybe it was more of a warning than an actual threat, besides Paul really was his friend. It was his wife that he had a problem with, but he meant to correct that.

Paul changed tactics. "Robert, you know how fickle the public is. It is political suicide to continue with this crusade and that's what the papers are calling it now. You do remember how the crusades ended, don't you? The Christian knights might have been right, but they lost anyway. Do you want to risk your re-election by refusing to make a simple change in strategy?" Paul had his attention now. All that Robert thought about was his political future.

"Let me think about it." Robert was hedging; he probably planned to put the Secret Service on alert or check to see if he had received any unusual threats lately. Presidents always angered someone. That was nothing new.

Paul continued as though he had agreed with him wholeheartedly. "Tomorrow morning. We'll have a strategy meeting with the staff, and we'll launch a new initiative. You'll see; I'm right about this." Paul held out his hand. Robert looked at it a moment before he shook it. What was that all about? Paul wondered if there was something going on that he didn't know about. He left Robert and punched in Alberto's number as he walked back to his own office.

As soon as Paul left his office, Robert went straight to the residence. He dismissed the baby's nurse the minute Robbie was put to bed. Then he asked the kitchen staff to leave when they finished serving the evening meal. They were puzzled but hoped that the President had a romantic evening planned. He was such a busy man, and he rarely spent time with his family. The romantics left smiling; the realists left wondering. Nothing was private in the life of a public servant, even the President.

Caroline didn't remark on the changes for the evening. They rarely talked; they simply coexisted. He performed his duties as President, and she carried out her obligations as First Lady. They acted the loving couple for state dinners and formal occasions. Those on the outside saw what they expected. Those on the inside chose not to see anything. Life had become predictable. Caroline hated every minute of it. It was a never ending prison sentence with no time off for good behavior, and she had been good. She and Paul hardly ever saw one another and then only with Robbie between them. It had become an unspoken agreement. That was the way it would remain as long as Robert was President, but she didn't have to like it.

Robert pushed his gold-edged dinner plate back and poured himself another glass of wine. He didn't offer Caroline any, not that she would have taken it. Still, she recognized the slight. He was trying to anger her, but she was determined that he wouldn't.

He sipped the wine slowly then set the glass down. "Who is Robbie's father?" He stared directly at her, waiting for her to deny the fact, ready to accuse her if she did.

"What does it matter? Legally, he is yours. That's all that should matter to you. He makes a nice campaign tool, don't you think?" She hadn't even flinched. She had been expecting something like this for ages. She was glad it was out in the open. She hated the lies and deceit. That was Robert's specialty not hers.

"Should I hazard a guess? Someone we both know—a family friend perhaps. Someone I trusted." His voice was rising with each word.

She could play this game as well as he. She stood at her end of the dining table and placing her hands on the table top leaned forward to emphasis each word. Did she realize how much like Paul she acted? "Someone who helped you meet the right people, who put you in the right places, who introduced you to the men who *make* Presidents. A family friend who has stood by and watched you risk your future on drugs and women, who saved you from ruin and your own stupidity countless times, who supplied your needs, who kept your dirty little secrets, who has worked to make you the man you are, someone who cares enough about you to continue to help you. That someone is the father of my son. I'm not ashamed of the fact. You didn't marry me out of love, but necessity. You had some indiscretion that had to be foiled before anyone found out, and you needed me to help you switch the public's attention in another direction. Well, I married you, and I tried to live up to my part of the bargain, but you couldn't do it, could you?"

She pushed her hair back from her face. Her velvet blue eyes glistened with unshed tears. "Once we were friends, but I wasn't enough, and I wasn't the kind of woman you wanted." She swung around. She would not let him see her cry. "Can you blame me for needing more than you offered, for needing more than pain and humiliation, degradation and suffering? That isn't living and it certainly isn't love." She walked into the living room and sat down. She didn't want to talk to him. She couldn't suppress her feelings like she once had. Things had changed. She had changed.

Robert went into the study. He had some thinking to do.

When Paul entered his office the next morning, Robert was sitting behind Paul's desk, tapping a pen like he always did. Paul recognized the habit, one he exhibited when he was weighing options. Was he contemplating Paul's ultimatum or something else? He had received a cryptic message from Caroline asking him to come by to see Robbie, but he knew there was something else going on. When he stared at Robert's face, he knew he was right.

"Out with it. We have work today." Paul wasn't in the mood to mollify Robert's overblown ego. He walked around his desk and stood waiting for Robert to get up from his chair. Paul had the feeling they were back in grade school and about to start daring one another any second. He wanted to laugh. The situation was ludicrous, but deadly serious, more so than Robert would ever believe. Paul had sent Alberto to talk to Raul and to gain more time. He hoped his plan would work. If it didn't, Paul wasn't sure what the future held for any of them.

Robert stood and smiled. "Did we both get what we wanted? You know back in college, when we made all those plans, did we get what we really wanted or did we settle for what we got?" He walked around the desk and sat in a chair in front of it.

Paul sat down. "That's an interesting question. I'm not sure I know the answer to it. What do you think? Did you?" Robert wasn't usually this introspective; something important had set him off. Robert didn't answer him. He just sat thinking.

"Okay, Robert, I know that something is eating you, what is it?"

Robert looked at him for a minute. "I just don't know how you could do that. She's my wife! Whether you like it or not, she's mine and I mean to keep her." He sounded as though Paul had taken his prize toy or something, a possession—not someone he should love and cherish. Did he even realize how he sounded?

Paul didn't deny anything or even act as though he didn't know what Robert was saying. He knew all right, and it was time to straighten out this mess. Pandora, she had been right.

"You've got to be joking. You don't love Caroline. You never have. You were always more in love with yourself than her. You liked the way she made you look. You liked the way men envied you. I don't think you know how to love anyone but yourself!" Paul was angrier than he had ever been. Robert didn't want to push him, not now, not ever.

"You're wrong. I did love someone once. She wasn't right for me, but she loved me—just me, not who or what I was. I turned on her. I made her think that I hated her, hated her for getting pregnant, for lying to me. But it wasn't her fault, not really. It was the dream I had in my head. The one I had worked so hard to achieve. I couldn't let her ruin it, could I?" He dropped his head in his hands, trying to block the memories that hid in the corners of his mind always waiting to slip out when he least expected to taunt him with what could have been.

"What happened to her, to the baby? You have to find out where she is and let me know. I need to know." He was pleading. Paul couldn't believe what he was hearing.

"Are you crazy? Any questions of that nature by anyone in this administration are sure to lead to problems. Have you forgotten she was a drug addict? Have you forgotten how you never wanted to see her again, begged me to do whatever it took to get rid of her? You've glorified a memory that can't possibly measure up to your ideal; in fact, they never do. Keep the memory and forget the girl. She and her baby are both gone. They can't bother you, and you don't need to know anything more about them. Is that understood?" Paul felt like he was instructing a callow school boy at times. Despite all his brilliance, Robert could often be amazingly naïve.

"Since you obviously need something to take your mind off these problems, call a meeting with Richards and the DEA. I want their department to wrap up operations and close the offices by the end of next week. Any pending investigations can be turned over to the appropriate local agencies and funding can be shifted to our new projects." Paul was adamant. He had to get Robert back in line fast.

Robert sat staring at him. "Is that an order or a suggestion?"

"Consider it whichever way you like, but for your own good, do it!" Paul pressed the intercom. "Call a staff meeting in fifteen minutes." He looked back at Robert.

"Well, what is it going to be?" He was tired of all the headaches, the deception, the animosity that was building between them. Maybe it was time to end this whole scheme. Things weren't working out the way Raul had envisioned. Paul was beginning to think that the distance and the difference in cultures were too great.

Maybe he was just too tired to think, but he didn't have time to bemoan his fate. He started shoving papers in his briefcase and opening drawers to look for personal items. He began tossing articles on the desktop. Robert frowned.

"What are you doing?"

"What does it look like? I'm cleaning out my desk. You can have your pick from a dozen good men who would be perfect for this job. They will follow behind you like sheep to the slaughter. They won't dare voice an opinion that is contrary to yours, so everything will be perfect again. You'll have just what you want, at least for a while." He laughed, but the sound of his voice raised the hair on the back of Robert's neck. He was serious.

Paul reached over and pushed the intercom. "Cancel all my appointments, including the staff meeting." He lifted his finger and looked at Robert. "Unless you want to have it, but I won't be leading this one. It's all yours now." He snapped his briefcase, shoved his chair back, and headed for the door. He was feeling better already. It was amazing how uplifting a little honesty could be. He almost smiled.

"Wait!" Robert's voice echoed down the corridor as Paul opened the office door.

Paul turned back to face him. "Why? You don't need me; you don't listen to my advice. I'm superfluous to this office, a weight around your neck. Get someone else." He turned again.

"Look, stop! I know I can be—," he hated to disparage himself in any way, "trying, let's say, but you have to admit that you have given me just cause to be upset. Let's talk this over before the others get here." Paul nodded to his secretary.

"I haven't called anyone yet," she whispered. Paul winked. She knew him well enough to recognize a maneuver. Robert had just fallen for his act. She liked Mr. Stevens. Someone else might not be as easy to work for. She grinned when she thought about how the President had looked when he thought that Mr. Stevens was really leaving. Maybe he was a better person than she thought. It was so hard to tell about him. Some days she thought he was a wonderful President, others she wondered what was going to happen to the country. Maybe that was the way every office surrounded by such powerful men felt, chaos and confusion, on a good day; a strong drink and a sedative on a bad.

Chapter 21

AMANDA COULD HARDLY WAIT for Tim to get back to the hotel. She had uncovered some very interesting land deals. One was extremely noteworthy. She had almost clapped her hands in glee like a little girl when she saw the owner's name. First she had investigated Billings and his property holdings, but on a hunch, she added Stevens' name to her search, and she had located several items. One was an estate situated in a remote area outside of the capital. Aerial photos and county land surveys revealed its rather isolated location and limited access. It would have been the ideal hideaway for a weekend rendezvous.

Billings' property was limited to a luxury apartment which he owned jointly with Stevens. They had disposed of the apartment once Billings became governor. Then he and Caroline had purchased a home, which they still owned. Stevens had purchase a condominium, which he had also retained. The house Stevens owned had been sold right before Billings ran for Governor, and the few smaller properties, he had retained as part of a portfolio of land holdings. Nothing stood out at first.

What caught Amanda's eye after a more thorough inspection were the transaction dates and their relationship to the dates Judy had been first seen in Little Rock and the date of her death. They were too similar for coincidence, especially given the other relevant facts. She had also located the previous owner of the estate who had recognized Stevens from his television exposure as part of Billings' presidential staff.

She had sold the home and several acres of land which were part of her larger estate. It had once been a quiet retreat for her parents when they visited for extended periods of time. She hated to see it remain unused, so she decided to sell it. Of course, she had placed certain restrictions on the buyer due to its close proximity to her home, but she had had no problem selling it. The realtor informed her that the new owner had no problem meeting her requirements and planned to use the home only as a quiet weekend retreat.

The elderly lady was very forthcoming with details that Stevens most likely had no idea she knew. He had bought the property through a realtor, but the lady just happened to be a friend of the agent's mother, and the realtor had shared much of the privileged information she had about the new owner. The fact that he was a prominent lawyer and political aid to the Attorney General only made him more intriguing.

Amanda realized after talking to her that she was what most people referred to as the nosey neighbor and had made it her business to check out the comings and goings at the house, especially since her land and home were adjacent to the property.

Given the rather remote location, Amanda could only wonder how she had learned so much about what transpired at the house, but Amanda soon learned during their conversation that the lady considered herself to be some type of amateur detective and spent a great deal of her time uncovering what she felt were suspicious details about other people's lives. The entire conversation would have been comical had it not been for the fact that she knew so much inside information about who had made a habit of visiting the estate and what had gone on during those visits.

More importantly, she had kept a diary of her observations complete with dates, times, and descriptions. Amanda was impressed. Had this lady been from a more modern generation, she would have made an excellent investigative reporter, which was exactly what Amanda told her. She was elated at the praise and gladly allowed Amanda to take her written accounts with her when she left.

Miss Maude, as everyone in the capital city referred to her, was a legend. She could trace her family back to the early French settlers who had paddled their way up the Arkansas River and helped to establish the trading post which later became a focal point on the river, easily recognized by its rock outcropping. She hadn't told Amanda, but she knew who Amanda was also. She was a sharp-eyed old woman who never forgot a face, and Amanda's was often seen at White House press conferences soft peddling some issue or another for the President.

Maude hadn't really cared for him as Governor, and he hadn't improved with age as far as Maude could tell. But, of course, her opinions were affected by the personal information she had on Billings.

Something about soft-spoken, sweet-tempered, little old ladies put people more at ease. It had been relatively simple for her to befriend the housekeeper. It had taken some doing at first, but the isolated area didn't lend itself to many visitors. So with a plate of warm cookies in hand, she had launched her campaign to learn about two of Little Rock's most important figures.

The housekeeper had been reluctant to talk much at first. She knew that the main rooms of the home were wired with surveillance equipment. Her private rooms had been left untouched, but she knew that to reveal any information about the occupants of the house was very dangerous. Miss Maude had seen the team of men installing cameras and other hidden devices before the owner actually took up residence. It had been that one event that had peaked Miss Maude's interest.

The house had been redecorated tastefully but not extravagantly, so the excessive amount of surveillance equipment seemed out of proportion to the need. When the men were in residence, cameras panned the outer perimeter of the estate and laser beams signaled any intrusion on the grounds, and guards were stationed both inside and outside the house.

With her every word and movement recorded, Miss Maude was sympathetic to the housekeeper's plight, but she was relentless. Soon she had the housekeeper visiting her home where she could speak more freely. Speaking Spanish to the lonely housekeeper had eased some of her loneliness and soon broke down her resistance. Before long, she was sharing woman to woman confidences about the people who visited the house on those wild weekends and all the things that went on. The drinking, drugs, and sex were commonplace happenings, but what Maude thought most interesting was that Stevens never attended any of the parties himself. The house seemed to be a hideaway for Billings and his playmates.

There had been others present usually, but the housekeeper referred to them only as business associates. She said it so quietly that Miss Maude hadn't pressed her for details. Obviously, their business wasn't something she wanted to talk about. The housekeeper did refer to Sr. Nunez rather often. Supposedly, he ran the show, but Maude could never quite decide if the housekeeper was in awe of him or afraid of him. According to what Maude did find out, those were *some* parties they held most weekends, discreet but definitely wild.

In Maude's younger days, she had been at quite a few similar ones herself, but things had changed, and alcohol wasn't the drug of choice any more. These young girls nowadays didn't have a clue what they were doing to themselves or just how much trouble they could get themselves into. That much hadn't changed. History just kept repeating itself generation after generation. Her silver curls shimmered in the bright sunlight coming through the windows in the upstairs parlor as she shook her head, sadden by the thought.

Amanda was so excited. She had a detailed record of the parties that had taken place at Stevens' estate and she had names. Things were beginning to shape up nicely. Her next step was to try to trace the vehicle and driver which was used to pick up the girls. The woman at Judy's apartment had said that the same car always came for them. Maybe with more time she could find out who it was, but at the moment she wasn't having any luck.

Richards wasn't fairing so badly himself. At the start of his investigation, he had decided to begin with the state drug task force. The captain recognized Richards as the organizer and director of the federal government's drug task force and was more than willing to pass along some recent information they had received. Richards was elated when he heard the news.

A recent drug bust by the state police and the narcotics division had uncovered a major cocaine distribution point. The travel agency that catered to the personal desires of its clients arranged transportation to several Central and South American countries. It operated mainly from a large, privately owned airstrip where numerous aircraft and hangars were located. Isolated in the foothills of northwest Arkansas, the airstrip provided the perfect means for bringing in drug shipments undetected.

Obviously, the backers of this enterprise had chosen the area for several reasons, the most important being its central location and easy access to several highway corridors for quick distribution. Likewise, a poor economic state like Arkansas would make it easy for those in power who needed a little extra funding to feel more inclined to turn a blind eye.

Richards assigned a computer expert to the task of uncovering details about the ownership and funding of the enterprise. Richards knew from experience that shell companies and dummy organizations shielded many unsavory individuals from public exposure. He wanted them all.

The DEA had received an anonymous tip probably from a disgruntled neighbor or a jealous local official who wasn't on the cartel's private payroll that a special shipment would be arriving on the next return flight. Because the travel agency booked frequent trips to and from Central and South American countries where drug smuggling was an art, their aircraft were routinely inspected, but drug agents knew that is was much too easy to pay off local and state officials in charge of such investigations.

A few special gifts and untraceable donations lined the coffers of many elected officials in return for information about scheduled inspections. The system had worked for years, but someone had finally tipped their hand. The DEA's special task force under the aegis of the President had moved in without giving local or state officials any warning.

The suspects had become so complacent about their activities that they were easily overpowered by the Special Forces team sent in to apprehend them and were caught in the process of dismantling one of the planes and removing the cocaine from special compartments.

They had seized the drugs, arrested the men, and impounded the remaining aircraft. They closed operation of the travel agency and issued arrest warrants for the owners and operators of the business. They knew that most likely, those in charge of the operation would have already been tipped off and were probably scurrying to get out of the country. But they would be able to round up several if they were lucky, since their operation had been carried out so quickly. This was another major strike for operation Slam Shut.

As director of the task force, Richards was allowed to interrogate the men who were brought in. They had been separated and held in isolation without charges, pending interrogation. Richards knew he would only have a short time to question any of them before they requested counsel. Most of them knew the legal system better than their lawyers, but if he was lucky he would catch one who didn't know the score, and he might get something.

Richards looked them over as they fidgeted in separate cells. One stood out. He seemed a little harder looking than the others. He would bet he was the one in charge. Richards figured the others would talk easily enough, but they wouldn't know the facts that he wanted. Richards had him placed in an interrogation room and let him sit there for several minutes before he entered. He could tell that he wasn't as brave as he wanted them to think. He kept looking at the door as though he expected someone to come in, someone he didn't really want to see. He had the look of fear all over him.

Richards understood his fear. He had seen the results of the cartel's displeasure many times in the past. It wasn't a pretty sight. This man had a right to be afraid, especially since he had carried out his duties so poorly. Richards knew that the cartel probably had a report on the DEA take down in front of them already. The responsible parties would be punished. The cartel didn't like to lose, and this little operation had definitely been lucrative.

He let the man squirm a little longer before he spoke. "Look, you know how this works. You help me and I help you. Who is the head of this operation?"

The man looked at Richards like he had grown two heads. "Are you crazy, man? If I talk to you, I'll die. You know that." He was beginning to shake.

Richards studied him for a minute. He was either panicked or in need of a fix—or both. Richards could see him begin to sweat. Both, he concluded. He continued as though the man hadn't spoken. "The way I see it is, you can tell me what I want to know and I'll try to protect you. Or I'll talk to the others and let them think that you have already talked and as soon as their lawyers arrive, you will be a marked man. When we release you, how long do you think you will you live? But it's your choice." Richards pushed back his chair and stood. He didn't make it to the door.

He knew the guy didn't have a choice; they both knew it. Either way the cartel would get him. They couldn't leave it to chance that he wouldn't eventually talk. His only hope would be to help them and pray that they could protect him long enough to give him a new identity and get him as far away as possible. Richards knew it wouldn't work though. The guy was hooked, and it would only be a matter of time before he would make a buy from the wrong person, someone who knew him, and it would all be over.

"Okay, okay, but I can't tell you much. I don't know anything. I just break down the plane and remove the shipment. We load it up and drop it off at different stops. It changes all the time." He was visibly shaking. He knew every word was putting another nail in his coffin.

"Can you identify anybody? Have you ever overheard any names?" Richards needed something to go on.

"No, Man. They're real careful. I just meet the pilots and guides. We help load the suitcases and equipment for the trips. Then when we get word, we strip down the plane when it gets back and unload the stash." Richards could see the man's legs jittering on the other side of the table.

"How do you get word?" Richards was puzzled. Did the pilots and guides know about the cargo or were they used as decoys to make the business look authentic? He would need to put his men to work on that right away.

"We get a call at the hangar. One of us has to stay there all the time. It can really be boring." He started to smile then realized that there was nothing to smile about now.

"Do you know who calls? Would you recognize the voice?" This wasn't helping at all.

"No, Man. Like I said, they're careful." He stopped for a second. "I did hear a name once, some lawyer, I think, Nunez. I think that was it." He frowned. "The man where we dropped off a load was high and griping about some big shot who had threatened him, if he didn't straighten up. He was so high I don't think he knew what he was saying. I got out of there fast. The guys around him were trying to shut him up and they were real scared. One of them muttered something about this guy being 'la Cara del muerto.' I didn't hang around to hear more."

The face of death, Richards had heard that name on the streets. When just a name could strike fear in the hearts of the tough guys he had seen, Richards knew, whoever he was, he was one heartless soul.

"Did you hear anything else?"

The guy's legs were practically jumping up and down where he sat. He didn't even seem to notice. "I heard the guy shooting off his mouth that night turned up in several pieces later. They never found his tongue." He swallowed hard. "I don't know anything else."

Richards knew he was wondering just what his own fate would be. "If you think of anything, let me know. We'll do our best to protect you, but you'd better tell us everything."

The guy nodded then dropped his head in his hands. He was shaking all over.

Nunez, Richards had heard that name before, but he couldn't remember where. It was a common Spanish name, but there was something else, some other connection. He just couldn't place it. It would come to him.

Richards sent one of his men into the interrogation room with a laptop and instructions to have the suspect look through their files of known drug associates. Maybe they would get lucky and the guy could identify someone, but he doubted it.

Richards went back to his temporary office and placed a call to a friend in Memphis. If anyone could find out, he could. He supplied him with the little he had and asked about the street name, la Cara del muerto. When his friend heard the name, he whistled softly.

"You **are** playing with the big boys," he emphasized. "He's the worst hombre I've ever heard about. Some Bolivian dude—makes Attila the Hun look like Mother Teresa—brutal. Nunez, you say?" He looked down frowning thoughtfully. "I'll see what I can find out, but you now the smart ones won't talk. Still there's usually someone who needs something; I might get lucky." He laughed abruptly, a sharp short sound. He was a street-hardened pro like Richards. He knew the score. Just asking could get results he didn't want.

Richards hesitated. "Be careful. Don't take chances with this one."

His friend laughed again. "You know me. I never take chances. I'll get back to you."

Richards hung up the phone and almost wished that he hadn't had to involve him. He rubbed his aching thigh. They had already tried to kill him. They certainly wouldn't be concerned about killing someone who was asking too many of the wrong questions.

Tired from the grueling day, Richards returned to the hotel. Amanda had already fallen asleep. He showered then slipped into bed beside her. She snuggled up next to him but never woke. He hugged her close; he would just have to wait until morning to share his good news. He felt hopeful for the first time.

When Amanda woke the next morning, she reached over and the hugged Tim. She knew he must be tired, but she couldn't wait to tell him her news.

Tim pulled the pillow over his head. "Can't a man get any sleep around here?" His voice was muffled by the pillow. Amanda dragged it from his hands and kissed him soundly. He flipped her over on her back and returned the kiss with a strong dose of heated passion, his hands roving up and down the slender body beneath him.

"You were saying?" He grinned at her confused expression, still moving suggestively against her. Then she remembered the real reason she had awakened him and sighed.

"This will have to wait. I have to talk to you. You're not going to believe what I found out yesterday." She grinned up at him. He suddenly became serious and moved to lie beside her.

When he didn't speak just waited silently for her to begin, she realized he was almost afraid to hope for good news. She hugged him quickly to reassure him and launched into her story. Several minutes later, he fell back against the pillows and stared blankly at the ceiling.

It was too good to believe. Now he understood why that name had sounded so familiar. Amanda had referred to him occasionally as part of Stevens' personal staff and an advisor to the President. She had mentioned that he didn't have an official role but seemed to have the run of the White House, and everybody carried out his orders without hesitation.

Richards remembered seeing him on occasion. He was good-looking and well-spoken, but he also remembered thinking he wouldn't want to get on his bad side. He had that look that Richards knew well from the streets, all business and no excuses. He would be a hard taskmaster. It was the eyes; even Amanda had said there was something missing behind those dark eyes. Richards knew what it was—a soul. He didn't tell Amanda, but he warned her not to say anything to anyone about what she had uncovered, especially the President.

Richards had a lot to think about. He read through Miss Maude's notes and almost became physically ill. Evidently, the housekeeper had told her everything. The music, alcohol, drugs, the sex, the physical abuse, she had left nothing out. She had witnessed it all. There was a profound sadness in the recounting of the events that led to the selling of the house. The housekeeper had witnessed the young girl's misery that last afternoon, heard her excited admission, seen Billing's reaction, and known the truth that the girl couldn't accept. She had seen her misery, her complete despair, and had wept for her.

On Miss Maude's last visit before the house was closed and sold, the housekeeper stated that she feared for the life of the young girl. She had been desperately in love with Billings and had suffered at his hands just to please him, but he had turned on her with a wrathful vengeance. She had not defended herself; she had not cried or pleaded with Billings, but the housekeeper had seen the total devastation in her soft blue eyes as she left minutes later with one of the other men. She heard no more about her, and Miss Maude never knew what had happened to her after that afternoon.

Richards did. He swallowed hard trying to dislodge the lump of pain threatening to suffocate him. Now at last he knew the truth. Now he knew who had been responsible for her death and for the baby, but what could he do? Only a sample of Billings' DNA would prove his connection to Judy, but that wouldn't prove that he had been responsible for her death. Yet, Richards knew there had to be a connection.

Amanda sat quietly allowing him to take in all that she had found out, but only he knew the whole truth, knew his sister's connection to Billings. He didn't want to share what he knew, but he had to. Amanda needed to know the type of men she was dealing with; they were dangerous, and she couldn't take chances by revealing anything she had learned. He had to make her see that.

Richards left Amanda packing for their return trip while he went to the DEA office. His team had been following the leads they had obtained the previous day. Richards added a computer search of Nunez's travel from the States using his passport documentation. He wanted dates and locations. He needed some way to connect him directly to the cartels. His informant had called him Bolivian, so they would start there. Maybe they would get lucky.

Another man worked on the airstrip angle searching for who had purchased the land and financed the business, when they had begun operation, where they traveled, anything they could find out. Everything was organized at first glance by legitimate companies in the States, but after hours of delving into records and tracing leads they began to see a pattern. Dates began to coincide with Billings' terms in office as Attorney General then later as Governor. The higher he climbed, the bigger the charter business grew, the more money the cartels made.

Reviewing campaign contributions led them to find that the charter business had made substantial contributions to Billings' election funds and had later financed several of his overseas trips. There was definitely a pattern of abuse of office and misuse of funds, but Richards knew there was more. They just had to keep digging. Billings was connected to the drug cartels one way or another whether he knew it or not. Richards just couldn't see him being that stupid. It was much too dangerous, but stranger things had happened.

Richards put a trace on Nunez's phone, but he knew that was probably a waste of time. Most illegal activity connected to phones was through throwaways. Still, they might get lucky.

A trace on his travel out of the country revealed several trips to the Caribbean. From there they were able to trace his continued travel by private jet to various South American locations. The private jets were registered to several different companies and locating a specific travel manifest became almost impossible. Richards was almost positive of his ultimate destination.

Nunez' role in the President's administration confused Richards. Why would a cartel kingpin help a president who had been adamant about destroying drug trafficking in the States? What was his connection to Billings? What did he expect to gain? It didn't make sense. They had to keep looking. They were missing something.

A special DEA report was forwarded to the President's office informing him of their progress and the success of their last operation. Robert was elated with the good press they were receiving. Paul was frantic. This campaign had to be stopped.

Robert had gone along with Paul's plan to call a halt to the drug operation, but this latest news made him reconsider that idea. Maybe they should wait just a little longer. He seemed to be getting excellent press for his drug initiative. The public was elated about the eradication of drugs on the streets and the potential for limiting access to them now.

Paul knew better than most that a limited supply didn't keep people from using; it just made it more expensive and created a greater likelihood of criminal acts being committed by those trying to support a habit.

Robert forced Paul's hand. He had no choice now but to use whatever he could to bring Robert to heel. He placed a call to Alberto. The calls were always short, but Paul was unaware of the trace on Alberto's phone and ultra high resonance recording device that had been placed to intercept Alberto's calls and record them.

Richards saw the number and knew that this might be the break they needed. When he heard the conversation, he sat trying to process what it meant. Nunez was supposed to contact someone and retrieve information, information that Stevens said would realign Billings' thinking. Ambiguous, vague, and hardly revealing, but just the connection Richards had been waiting for. Stevens was calling the shots, so what was his connection to the Bolivian drug cartel? That much remained to be seen.

Richards immediately put his team to work on researching the background of everyone associated with the President. He couldn't single out one person and not give away the game. It was time consuming and frustrating but they had to be careful. They didn't want anyone on the inside to become suspicious. Routine background checks were a part of the Secret Service system. No one thought anything about having their records requested, and they didn't have time to notice that all their records were being scrutinized.

It was going to be tricky, but Richards wanted to get a copy of whatever Stevens had requested. He put his best computer whiz to hacking into Nunez' personal computer system. They had to be careful. Anyone associated with the cartels had the best of everything. Government entities were always trying to play catch up, but Richards had an ace in the young recruit to his department. They had rescued him from a lengthy prison sentence for hacking into financial accounts on Wall Street just for the fun of it. If he hadn't talked about it to his friends, no one would have ever known. He was a genius at subverting fire walls and security systems and redirecting systems analysis so that no trace of his intervention would ever be detected. Richards prayed that he could perform his magic for them this time too.

The computer expert at the DEA was whistling softly as he downloaded Nunez' files. It had been a challenge hacking his system, but a thrill when he succeeded. Richards was more than pleased.

Alberto copied the file and downloaded the pictures. He made a back up disc complete with audio in case Billings got the bright idea to try to deny his culpability. Alberto knew how his mind worked, and he was prepared to add more fuel to the fire if Billings got too smart. It was time that he realized that he was a bought man, one who could easily be asked for a permanent refund of their investment. He brought the pictures to Paul himself. He wouldn't trust anyone else with something this damaging.

Paul and Alberto entered the Oval Office after a cursory knock. Robert glanced up, but returned to signing the papers in front of him.

They waited until he finished. Robert placed the papers in a stack and slid them aside. "Do we have a meeting scheduled?" He motioned for the men to be seated. They remained standing. Robert frowned. "This must be bad news. What is it?" He motioned to the folder Paul held.

Paul stepped to the desk and handed Robert the folder, "Nothing that we can't fix."

He waited until Robert opened the folder and took out the photos. Robert paled when he saw the identifying scar on the man's back. He was almost certain that he had never done anything of this nature, almost, but not completely. He glanced up at Paul. He knew Paul recognized the scar. They had spent too much time in locker rooms and gyms in college for him not to have seen it before.

"I don't understand. I wouldn't do this, and you know it." Alberto stared at him with those cold, piercing, black eyes, and Robert knew Alberto didn't believe a word he spoke.

"How can you deny it? Even I recognized the scar. Don't you think others will too?"

Robert stood and began pacing the room. "I know those can't be of me. I know I have never done anything that despicable. That's a kid for Christ's sake." Robert felt physically sick. What was he going to do? He turned to face Paul. "Where did you get those?"

"They were sent to my office with a note demanding that you stop your campaign against cocaine trafficking, lessen your stand, choose another issue to attack, but do it now, or the pictures will be sent to the press." Paul waited while Robert considered his options. There weren't any, not any which would leave him with a political career.

Robert thought about how much younger he looked in those photos. When had they been taken and how? He couldn't figure it out, but there had been times when he got high in college, maybe he had done something then. No, he wouldn't believe it; he couldn't believe it. He slumped back in his chair for a minute thinking then leaned forward and pushed the intercom.

"Send the DEA director in to see me as soon as possible." He looked back at Paul."How do we know that this will satisfy them and that they won't ask for something else later?"

Paul stared directly at him. "We don't. We just have to trust them. It's all we can do." He reached across the desk and picked up the photos, pushing them back into the folder. "You realize this could be the end of your political career, not to mention the possibility of prison, if these kids could be identified." He wanted Robert to truly understand how desperate the situation was.

Robert stared at Paul helplessly. What could he possibly do? "Can you help me?"

"I can try. Just take care of this immediately." He wanted to add that he had tried to warn him, but he knew Robert wouldn't appreciate that fact at the moment.

When the DEA director called Richards later that morning, he assumed that there was a new development in the case. He hurried to his office. This case was consuming his life. There were so many angles and so many people connected in multiple ways that it would take a month just to file the paperwork. The director wasn't smiling when Richards entered his office. He motioned for him to sit. Richards knew that he wasn't going to like whatever he was about to hear. Obviously the director was not pleased either if the scowl on his face was any indication.

"We've been ordered to close down our operation. The President has deemed our investigation complete and the drug trade crippled enough to cause him and his advisors to decide to spend their money on another issue, one foremost in the minds of the public." He was practically snarling by the time he finished his little recitation. "That's hogwash, and we both know it. But there's nothing I can do about it. As of now the operation is closed." He paced back and forth behind his desk, his hands tightly clenched behind his back. He stopped and turned back to Richards and smiled. "There's nothing to say that you can't investigate this simply as a departmental inquiry. Of course, you'll have to keep things quiet. Hold off on any major strikes for a while. Let them become complacent again. Then we'll hit them."

Richards laughed and stood to leave, "You got it, Boss." So now he knew the connection. Stevens and the cartel were backing the President and the photos had been their way of bringing him back in line. Their operation must have really inflicted some heavy damage to the cocaine rings. Now Billings was being forced to call off the DEA's investigation.

That still didn't explain how Stevens was connected to the Bolivians, though. Richards hurried back to his office. Maybe one of his team had uncovered something that would help answer that question. Richards called a quick meeting and instructed his team to continue work on the personal files of Stevens, Nunez, and Contreras.

Several hours later, one of his men called him over. He had discovered that Stevens had been adopted. He found nothing unusual about it, until he had investigated the adoption agency. He found that it no longer operated, but after a lengthy search of records, he discovered that it had once been a subsidiary of a larger company working in imports and shipping, mostly from South and Central American countries. That caught his interest, so he traced the nationalities of the adopted babies and found they had all been part of a Catholic Church agency in Bolivia, which specialized in securing homes for children of unwed mothers.

Private adoptions had been arranged through the agency with wealthy couples willing to take children of mixed Caucasian and Hispanic origin. Further investigation revealed that the children had been placed with prestigious families. As a matter of routine, he had run several of the other names he had found and had identified the First Lady also as having been adopted from the same agency. Richards didn't know what to make of the information, but he realized that it was an important element, another piece of a very confusing and complicated puzzle.

More information poured in from the personal files. Billings and Stevens had been friends since their days in college. They had practiced law together, and Stevens had functioned as Billings' advisor and confidant through his entire political career. They had been inseparable.

Stevens' connection to the First Lady wasn't as clear, but his sources revealed that she had been introduced to Billings by Stevens during college, and like the men, she had practiced law for several years in Arkansas. The trio had been prominent in both Arkansas politics and society. Richards noted that their marriage had taken place a short time after Judy's death.

Richards was certain that Judy had been killed to keep her from causing problems to either Billings' political career or his personal life. He had been Attorney General at the time and soon after that had entered the race for governor. Taken with his sudden marriage to Caroline, Billings became the front runner in having a motive for Judy's death. Coupled with the fact she had been pregnant with Billings' child, according to Miss Maude's investigation, she had become a definite liability to an up-and-coming politician with his eye on the White House.

Proving who was responsible was another matter entirely. He might know why she was killed and who he thought was responsible, but he was quickly realizing that he had no way of proving anything. He couldn't see Billings involving himself in anything of that nature, and as much as he wanted to blame Stevens, he didn't think he would do it either. No, he would bet anything it had been Nunez. He had seen the way his good looks and that aura of danger drew women to him, while those same qualities made men move aside. He was dangerous and deadly; that much Richards knew for a fact.

Richards only option at this point was to turn one of them against the others. He wanted Billings more than anyone else for personal reasons. It wasn't strictly by the book, but he didn't care. If he could get Billings, there might be a way to draw Contreras in. With him in custody, they could lessen the influence cocaine had in the States. Richards knew any progress they made would only be temporary, but progress of any type would be preferable to allowing the cartels to continue their growth unchecked.

Chapter 22

PAUL HADN'T HAD ANY spare time to contact Caroline since this problem had begun. He wanted to sigh in relief, but somehow he knew that things weren't anywhere near a point where he could take a deep breath. He felt trapped, suffocated by the constraints placed on him by his father, by his friendship, by his loyalty. He wanted to simply throw up his hands and quit, but there wasn't any way that he could ever do that. He might be Raul Contreras' son, but his life was just as expendable as the next man's, if he went against the cartel's best interests.

Raul had achieved his goal, but nothing was working as he had planned. Raul had his man in the White House, but Robert had done nothing but cause problems so far. Raul owned men in Congress, the court system, state officials, local governments; what more did he want? At some point, just like Caesar's empire, it would become unmanageable, impossible to rule over and fall to chaos and ruin.

Paul was feeling the last gasps of a dying dream. He couldn't imagine his father going quietly, losing with dignity, folding his hand and walking away. It went completely against everything he had ever worked for. Both he and Rafael had spent their entire lives working for this moment. They had achieved it—now what! What was his role in this scheme now? He had shaped and pushed Robert to this point, but he was tired. He hated the deception that had caused him to betray his friend, to deny his feelings for Caroline, to allow his son to become another man's. He was disgusted by his actions and disillusioned about his future prospects.

Money could only buy so much; power could only dominate so much. There came a time in every man's life when he must choose which path he would take, which road he would follow. Paul had never been given that opportunity, never allowed the choice. His life had been dictated for him, his path chosen. He had never experienced the feeling of real satisfaction of having done something well just for the sake of doing it. Everything he had done since his first meeting with his father had been obligatory.

Suddenly Paul couldn't force himself to do another thing just for his father's sake, just to see his vision become a greater reality. He wanted to be his own man, not someone else's puppet. He wanted to make choices because he felt they were right. He shook his head. It was an impossible dream. He had no power over his life, his future. He never had, not from the time he was born, definitely not now when he had the woman he loved and his son to consider.

Richards had devised a plan that might work, but more likely it wouldn't. It was a true long shot. At this point they really didn't have anything they could go on, so his plan was to bluff Stevens with the little information he had and pray that he could shake his composure enough to create doubt in his mind. He had the leverage he needed. At least, he hoped that he did. Maybe a little coercion and blackmail would gain the support he needed, because without Stevens' help, the whole plan would fold. Right now, he had nothing to lose.

Richards had already placed the call requesting Stevens to drop by his office, unofficially, of course. He had made the message deliberately ambiguous, trying to entice him to come just to find out what it was all about. Curiosity and the cat, he hoped. Stevens was an extremely busy man. His time was limited because of his position in the White House, but Richards knew that there had been too much trouble between the cartels and Billings for his Chief of Staff not to check out anything that might be another problem for him. He was counting on it. It would all depend on how much hold the Bolivians had on Stevens. All Richards could figure was that it had to be substantial. He just didn't know what.

Paul looked at the message and started to toss it aside, but at the last minute he told his secretary to place a call and inform Richards he would be there around six. It was late, but he had a lot to do before he could call this day over. He was mentally exhausted and frustrated with Robert and the problems he had caused. He wanted to take Caroline and his son and disappear from the face of the Earth. He pushed his hand through his hair. That would never work as long as their fathers breathed. He sighed, took the next set of papers from the stack on his desk, and went back to work.

Richards' team was continuing their search for any information that might explain the connection between Stevens, the First Lady, and the Bolivians. Richards needed all the leverage he could get, but he had ruled out Billings who seemed to be more of a pawn than a real player. Richards couldn't find any direct association between Billings and the cartel other than through Stevens and possibly the First Lady.

Richards hadn't given up on bringing Billings to justice; he planned to make sure he brought him down any way he could, but he had to put that aside for now. The Bolivian cocaine cartel was his top priority. To get it, he knew he would have to use Stevens and his ties to the First Lady and her son—their son—dirty pool, so to speak, but a necessary evil in this war.

It was already after six. Richards was beginning to think that Stevens wouldn't show. He started putting his desk in order. He might as well go home. He looked up at the brief knock on his open office door. Stevens stood in the doorway, frowning.

"I take it that this meeting was not important. I see that you're about to leave, so I won't keep you." He turned before Richards could speak and started to leave.

"I guess it all depends on your perspective. It concerns your son." Richards had rolled the dice. Now all he could do was pray they didn't come up snake eyes.

Paul froze. How did he know about Robbie? He turned back to face Richards. "What is that supposed to mean?" He wasn't going to confirm or deny his statement.

"Why don't you come in and have a seat? I was just finishing up a report, but it can wait." That was a lie. It didn't matter. He knew Stevens didn't believe him or care. He walked around the desk and closed his office door as Stevens sat down in front of his desk. Richards took his time walking back to his seat. Let him stew a few minutes.

Paul didn't rush to question Richards but sat waiting for him to speak. This was a power struggle and neither of them wanted to cry uncle. Paul would sit there all night if necessary. He knew Richards had to make the first move; after all he had called for this meeting.

Richards was impressed, but he should have known that a man in Stevens' position would be a pro at verbal strategy. He certainly wouldn't be intimidated by a lowly public servant like Richards. He was Chief of Staff to the President; he knew more powerful people by their first name than Richards would ever know period. All Richards could hope for was a sliver of conscience, a miniscule amount of compassion, and a little honesty.

Richards stared at Paul for a minute trying to understand how a man of his stature, his background had become entangled with the cartel. He wanted to ask, but he didn't think he would get a straight answer right now.

"Look, I won't insult your intelligence or waste your time with pointless questions. I know that you personally had some rather explicit photos of the President in, let's say, a compromising situation sent to you from Raul Contreras in Bolivia. How he got them or why he had them, isn't the issue now. I know that you used those same photos to convince the President that it would be in his best interest to terminate our cocaine operation. I'd say right now you're looking at coercion, blackmail, and possibly treason just to get started. That is some serious prison time. I also know that with enough money you can drag out any trial until we all face retirement, but it won't change the facts. During that time you will have subjected your family, the First lady, your son, and even the President to an unmerciful trial by public opinion. The press would love nothing better than to unearth a scandal like this. Do you want to subject them to this type of scathing publicity, personal scrutiny, and public humiliation?"

Paul sat quietly weighing his options. He wasn't rushing to answer any charges right now. He needed to think.

"Consider this. If we can find out that Robbie is your son and not the President's, others can too." He let that fact sink in. "Once any type of investigation is made public, the media will be on you like a pack of hungry dogs. You know that; you know how they work." He leaned toward Stevens and spoke quietly, confidently. "They'll write anything to sell news whether it is fact or fiction, and you know as well as I do that once fiction is reported, it becomes fact, especially in the minds of the public. Do you want that stigma following your son and his mother for the rest of their lives? Is that the legacy you want to give them?"

Paul was amazed at how much and yet how little Richards had learned, but it was enough. He was right in everything he said, so why was he saying it? What did he want from him? He might as well ask. He wasn't admitting anything; he was just listening to his options.

"So what do you want from me?"

"That's easy. I want Contreras, Nunez, and Billings. If I thought that Billings could land me the others, I wouldn't be talking to you, but I know he is just a pawn in this game you're playing, and I want the king and all his court. I'll get them eventually, with or without your help. So what will it be?" He sounded so adamant, so confident. Paul really felt that he could make it all happen. He couldn't keep a frown from his face. He was asking a lot, more than he could ever imagine. Could he turn against his father, the family? What would Alberto do if he realized what was happening? Whose side would he be on?

"I can offer you a new start, a life with your son and his mother, if that's what you want. But you'll have to give up everything you have to get it. You might think the sacrifice is too great, some people would. Think about it. I'll give you until tomorrow morning."

"Aren't you afraid I'll skip the country or talk to someone? A lot can be destroyed in a little time." Paul wasn't sure what game Richards was playing. Could he trust him? His life might hang in the balance.

"No, I have enough evidence to make a conviction stick, with or without your help. You're the one who might want to be careful. I know the cartels; I know how they feel about mistakes; I wouldn't want to be in your shoes. This was a big mistake, letting us get this kind of information." Richards smiled slightly. He wanted Stevens to feel the touch of fear that mishandling any problem for the cartel elicited. It didn't matter how high up in the organization you were, errors were punished severely; mistakes were a death sentence.

Paul only smiled. He had an inside hand. Richards didn't know that though. Raul wouldn't be happy, but he wouldn't punish him the way Richards thought. At least, he didn't think he would. He frowned slightly as he recalled his last conversation with Raul. Something had been different. He couldn't figure out exactly what it was, but there was a difference. That was one reason he had sent Alberto down to talk to him personally. He had sounded uncertain, confused somehow, totally unlike the father he knew.

When he returned, Alberto mentioned that Raul seemed a little under the weather, that he hadn't been well, and that a specialist had been called to come to the compound. When Paul called later that week, Raul had seemed fine and said that nothing was wrong.

Still, it was a strange feeling; Paul couldn't remember his father ever being sick. He had always assumed that Raul simply refused to be; therefore, he never was. Raul had that type of strength, a mind-over-matter mentality. Paul couldn't help being concerned. He hadn't seen his father in years. Their conversations were always brief, business-related never personal.

There was no time to fly down for visits as there had been in previous years. Summer visits had ended with his twenty-first birthday. His life was so regimented now; free time came with too high a price. It was easier to work and stay up with the constant demands than to struggle with the workload when he returned. More importantly, he couldn't take the chance that, no matter how careful they were, someone would make a connection. Paul was too well-known. He would have to wait. His plan was to enjoy life once Robert was no longer President.

He laughed. That might be sooner than they had imagined. Richards raised one eyebrow in question. Paul just shook his head, "Private joke."

Richards looked at him hard. It might be a joke, but Stevens certainly didn't look very happy about whatever it was. "Is there anything you want to tell me before you leave?"

Paul shook his head, "No, let me think about this. I'll give you my answer in the morning. There's more involved than you realize." He smiled, trying to be philosophical about the mess his life was now in. Pandora, she had been right.

"There always is." Richards spoke from experience. Nothing was ever easy in life and anyone who thought so just hadn't lived very long. Richards nodded to Paul as he stood to leave, "Whenever you can—tomorrow." Paul left; he had a lot to think about. He wasn't sure one night would be nearly enough time.

Could he do it, could he give them up to have a future with Caroline and Robbie? What future would he have knowing what he had done to get it? He wasn't like Raul. He couldn't disassociate himself from his feelings, his emotions. He had never been able to do that. He needed someone to talk to, but who was there? He certainly couldn't involve Caroline, not now, later maybe, once he decided. He knew what he had to do, but if he was wrong then he might be signing his own death certificate.

Alberto knew there was a problem even before Paul called. He had set up a new security system on his computer and it flagged the files which had been downloaded to a second system. It didn't take him long to find the source. He had tried to warn Raul about transmitting documents over the internet. It was too risky no matter how great your protection was. But Raul hadn't been himself lately. Alberto couldn't reason with him. Rafael had his hands full with an uprising in the coca fields. Workers backed by guerrilla leaders from several groups were joining forces to demand higher wages and greater profits.

Workers at the compound were sending their children off to receive their educations, and they weren't returning to work for Raul as they once had. With each new generation, loyalty to the cartel was weakening. Rafael could feel the power slipping from their hands. His trained forces were aging just as he and Raul. With fewer problems requiring the tactics which had once instilled fear in the hearts of all, fewer young men wanted to spend their lives pursuing that type of career. Times were changing, but Raul refused to see it.

Always a visionary in the past, Raul had become blinded by his own power. He failed to see that his cartel was no longer the dominate force in the world of drugs. They were now available in every part of the world. They were competing in a global market for their share. Countries whose economies were failing with legal exports were challenging them with their own production of illegal contraband. Cocaine had become a worldwide commodity. Raul's share of that market was dwindling. The power base of intellectuals he had established around the world was branching out, joining with others seeking their own fortunes, their own way.

Names that had once inspired respect and loyalty now were viewed with disdain. They were still the strongest and most powerful cartel in Bolivia and their fortune was such that it could supply their needs for generations, but there was a constant and slow decline taking place over all of their holdings. The battle they were waging in the States had weakened their influence in South America. Rafael didn't know what to do to stop it. He wasn't worried, but he hated to see the power they had slip away. Raul thought that everything would be fine, that Paul could force the President to withdraw from his continued campaign against cocaine. Rafael was more realistic.

Times change and the wise change with them or get left behind. Rafael could see that happening; Raul couldn't. He was impossible to talk to. He ranted and raved about things no one understood. He seemed caught up in some battle in his mind and couldn't fight his way out. Rafael wasn't worried about the cartel; it could survive without either of them, but he was worried about Raul. He had tried to get Raul to let him contact Paul, but he refused.

Against Raul's wishes, Rafael had sent for a specialist, a family friend. After treatment and medication, Raul seemed better, but there were still moments, flashes of anger, confusion, and disorientation. Rafael knew that Raul was far from well. He refused to discuss it with Rafael.

When Alberto called, Rafael confirmed what Alberto suspected. Now the problem was how to handle the situation.

Paul tried to make a decision, but he couldn't. He knew that his loyalty should be to his family, but Raul had never treated him like a son. He regarded him more as an extension of himself. Raul had supplied him with every possible advantage and had made it possible for him to have everything he wanted, except what he wanted most—Caroline and Robbie.

If he didn't do it, he would lose them both, and they would be left to face an uncertain future. How could he fail them? He pushed his hands through his hair. He had to talk to someone, and there was only one person that he had ever been able to confide in. He would just have to face the consequences. It had been his decision that had brought all of these events down on them. He had no choice. Paul reached for his phone and punched in the number. It only rang once. He had been waiting for his call.

Paul arrived at Richards' office early the next morning, much sooner that Richards had imagined. He was glad. He didn't want to force him to do anything. People were much easier to manage if they felt they had freely chosen to follow a certain path. In this case the choice was between two equally difficult roads, but at least there was a choice. He motioned for Stevens to be seated; then he pulled a file in front of him.

"This won't be easy to pull off, but I think we can make it work for everyone involved." He frowned as he spoke; he wasn't sure that it would all fall into place like they planned.

"I understand the risks. They're acceptable given my choices." He sat calmly waiting for Richards to lay the groundwork.

After several hours of negotiation, discussion, and phone calls, Richards was pleased with the plan they had formulated and the results they hoped to achieve. Now all that remained was for Stevens to carry out his part. The plan itself was complex, carrying it off would be a strategic nightmare, but Stevens seemed to feel that it could be done. Richards prayed he was right.

Paul left Richards' office later in the day. He had warned Robert that he wouldn't be available for most of the day. He had felt his phone vibrate on and off all day. He knew it was his office; he would get back to them later, if there was a later. He shook his head. It was hard to believe that so much had happened all because Robert failed to relinquish even a little bit of power. Had he followed Paul's advice in the beginning, none of this would be happening, but maybe it was for the best. He was tired. Keeping Robert in line for over ten years had become a full time occupation, and the most exhausting and frustrating thing he had ever undertaken. But that was over; from this evening on Robert would be someone else's problem. He was relieved but saddened to think their friendship would end like this. Paul laughed a humorless sound. He knew Robert. Robert would come out on top regardless, if he could restrain some of his less admirable proclivities. Without Alberto, he might be in trouble.

Paul went straight to the Oval Office. He knew Robert would still be there. He knocked briefly and entered. Robert was kicked back in his chair elbows resting on the chair arms and his fingers laced together in front of him."I've been trying to get in touch with you all afternoon. Where have you been, and why weren't you answering your phone?" His tone radiated his impatience.

"Are you sure you want to know?" Paul was mocking him, and he let it show by the grin on his face. His days of catering to Robert's ego were finally at an end and it couldn't come any too soon. If it hadn't been for Raul, Paul would have ditched him years ago, friend or no friend.

"I wouldn't have asked if I didn't want to know." Robert let his anger show. He was tired. His day hadn't gone well. He had needed Paul's advice to help him make some crucial decisions, and he hadn't been able to locate him.

On his way in, Paul had ordered a tray sent up from the kitchen. He was hungry now that everything was decided. He waited as the waiter sat up a side table and uncovered the dishes. When he left, Paul walked over and sat down. "You might want to join me. We may be here a while, and we have to wait for someone to arrive." He began filling his plate and poured himself a glass of tea. Robert could suit himself.

"What if I don't want to?" Robert was being petulant, like some cocky little school boy.

Paul laughed. "If you would take my advice, which you never do, I might add, you would eat now. You never know when you will get another chance." He laughed again then took a bite of his food. Now that he had made his decision, he was relaxed. It was an odd feeling considering everything that was about to happen.

Robert refused his suggestion and sat fuming until Richards was shown into the room. Now they had his full attention. He frowned. He didn't like the look on either of their faces.

Several hours later, Robert sat too stunned to move. He had a stiff drink in his hand, but he couldn't even raise it to drink. How could he have been so blind, so stupid? They had deceived him completely and now he was going to have to pay the price for his ignorance—him, one of the smartest people around. His remarkable IQ and phenomenal memory hadn't done him a bit of good. He had been outsmarted and outmaneuvered by pros. They hadn't given him any choice. Everything had been decided and was being arranged right now. In less than four days, he would be a dead man. He sat without moving for hours, his mind working at warp speed but traveling in a continual circle.

Once the President was advised of the plan, Richards had to make things happen very quickly. They didn't want any time delay, if possible. The sooner everything took place, the safer they would all be. He almost felt sorry for Billings, almost. He had never really liked him, but Richards was certain that he hadn't expected his life to take such a dramatic turn. He had been completely astonished by the facts they presented and speechless when he heard the complexity of their plan. It was all out his hands. He could agree or not, but ultimately they had given him no choice.

Richards began work on the plan that evening. He contacted the head of Presidential security and together they arranged for the President to leave the next morning for Camp David. He and his family would spend a few days in retreat before returning to Washington. Caroline was advised on the change in plans and was astonished at such short notice, but she altered her schedule a breathed a sigh of relief to have a few days alone with Robbie.

Ms. Martin had them all packed and ready before Caroline had finished breakfast. Caroline thought she was a wonder and Robbie loved her dearly. She would be traveling with them; Caroline couldn't imagine life without her. She was fast becoming Caroline's confidant and a strong shoulder for her to lean on. Robbie would have been lost without his Marty.

Robert was unusually distracted. He spent very little time with his family. He wondered the vast area surrounding Camp David as though in a daze. Caroline had tried to talk to him, but he had brushed her concern aside with a snide remark, telling her that she would soon have her heart's desire. Caroline was at a complete loss; she had no idea what he was referring to, but she left him to himself for the remainder of their stay.

When they left to board the helicopter for the return flight to Washington, Caroline was completely baffled by the last minute change in their plans. Instead of boarding the helicopter, their limo stopped momentarily near the helipad then left the retreat by a back road. The look on Robert's face kept her from asking about the change. Instead she sat silently and waited. No one was talking. Even Paul seemed distracted. You would think someone had died. She supposed she would find out soon enough.

She sighed as she glanced at the countryside rushing by. It was so much like her life. It seemed to be racing headlong passed her, and she didn't even have a moment to enjoy it. What would it be like to take a simple walk without half a dozen people following along? Or to have a phone conversation that wasn't recorded? Someday, if she was lucky, maybe, she smiled.

Kenny Eliot, a thirty year veteran of the CIA, and one of its most trusted members, waited patiently in the rural countryside several miles from the compound. He had everything in position; all that remained was for the helicopter to top the ridge of trees and his mission would be over in a matter of seconds. The shoulder-launched, anti-aircraft missile, easily identified by its Middle Eastern markings, was situated for a direct hit.

The roar of the rotors alerted him to the craft's approach; he marked his target and fired. A giant ball of fire lit the early morning sky rivaling the brilliance of the sun. Black smoke poured from the wreckage as it impacted the earth. Eliot dropped the launcher and raced to the waiting truck. He had only moments before the military strike force would converge on the area. He had to be as far away as possible.

He took a deep breath as he sped away; every mile meant greater success. He hadn't been detected. He was ready when the call came. He simply turned his vehicle around and retraced his route, secure in the fact that he would be part of the investigation and able to destroy any betraying evidence, if need be, with no one the wiser.

It had been an unusual assignment, but he had taken part in others just as strange. Still, he had liked the President. He hated to see his Presidency end in such a way, but he was sworn to secrecy, and he would never betray his sworn oath.

Richards' hand-picked, special response team rushed to the scene. The area was immediately cordoned off and local and state authorities were issued procedural orders, as the military arrived to help in the search for bodies and to seal off sites of debris. They were quickly collected and taken to a military facility to safeguard the remains.

Under the strict supervision of the military, the remains were identified and autopsy reports issued. The deaths had been instantaneous, most likely from the force of the missile strike or impact with the earth, which had taken place within seconds. A special Green Beret unit stood guard, securing the bodies until they could be transported back to Washington. Due to the extent of damage the bodies suffered from the initial explosion and subsequent crash, the caskets were sealed before leaving the facility in preparation for burial.

Within hours of the crash, the search team located the missile launcher and identified its betraying markings. News flashes interrupted every channel with reports of the deaths and initial findings. Even while the nation prepared to mourn the death of its President and his family, they demanded action against those responsible. The war on terrorism gained unprecedented support from both parties in Congress, and the military began an immediate campaign to eliminate the most well-known terrorist proponents and their supporters.

Within minutes of leaving the compound, the Presidential limousine had turned onto the main highway and raced toward a waiting 18 wheeler stopped further ahead. As they approached the semi, Richards contacted the driver; the back doors opened, a set of ramps extended from the truck, and the car drove up into the trailer. The ramps retracted and the doors closed. Interior lights illuminated the space. Caroline's door opened, and she was asked to step out of the vehicle; she felt like she had gotten trapped in a weird science fiction movie or crazy spy thriller. She wanted to laugh at how bizarre it all seemed until she looked first at Robert then Paul. They weren't laughing.

They spent the next few hours relaxing in a well-furnished sitting area equipped with magazines, books, food and drink, even bathroom facilities. Only no one seemed to be relaxing. Caroline was impressed, but definitely confused. At some point someone was going to have to talk to her, and explain what all this cloak and dagger stuff was about.

Later when she thought of Robbie, she wanted to panic. He had been left with Ms. Martin who was returning to D.C., by car with Robbie. He didn't like the noise of the helicopters, and the drive was reasonably short. Caroline knew that Ms. Martin would take care of him, but she wanted to know how long she was going to be away from him. Somebody better start talking and soon. She glanced at Paul. He shook his head and nodded toward the Secret Service men stationed at a tactful distance from them.

As the semi raced toward its destination, Richards took a deep breath. So far things had gone as planned. The three had been removed safely from the scene. Substituting the appropriate helicopter the night before had been the most harrowing task so far, but the Secret Service had provided the necessary delaying tactics and subterfuge to carry it off. The decoy helicopter, which had been flown remotely by one of the military's best computer technicians, had been destroyed with the bodies supposedly of the crew, President, First Lady, and Chief of Staff aboard. The bodies had all been obtained discreetly from local county morgues under the pretext of use for scientific and medical research.

Now the living corpses, sat together in the enclosed space, racing toward their ultimate destination. No one felt like speaking, and Caroline had been in politics long enough to know when not to ask questions, but she was becoming concerned. It showed in the frown creasing her brow. The men continued working on papers spread out on the low table in front of them.

Robert sat across from Paul; he looked at Caroline for a moment. She sat a short distance away, trying to pretend interest in the magazine she held, but it had dropped from her hands to her lap, and she was staring blankly at the far wall.

Robert smiled sadly. Their divorce papers lay spread out in front of him. Paul had thought of everything as usual. Robert wanted to be angry, but he knew he was probably still in shock. He couldn't feel anything, not regret, anger, nothing. He grabbed the pen and scrawled his name across the bottom of several pages. His life was dissolving all around him, and he had absolutely no way to stop it.

Caroline glanced up. She still didn't know what was happening. They couldn't really talk about it until they reached their destination, wherever that might be. She frowned questioningly at Robert when he looked at her.

He shook his head and continued signing the last few pages. She didn't even know it, but she was a free woman. He had relinquished all claims to her son and ended the sham of a marriage they had. Now they could both start over; maybe this time he could get it right.

He studied her profile turned away from him. He had once been impressed by her talents and attracted to her beauty. She had captured his interest with her poise and confidence; she had stunned him with her ability to challenge him and hold her own. He liked that about her. She never gave in gracefully if she thought she was right; she fought to the last.

Their marriage had been anything but dull, but there had never been any real depth of feeling for either of them. He knew that; she knew that. He didn't dislike her; he just didn't love her, and that had been their problem. He had hurt her. He hadn't really meant to; he just couldn't stop himself sometimes. She had tried to be a good wife to him, but she couldn't accept the man he was, the needs he had. He didn't blame her. It was no life for either of them.

Only one person had ever really understood him and accepted him just for himself, failings and all. She had truly loved him unconditionally, but his anger had forced her away. She was gone from his life forever, she and their child.

He didn't hold Caroline responsible for their problems. He had brought his frustration and anger to their marriage. He felt pushed into marrying her, and he punished her for it. She had been an innocent victim of his foolishness, and he had hurt her because he couldn't face what he had done, what he had thrown away. It was easier then to blame her and hide from the truth. He had brought this all on himself, and on some level, he felt he was paying for his sins. His mother would have said that he was reaping his just desserts. He was glad she wasn't here to see how far her son had fallen.

He shoved the papers back in the folder and handed it to Paul. He still couldn't believe Paul's part in all this. It was incredible, but once he knew, it made so much sense. He still couldn't fathom his own stupidity. "Be careful what you ask for." He had asked, and he had received, and he had gloried in his achievements; now he would suffer for his mistakes and pay for his folly. Like so many men before him, his excessive pride and blind ambition had been his downfall. He leaned back in his chair and closed his eyes, trying to block out all the memories.

Vice President Chambers was sworn in as the next President as soon as Billings' death was officially confirmed. Richards had in his possession Billings' resignation signed that morning before they left Camp David for Washington. Everything had been done legally, so there could never be any issues of legality at a later date. Billings' sworn and witnessed resignation would be placed safely in a Washington, D.C., bank vault where it would remain until Billing's actual death at some future date. Then when necessary, it would be placed among the appropriate Congressional documents, a brief and scandalous footnote in the history of the United States.

A military honor guard traveled with the bodies of the President and First Lady in their secured coffins to Washington, while Stevens' body continued on to his home state of Texas for a private service there, and the nation gathered to mourn its unprecedented loss.

As soon as the caskets were placed on display in the capitol Rotunda, the grieving American public began filing passed the double coffins, a first in American history, the President and the First Lady. People lined the streets for hours; lines wrapped around the city blocks. Thousands of mourners paid their last respects to a man who not all had agreed with, but who had been taken before his time in an unheralded and brazen act of injustice. News reports and written accounts described the story of his life and his meteoric rise in politics to the Presidency. Political analysts worked around the clock to predict Billings' loss to America.

When Billings later heard the reports, he was gratified to hear his life praised, but he wanted to shout as Mark Twain once said, "The reports of my death are greatly exaggerated," but he was forced to remain silent. Robert Billings no longer existed. His life as he had known it was over; his future looked decidedly bleak.

The secluded estate in the upper regions of Pennsylvania had been the best choice for the next stage of Richards' plan. Confiscated from a drug baron as part of the DEA's operation, it had everything they needed, most importantly, complete privacy. For the next several weeks, it would become their home, and it was equipped with its own private airstrip which made travel back and forth between locations possible for Richards and Ms. Martin.

They had gathered in the luxurious living space on the lower floor of the house. Secret Service men were stationed at a distance from the group. Well out of hearing, Caroline noted. Moments later she was glad. As Richards began what he called catching her up to speed, she had been stunned, but it had only gotten worse.

When he revealed his plans for Caroline, she had almost fainted, and she was not the fainting kind. Her mind had been swamped with so many contradicting thoughts that she actually felt giddy. She didn't know what to say because she didn't really know how much Richards knew. She realized immediately that he had many of the facts, but he was also missing several key elements. She didn't want to inadvertently supply him with additional information.

She didn't know who to look at Paul, Robert, or Richards. Each man was playing a different role in her life and none of it made sense. She tried to sort through the information and put it in some type of order as Richards explain why they were in isolation from the rest of the world. He kept things basic; questions could be asked later, if she wanted more details.

Richards began by informing her that Paul was tied to a drug cartel in Bolivia and had been responsible for giving the DEA the leverage it needed to bring down the President. Robert had allowed the cartel to infiltrate the United States through its land holdings in Arkansas.

They had financed much of his campaigns over the years, and he had withdrawn support for the DEA's investigation into the cocaine cartels based on his connection to them.

Richards didn't explain how the cartel had forced the President's support; he felt she could be spared that. Richards had forced Robert to resign his Presidency or face criminal prosecution. Once that decision had been made, it became apparent that if the cartels realized that Robert or Paul had turned against them, they would most likely retaliate. Their lives and the lives of those they loved would be at constant risk. To remove that fear, they had decided to fake their deaths, which would allow them to start new lives with new identities. The problem was they would be recognized because they had been such prominent public figures.

When Caroline heard the next part of their plan, she felt physically ill. She wasn't sure that she could do it, but she didn't have a choice. She had Robbie to think about. She looked at Paul. Was this really the way their lives were going to end? But it had already been decided, and she hadn't been asked. Paul would have considered every avenue before choosing something this radical.

There must be something more than she knew, more than Richards knew. She realized that Richards definitely hadn't made their personal connection to the cartel. She was confused by his lack of information, but he had enough to make their lives impossible. That was really all that mattered.

Paul was the big question. She understood him better than anyone, but this had her completely puzzled. Still, she would trust him. She smiled rather sadly when she looked at him, trying to let him know she would do whatever he asked because she knew he would do whatever was necessary to protect her and their son.

Robert listened to Richards recounting of the events for Caroline and still couldn't believe he was talking about him, about his life. None of this seemed real. He was dead, yet he wasn't. How did he rationalize that? His mind couldn't fathom the events that had taken place in the last four days. Four days—had it only been four days? His life and everything in it was gone, and it only took four days to end it all.

He had seen some of the news broadcasts, but he couldn't actually watch them. The man they were talking about didn't exist anymore. He had to start planning his future, a future without politics, without notoriety, a quiet existence where no one would ever know him. He sat with his head in his hands. He didn't care what anyone thought. He didn't need to impress anyone ever again. He had made his choice; now he had to live with it.

Richards had outlined a possible scenario for him to follow. It was decent. He would have an adequate life, but he would never again be allowed to rise to the heights of power he had once enjoyed. He had to accept his future if he was ever going to survive; he knew it was going to take time, but he didn't have much of that. Within a few weeks, he would begin again.

Paul was worried. He tried not to show it. There were so many considerations to take into account. Any one thing could cause the whole scheme to fall apart. He hated to put Caroline through the next weeks, but he could see no other solution that would allow all of them to have a peaceful future. All he could do now was pray that she wouldn't accidently reveal something else to Richards. They had taken her completely by surprise.

There had been so much to do beforehand, and he couldn't risk her revealing anything. Now there was no time, no privacy, nothing that he could do to warn her, to explain. She had to trust him; only this was blind trust. He just hoped she could read the love he felt for her in his eyes. It was the only way he could communicate. He smiled slightly; she had regrouped nicely. He could see his spitfire rising to the challenge as Richards began talking again. She definitely had her father's tenacity and determination. She would need both in the weeks to come.

When Richards mentioned Contreras, Caroline's eyes instantly flew to Paul. How much did Richards know? As he continued to outline his plan, Caroline turned back to face him. She couldn't decide if she was hearing him correctly. They were going to lure Raul to the States with her son. Were they crazy? No one was going to use her son for bait! She was all primed to interrupt him when she felt Paul's eyes on her. She glanced briefly in his direction. He shook his head slightly. She almost collapsed with relief. She sat back in her chair.

She interrupted Richards. "Stop, I have to have something to drink. I can't take in any more of this right now. Give me a few minutes." She was about to scream; she was totally confused and so lost in whatever was transpiring, she couldn't stand to hear another thing.

Richards walked to the opposite side of the room and found a soft drink in a concealed refrigerator under the bar; he handed it to her. She placed the cold bottle to her face. How could she possible know how to react, what to say, when she had no real idea of who was leading this crazy parade and who was following? "Just give me a minute. You have all obviously had days to take this in, just give me a minute."

No one spoke. Caroline didn't look at anyone. She sat with her eyes closed and tried to breath. It was like swimming in a fog. She didn't have any idea where the shore was. She felt completely lost. Then she took a deep breath. She had never let anything defeat her before, and she wasn't about to let a little confusion do it now. She would piece this all together later. Right now, she needed to know exactly what Richards knew or thought he knew.

She took a deep breath, held it for a second, exhaled, and looked first at Robert, then Paul, and finally Richards. "Okay, let's hear the rest." Richards gave her a second more. She took a sip of her drink hoping to be able to swallow whatever was about to be forced on her and prepared to be shocked some more. She wasn't disappointed.

Richards glanced at Paul. "Look, I might as well put all my cards on the table. We know that Robbie is Stevens' son. That information is only relevant in so far as it impacts the future arrangements we have had to make. However, since your husband already knew and has agreed, we have had matters simplified." He nodded toward where Robert sat. "Billings has already signed the divorce decree. All that remains is for you to sign the papers, and your marriage will be officially dissolved."

Caroline turned to Robert. "Is this true? What about custody of Robbie? Will there ever be any future problems?" She sat waiting for Robert to speak. He looked at her sadly and shook his head.

"No, it's all taken care of. You will both be better off, and you won't have me dragging you down. I never was the man for you." And you weren't the woman for me, he finished silently.

Caroline didn't know how to respond to that. He was right. They were never right for each other. They both liked power too much. She almost laughed. She tried to manipulate things with Paul, but he just quietly took over and never gave her the opportunity to refuse or argue. She would bet his fine hand had been pushing all the pieces into place in this little game too. Richards would never know how little he had influenced whatever was about to happen.

Paul was brilliant at letting others feel as though they were making the decisions, when all along he was. He was so self-assured that he didn't need anyone to know how he worked behind the scenes. She loved that about him, his quiet assurance, his confidence, his willingness to let others shine in the spotlight, his ability to move mountains. She smiled at him. This was some mountain he had moved. She was impressed.

She glanced at Richards. "Let's get that out of the way. Where are the papers? I might as well sign them now." He motioned to the table between them. She reached out and took them out of a folder. She held her past and her future in her hands. How insignificant it all felt. She only gave a cursory glance at the documents. She knew what they would say and all she cared about was Robbie. She finished the last one and handed the file to Richards.

"These will be discreetly filed and secured to insure your safety. You need never worry about any future legal decisions you might make. This is official and irrevocable." He sat the papers beside him. Those along with a few other documents would be safeguarded by the Secret Service.

"We have a team waiting, specialist chosen because they can be trusted. These teams have reshaped the future of some very important people. But for their safety as well as yours, each team will only do one procedure. No one will ever see the finished products. As each takes place, the remaining areas will be completely covered. This is simply added insurance that once you leave this estate and go your separate ways, no one will be able to supple information even if forced to do so." He hated to emphasis the necessity for this, but it was crucial that she understand the gravity of their situation.

Caroline could see that he was truly concerned with her wellbeing. She was touched, but she wasn't worried. Paul would take care of them. He was right; they could never return as the people they had once been. That life had ended.

Richards looked directly at her; there was no way to soften the blow. "One of the problems with this type of enterprise is that loved ones are victims of our choices. Your parents believe that you perished in that crash. There is no way that we can apprise them of anything different. To do so would compromise the entire plan." He hated this. She looked at him, obviously in shock. She hadn't thought of them yet.

"Oh, my lord, they will be devastated." She wanted to cry from the injustice of it all but knew she couldn't. They would survive, and maybe someday she could explain, maybe. Her life seemed to be based on that one word. Nothing was ever certain.

"What about Robbie?" How were they ever going to work out all the problems?

Richards was not as certain about this aspect of the plan, but Stevens had been adamant. He knew that the only way she would go along with this plan was if she had Robbie with her as much as possible.

"We felt that for the time being, he would be better suited to staying with Ms. Martin. She has received custodial care of him while she and Robbie reside with your parents. Official custody at the moment is with your parents as prescribed in the directive of your will." He stopped and let her assimilate this last bit of information. He didn't really think that she had come to terms with her supposed death and all of its implications.

She looked up. "Then what, how do I get my son back?" She looked directly at Paul. He better have this worked out.

"This is where we have to tread lightly. Your parents believe that your death was caused by a terrorist faction, not all of whom have been captured. We will assure them that for the time being it is necessary that we remove Robbie from their care, along with Ms. Martin, so they can be protected until we are certain that he will come to no harm as the son of the ex-President.

"We have assured them that Robbie will be safer for the time being if placed in protective custody. We have guaranteed he will receive the best of care and will have Ms. Martin with him continually. Your mother was extremely upset by the news but your father convinced her that it was in Robbie's best interest to allow us to follow through with this plan." He hated this part of his job, but in this case they were definitely limited in plausible excuses.

"Do you think they really bought that?" Caroline was skeptical. He could hear it in her voice.

He understood her feelings, but she hadn't seen the news reports or the videos of the crash site or the thousands of people who even now, as they were planning new lives, were mourning their loss and the tragic circumstances of their deaths.

"Yes, after they flew to Washington and met with the Secret Service, they understood the situation better. They weren't happy about it, but they understood. They were allowed to spend a few hours with Robbie before he and Ms. Martin were escorted to a secure location in preparation for traveling here."

"What about Marty, what will she be allowed to know?" Caroline could think of more questions than answers, and her head was beginning to pound from all the stress this had caused. Paul quietly moved to the bar and returned with a glass and held out his hand to her. She looked at him blankly for a second and frowned, not understanding. He took her hand and placed two aspirin in it and handed her the glass of water.

"You're rubbing your forehead. It's enough to give anyone a headache. I think we have all had one since Monday." He glanced briefly at the two men. Robert was self-involved as always. He wasn't paying the least bit of attention to anyone but himself. Paul was letting Richards do all the talking. That way he wouldn't let anything slip. He tried to make light of the situation for Caroline's sake, but it was a forced effort; still, she seemed to appreciate his attempt.

She smiled briefly. "Thanks. I didn't realize that I was, but what about Marty?" She had turned back to face Richards.

"Stevens swears that she wouldn't want to leave Robbie and would gladly accompany you to your final destination, and he also beliefs that she can be trusted implicitly. This will have to be your decision. After all it's your life that will be in danger if she ever talks to anyone." Richards wasn't nearly as confident about the baby's nurse as Stevens. He could foresee a thousand scenarios and none of them good.

Caroline really had a headache now. She loved Marty and trusted her completely, but why did Paul think that she would want to give up her life and follow them wherever they went? Why would she want to accept such a heavy burden of responsibility just for them?

"What are my other choices?" Caroline spoke directly to Richards; he looked a little pale. He didn't really want to tell her.

"There aren't any that you would like. The only other options are that we fake Robbie's death somehow, or you could leave him in the care of your parents and go on with your life again without him."

Caroline shot to her feet before he even finished his sentence. "If you think that I will leave my son behind then you don't know me. I don't care if this whole plan blows up in your face. I don't care if Robert is found out and spends the rest of his days in prison, but you will not give my son away." She was fighting mad now. She stared directly at Richards, her hands clenched into tight fists by her sides.

Richards felt that she was about to take a swing at him. She was something when she was mad. She didn't even look like the same woman. He could actually feel heat radiating from her body. She seemed ready to burst into flames any second. He wouldn't want to make her too angry because she looked like she could burn him to a crisp for even suggesting such a thing. Stevens had been right. He certainly knew how to read this woman.

Paul smiled. He tried to warn him that he would never convince her to leave Robbie.

Caroline sat down suddenly. She was really getting sick. The room seemed to be spinning in crazy circles. She tried to focus on Paul's face, but it was weaving in and out.

Caroline turned deathly pale. Paul was at her side instantly. He was afraid this was too much to deal with at one time. They had had days to think about all the problems; she was getting hit over the head with them, and none of them had been of her making. She had a right to feel sick. This whole plan was a logistics nightmare. She must have just realized that if she took Robbie, her parents would lose them both. He knew he was right when he saw her lower lip quiver slightly. She wouldn't cry; she was too tough for that, at least not in front of them.

Paul took her hand in his; it was ice cold. She leaned her head back against the couch and closed her eyes. She wished that when she opened them, her world would be normal again. She knew it wouldn't; it never would be again.

"Marty comes with us." Her voice was flat, almost defeated. He couldn't blame her for feeling that way. Both his parents and Robert's had passed away. They didn't have the concerns of family to worry about. Caroline did. He knew she was considering how all of this was going to affect her mother's heart condition. He had thought of that, and as soon as he could, he was going to make sure that she was all right.

"Try not to think about this too much. We have it all worked out, and Richards will make sure that your mother isn't unduly upset." This was a crock, and they all knew it. Her mother would suffer more than any of them could possible understand. Caroline was her daughter, her child, even if she was adopted, and she believed that she was dead. Nothing could be worse unless it was taking her grandson, too.

When Richards started to speak again, Paul shook his head and nodded for them to leave the room. This was enough for now. Robert frowned as he looked at them. Paul just stared him down until he turned and left behind Richards. He probably wasn't too pleased that Caroline was willing to toss him to the wolves. Robert seemed to think that she owed him her loyalty. He had never understood that trust was something you earned. It didn't come with the wedding license. It came from being trustworthy, and Robert wasn't now and never had been.

Once the men had left the room, Paul put his arm around her and pulled her to him. She leaned her head on his shoulder. He whispered to her. "I have it all figured out. Try not to worry. Let Richards run the show for now. It will all be taken care of, I promise."

Caroline slipped her arms around his waist and hugged him. If he promised then she was certain that everything would be all right. She couldn't see how, but he obviously did. She would take his word.

"I'm hurting so many people. I feel so utterly selfish. How will we ever be able to take Robbie and not cause my parents irreparable hurt?" She looked up at him; his eyes were on her face. He was smiling slightly, his eyes shining with love. This was the closest they had been in weeks, and all he wanted was to hold her in his arms for the rest of their lives. He pulled her back to him and held her for a few minutes. Neither of them spoke. She needed this more than words, more than answers to unanswerable questions. He understood.

After several quiet minutes, her color improved, and he felt she might be better prepared for the next few weeks if he could reassure her as much as he could. That was the problem. There was very little that he could say for fact; everything was contingent on something before it happening as they planned. The crazy little homely about the best laid plans of mice and men kept running through his mind.

Of course, Robert had withdrawn from all involvement. He simply functioned as told and spoke very little to anyone. Paul would have been concerned if he had the time, but that was fast becoming a commodity in short supply. The medical teams were scheduled to arrive tonight, and they would begin tomorrow morning.

That was another reason he needed Caroline fighting fine; he wanted her recovery to be speedy and as painless as possible. She needed to regain her old spirit. He had seen glimpses of it today, but they had thrown her one curve too many.

Before he had time to consider all the issues at hand, he turned her face up to his and kissed her with the depth of feeling that only a person who has found their other half can. He poured his love and his longing into the kiss. He molded her body to his and held her with such tenderness that she felt her very soul tremble.

She wrapped her arms around him and shaped his head with her hands holding him fast to her. She wanted the moment to last forever, to block the confusion and sorrow that she knew the next weeks would hold. She returned the kiss with the passion of a hundred lonely nights and the promise of a lifetime to come.

When their lips parted at last, Paul rested his forehead against hers and just held her. He could feel her breath on his lips, his heart pounding in his ears. She would forever be his and his alone. She would never be a bargaining chip in anybody's plans again. She inspired him to want to go out and slay dragons. He smiled. The problems ahead were more on the scale of Medusa, so many heads that he might be fighting them for the rest of their lives. She and Robbie would be worth the fight.

He leaned back and drew her against him. With one hand he slowly drew his fingers through her hair. He loved its silky feel and the soft fragrance that always reminded him of spring. "Before they return, all you need to do is follow Richards' plans. If I don't agree with anything, he won't be allowed to do it, so don't worry about any of this. I **will** take care of everything. I can't tell you any more than that. You must trust me." She turned in his arms and placed a soft kiss on his cheek.

"Don't I always?" She held him tightly. She knew that their brief time together was almost over, and they wouldn't have any more for several weeks. They would be isolated from one another in separate wings of the house and remain there until their plans were finalized. Their separation was necessary for their protection, Richards had said, and so the medical teams would not be aware of anyone else's presence and somehow piece together their identities. He had assured her that the chance of that happening was remote, but he didn't like to tempt fate.

She sat up suddenly and turned to face Paul. "What if you don't like it?"

He laughed. It certainly had taken her a long time to think about that aspect of this little project. He grinned at her, the silly little lopsided one she loved so much. "Don't worry. I've already taken care of that. I chose everything myself. I think you will be pleased." He really grinned then. "I know I will." He kissed her soundly before she could speak then stood and drew her to her feet. Holding her hand tightly in his, he walked purposefully toward the stairway. "Come on Sleeping Beauty. When this is all over, I promise to wake you with a kiss, and everything will be fine."

She jerked him to a stop and stared into his dark eyes, so much like her son's. "You promise?"

He squeezed her hand then brought it to his lips and kissed it tenderly; the laughter was gone from his eyes and all that remained was the love he felt. "I promise," he whispered softly.

Chapter 23

Ms. MARTIN ARRIVED EARLY the next morning with a wiggly little boy in tow. When Robbie saw his mother, he squealed with glee and toddled to her as fast as his chubby, little legs could go. They spent the morning playing and laughing. Caroline held him all through his nap. She was dreading the next step, but she had been assured that between the minor procedures they had planned for her, she would be allowed time with her son. Only that and her fear for their future happiness gave her the strength to carry on.

Actually it wasn't as bad as she had anticipated, but she was always a wimp when it came to pain. Everyday Marty brought her books and flowers and silly little surprises from Paul. She didn't know where he was getting all of them, but she loved the reminder that he cared and was thinking of her. It kept her from feeling so alone, but it also made her feel sad. Robert had never done anything to surprise her. He had given her the requisite birthday and anniversary gifts, but never anything just because he wanted to please her. Paul understood her. It wasn't about money; it was about caring, sharing, loving. That had been Robert's problem; he couldn't get passed himself. There wasn't room in his life for anyone else.

She wouldn't have made it without Marty. She kept her in touch with her son and her sanity. She wasn't used to sitting around doing nothing. She liked action, but she was learning to adjust. She hadn't read so many books since her college days, and she found that she rather liked the experience. Marty kept her well supplied from the extensive library downstairs, and she spent much of her free time discussing them with

Caroline. Though Caroline never asked her particular political leanings, she easily surmised that Marty hadn't been especially impressed by Robert, but then the more people really got to know him, the less they usually liked him. He could be overbearing, superficial, and self-involved. Caroline had to admit, however, that could be said of most powerful men and women, especially in politics. She preferred the quiet men who worked behind the scenes, who really made the decisions. She smiled as she thought of Paul.

Caroline hadn't asked Marty why she had chosen to give up her life for them; she didn't ask anything of anyone, but she had expressed her gratitude to her on several occasions. The only other people she saw were medical staff and Richards. She would wait for answers when Paul could tell her what his plans were. She had learned early in her life, not to ask questions. The answers weren't always easy to accept. Sometimes ignorance really was bliss. She had learned that firsthand from Rafael. Once had been enough.

Caroline had too much time to think. She couldn't shake the feeling that she had to make some effort to contact her parents somehow. It became such a burden that she began losing sleep and not eating. The thought of how they might be suffering was unbearable, and she had added to their suffering by taking Robbie from them. She felt ungrateful and selfish and became so distraught that Marty finally told Paul.

Ms. Martin was the liaison between them, but she only spoke to Paul under the strictest circumstances. She was extremely cautious about anything she said, and their conversations were always rather ambiguous. Paul recognized the problem at once. He sent a verbal reply to Caroline stating that he promised they were safe and happy. Marty wasn't exactly sure how he would know that or how they could possibly be happy under the circumstances, but she relayed the message anyway.

Caroline seemed a little confused by it at first; then she smiled and that was the end of her concerns. Ms. Martin assumed that it was a private understanding they had and didn't pry. She was glad that Caroline was eating and resting again. She would need all her strength to handle Robbie in a few days. He was ready to see his mommy and was an exuberant little bundle of energy.

She smiled as she watched him play. She loved him so much; she was glad that she had chosen to work for them. She had been hesitant at first and uncertain about how she would manage the daily interaction with them all, but it had been the best decision of her life. She would always be grateful for the circumstances that had forced her to take the position. She hadn't realized just how much her past had kept her from living until she witnessed the love that Paul and Caroline shared with Robbie. She was so thankful to be able to be a part of all their lives.

She laughed as Robbie demolished his block tower again just to stack them over. He was so easily amused; he would play happily for hours until he became hungry or tired. Then like all little boys, he wanted immediate attention. She was more than happy to see to his every need. He returned her care and affection with the uncomplicated love and trust that only a child can give. She felt truly blessed. Giving up her life was no sacrifice for her. They were her life now.

Caroline wondered about Paul. Would she know him? Would their lives be the same? Then she would laugh at herself. She would always love him. None of the other things mattered, only Robbie and Paul. She had had it all before. Anything that money, power, and prestige could buy had been hers. She had always known that those weren't the things that really mattered. She had been blessed; she had found true happiness, true love. She didn't need anything more.

Caroline picked up another book and laughed. When this was all over she was certainly going to be well read. Ms. Martin heard her as she came in and smiled. Laughter was always the best medicine.

Richards had trouble understanding what Billings' wife had ever seen in him. He was the most insufferable man he had ever dealt with and that was saying something. He couldn't remember anyone other than Strong maybe who had such a colossal ego, but he would admit that Billings was in an unenviable position. Then he would remind himself that this entire situation had been of Billings' own making.

The medical staffs were working efficiently to carry out their plans as quickly as possible. Stevens and Ms. Billings' had been relatively minor compared to Billings. He, of course, would require more radical changes in order to protect his safety. Richards was beginning to feel that Billings might be worried about making it on his own. Apparently, Stevens had been working for him since college and Billings had become dependent on him. That might be more difficult for him than many of the other aspects, but Billings was a brilliant man. He would survive; Richards was certain of that fact. His kind always did.

Richards' felt confident that they were going to be successful in luring Contreras to the States. Things were progressing nicely. Through his sources, Richards had learned that Contreras planned to visit the States within the next week, reportedly to finalize some rather important business negotiations. Richards knew Contreras had multiple legitimate enterprises in the States but rarely traveled to the country himself. Richards also learned that Contreras' health was failing although that had not been officially confirmed. When he mentioned the fact to Stevens, he had only shrugged. Richards couldn't shake the feeling that he was missing a big piece of the puzzle, but he didn't know how to find out what it was.

His men had been unable to connect the adoption agency to anything in Stevens or Ms. Billings' pasts, so he had written it off as coincidence. Still, he didn't believe in coincidences, but the agency had been closed for so many years that there was no way to track personal information other than through court documents. They had followed that lead until there was no where left. He couldn't really drag grieving parents in to ask about their daughter's adoption or why they had chosen that particular agency. As luck would have it, both of Stevens' parents, having been much older when they adopted him, had passed away some years before.

Amanda hadn't had any better luck in tracing a connection. Like him, she felt that there must be something, but she couldn't discover what it was. She was confused about why Tim wanted to pursue such an investigation after the concerned parties were all deceased, but she didn't ask. She knew he was still frustrated that he hadn't been able to bring Billings to account for Judy's death and Billings' part in it. Tim really wanted to believe that Stevens had had something to do with it, but there was no proof of that. He had owned the house, but even according to Ms. Maude's notes, he hadn't taken part in the events that had transpired there. Amanda had always liked Stevens; she really hoped her loyalty to him hadn't been misplaced.

Richards had received the final reports from the medical staffs. Their jobs were complete and their patients pronounced ready to assume their new lives. According to Stevens, he, Caroline, Robbie, and Ms. Martin would be traveling to Canada, where he planned to obtain his license and open a law practice in a small town well away from the cities. They planned to recoup in a semi-isolated locale for the next several months as he prepared for the bar exam.

Billings had been given his choice of identity and locations. He had chosen Chicago where he would open a private law practice suited to his expertise. He liked the Windy City and felt he would be able to adjust nicely there. It was cosmopolitan enough to offer a variety of interests and, provided he stayed away from politics or public office of any type, he was a free man as far as Richards and the DEA were concerned, but free was a relative term.

They all planned to leave the following day at separate times. It was crucial that none of them see the others to maintain the safety of each. No one objected. Robert had nothing to say to either of them, and Caroline had already said all she wanted to. Paul was certain that if he ever needed to contact Robert, he would have little trouble, so he didn't voice any objection.

Caroline, Ms. Martin, and Robbie would travel to Quebec where they would stay in a luxury suite downtown for several days while Paul contacted realtors and arranged for suitable housing. He would be staying at a different location, and they would meet once he had made arrangements for them. Caroline was anxious. Paul was relieved. So far things had gone relatively smoothly.

Richards had released them, wishing them well more for Caroline's sake, and advising them to remain out of the country for some time. Paul knew that Richards really wanted to bring some type of retribution down on him, but he simply couldn't find enough to do so. His connection to Raul had been more of a legal nuisance than a real problem for Paul, but he let Richards believe otherwise because it suited his plans. Alberto had left the country as soon as he talked to Paul. Without Alberto they really had no case; Paul could always plead innocent of the charges or of the information contained in them. He could always say that he was only following the advice of an anonymous source that had encouraged him to request a copy of the damaging files, allowing him to advise the President in order to stave off a political scandal which could possibly threaten the safety and good standing of the United States.

Paul was a good lawyer. He could take the most damaging information and twist it to suit his needs. Richards knew there was more to the events than he could uncover, but he had to be satisfied with bringing down the President and in some minor way making him pay for his sister's death. Paul understood his motivation. He had had

Richards investigated as soon as he became a player in the game. Paul knew a lot more about Richards that Richards would ever know about him.

They arrived by different flights to the city of Quebec. Caroline, Ms. Martin, and Robbie were taken to their hotel and dropped off. They were no longer the concern of the DEA. Richards had made all of the arrangements, and his responsibility ended at the border. Even though he had to admire Caroline's fortitude, he knew that her future was still very uncertain. Stevens seemed more than capable of handling anything that might happen, so he didn't feel as badly about leaving Caroline. She had more than adequate resources, and she knew that if she should ever need his help, she could contact him. With that, he had watched her board the plane and set off to start a completely new life.

Ms. Martin retained her identity and accepted the position as nurse to her new charge, Bobby. It was agreed that the minor change would be easier for all concerned, especially Robbie. Caroline knew that they would all need time to make the necessary adjustments, but she had a lifetime for that now.

She wasn't quite sure how she felt about her looks. They hadn't made drastic changes, but more subtle differences. Her appearance had changed enough, however, to cause Robbie to look at her strangely for a minute when he first saw her, but as soon as she spoke, he came running to her, laughing happily. She was so relieved that she actually cried, which, of course, caused him to cry. Then she couldn't help but laugh, and everything was fine.

Caroline wondered what changes Paul had agreed to as she dressed to meet him that evening in the hotel restaurant. He had never been overly concerned with his looks or what others thought of him. She had thought him quite handsome that first summer and completely hers. She soon learned just how little she knew. That seemed so long ago, so much had happened in their lives since then.

She smiled when she remembered their first headlong flight through the jungle in his old, beat up, dust-covered jeep. He had scared her almost to death, but she would rather die than ever let him know. She had felt honored when they arrived at the final destination. She knew instinctively that this was his secret oasis, somewhere he came to get away from the expectations and the restrictions of his life. She recognized his need because she felt the same at times. The world lay at her feet, but it was a world of someone else's making, not hers.

With a nod to Marty, Caroline slipped quietly from the suite and walked to the elevator. Within seconds she was watching the doors glide open. The hotel's luxurious foyer lay before her, but she wasn't concerned with anything except meeting Paul. She walked confidently across the open expanse, smiling politely to those she encountered. Only after she had walked passed a man standing at one side of the restaurant entrance did she stop and turn. Her heart beat faster; her face flushed; her eyes filled with tears.

He was her Paul as handsome as always with his dark hair and laughing brown eyes, but his dimples were more pronounced, and the bump on his nose was gone. She hadn't minded the bump; a reminder to duck faster, he once told her, laughing. In fact she thought it added character to his classical good looks. Now his face was more defined, more mature, but more importantly her Paul's.

She didn't need food. She had everything standing across from her and laughing at her as always. She had walked two whole steps passed him before she recognized him. She would never live it down, but then he had an advantage. He knew what she would look like. He walked to her, took her hand in his, and led her to a private alcove where their table was secluded from the view of others. An elaborate arrangement of lavender and violet orchids, her favorite flower, graced the table. A bottle of champagne rested in a container of ice. The soft glow of candles illuminated the area. Caroline was afraid to speak; she didn't want to break the spell. She felt like a pampered princess waiting to be kissed.

Just as that thought crossed her mind, Paul pulled her into his arms and kissed her with all the passion that he had longed to share with her for weeks. She melted into his embrace and pulled him closer. Caroline hadn't even considered where they were. She was overwhelmed with emotions that only weeks of anxiety can produce, but Paul had insured their privacy. The waiters had been instructed not to disturb them until he signaled. Paul had plans for this evening, and the kiss was only the first step.

"Wake up, Princess." He smiled slowly, his eyes shining with love. "You didn't think I would forget, did you?" She smiled in return then laughed when she remembered.

"No, not a promise," she replied softly. She wanted to hold on to him forever, but he turned her around and pulled out the chair for her. She didn't want food, but she knew he had gone to a lot of trouble to make this evening special. She loved him for the thought—but.

"Do you have any idea how beautiful you are?" His voice carried such sincerity she was caught off guard. He could tell she didn't really know how to respond. But she never failed him.

"No, but you can spend forever telling me, if you like." She was trying very hard not to cry, but she was so relieved that they could finally be together that seeing him at last was overwhelming. She couldn't seem to cope. She had never dreamed that there would ever be a time when they could be themselves, not part of some grand scheme, or some plot or other, just themselves, free to love and laugh and be together, free to start their lives fresh, a new beginning.

She stared at him, her eyes glowing with love. So like her Paul, still handsome, still debonair, yet different, but his looks didn't matter. It was the man within she loved. He reached across the table and took her hand in his. He warmed her cold fingers and lifted them to his lips. He never took his eyes from her face. He smiled as he lowered her hand.

"Caroline, will you marry me, for better, for worse, for richer, for poorer, 'til death do us part?' He spoke so softly Caroline wasn't sure that she had heard him correctly. She hadn't expected anything like this, maybe at some later date, but not now.

When she sat there speechless, he tried another tactic. "Okay, I know that we have never talked about anything like this, but you know my family and I know yours. You know my faults and—," he stopped. She had raised one finely arched brow as he began to finish the comparison. "And you don't have any." She smiled broadly. He was learning already. She was beginning to enjoy this.

Paul smiled to himself. She was looking much better. No longer the pale, nervous woman who had stepped off the elevator, but his Caroline, a little opinionated, obstinate, and head strong, still he would never tell her that. He wouldn't want her to change. He loved her just the way she was—his!

"I think you know that I can provide for you and Robbie, uh, Bobby, and I hope that you know I love you more than the very air I breathe." He coughed twice for emphasis. "My life is meaningless without you in it. I was always searching for something, but I didn't know what it was until you sashayed down the stairs that day. My life has never been the same since." He shook his head in regret and sighed eloquently, his laughter barely held in check.

She almost expected him to break into song at any moment. She hid her smile.

"Is that a good thing or not?" She seemed a little perplexed. Her brow was rising higher with each testimony of his love. He was being so silly she couldn't take him seriously.

He laughed, trust her to be nitpicky. "Which part? You know you're ruining a well rehearsed speech. I spent countless *seconds* preparing this. How can you be so heartless?"

"Obviously and easily, in that order," she countered. There went that brow again. Did she practice that or was it natural? He'd better not ask right now, later maybe. He was happier than he had ever been in his life. He felt free for the first time.

"When do we get to the good part?" She questioned.

"What part is that?" Now he seemed a little confused. He knew what he would consider the good part, but he wasn't as certain about her. She erased any doubts.

"The part where I get to rip your clothes from your body and make wild, passionate love with you until you can't stand it anymore, part." She was smiling so sweetly, so innocently, that it was difficult to believe she was saying what he was hearing.

"Oh, that part." He tried to act nonchalant, but he was beginning to sweat. This verbal repartee could easily backfire on him if he wasn't careful. He was having trouble not visualizing what she had described. They needed to turn up the air-conditioning; the room was becoming decidedly warmer. He had better reign in this conversation and his thoughts if he expected to make it through dinner.

He cleared his throat. Caroline smiled sweetly. "Back to my original question, is that a yes or a no? Just to clarify. I mean if you need time to think about it, or if you would like to enjoy your freedom now that you finally have it, I can understand." He hesitated. "I won't like it, but I'll try to understand." He stopped then looked directly at Caroline. His eyes weren't laughing any longer. "No, I won't! I won't like it, and I can't possibly understand why you would not want to marry me. I'm not that bad looking and I have money, not that you need any. Besides, I love you, and I want to spend the rest of my life showing you just how much. I want us to be a family—you, me, and Robbie." He was practically glaring at her when he finished.

Caroline started to laugh then she realized that he was serious. He had talked himself into a good case of righteous indignation and had not even given her a chance to respond.

Men! She let him stew for a minute. "Yes. Now can we eat? I feel the need for a substantial meal." She smiled that little butter-wouldn't-melt-in-her-mouth smile. "I have an exercise program planned for later this evening. You are welcome to join me, if you like."

She was definitely laughing now.

"Really? It might be interesting to see how you pull that off by yourself." He was laughing too.

"Oh, there will definitely be "pulling things off" one way or another." She was so happy she fairly glowed. Paul couldn't have been more pleased. He slid his hand across the table and took hers. With the other he slipped an emerald-cut, diamond engagement ring out of his pocket and onto her finger.

The tears did fall then, but neither one of them cared. They were tears of joy, a celebration of their love. He pulled her to her feet and held her close as they moved in harmony to the soft strains of a violin. Their world was perfect for the moment, and moments are sometimes all anyone has.

Chapter 24

RICHARDS LEFT HIS OFFICE that evening and went home to his wife. He and Amanda had married quietly after Billings' death. President Chambers had asked her to stay on as his press secretary and she had. Her job was still demanding, but the entire White House, once it had overcome the shock of Billings' death, had become a much easier and peaceful place to work.

Amanda was amazed at the difference in personality between the two men. She hadn't really liked Billings nor approved of his choices, but she had never known what each day would bring. Working with him had been a real challenge. Chambers was more reserved and soft-spoken, but he was still a man who could get the job done.

It was a refreshing change, especially for a woman trying desperately to keep a secret from her husband. She only hoped that when she told him tonight, he would be pleased. She had a special dinner prepared. She had taken off work early and had everything ready when he walked through the door.

Tim knew that something was up as soon as he saw her face. She wasn't very good at keeping secrets, but he wouldn't spoil whatever it was by trying to guess. For a woman who could command the respect of millions of television viewers, he was always amazed that she would love someone like him. He felt truly blessed that she was part of his life. He wished that Judy could have known her. He knew they would have been great friends. He had to let the pain of her death go. He couldn't do anything more. It was time to start fresh. It was time to focus on his life with Amanda.

Amanda was wondering if he was color blind by the time they had finished dinner. She couldn't have been more obvious if she had tried. Everything on the table was either pink or blue. She had bought special dinnerware, glasses, even dessert with those two colors. Tim had sat there quietly eating his dinner, looking a little lost. She had heard the news reports; she knew what it would mean to him, but surely he could see what she was trying in a very non-discreet way to tell him.

When she placed an elaborately decorated pink and blue cake in front of him, he looked up and smiled. "Are you trying to tell me something?" He didn't need cake. He had something much sweeter. He held out his arms, and she rushed into them. She was laughing and crying, happy and scared, all at the same time. He had understood her less-than-subtle message almost at once, but he played along. He had been so pleased that he had hardly been able to force down his food. They were going to have a baby—a baby! He could hardly wait to tell the world. In the grander scheme of things, it might not be earth-shattering news, but to him, it was truly amazing.

Paul completely surprised Caroline. He gave her the choice of remaining in Canada or beginning their life together in a completely different location—Australia. She opted for the new environment. She wanted as far away from her old life with Robert as possible. Although she would have some very fond memories of their brief stay, Canada was too close to the States for her peace of mind. Paul laughed when she told him.

"Good because I've already bought the land and home." He gave her a smug little grin.

"What if I said I wanted to stay?" she countered.

"Then I would say, what has been bought can be sold. Problem solved. I don't care; whatever makes you happy makes me happy." He wrapped his arms around her and kissed her soundly. "Don't you want to know where it is?"

"Not really. This is the only place I care about being." Then she kissed him. "Maybe later, I have some business that needs taking care of right now." She grabbed his hand and began pulling him toward their bedroom.

"It's a good thing we're married. This would be a terrible example to set for our son." He pretended to lag behind until he reached the door, then he swept her into his arms and tossed her on the bed. He was beside her before she could catch her breath. Then he took her breath away with a kiss that would have smoked the devil himself.

Marty only smiled when she heard giggling coming from the master bedroom. Newlyweds! She couldn't have been happier for them. She had finally found peace in her life. Alberto had always known what a terrible ordeal her life had been. Now that was all behind her, and she could look to the future, not worry about the past.

Alberto had never abandoned her, even after she was forced to leave. Years later she realized that she was not meant to survive the trip, but Alberto had broken a cardinal rule and made plans of his own. He had taken her to live with a family in the northwest, as far removed from her previous life as possible. He had told her what she would do and how she would do it. There were no choices, no excuses, and no mistakes. It was his way or no way. She chose his way. She had worked hard to obtain her nurse's degree. As a pediatric nurse, she found immense pleasure in helping children in need. She had never regretted her decision. Her only regret was the loss of her child, but over the years, she had learned to cope.

Now, everything was right in her world. She would bide her time and wait for Alberto to decide if and when the time was right to reveal her past. But she was content if that time never came. She had a full life with the people she loved most in the world. She smiled as she watched Robbie toddling across the room chasing a bright red ball.

She would join the newly-weds once they had everything set up on their new cattle station in the outback. Marty felt they would all be in for a few surprises, but those would only keep life from being predictable. Change was good—well, most of the time. She laughed.

Rafael stood before the bank of flickering computer screens and surveyed the progress his men were making. Remote installations now provided continual surveillance of the perimeter of the compound. His men patrolled the outer reaches and schedules were constantly altered. The rebel-instigated uprising had revealed a need for improved surveillance, a venue prior to this which fell under Raul's domain. Things had changed. Raul was fighting a different war, and it was up to Rafael to hold their empire.

Alberto had returned to Bolivia as soon as he and Paul had spoken. From there he had arranged for Caroline's parents to be notified with an altered version of the facts surrounding their daughter's supposed death and their need to keep those details secret. To safeguard Robbie's and her safety, they must continue with their lives as though she had died. Due to her mother's failing health, Caroline's parents would be able to tell anyone who pried too deeply into their affairs that Robbie was being taken care of by both families, and Robbie's frequent trips to see them with Ms. Martin would allow them to continue this deception.

Once Paul's decision was made, it became apparent that he could no longer maintain ties to the cartel, at least for the present. If as Alberto warned, drastic steps weren't taken immediately, the empire Raul and Rafael had built would be in jeopardy. He had advised Paul to follow Richards' plan and assume a new identity as a safeguard against reprisals in the event that trouble in Bolivia manifested itself on the scale that Alberto felt was inevitable. As Paul had become more and more involved in achieving Raul's dream, he had become further removed from the events in Bolivia. He could hardly believe what Alberto was saying to him.

He was not concerned for himself or Caroline. He had placed most of his personal income and funds from his parents' estates, as well as much of the money Raul provided for his use in numbered accounts in various world banks just as a safeguard against anything happening in the future. That future was now, but he was prepared.

Paul realized now that Raul had deliberately hidden the problems growing within the cartel from him. In the past, Raul had had no difficulty in maintaining rule over his empire. With the help of Rafael, they had held sway over the entire country. Now younger men were pushing at their defenses, testing their strength, trying their endurance, making life difficult. Raul had invested so much time and energy in achieving his heart's desire that he had failed to see the potential problems developing in his own country and the weaknesses seeping into the cartel.

Left to grow unchecked, those problems had gained strength and power and support within the Bolivian government. Where once men feared reprisal from Raul, now with their own advanced global influence, built many times from the very money Raul had supplied, those same radical groups were pressing for their stake in Bolivia's illicit drug trade. One group alone would have posed little problem to Raul or Rafael. Several at once were playing havoc with their resources and manpower. Rafael's men were stretched thin, trying to protect and defend, and recruits from the outside could prove unreliable.

As his illness had progressed, Raul had become obsessed with the future and had ignored one of his own cardinal dictates. He had overlooked the present. The past could not be changed, but to shape the future, the present must be dealt with. With his health affecting every decision, Raul had failed to take into account the changes taking place. He had continued to fund the education of young men seeking a new way of life; now they were using that education against him. He had spent money to provide for his people, but he had failed to give them a say in their happiness. Once he would have lived for the challenge to assert his power, but Raul now moved around in a daze, uncertain of his next move, unsure of his next step, lost in dream of achieving his goal.

For his part, Rafael had failed to see the changes in Raul's health; they were insidious and had crept in slowly and only became apparent to others much too late. Rafael blamed himself for not realizing what was now so obvious. He could do nothing to change what had already happened, the decisions Raul had already made, but even more troubling, he could do nothing to help his friend.

Alberto, who rarely traveled to the compound once Robert became influential, had seen the extreme changes and had tried to warn Rafael, but he had brushed Alberto's concerns aside, believing that Raul was just becoming temperamental in his advancing years blaming Raul's lapses on the debilitating headaches he had begun suffering. Like Paul, Rafael could not fathom a man as intelligent and forceful as Raul allowing a simple failing of his physical body to affect the acuity of his mind. But Rafael had always been more the brawn behind the brains and had misinterpreted those first warning signs.

When Rafael had first learned of the terrorist attack, he had refused to allow anyone to see that the knowledge of Caroline's reported death had affected him greatly. Like Raul, his life had been built around achieving greatness through his daughter. When he thought that dream was taken from him, that she had been taken from him, his life had looked bleak, empty, and meaningless. But there was still hope with the child, with Robbie. He became Rafael's focus.

Rafael had turned his energy to protecting their empire for their grandson. At this critical time, any show of weakness was one he couldn't afford. With their empire under attack on so many fronts, he wondered if it would be possible to hold it together much longer. The unexpected moods and almost violent behavior Raul had begun exhibiting forced Rafael to assume responsibility for both of their jobs. Alberto's return had given him the additional assistance he so badly needed. If anyone could help save the cartel, it would be Alberto. Raul had trained him for just such a role.

Trouble was brewing on several fronts, none more important than with Raul. Once Raul learned that Robbie was Paul's son, he insisted on bringing him to Bolivia to live. Rafael didn't think it was a good idea as things were, but he realized that Raul thought his time was short, and he desired to be with his grandson while he could.

Rafael felt there could be problems with Caroline's parents. Raul assured him that no one would stand in his way in assuming custody of the boy. He had procured enough information over the years relating to Caroline's father to insure his complete cooperation. That was the thing about politicians; they always had a few skeletons rattling around somewhere if a person looked long enough, hard enough, and deep enough in the back of their closets. Raul had had years to search, and his investment had paid off.

Raul also knew that Caroline's mother had a weak heart. He didn't really want to reveal anything to her about her husband's past unless he was forced to do so. He must be getting soft in his old age. He almost laughed. A little added insurance was always a good thing to possess. Once he made his position clear to them, Raul was certain they would see things his way. He was confident that his success was guaranteed.

Together Rafael and Alberto worked out a detailed plan for Raul's travel to the States where he would assume custody of Robbie. Rafael had just finalized the last details, and Raul was upstairs preparing for the trip. His headaches had returned with a vengeance, but he wouldn't allow anything to interfere with his plans. He swallowed another handful of pills and wondered just how much time he really had. He could hardly wait to see *his* grandson.

When Rafael stopped by Raul's suite to tell him that everything was ready, he knew that Raul was in severe pain. He had witnessed the daily changes which affected Raul's behavior. The medication was only a deterrent to the debilitating pain; it could do nothing to erase the problem or stem its progression. Time was limited. Rafael was glad that Raul meant to see their grandson. He knew this might be Raul's only opportunity, so he had gone along with Raul's plan without further dispute.

Alberto and Raul would travel together. Their private jet had been readied, the flight plan filed, and the men were set to leave within the next few minutes. Things were coming together nicely, but Rafael always expected last minute problems. He was rarely disappointed. He received the phone call just as they were leaving for the airstrip.

He shook hands with Raul and clasped one hand on his shoulder. They stared at one another briefly seeming to see each other clearly for the first time in years. They had always understood one another. There was no need for words. Raul smiled; he knew. Rafael stepped back and wished them good luck at the door then turned and hurried back inside to take the call.

He watched the live remote feeds showing everything taking place at the airstrip as he talked on the phone. Alberto and Raul boarded the plane. A baggage cart with their luggage and several large boxes being shipped to the States drove up next to the jet, and men began loading the items into the cargo area of the plane. After several minutes, the jet taxied down the runway and lifted off. Alberto turned and pressed a key on his laptop to close the screens.

Rafael stood, pondering the unusual nature of the phone call he had just received. An associate had called wishing to speak to Raul. When Rafael told him that he had just left on a flight to the States, the man had seemed relieved. Rafael could almost hear it in his voice. Why would he be concerned about Raul's whereabouts? Rafael didn't like unanswered questions. He would definitely have to check this out. He was still contemplating the strange call as he left his office.

As fate would have it, Rafael had closed the screens only moments too soon. Another few seconds and he would have seen the outer perimeters being surrounded by a phalanx of DEA officers and Bolivian troops.

Unaware of what was happening outside, Rafael continued down the corridor on his way downstairs when the compound sirens began screaming. He raced outside to see a heavily armed contingency of men breaching the distant outer walls. Where were his men and why had they not been warned sooner?

There was no time for questions. He ran across the open expanse between the house and the computer center. Once inside he would be able to detonated hidden arms which would hopefully deter the invasion. He raced toward the outer doors, reaching them just moments after they had been locked down. No one could enter until the workers opened the doors from inside. He slammed his fist against the heavy metal, pounding with all his strength. He had to enter in order to activate the switches. At last someone opened the outer doors; he flew through the halls to the central surveillance room. Computer screens revealed a break in their perimeter at several key locations.

The recent insurrection led by the rebel forces had diminished their stockpile of munitions, which hadn't been replenished as yet. His men had been fighting in the jungles for weeks and were exhausted. He had promised them a few weeks of rest. Now their very lives depended on their quick response, and they had been caught unaware. How could this possible happen?

He had to implement counteractions fast. He began typing in the codes only to find that the programs weren't responding. He had no outside help. They were trapped. All along the perimeter, his men were fighting valiantly, but they were greatly outnumbered. Rafael had never let them fight without him. He broke open the arms cabinet and tossed rifles to all the men in the room. As one they raced outside to combat a force of staggering proportions. Rafael could only wonder why these men, men he had helped so many times before, would turn against him in this manner. That was his last thought. There was no more time for thinking. All that was left was action.

He fought as he had never fought before, but it was useless. Still he and his men continued until their last bullet was spent. Their lives, their futures were over. Death was preferable to the disgrace of being taken and the agony of possible torture. Rafael led the last charge as they pressed the men in front of them back toward the outer wall, only to be surrounded themselves by other forces and escape denied them.

Rafael's last thought was someone had sold them out. He quickly scanned the military troops before him. There he saw him. Rafael couldn't believe that he would have done such a thing. The man smiled as he watched the bullets rip into Rafael's body; he shouted as he saw him fall, blood quickly spreading around him in a crimson pool. The firing ceased; he walked over to Rafael's body and stared down at the man he had witnessed savagely kill his brother and spat on the ground.

Memories of that day filled his mind. Because of his young age, he had been forced by his brother to remain hidden in the dense cover of the jungle. His brother and his troops had launched an attack on a young boy's Jeep. At the time they had believed the vehicle belonged to a rival rebel faction. They had attacked the Jeep, only to be confronted moments later by a larger group under Rafael's leadership. After a bloody battle, his brother and his men had been taken by Rafael's forces, and the young boy had watched as the men had all been unmercifully killed, jutted like wild pigs at the slaughter. The stench of death had filled the air.

He had stumbled back to their jungle camp and waited with the remaining few for the arrival of Rafael's men. He knew that they were known for making reparation whenever they could. His anger was not something that could be appeased by money. Only blood for blood would ever repay the injustice of their deaths, but he had taken their money, and when he became older, he had gone to the compound and sought employment. It had taken him years to infiltrate their organization to the point that he was allowed access to the information he needed, but he had succeeded.

Today the victory lay with him. He had waited years to avenge his brother's death, and he had succeeded at last. He rolled Rafael's body over with his boot and stared at his sightless eyes. He was glad that Rafael's last vision had been of his victorious face.

The compound swarmed with DEA officers and Bolivian troops. The computer center was quickly overrun and the computers, files, tapes, discs, and any other relevant material seized. Everything they needed to destroy Bolivia's largest and strongest drug cartel was now in their possession. Together with the Bolivian government, the DEA had carried out the final objective of Operation Slam Shut. With President Chambers' backing, they had used the intelligence they had obtained to dismantle one of the major supplier of cocaine to the States.

When Richards heard the report, he was relieved that they had finally achieved success. With the files and computer records the cartel had kept on their sources in both federal and state governments, the judicial system, and law enforcement agencies across the nation, the DEA would need months to bring justice and order to the ranks. A wholesale sweep would be logistically impossible, but those in influential positions would be brought to account immediately.

Raul's jet landed without incident, and he and Alberto made their way through the terminal after clearing customs. Raul had everything he felt would be needed in his briefcase. They had received word that Robbie was staying with Caroline's parents. He had brought a file of the evidence he had against Caroline's father as an insurance policy. He never doubted that Robbie would be returning to Bolivia with them the next day. Alberto wasn't as sure. Raul didn't have the same effect on people as he used to have. Once he had held people's attention simply by walking in a room, now he struggled to maintain focus on his own thoughts.

Alberto was worried. Rafael needed him at the compound. Alberto could tell that he was overwhelmed with the responsibilities of both jobs. But he had promised him that he would accompany Raul and take care of him. Raul would have been belligerent had he known and would have refused his help. The old Raul wouldn't have needed any, but, at times, this Raul was a different man entirely.

As they exited the terminal and approached the waiting limousine, Alberto felt the hair rise on his neck. He quickly glanced around but saw nothing unusual. Still the feeling persisted. He took Raul's arm and began walking away from the car, trying to move them away from the entrance. Raul looked at him strangely then pulled his arm free and walked purposefully toward the car.

"Wait, Raul, I forgot the flowers for your sister." Alberto knew something wasn't right and tried to stop Raul, but he didn't understand. He didn't remember the warning.

Raul turned to him with a frown. "What's wrong with you? I'm in a hurry. Get in the car." Alberto didn't know what to do. Raul didn't remember the signal. Alberto knew someone had set a trap for them and Raul was headed right for it. He raced in front of Raul and stopped him.

"You have to listen. Come with me quickly." Alberto was glancing around. He knew that no one would do anything in the busy entrance. He had to keep Raul from entering the car. Once they were in the vehicle, they would have little recourse for escape. Their luggage was being loaded in the truck, and the driver held the door open, waiting patiently at the side, and Alberto knew it was a trap. The man didn't have the feel, didn't have the deference of family.

Raul knew that Alberto would never hurt him, so he pushed passed him angrily. "I don't have time for this now. I have to see my grandson." Alberto had little option left but to go with him to face whatever awaited them. He knew that it wouldn't be good.

Alberto stepped into the vehicle knowing he was about to meet his fate. Raul had once saved his life; Alberto would do whatever he could to repay his debt. He glanced at the driver as he shut the door and nodded. The driver held his breath; the face of death stared back at him, and he knew that he had stepped into a trap. He could have easily gotten away, but he had chosen to accompany Contreras. Honor among thieves? He doubted that. Besides these men were worse; they were drug dealers. Everyone on the force knew Alberto's reputation. Even with the bulletproof glass separating them, he wouldn't feel safe until they were taken into custody.

Alberto knew his fate was sealed the second he heard the door locks click, but Raul was clutching his forehead as though the strain of the last few minutes had been too much for him. Alberto was worried, not about himself, but unsure now if Raul would ever see Robbie. Alberto took the bottle of pills and gave two to Raul. Raul looked at Alberto as though he were a stranger, as though he had no idea who he was. Then his eyes cleared. He laughed a humorless little grunt.

"I messed up, didn't I? It's not the first time, but it may well be my last." He tried to instill a little humor in a deadly serious turn of events. "I should have listened. That's always been my failing, not listening enough to good advice." He sighed. "It's just a matter of time now anyway. You did your best. You should have left when you could." He turned to face Alberto and clasped him in a brief hug, then sat back against the seat and closed his eyes.

Alberto was shaken. He had never known Raul to show emotions or sentimentality of any kind except one other time. He smiled as he thought of Paul and hoped that he had taken his chance to begin again. Raul would be proud to know that Paul had deceived them all and escaped. When the time was right, he would tell him.

Richards couldn't believe their plan had worked. He held two of the world's worst drug traffickers in his interrogation rooms, and he still couldn't believe how easy it had been. Once he received the driver's report, he realized just how lucky they had been. Only Contreras' poor health had allowed them to take the men without a fight. Nunez had known but had chosen to go quietly with Contreras.

Richards had enough evidence to arrest Nunez and hold him for trial on several federal charges. It could have been a lengthy process, but Nunez had agreed to give them whatever they needed for one concession. After a lengthy debate, Richards agreed. Raul would be allowed to spend a day with Robbie once it could be arranged. He would contact Ms. Martin to make the arrangements. Robbie would be accompanied by her and preparations were made to have the pent house suite of a local hotel cordoned off for their use. Nunez urged him to make the arrangements quickly.

Richards doubted Contreras would make it to trial. It was obvious to him after several hours of interrogation that Contreras was physically unfit. The physicians only confirmed his feelings. Contreras' memory seemed to slip in and out, and he easily became angry and aggressive. Richards only agreed to his visit with Robbie under the strictest of conditions, one being the presence of a physician. Richards was afraid he might try something when he was in one of his strange moods, and he didn't want to jeopardize Robbie's welfare in anyway.

Of course, Robbie had never been at Caroline's parents in Texas nor had either of her parents. Richards knew the best plans could fail, and he had planned accordingly. Robbie was secluded with Ms. Martin in an apartment in New York, while Paul and Caroline set up their new home. Richards had advised Caroline's parents to take an extended vacation somewhere far removed from the States for the next few months. They had received a touching note from distant relatives in Australia asking them to join them at their cattle station while they recovered from their recent bereavement, suggesting that a change of scene might help heal the pain of their loss. They had decided to take up the offer and planned a lengthy stay.

From the files they had removed from the Contreras compound, the DEA had been able to identify several top-ranking politicians who were in league with them either through financial support or special favors. Their computer experts were still working to break the codes for many of the computer files they had retrieved. It was frustrating, but any step was a step in the right direction. Each day brought them more evidence of corruption, and more arrests were made. They had crippled the supply chain for the present time at least.

The press noted that there seemed to be an epidemic of health issues sweeping through the federal government and questioned if the "new blood" being brought in would bring a better state of political health to the country at large.

Federal judges, high-level state officials, and lowly public officers in states all across the country found they needed to pursue other avenues of public service. Change swept through the nation, cleaning and purifying, removing the staid, old incumbents from political office.

The DEA was losing one of its best men, but Richards felt it was time to make a change. He didn't want to live his life with the constant fear of reprisal in the back of his mind. He had a family to consider now. They came first.

He was pleased with his final part of their investigation. They had Contreras locked away in the hospital ward of a federal prison. It was only a matter of time. The tumor on his brain had increased in size, and he was no longer able to function in any capacity. Such a powerful man, who once ruled a vast drug empire, brought down by the failings of the human body. Maybe there was justice after all.

Richards left his position feeling that he had accomplished something worthwhile, maybe not lasting, but it was a beginning. Congress passed legislation requiring stricter enforcement of restrictions placed on campaign finances and political gifts. Richards felt he had appeased some of the guilt he felt concerning Judy's death. Amanda wanted to name their child, if it was a girl, after Judy. It was a kind and generous gesture, and he loved her even more for making the offer. He had found what many never did, true and lasting peace and love.

It wasn't like anything he had left behind, but it gave him a sense of accomplishment to know he had earned it. It wasn't bought to create an image, to project the man, to establish his position in society. He had bought it just to please himself.

The upscale condo on the shores of Lake Michigan was simply furnished and maintained by a housekeeper and cook. Roger took most of his meals at home. He had met many people in his new job and had made a few friends, but he wasn't the outgoing firebrand that he had once been. He had learned to step back and let others shine, to listen and learn from what others said, and often more importantly from what they didn't say. He had put together a client list that was worthy of the best lawyer, and he could argue any case with passion and dedication. His clients loved him, and his bosses appreciated him, and he was miserable.

He had joined several service organizations and civic groups. His days were filled with work and his nights with activity, but he was a lonely man in a city made for fun. He just couldn't connect the way he once had. People enjoyed listening to him speak, and he could debate any topic for hours, but there was no fire. He had lost his spark, his ambition. He had accomplished his goal in life only to have it torn from him. He blamed everyone but himself.

He became tortured by what he felt was the injustice perpetrated against him. His mind became filled with ways to avenge the wrongs done him by those in charge. He began researching ideas and methods of retaliation. He plotted and he planned, and the fire began to burn once more. He spent every spare moment creating his master plan. He had names and dates and he began computer searches for information that he thought might be relevant. He followed the trials of those indicted by the DEA. In his mind, he began to see the larger picture.

He spent hours each day working at his computer. He became isolated from everyone and worked only enough to keep his clients and bosses happy. He didn't seek advantages or curry favor. He focused with the dedication of a zealot on his plan.

He began sleeping less and less. He lost weight and couldn't concentrate. He knew what he needed, but he had no way of acquiring it. He began drinking, but that only created another set of problems. He became despondent and seriously considered revealing his darkest secret to the world just to put an end to the anger he felt. In his more lucid moments, he realized he would be the one to suffer by any revelation of his past. No one would believe him.

His anger finally caused him to speak too aggressively in court. The judge who had been fed up with his condescending attitude finally cited him for contempt and sentenced him to a day in the local lock-up.

Roger Bennington was angrier than he had ever been in his life to think that *he* had been placed in jail like a common criminal. Of course, later he considered the event a blessing because that was where he met Javier. They had no idea who they were dealing with, and that was what angered him most. He couldn't tell them.

When he had calmed down enough to be coherent, Javier had struck up a conversation. Roger revealed that he was a lawyer, and Javier had solicited a little free advice. Of course, he had no means of repaying Roger, but he had given Roger his address and told him that he could fix him up if he ever needed anything.

When his legal advice was proven correct, Javier of the golden teeth, as Roger referred to him, became Roger's good friend. He supplied Roger's every need and fulfilled his every wish. Roger found what was missing in his life. He lived for the moment, filling every minute away from his office with sex and drugs. Before long, the drugs slipped into the workplace and he needed a hit to make it through the day, then another to get home.

From there he would head to Javier's rundown apartment to score again and meet up with whoever might be available. Someone was always around, wasted, unconcerned about his perverted demands. As long as he paid well, pain only added to the pleasure of securing the next fix. He always paid well.

His life became a predictable pattern of use and abuse. Moments of lucidity were reserved for work. He didn't need to concern himself with anything other than that. He simply existed, and it began to show. His boss called him in to reprimand him about a mishandled case, but he refused to listen. He stormed out of the office and headed straight to Javier's. He wasn't home, but he had shown Roger where he hid the key. Roger let himself in and slumped down on the faded couch. He needed a fix bad.

He got up and started rambling through Javier's belongings looking for a score, for anything to take the edge off. He laughed when he found Javier's hidden stash. In seconds he had the dust cut and spread and filled his lungs. He could relax. He could be himself. He could wait for Javier now. He felt so good; he decided to take one more line. It wouldn't hurt. He liked the feeling; he was almost there. Paradise was just beyond his reach. He took another line and then another for good measure.

He leaned back and closed his eyes. He could see Judy; she was calling him. He wanted to say he was sorry, but she turned and walked away. He stood to follow her but tripped over the low table in front of him and crashed to the floor.

Javier pushed open the door to his apartment slowly. He didn't want to walk into an ambush. Everyone knew he dealt. It wouldn't be the first time someone had tried to take him down. He eased further in the room. Then he saw him stretched out across the filthy floor. Roger had found his stash. It littered the floor around him like a white cloud. How much had he done?

Javier looked at the powder and then back at Roger. Fool, he thought. He hadn't had time to cut his last buy yet, and Roger had found it. Too bad, he was one of his best customers. What a loss. He went to the door and looked down the hall. No one was around at this time of the day. Why had he been here anyway? He shrugged; he would never know.

He searched Roger's pockets and removed everything of value. If he didn't, someone else would. Then he grabbed Roger's feet and pulled him from the apartment and down the hall. He shoved him into the elevator and pushed the button for the basement. The doors opened on the dank-smelling, trash-filled room which opened onto an alley. Unceremoniously, he dragged Roger's body through the filth and dumped him outside near the overflowing trash containers.

There would be questions. No one would talk. Most couldn't remember their own names. Javier would be a suspect, but he was about to take a short vacation. He hurried back to his apartment. Roger had always paid well. This time it had been with his life. Javier shook his head. Greed, people were never satisfied with just a little; they always had to have more. But too much of a good thing could be very bad. Roger had learned. What a shame that it was his last lesson.

Javier smiled as he counted the money. He could sell the watch and ring for a little. If he hurried, he could use the credit cards in the next city. There were always places where no one asked questions.

He flipped the watch over. Solid gold, he just might keep it. He looked at the engraving inside then frowned as a distant memory tugged at him. "Congratulations, Mr. President, love Caroline."